DEBORAH GRACE WHITE

A Shattered Reign

HEARTSONG BOOK THREE

RIVER OND
ONDFORD
OLEAND
SUNDERING CANYON
PORT TARAN
ZEV'S HOLDINGS
TARANDON
AELTAS
The Sovereign Realms
W
S

Marieke

"I think I'll tell them I can't go." Zev nodded. "Yes, I'd better stay."

"Zev, don't be ridiculous," Marieke scolded him. "I'll be fine here with your mother for one day."

Zev frowned. "I told myself I wouldn't let you out of my sight. Taking the bull to a farm two hours away for the whole day is the opposite of that."

"Azai needs your help," Marieke said. She cast a quick glance around, confirming that they were alone in the yard before laying her hand on his cheek. "Life has to go on, Zev. The farm still needs to be run."

Zev let out a long breath, silently acknowledging her reference to the loss of his father. It had been a week since Gideon's funeral, and the strangest part about it was that while nothing felt normal, so much of the farm's routine continued unchanged. The steady stream of family members who came and went each day helped fill the gap in the workload left by Gideon. Even as they spoke, Zev's aunt and cousin were in the kitchen with his mother, although dawn had barely broken.

Of course, nothing could fill the indefinable sense of emptiness left by Gideon's absence. It was a constant gaping hole in everyone's awareness. Marieke felt it with every breath, so she could only imagine how much more strongly the hollow feeling gripped Zev and his family.

"I know life has to go on." Zev's voice was a steady murmur. "But I don't like being away from you."

"I don't like it either," said Marieke, moving her fingers along the scratchy shadow that covered his jaw. "But it's only for the day. You're usually out in the field half the day anyway. It's not so different."

"It's completely different," Zev told her. "I know when you're nearby. I can just tell."

Marieke leaned her head against him, hiding her smile in his chest. "I know what you mean. But you're still going."

Zev let out a sigh of defeat, sweeping an arm around her and squeezing her close for a moment.

"Oh, my apologies." The dry voice of Azai broke into the moment. "I didn't realize you two needed privacy." His icy politeness was worse than shouting. "In the middle of the yard."

Marieke made to pull back, but Zev's arm remained unyielding around her. He ignored his brother completely, shifting only enough to lower his face to hers.

"I'll see you tonight, all right?" His eyes searched hers for a moment before he pressed a brief kiss to her lips.

"Be safe," she told him, her hand lingering on his chest for a moment longer than necessary as he at last let her step back. "And try not to murder your brother."

Zev's lips quirked up in a grin at that, and he turned away with a chuckle.

"No promises."

Marieke watched the brothers stride toward the barn, their conversation too low for her to catch. When they disappeared from view, she hurried back into the house, eager to get out of the cold morning air.

The sound of voices issued from the farmhouse's kitchen, and she made her way there. When she entered the room, Narelle was in the act of rising to get the water off the fire, and Marieke quickly waved her down.

Wrapping a towel around her hand, she lifted the water carefully. She had no need to ask Narelle for assistance as she pulled clay mugs down from the cupboard. She was familiar enough now with the kitchen that she was more than capable of making the tea for their visitors so that the grieving widow could sit for a moment.

It felt like the very least she could do.

The familiar lump rose to Marieke's throat, as it did every time she thought about what had happened to Gideon. Zev refused to hear any apologies, rejecting all suggestions that she'd had a hand in his father's death. But she couldn't help feeling guilty. Much as Jade might seem more interested in Zev than in Marieke now, Marieke was painfully aware that it was her involvement with Zev that had ultimately led to Jade finding them.

In short, her presence in Zev's life had produced exactly the outcome his family had feared it would: exposure and attack.

And now his father was dead, and Zev carried all the weight of the family's expectations. Generations of expectation, and she could see how much it burdened him.

Marieke poured out the tea, listening absently to the conversation being carried on heroically by Zev's Aunt Fiona. She was Gideon's only sister, and she'd come with her eldest daughter, Sara, to sit with Narelle. She came most days, and the company usually seemed to help. But today, Marieke had the sense that Narelle was tired, and would have preferred solitude.

Not that she blamed Fiona. She was grieving her brother's

death as well, and trying to comfort her sister-in-law on their shared loss in the only way she knew how. No one could ever truly know the right thing to do or say in response to death. It was a kind of pain words couldn't fix.

Aunt Fiona let her words peter out, apparently out of ideas for what to say. There was a moment of silence, then Sara spoke up.

"Have you updated the family records, Auntie Narelle?"

Marieke glanced around, her interest piqued. "The family records?"

"Like most families, we keep records of births, deaths, and marriages," Aunt Fiona said smoothly. "It's a common practice around here."

"Mother, you don't need to speak carefully," Sara said. "She knows, remember?"

"Oh." Aunt Fiona put a hand to her forehead. "I keep forgetting. My apologies, Marieke."

"No need to apologize," said Marieke.

But Aunt Fiona was still waving a hand. "Foolish of me to forget. It's just that none of this generation have married yet, although one other nephew is engaged. We're out of practice with welcoming newcomers into our secrets." She cast an eye over Marieke. "And we've never had an Oleandan among our number before."

"Oh, leave the girl be, Fiona," said Narelle. "If she's Zev's choice, it's not ours to stand in his way. No one has the right to tell him what he is or isn't allowed to do."

"I meant no offense," Aunt Fiona clarified. "And I'm not trying to dictate anything to Zev."

"It's still so strange to think of Zev as the patriarch," said Sara, her voice hushed. "He doesn't seem nearly old enough."

"He isn't old enough." Narelle stood, turning away to bustle with the tea.

Marieke relinquished the task, recognizing that the older woman needed something to occupy her hands. "So the family records," Marieke said quickly, hoping to distract the other women and give Narelle privacy.

"Yes." Aunt Fiona nodded. "We keep meticulous records of our family tree. Zev's ascension to the position of patriarch—that is to say, rightful holder of the royal title—should be noted as soon as possible."

"It has been, of course," Narelle said. She turned back around with a pitcher of milk. "The night Gideon died." Her smile was twisted. "Certain duties can't be neglected no matter what's happening." She glanced out the window at the early morning light now bathing the yard. "Such as the cows being milked, incidentally."

"I'll do it," Marieke said, standing. "I'm sure it must be my turn."

"No, let me." Aunt Fiona waved a hand. "Gideon would be ashamed of me if I sat here prattling instead of helping out at such a time." She fixed her daughter with a pointed look. "And I'm sure Sara can make herself useful in here."

"Yes, of course." Sara stood as well. "I can finish preparing today's dough, Aunt Narelle."

Before Marieke could blink, the two visitors had set to their tasks, leaving her and Zev's mother with nothing to do but sit. She looked over to see Narelle smiling ruefully at her.

"As if idleness is what I want."

Marieke chuckled, the sound a little awkward. "I know what you mean. When I'm troubled, I much prefer distraction."

"I'm good at providing that," said Sara cheerfully. "Or so the aunt assigned to tutor me on our history always said. She claimed I was the most distractible student she'd ever taught." She gave Marieke a friendly smile. "No one really minds that you're Oleandan, you know. Everyone is just adjusting."

"I know," Marieke assured her.

She refrained from sharing her suspicion that her status as a singer was more responsible for the sideways looks she still got from most of Zev's family. Azai, in particular, found it hard to hide his reaction every time she walked into the room.

"Personally, I think it's very exciting to have someone find out who we are," Sara said. "We grow up being told we're special, but what's the point of being special if no one else knows about it?"

"We know," Narelle said. "That's what matters."

"Is it, though?" Sara sounded doubtful. "That doesn't give me much scope to show off, Auntie Narelle."

Marieke chuckled, warming to the young woman.

"Zev didn't tell you, anyway, did he?" Sara said. "That's what my father said, when my brother asked why Zev didn't get in trouble for telling a girl outside of an engagement. He said you figured it out."

"Oh." Marieke fiddled awkwardly with the fabric of her sleeve. It was a little unsettling to know that she—and the status of her relationship with Zev—was being discussed in such detail. "Yes. I suppose I did."

"What was that like?" Sara asked. "How did Zev react when you told him?"

Marieke considered the question. "Honestly, I think he was relieved. I could see how heavy it was for him, carrying the secret."

"I remember when Gideon told me," Narelle said, her tone taking on a reminiscent note Marieke rarely heard from the practical woman. "It was a week before our wedding, as is traditional. Close enough to the marriage being sealed that he was pretty confident of my devotion to him, but with still enough time for me to cancel if I didn't want to tie myself to the situation." She chuckled. "I nearly did cancel, too."

"Really?" Sara abandoned her task temporarily, turning fully to face the others. "I haven't heard this story."

"Were you overwhelmed at the thought of marrying into the bloodline of the royals?" Marieke asked.

Narelle shook her head. "No, not at all. I just didn't believe him. I thought he must either have lost his mind or be a liar. And a very arrogant liar at that, to be making up such a self-glorifying tale."

"How did he convince you?" Sara asked.

"He showed me the records," Narelle said. "It wasn't strictly allowed, given we weren't married yet, but," she smiled, "he really wanted me to stay."

"Of course he did," Marieke said. "He was a wise man."

"Well, I certainly don't think he ever regretted his choice," Narelle said. "In any event, the records were enough to convince me. I never looked back after that. This family's identity became mine as well." Her eyes held Marieke's. "Which is no small thing, incidentally. I don't know if anyone's asked you whether you're really ready for that."

"I haven't been ready for most of what's happened over the last few months," Marieke said simply. "It hasn't stopped it coming at me, and it hasn't stopped me from dealing with it in the best way I know how."

"Yes, well, there's something in that," Narelle agreed. "I suppose when we think we're ready for anything, that's probably when we're most at risk." She eyed Marieke. "Do you want to see the records?"

"Am...am I allowed?" Marieke asked uncertainly.

Narelle shrugged. "I don't think Sara's going to stop us."

Sara shot Marieke a wink. "Go on. I won't tell on you."

Marieke smiled back, following as Narelle rose. She had the sense that the older woman was making an impulsive decision, and she didn't want to discourage the instinct toward openness. She wanted Zev's mother to like her, but it had been very hard over the last couple of weeks to know when to put herself forward and when to hang back. Being an outside observer to family grief when that family was forced to keep her nearby was an awkward experience for all involved.

The two women left the kitchen, making their way down the hall toward a wooden door on the ground level. Marieke had heard Zev refer to it as their library room, but she'd never been inside it. She watched with interest as Narelle fished a key out of her pocket and unlocked the door.

"I locked it for the funeral and haven't had reason to unlock it since," the older woman commented. "We don't usually keep it locked. That would be more suspicious than a farmhouse with a library, probably."

When the door swung open, Marieke was met with the sight of a small but pleasant room. It wasn't as light as the rest of the house, because the glass of the window was mullioned for privacy, but it still let in the cool morning sunshine.

As she moved across the space, she realized it wasn't as small as she'd initially thought. She'd only had that reaction because she'd been expecting a library, like a miniature version of the ones she'd visited at the Oleandan and Aeltan Academies of Song. For a room in a house, it was actually quite spacious.

There weren't rows upon rows of shelves, but bookcases lined one wall and crates the other.

"The crates have farm records in them," Narelle said. "Recording our harvests each year, and other such details."

Marieke nodded politely, inwardly hoping that she wouldn't be expected to rifle through them and feign interest.

Narelle's smile suggested she had some idea what her companion was thinking, but she didn't say it. Instead, she let her gaze wander to the large but simple desk pushed against the wall directly under the window.

"That's where the boys did their study. Zev excelled at it. Azai was also perfectly capable, but he didn't like it, so he didn't apply himself as much. He would have preferred to be out in the fields or with the animals."

"He's excellent with the animals, isn't he?" Marieke said. She smiled tentatively at Narelle, glad to have something genuinely positive to say about the son who hated her but was —naturally—loved by his mother. "It stands out to me, since my father works with animals for a living. Some people have the right manner with them, some never will. And Azai clearly cares for the animals on this farm. He understands them."

Narelle nodded, looking pleased. "That's very perceptive of you. You're right." She gave Marieke a sideways look. "He cares for people as well, you know. Sometimes he's just too proud to show it."

"I don't think he is," Marieke said. "His love for you is evident even to an outsider like me."

"He loves Zev, too," Narelle pressed on, disregarding the polite words. "Those brothers are devoted to each other, have been since they were children. I trust they'll never forget it." There was the tiniest hint of sternness in her voice. "I trust you won't let them."

Marieke bit her lip, discomfort roiling in her stomach. The last thing she wanted was to create a rift between Zev and his brother. But she didn't know how to prevent it. Short of disappearing from their lives altogether, she doubted anything she did would please Azai. And that route, apart from being unthinkable for her personally, would placate Azai at the cost of Zev. It would be at least as likely to lead to a permanent breakdown of the brothers' relationship.

"Anyway, the ancestry records aren't up here for anyone to stumble upon, of course," Narelle said. "They're hidden away." She pulled open the desk's single drawer and withdrew a flint before leading Marieke to one end of the large bookcase. "See here."

She bent down and shifted some books off the bottom and second-to-bottom shelves. Marieke watched with interest as Narelle lifted the second shelf upward and removed the plank that formed the bottom shelf altogether. Then she slid the wooden back of the bookshelf across—apparently the bottom part of the structure wasn't attached to the rest of it. What was revealed was a cavity in the wall behind the bookcase, with a trapdoor that extended partway under the now-removed bookshelf base.

"We don't go down here often," Narelle said, as she lifted the trapdoor by means of an iron ring set into it. "As you can see, it's a bit of a process."

"It's amazing," said Marieke. "It's very cleverly designed, the way all the joins are hidden in the structure of the bookcase. I would never have guessed it wasn't just an ordinary piece of furniture."

"That's the idea," Narelle said, turning around so as to descend a very narrow, very steep set of stairs. By the time Marieke followed her, she'd retrieved a lantern from inside the hidden basement and lit it with the flint. "I should replenish the oil," the older woman commented absently. "Looks like it was left a little low last time."

She lifted it to reveal a larger space than Marieke had expected. It wasn't as big as the library room above, and obviously it had no windows. But it was clean and neat, devoid of cobwebs or excessive dust. The walls were of stone bricks, and the chests lining the space seemed to be properly sealed against moisture.

"This is where we keep any record relating to the royal line," Narelle said. "Or even documents detailing life before the coup. Some of Gideon's predecessors made a project of acquiring such records. Gideon was familiar with the contents of all the ones left to him, but never had much interest in expanding the collection."

She crossed the space in a few strides, lifting the lid from one of the crates.

"This is the family tree. The original page that the survivor of the coup brought with him—or rather, his nursemaid did—is encased in glass at the bottom. But our own records are just bound in leather."

Marieke waited, fascinated, as Narelle lifted out the first of several tomes from the chest and flipped open the cover.

"It's not just names. There's a book with nothing but names and dates of birth and death, but this one has details of the lives of everyone in the direct line." Her eyes became unfocused as she stared at the page in front of her. "There are two entries in a row now that are much shorter than the ones before them."

She handed the book to Marieke, her eyes on the younger woman's face as Marieke turned the pages carefully, scanning the names and dates.

"When my fears get the better of me," Narelle added, "I worry that there will be three such entries in a row."

"I won't let anyone hurt Zev," Marieke said fiercely. "Not if I can possibly prevent it."

"It's that *if* that worries me," Narelle sighed. "I know you don't wish him harm, but I confess, I wish he wasn't caught up in Oleand's troubles." Her eyes were weary as they searched Marieke's face. "What's your plan? What do the two of you intend to do next? I've gotten nothing much out of Zev."

Marieke sighed. "I imagine that's because there isn't much to tell. Truthfully, we don't know what to do next. It's my fault we're stalling. If Zev is right, and we really have figured out the true cause of Oleand's deterioration, we need to warn the Council of Singers. But I don't really know how safe it is for me to go back to Ondford. I didn't leave quite…honestly."

They'd also been in no hurry to leave Zev's mother and brother after their recent loss, but Marieke didn't say that. The last thing she wanted was for Narelle to think she resented delaying on the family's behalf. On the contrary, Marieke was relieved to have a valid reason to postpone the inevitable moment when she had to once again set out on a seemingly impossible quest to save Oleand from falling apart.

At least she wasn't alone in it now, she reminded herself, warmth seeping through her at the thought. Zev would be with her.

The sound of something falling above them made both women look up. Narelle had taken half a step toward the staircase when a voice called down.

"Aunt Narelle?" It was Sara's voice, and she sounded worried. "There's someone here."

"Come on." Narelle took the book back from Marieke, shutting it with a snap and replacing it in its crate, her lips stretched tight in concern. The two of them hurried up the ladder and emerged blinking into the library room.

"Sorry, I knocked the stack over," Sara said, grabbing a pile of books in her arms as Narelle quickly replaced the planks of the bookcase.

"Never mind about the order," Narelle said. "Just put them in neatly, so they don't look like they've been disturbed."

With Marieke helping, Sara had the books back on the shelf in no time.

"Who's here?" Narelle asked, as she straightened the whole set up, assessing it with a critical eye before returning the flint to the desk.

"I don't know, but they look official," Sara said nervously.

"They were at the gate when I came to get you, but they might have come in by now."

Sure enough, as soon as they entered the hallway, they heard a firm knock at the door. Fully master of the situation, Narelle strode forward to answer it. Marieke had to admire her self-possession. Nothing in the older woman's manner as she greeted the two strangers on the other side gave any hint that she'd just been interrupted in a highly secret task.

"Good morning," one of the men said. "Is this the farm of Gideon and Narelle, and their sons Zevadiah and Azai?"

"You've come to the right farm," Narelle said, her voice steady but cool. "But the farm belongs to Zevadiah now. Gideon was buried a week ago."

"I'm sorry," the stranger said, taken aback. "I was unaware."

Narelle eyed the man and his companion. Both wore blue tunics with the familiar budding tree embroidered onto the shoulder in bronze thread.

"I didn't realize we were expected to notify the Council of Singers of our loss."

"You weren't, of course," the man said, his forehead crinkling in a frown. "I only meant that I'm sorry to intrude on you at such a moment."

The other man nodded. "Our condolences."

"Thank you," said Narelle. "Is there something I can assist you with?"

"Actually, yes." The two council representatives exchanged a look, seeming reluctant to continue. "We're here on behalf of the survey team. We—"

"Someone already came by regarding the survey," said Narelle. "We're aware that there was a malfunction that prevented our property being assessed, and we provided the details of our harvest and property as requested."

"We know," the other man said. "That's all in order. But we're under instructions to ask some further questions. The survey parchment's been thoroughly checked, and there was no obvious malfunction." He shifted a little, trying to look around Narelle, who was blocking the doorway. "Is Zevadiah here?"

"He's not, actually," Narelle said. Her voice was still calm, but Marieke could detect the edge to it. "He's away from the farm for the entire day, I'm afraid. Why do you wish to speak to him particularly?"

"You said it's his farm now, didn't you?" The council employee's casual tone was unconvincing. In face of Narelle's expectant silence, he relented. "Our visit has two purposes, actually. And the second purpose requires us to speak with Zevadiah."

"What purpose is that?" Narelle asked, her voice far from encouraging.

"We'd hoped to discuss it with him, but..." The man trailed off, shooting a look at his companion. "Perhaps you can help us. I understand that Zevadiah has been known to travel with a young woman, a singer from Oleand."

Marieke stiffened in alarm. She should have gone into the kitchen or up to her room before Narelle answered the door. She debated slipping out of sight now, but thought the movement would be more likely to catch the men's attention.

"Oh?" Narelle's reply gave little away.

"She's a very young woman, not long graduated from the academy," the stranger pressed. "About your height, with dark hair and blue eyes."

"What about this woman?" Narelle said, her calm tone more forced by the minute.

"Well, the Oleandan Council of Singers is looking for her," the first employee said. "They've requested us to make inquiries as to—" He'd been shifting as he spoke, and he broke off as he caught sight of Marieke. "Oh. Hello. What's your name?"

Marieke's mind raced as she tried to decide how to respond. Clearly he'd seen that she fit the description he was looking for.

"She's a guest in my home," Narelle said before she could speak. "If there are any issues, feel free to discuss them with me."

The man clearly took this as the confirmation it was, and his demeanor changed.

"I'm afraid you need to come with us to the capital," he said, his words directed to Marieke.

"She needs to do no such thing," Narelle said darkly. "As I said, she's—"

"It's all right." Marieke held up a hand. She stepped forward, frowning at the council representatives. "Am I under arrest for something?"

"Of course not," the second one said easily. "But your assistance is requested." He paused. "Strongly requested."

"She's not going anywhere." Narelle spoke again, and to Marieke's dismay, she reached surreptitiously toward the coat cupboard by the door as if seeking a weapon. For all Marieke knew, there *was* a weapon stored there. She wouldn't put it past Zev's family.

"I'll go," Marieke said quickly.

"Marieke, no." Narelle scowled at her. "They have no right to come here and demand—"

"They won't see it that way," Marieke said, too quietly for the men to hear. "In fact, that's the opposite of how they'll see it. In their minds, they have the might of the Council of Singers behind them."

What she didn't say was that she could feel the magic starting to pool to the council employees. Naturally, they were both singers, and they surely wouldn't hesitate to use songcraft to incapacitate Narelle if she tried by force to stop them from taking Marieke. Marieke absolutely refused to be responsible for Zev's mother being attacked in her own home. She could try to pit her own songcraft against the council singers' magic, of course, but it was two to one, and even if she was successful, it didn't seem like a path that would lead to any good outcome.

"My son left you with me because he trusted that you'd be safe here," Narelle said, her distress clear on her face.

Marieke shook her head. "No. He left me here because he trusts me to take care of myself. Which I fully intend to do." She laid a reassuring hand on Narelle's arm. "I'll be all right." She turned to the men. "Please give me a few minutes to gather my things."

Their nods of assent were terse, and she could feel their eyes on her back as she climbed the staircase. The sooner she got them away from the family farm, the better. They clearly already had too many questions about the unusual family of farmers. Her mind raced as she gathered her things, wondering what the Aeltan Council of Singers really wanted with her, and how big a trap she might be walking into. She would have to keep her wits about her and take nothing for granted.

When she came back downstairs, both Narelle and Sara were waiting, the former grim and the latter wide-eyed. Marieke kept her goodbye brief, Narelle's murmur following her out the door.

"Take the mare, Sara. Go get the boys. Right now."

Unease swirled in Marieke's stomach as the men led her across the farmyard toward a waiting vehicle. And only half of her anxiety was for whatever was awaiting her in Tarandon. She'd managed to persuade Zev's mother not to do anything rash. Now she just had to hope that Zev would have the sense to refrain as well, without her there to talk him down.

She didn't claim to be confident in that hope.

TWO

Zev

Zev secured the latch on the now-empty back of the cart, turning to watch as Azai and the owner of the farm led the bull away. Moving around to the large storage area under the cart's bench seat, Zev hefted up one of the bags of grain they were selling to the dairy farmer. He was glad to have the mindless job of transporting the heavy sacks. He was in no humor to be friendly with a near-stranger, or to haggle over the price of the bull's services. He'd leave that to Azai—after all, the whole exchange had been his idea.

Zev was returning for the tenth sack when he heard the unmistakable sound of hooves pounding into the yard. Whoever was riding in was pushing the horse fast, and he paused to watch their arrival. His heart jolted at the sight of his cousin Sara on his favorite mare. Even without the method of her arrival, her face would have told him that something terrible had happened.

Dropping the sack on the ground, he strode toward her as she slid from the horse's back. His steps had become a run by the time he reached her.

"What is it?" He grabbed Sara's shoulders. "Marieke?"

She nodded, swallowing visibly.

"What happened?" Zev demanded, panic rising. "Did Jade come back?"

"No." Sara shook her head. "Some men from the Council of Singers came. They said she had to go with them. Auntie Narelle tried to stop it, but Marieke insisted. She went without even fighting."

Zev let out a low groan, berating himself for going against his instincts and leaving Marieke behind at the farm.

"How long ago was this?"

"A couple of hours," Sara said. "I rode straight here, but—"

"It's not your fault," Zev cut her off, seeing her distress. "Tell me everything, what did they say?"

He listened with growing anger to her account. It wasn't a surprise to him that interested inquirers had been able to discover the connection between him and Marieke. What angered him was the gall of the Oleandan Council of Singers, using the Aeltan council to seek her out. Marieke had told him that she'd left Ondford in defiance of her council's instructions, but pursuing her through diplomatic channels like a wanted criminal who'd fled across the border was too far.

"Look after the mare," he told Sara shortly. "I'm going to get Azai."

He strode in the direction Azai had disappeared, his pulse thundering in his ears. He didn't trust either council, and the fact that Marieke had gone without a fight didn't reassure him at all. By the time he found his brother, his fear and impatience were barely contained.

"Azai." He pulled his brother aside. "We have to go. Now."

"What?" Azai stared at him. "Zev, we can't leave yet. We're supposed to take our bull home at the end of the day."

"We'll just have to trust them to return it," Zev said. "We have to get back. Marieke—"

Azai's groan cut him off. "Zev, she'll be fine. You're acting like a lovesick fool."

"No, Azai, listen to me!" Zev was growing frustrated. "She's gone. Sara just arrived, and she said Mari was taken."

"What?" Azai stiffened, anger passing over his face. Any belief Zev might have held that his brother's outrage was on Marieke's behalf was swept away by his next words. "You're telling me that Jade came back? I thought you and Marieke were convinced she wouldn't show her face again until her plans were ready."

"We're not convinced of anything," said Zev grimly. "But no, it wasn't Jade. It was some men from the Council of Singers."

"Oh." Azai frowned. "You should have started with that."

Zev held in the retort that rose to his lips. He couldn't even be mad at his brother's distraction from the main point of Marieke's welfare. He fully sympathized with Azai's fury at the thought that he'd missed a chance to take revenge on their father's killer.

"I don't like that they're still sniffing around," Azai said. His grimace was slightly begrudging as he met Zev's eyes. "And I can understand you being worried that they took Marieke. But I don't see what it will achieve for us to go racing back."

"I'm going after her, obviously!" Zev said. "Azai, she was a guest in our home, and the council came and seized her right out of it. On *our* property! You really want to just let that stand?"

Azai's brow lowered as he listened to this speech. "No, when you put it that way, I suppose I don't. That's overstepping, even for the council." He sighed. "I'll speak to the farmer."

Zev didn't stay to hear whatever explanation Azai would come up with. By the time his brother rejoined him, he had the mare Sara had ridden ready to go, along with the horse who'd pulled the cart on the way there.

"You'll have to ride double with me, Sara," he told his cousin. "It will be a stretch for the horse, but still faster than pulling the cart."

Sara didn't dispute it, and soon the three of them were cantering along the road. Zev's tension grew as the ground passed too slowly under them. He had to pace their journey for the sake of the overburdened mount, and it chafed him. It was almost three hours from Sara's arrival that they finally rode between their own gates. The singers from the council had five hours' head start on them, which meant there was absolutely no hope of catching them before they reached the capital.

"Mother!" Zev threw open the door to the house as the others led the mounts to the barn. "Mother, where are you?"

His mother appeared from the kitchen, Aunt Fiona with her. Both women's faces were drawn and serious.

"Is there more that Sara didn't know?" Zev asked curtly.

His mother shook her head. "She said she could take care of herself, Zev. She didn't seem to think she was in physical danger."

"I'm going after them," Zev said, disregarding his mother's reassurances. He knew better than anyone that Marieke was capable of taking care of herself. But the question was, would she? By going unresisting to avoid a fight, she'd already demonstrated to the council that she could be manipulated by the unscrupulous. "What should I expect?"

"I think it was only the two," his mother said quickly. "But they looked very official, and they carried themselves like singers. They loaded Marieke into a carriage."

"Did they tie her up?" Zev asked darkly.

"No. I didn't see any form of restraint. But I wouldn't be

surprised if they have some means of incapacitating her voice for the journey."

"I don't need songcraft to free her," Zev said, his hand flexing toward the sword he'd taken from his father's side.

"Be careful, Zevadiah." His mother's voice was sharp. "They're trained singers, and they asked for you by name. For all we know, they'll be looking for a reason to bring you in as well."

"I'm not going to just leave her at their mercy, Mother," said Zev.

"I wasn't expecting you to," she informed him calmly. "But don't be foolish about it."

"I don't intend to be," said Zev. "But I don't know what I'm walking into, Mother. I don't know how long I might be gone." He paused. "And I want to take Azai with me."

Surprise flashed through his mother's eyes, but she didn't look displeased.

"I think that's a good idea."

"But that leaves you—"

"Don't worry about your mother," Aunt Fiona said. "Or your farm. We'll keep things in order."

"Thank you." Zev nodded to her, knowing that she spoke for the whole family. He could trust them not to leave his mother alone or let his farm fall into disrepair.

"Get yourself organized," Aunt Fiona went on. "By the time you're ready to go, we'll have food packed for you."

Zev was already halfway out the door. It took very little time for him to gather what he needed, and by the time he emerged from the house, Azai was still returning from the barn. Zev ran down the porch steps, meeting his brother in the middle of the dusty yard.

"Leaving, are you?" Azai cast an eye over Zev's traveling

gear before glancing at the sun. "It'll be dark before you reach the capital."

"Can't be helped," said Zev.

"You could have gotten home faster if you'd ridden back on the mare and left me to follow with Sara and the cart, you know," Azai said. He was frowning, as if the thought had been playing on his mind for a while. "Why didn't you?"

"Because I needed you to come," Zev said steadily.

Azai raised an eyebrow. "What do you mean?"

"I mean that our enemies have taken the woman I love captive, and I need my brother's help to free her."

Something flashed in Azai's eyes, some glimmer of the way things used to be between them. Maybe a realization of how inconceivable their younger selves would have found it that either brother would have the slightest hesitation in responding to that call from the other.

Azai let out a breath. "You're really worried, aren't you?"

"I am," said Zev. "You don't realize the danger she's in. She's almost died in front of me multiple times. I know for a fact at least one member of the Oleandan council would be happy to see her dead, and I wouldn't be willing to vouch for a single member of the Aeltan council. She's asking questions they don't want answered, and she had to flee her own country to avoid consequences for it last time. And all of that doesn't even take into account the fact that Jade swore to me that she'd kill Marieke the next time she saw her. There's every reason to have real fear for her safety."

Azai gave a slow nod, then raised one arm to grip Zev's shoulder. "I'll be with you."

Relief and gratitude surged through Zev. He'd once considered himself and Azai inseparable, and capable of taking on the world. He was a child no longer, and he knew many things he hadn't known then. But he'd give a great deal to feel that way again.

They didn't waste time. Within fifteen minutes, they were riding out the gate on fresh mounts. Zev couldn't bring himself to look back and see his mother's expression as she watched the last of her family members leave. They would be back. He had no intention of letting himself or his brother be killed by the council or anyone else.

It wasn't just idle determination, either. He felt stronger than ever as he urged his horse southwest, toward the capital. He could feel the solidity of the ground beneath him, almost as though it was ready to rise to his aid in the same way magic rose to Marieke's at her command. He hated to think of any benefit attaching to his father's death, but there was no denying that since his father's position had passed to him, Zev had felt his connection to the land intensify. He knew he wasn't invincible —that connection hadn't saved his father. But since entangling his fate with Marieke and her songcraft, Zev had seen the power of his heartsong respond to him in more potent and tangible ways than he'd ever heard of his ancestors experiencing.

The hours passed interminably, but eventually, they reached Tarandon. As Azai had predicted, the sun was setting, but mercifully the city gates were still open. They rode straight through, steering their horses toward the building that had once been the royal castle but now housed the Council of Singers and Academy of Song.

Zev was braced for the gates of the complex to be barred to them at the late hour, but what he hadn't expected was to be hailed by name before he even reached them.

"Zev?"

He pulled his horse up, turning in surprise to see a young woman standing just outside the gate, her pale hair haloed by the light of a nearby street lamp. She was squinting up at him as if unsure she had the right person. With good reason. He'd never seen her before in his life.

"Yes, I'm Zev," he said cautiously. "Who are you?"

"Oh, that's a relief." She relaxed visibly, a smile spreading across her face. "I didn't know how much longer I'd have to wait, and it's getting cold now the sun's gone down." She sent a conspiratorial look at them. "Plus I'm not as confident as Marieke—it's terrifying having to accost random strangers in hopes they're the right person."

"You know Marieke?" Zev demanded.

"Oh, yes, sorry." The girl straightened. "I'm Veronica. I was assigned to Marieke when she came with the Oleandan delegation a few months back, and we struck up a friendship and have stayed in touch a little. She got a message to me earlier today, when she arrived."

"So she is here?" Zev said eagerly. "What was the message?"

"She asked me to stop you from doing anything rash," Veronica said. She stared him down—her attempt at severity would have been comical if Zev hadn't been so tense. "And I intend to do my best, so please don't be difficult."

Zev let out a breath. "I make no promises," he said darkly. "Where's Marieke?"

"I don't actually know," Veronica admitted. "But from what I can gather, she was brought in by some council employees for questioning." She shook her head. "What have you all been up to, anyway?"

"Who says *we've* been up to anything?" Azai protested.

Veronica shrugged. "Marieke doesn't really seem like the trouble-making type. But you..." She eyed Azai speculatively. "You have the feel of someone who's looking for an excuse to fight then blame it on someone else. No offense."

In spite of his anxiety, Zev couldn't help the dry laugh that escaped him. "She's figured you out in one glance, Azai."

"That's not my feel at all," Azai said, outraged. "I'm just trying to peaceably get on with my life. It's not my fault the council insists on abducting people off my farm."

"Hm." Veronica didn't look convinced. "Was it really as dramatic as an abduction?"

"It may as well have been," Zev said, trying to steer the conversation back on track. "We're here to free her, anyway. The council has no right to hold her."

"Well, I don't know about that," said Veronica. "I suppose they have the right if they think she's committed a crime or something. Which doesn't seem like Marieke. But I don't even know if they're planning to hold her."

"How can we find out?" Zev pressed.

Veronica jerked her head. "Dismount and follow me. My family lives nearby, and you can hire stalls in the public stable we use."

"Aren't you a student?" Zev frowned. "I thought you'd live at the academy."

"I'm not a student anymore," Veronica told him. "I finished my final examination a week ago."

"Wait, you're a singer?" Azai raised his eyebrows. "You didn't mention that."

"I didn't think I needed to," Veronica answered, seeming oblivious to his tone. "Marieke's role with the delegation was to learn from our Academy of Song, so naturally the person they assigned to her was a student. Besides, it's not a good look to go around boasting, is it?"

Azai narrowed his eyes at her, clearly debating whether to correct her assumption that he saw her status as singer as something to be proud of. To Zev's relief, he decided not to. Zev had no patience for further distractions from their purpose.

Veronica came alongside him as they walked down the darkened streets. "Marieke's told me about you, you know," she said. "She mentioned your…time together in Oleand."

There was a suggestive note to her voice which had Zev eyeing her sideways. What exactly had Marieke told her friend?

"You know," he commented, "you claim not to be as confident as Marieke, but you seem bold enough to me."

Veronica laughed self-consciously. "I deserved that," she said. She bit her lip, glancing around before lowering her voice. "You know, I told your brother that Marieke doesn't seem like a troublemaker, but that was partly because I couldn't resist the temptation of baiting him." She glanced at Azai, leading his horse behind and not quite within hearing range. "He strikes me as extremely baitable."

Zev acknowledged it with a grunt.

"But to tell the truth, I wasn't completely surprised by Marieke's message. I had the strong impression last time we met that she was in some kind of trouble."

Zev frowned. "When did you last meet her?"

"At least a month ago now," Veronica said. "She'd hitched a ride to Tarandon with a trading convoy and was preparing to go down into Sundering Canyon all by herself. Or at least, to try."

"She succeeded," Zev said. "Although not by herself. I went with her."

"Really?" Veronica brightened. "I'm glad. I told her she should contact you rather than going off on her own."

"Well, I'm grateful to you," Zev said. "Going in there alone would have been a bad idea, as she obviously knew, even if she was too stubborn to admit it in so many words. But why did you think she was in trouble?"

"She implied that she'd gotten on the wrong side of the Oleandan Council of Singers," Veronica said, her brow furrowed. "In fact, she said a lot of strange things, about the situation in Oleand not adding up, and some mysterious people in the canyon having answers that we don't have up here. But she refused to explain herself properly. She said she didn't think I'd want to know."

"She was probably right," Zev said dryly.

"I think she was at the time," Veronica admitted. "I certainly didn't press her as much as I should have. In my defense, I was pretty consumed by examination prep. But once that was behind me, and I'd still heard nothing further from Marieke, I started to wonder. And to worry. It's been playing on my mind, to tell you the truth. I don't want to ignore important truths just because they're inconvenient."

"Then you must be an anomaly among your kind." Azai's voice surprised Zev. He hadn't realized his brother had moved close enough to join their conversation.

"My kind?" Veronica repeated blankly. "I thought you were Aeltan, too."

"We are," said Azai, his tone bordering on offended. He really was absurdly baitable, Zev reflected. "I meant singers."

"Oh." Veronica considered his original comment. "I don't think so. Singers all go through the academy, and a big part of what we learn is *how* to learn. And learning involves digging deeper, asking questions, pursuing the truth. No one values knowledge like the Academy of Song."

"That's what they teach you at your academy?" Azai said skeptically. "To pursue the truth?"

"Of course," said Veronica.

Azai's expression showed that he doubted it, and she raised an eyebrow.

"Do you have a problem with me...what's your name again?"

"His name is Azai, and don't take it personally," Zev said. "He has an unreasonable prejudice against singers."

As Zev had known he would, Azai spluttered a protest. "A prejudice you shared until a certain someone got into your head, so no need to sound so high and mighty. And I can speak for myself." He directed his next words to Veronica. "I'm Azai."

Veronica came to a stop, eyeing him with astonishment. "You openly acknowledge that you're prejudiced? That's bold."

"Yes, it's true, I don't like singers much," Azai said, lifting his chin in a defiant posture. "Zev is always telling me to keep it to myself, but since he's seen fit to announce it to the world, I suppose I can speak freely. Surely it's better to own our opinions openly than to pretend we don't have them but still let them affect everything we say and feel."

"Huh." Veronica tilted her head to one side. "I suppose there's something in that." She stared at him. "But why don't you like singers?"

"Isn't it obvious?" Azai raised a shoulder. "They have all the power and no accountability. They think they have the right to rule just because they can access songcraft, but that capacity is no guarantee of integrity or even aptitude to govern. And they're hypocritical—they claim that the system under which the Council of Singers operates is in everyone's interests, but it's not even vaguely representative of most of the country."

"Mm, yes." Veronica nodded. "You do have a point there."

"I—I do?" Azai had clearly been ready to launch into another argument, and he fumbled over his words based on the unexpected reply.

Veronica stared at him like he'd lost his mind. "Didn't you think you had a point?"

"No, obviously *I* know I had a point," said Azai, growing agitated. "I just meant that I didn't know that *you* knew that I had a point. I mean, that my point was...you know, good."

Veronica was still blinking at him with a perplexed expression, and Zev couldn't help leaning in to mutter to Azai.

"You're doing great, little brother, really upholding the family honor. Keep at it."

"Shut up," Azai hissed.

"Well, it is a good point," Veronica said, taking pity on him. "And I'm not an anomaly for thinking so. It's a matter that I've often heard discussed around the academy. Lots of students raise it during the lessons around governance—there are always some students from non-singing families and rural areas, you know—and the instructors usually agree that they have good points. The trouble is, changing a system of governance is never simple. Even if everyone agreed the current system wasn't working right—which is a big if—that doesn't mean they would agree on what system would best replace it. So the debate goes on, and things stay as they are in the meantime because, let's face it, the way things are is at least working for the most part."

"That's..." Azai looked frustrated, but he didn't seem to have any words to contradict her.

"Uncomfortably reasonable?" Zev finished for him. "Get used to it." He turned to Veronica. "I don't mean to be rude, but—"

"Oh yes, of course," she cut him off. "I stopped because we're here. That's the stable. And that," she pointed to a different building, "is my parents' home. I'll let them know to expect you, then I'll go back to the council while you're dealing with your horses, and see if I can find out what's going on. I should be able to get in through the after-hours students' entrance, even though I've graduated." She cast an eye over their large, muscled forms. "Bringing strange men in after dark would most definitely not be allowed, though. That was against the rules even when I *was* a student."

She saw Azai raising an eyebrow at her, and flushed.

"Not that I personally ever tested that particular rule, of course." She cleared her throat. "I'll be back."

She hurried off into the night, Azai staring after her.

"She's even worse than Marieke," he said emphatically. "*Not as confident.* Hah!" He let out a scoff that Zev found unconvincing.

Zev just grunted as he led his horse into the public stable. He had no interest in discussing Veronica. In other circumstances, he would have been glad to get to know a friend of Marieke's, but until he was reunited with her, he didn't seem able to care about anything else.

They saw to their horses quickly—too quickly, because when they entered Veronica's family home, there was still no sign of her. Her parents were out, it transpired, but the housekeeper made them tea and left them to their thoughts in a pleasant parlor.

As the minutes ticked by, Zev could barely keep himself in check. The hours of riding had been hard, but at least he'd been moving. At least he'd been taking some kind of action. Sitting and waiting was unbearable.

After an hour had passed, he stood. "I can't take this," he told Azai. "Something's gone wrong. I think we should go back to the council building, and—"

The sound of approaching footsteps cut him off midsentence. Azai rose quickly as well, both brothers turning to face the door. Zev relaxed when Veronica appeared, but her expression quickly drove away any relief he felt at the sight of her.

"What is it?" he asked.

"I'm really sorry," she said. "I feel bad that I urged you to be cautious and wait, but I swear I didn't know what they were planning."

"What do you mean?" Zev could feel the tension radiating from him. "Where's Marieke? Is she all right?"

"I don't have any reason to think she's hurt or anything," Veronica said quickly. "It's the *where* that's the problem. It seems our council didn't question her like she was expecting. They were only acting on a request from the Oleandan council. As soon as she arrived, they loaded her up and sent her for the border." She winced. "She would have been gone long before I even gave you her message."

"What?!"

Zev found himself pacing, his fist clenching and unclenching. The Aeltan council was bad enough, but the Oleandan one was worse. They had Marieke in their sights in a way the southern country didn't. Not to mention the journey provided ample opportunity for Jade to catch Marieke in the open if she caught wind of what was happening.

"But how?" Azai asked. "I thought the bridge was still closed. Are they taking her around by the coast? That's a long journey. Maybe we can catch up to them before they sail."

Veronica shook her head. "The bridge is still closed to regular travelers. But I've heard that the council has started using it again, with small groups crossing on foot, using magical reinforcement."

"If they can use it, so can we," said Zev, clenching his fist one last time. "The land won't give way under my feet."

Veronica raised an eyebrow. "You sound confident."

"I am," he said shortly. He looked at Azai. "You ready?"

His brother nodded. "I'm with you."

"So am I," Veronica said unexpectedly. She met their stunned looks with a defiant toss of her head. "I know I wasn't invited, but I'm invested now. I'm not going to abandon Marieke, and I'm not going to pretend none of this happened. I want to know what's going on."

Zev eyed her. "What kind of songcraft do you do?"

"Healing song and structural song are my areas of focus," she said promptly.

Zev nodded. He expected Azai to protest, but his brother said nothing.

"All right, as long as you don't slow us down. The Oleandan council thinks Marieke is alone and vulnerable, and they're about to find out how wrong they are." His voice darkened. "I'll burn the whole council down if that's what it takes to free her."

He didn't wait for the others to reply to his dramatic declaration. He was already halfway toward the door.

Marieke

"This way."

Marieke held her head up as she followed the guards through an entrance to the council building that she'd never used before. A back entrance reserved for servants and those under trial, she suspected.

If she'd been told six months ago that she would be under arrest by the council and marched through her old academy grounds like a criminal, she would have been mortified. But after the seemingly endless journey from Tarandon to Ondford, she was too exhausted to feel much humiliation. She was too exhausted to feel much of anything. They'd been on the road so long, she'd even become numb to the noticeable deterioration of the land since the last time she was in Oleand. She'd barely taken in the familiar streets of the capital as they'd passed through them.

Hopefully wherever they were taking her had somewhere comfortable to sleep.

She was dismayed when the guards led her down a flight of stairs. They'd entered at ground level, which meant they must be going into a basement. Did the council building even have dungeons? They must, if they used to be a castle. She remembered tales of the monarchs of the past locking up dissenters.

Of course, whether those tales were true was another matter, she reminded herself. Partially true was probably the most likely option.

"Where are we going?" she asked, deciding to be bold. Her imaginings were worse than reality would be. Hopefully.

"The holding rooms," one of the guards told her. "It's not far."

As they descended the last few steps, Marieke contemplated running for it. But she wasn't yet desperate enough to do anything that would mark her indelibly as a fugitive. Plus, one of the guards was a singer, as evidenced by the quiet unlocking song he'd released when they entered the building. She couldn't assume she'd be able to escape cleanly.

She didn't need to fear prolonged captivity, she reminded herself. If they held her for long enough, Zev would come for her.

When they reached the holding rooms, Marieke was both relieved and disheartened. Disheartened because the close, slightly dank basement level had certainly once been a dungeon. Relieved because it had been made significantly more habitable since that distant time. The cells had been converted to rooms with actual doors, albeit ones that were lockable from the outside. The room into which Marieke was ushered was furnished with a basin and a bed, and some attempt had been made to insulate it against the chill of the damp air. They were clearly expected, because the basin was full of fresh water, and a tray of simple food awaited her on the bed.

The guards offered no explanation, withdrawing with the unmistakable sound of the door being locked. Marieke was too weary to care much. She ate the food mechanically, reflecting that its uncovered state was an encouraging indication that whoever had left it didn't expect rats.

The air felt unnaturally still in the holding room, almost stifling. Marieke drew in a deep breath, wondering why it seemed difficult to fill her lungs. It was only after the guards had retreated and she decided to do a quick assessing song that she realized the cause. It wasn't the air that was lacking. It was the ground. No magic stirred beneath her feet where they rested on the worn rug.

Marieke cleared her throat, whispering quietly into the stillness. Her voice was working fine for speech. But when she tried to sing, she couldn't get magic to pool to her. There was no magic to respond.

For a moment, panic flared. Had Oleand's deterioration progressed so rapidly in her absence that the magic was gone from the land? But no, she'd felt it on her journey north. More likely the absence of the magic was a construct of the council, designed to affect only the holding rooms. Marieke had no idea how they'd done it, but it was effective. Her songcraft was silenced.

She didn't like being defenseless, but it was a problem for tomorrow. The simple bed was calling to her, and she sank gladly into it, surrendering to a dreamless sleep.

When Marieke woke, thin morning light slanted down from a tiny window high up on the wall of her room. She hadn't even noticed the window there the night before. No wonder the room was so cold in spite of the insulating rug and other furnishings. She sat up slowly, all the unease she'd been too exhausted to feel the night before washing over her.

She was a prisoner. It didn't matter how comfortable the room was, she was locked into it with no access to her song. And it wasn't the Aeltan council she had to contend with—it was her own council, who'd already shown they were suspicious of her.

Marieke tried not to let panic creep in as she washed up and used the chamber pot that had been provided. At least they'd allowed her to have her bag of possessions, meager as they were. Her stomach was just starting to complain when she heard footsteps approaching through the still basement.

A pair of eyes appeared in the tiny window cut into the door.

"Mari? It is you!" The voice was familiar, and Marieke's heart lifted.

"Kaine?"

"Move back a little, we're coming in," Kaine instructed, and next moment she heard keys turning in the lock.

Marieke moved obediently out of the way, apprehension returning as she wondered who *we* meant. But she needn't have worried. When Kaine stepped into the room, a tray of food in his hands, he was closely followed by Solomon. The guard looked grim, the assistant instructor shocked.

"Mari, what's going on?" demanded Solomon. "I could hardly believe it when Kaine told me he thought you were locked in the dungeon!"

"They said a rogue singing graduate had been apprehended in Aeltas," Kaine nodded. "I had a bad feeling about who that might be, so I volunteered to bring your food this morning so I could make sure."

"Thanks," said Marieke, taking the tray from him and sitting down on the bed. "I appreciate the friendly faces."

"Why are you being labeled a rogue graduate?" Solomon protested. "What in the world have you been up to?"

"Nothing nefarious," Marieke said. "You know me, Solomon, do you really think I'm concocting some evil scheme?"

"I was a little surprised to hear it," Solomon said.

She gave him a look. "Thank you for that strong endorsement of my character."

"Don't blame Solomon," said Kaine shortly. "He's right that you have some explaining to do. Why did you run off last time, Marieke? From what we were told at the time, you'd been ordered by the council to stay in the city, and you slipped off in defiance of those orders. It took the investigators weeks to find your trail."

Marieke raised an eyebrow. "They had investigators hunting for me? I didn't realize I was so important."

"This isn't a joke, Mari," Solomon said, his stern tone amplifying his instructor status. "They've locked you up like a criminal! Why?"

"Ask them," Marieke said shortly. "As far as I'm concerned, I've never done anything worthy of being arrested. Instructor Rafael and the others are angry with me for asking questions they don't want me to have the answers to."

Solomon looked confused, but Kaine spoke before he could ask for explanations.

"It's not just that," the guard said. "When we were told to scour the city for you after you snuck out of the council building, they said you were wanted for questioning regarding a series of destructive fires."

Marieke let out a frustrated breath. "I had nothing to do with that fire! I helped stop it. I just happened to be in the right place at the right time."

"No offense, Mari," Kaine said, "but running away when you're told to stick around for more questioning doesn't make you look innocent. And the disasters continued after you escaped."

Marieke scowled at them. "I'm not behind any of the disasters, either before or after I was questioned. How can you think

I would attack people and destroy farms when times are already so hard?"

"We don't think it, Mari," Solomon assured her. "That's why we're here. But that's because we know you. We just don't think it's completely unreasonable for the council to be suspicious."

"They're very eager to identify who's behind the disasters," Kaine said. "And I can understand their point of view. Things are getting bad, Marieke. Really bad. People are already starting to blame the council for the state of the country, and then you add a never-ending series of unrelated catastrophes on top? Of course the council wants to quash this persistent rumor that the disasters are acts of nature and therefore further evidence of the land's deterioration."

"Oh, they're definitely not acts of nature," Marieke said. "Although I don't think you can call them unrelated. At any rate, I can tell the council who's behind them. It's Jade."

"Jade?" Solomon repeated, astonished. "You mean the student we've talked about before, the one who was expelled?"

Marieke nodded. "That's the one. And she's not finished causing trouble. I don't know exactly what her plan is, but she definitely has one. Part of the reason I didn't resist being brought here is because I always intended to find a way to warn the council about her." She sighed. "I just didn't intend to do it from behind bars."

Solomon ran a hand through his hair, setting it on end and intensifying the eccentric professor look that he naturally tended toward.

"This is beyond my level," he said. "We need to get someone higher up. Instructor Rafael needs to hear what—"

"No." Marieke cut him off at this mention of the academy's Head Instructor. "Not Instructor Rafael. I don't trust him."

"What do you mean?" Solomon frowned.

"They've been teaching us lies, Solomon," Marieke told him. She sagged wearily. "Unless you're part of the lies, of course, in which case I suppose they haven't been lying to you."

"I'm not part of any lies," Solomon said, affronted. "What are you talking about, Marieke?"

She studied his face. "Are you sure about that? You've never been asked to teach anything that isn't quite accurate?"

"Of course not." Solomon looked shocked. "The whole point of teaching is to impart knowledge. Accurate knowledge."

Marieke examined him for a moment longer before nodding. She believed him. It had never matched what she knew of Solomon to imagine him embroiled in a web of deceit.

"That should be the point of teaching," she agreed. "I'm glad you're not being dishonest with the students, Solomon. But that doesn't mean you're not part of any lies. It just means you're not *knowingly* part of it."

"I don't understand what you're talking about, Mari," Solomon said.

She nodded. "I know. And I can't fully explain it." Not without exposing Zev's secrets, anyway, and she wasn't willing to do that. "But I can tell you some of what I've discovered. It's the same thing that Jade discovered, and it's why she was expelled." Marieke felt her brow lower in anger as she gestured to her prison. "The second time around, they seem to have decided to get more serious in their reaction."

"Can you blame them if the reaction of the student they only expelled was to mount a series of magical attacks on the countryside?" Kaine asked reasonably.

"Jade isn't attacking the country because she was expelled," Marieke said. "I doubt she cares about that, to be honest. She cares about the fact that the Council of Singers is lying to us about what happened during the coup, and therefore about their own origins."

"What do you mean?" Kaine asked sharply.

Marieke met his eyes. "The monarchs weren't exiled like we were told. They were slaughtered while attempting to flee."

Solomon stared at her. "That can't be true."

"It is," she said simply. "The evidence is still there in Port Taran, for anyone who knows how to look. And…" She hesitated. She was straying into territory that might endanger Zev's secrets, and she needed to be careful what she said. "And I have reason to think that what happened back then might be contributing to the land failing."

Solomon thought this over, his face once again pale. "But even if you're right," he said, immediately reaching the obvious conclusion that had stumped her for months, "that was so long ago. The land has only started failing in the last couple of years. You must be wrong, Mari."

"I'm not," she said. "I can't prove it all to you right now, but maybe I will be able to in future. The point is, I'm a danger to the council because of what I know, not because of anything I've done."

Both her listeners looked very troubled.

"I would hate to think the council I serve is in the habit of locking up dissenters," Kaine said. "It's not something I've witnessed before."

Marieke sighed. "I don't know how deep it all goes. But I know for certain that Instructor Rafael knows things he isn't being open about."

In fact, she reflected silently, that's where it had all begun for her. With overhearing Instructor Rafael's mention of heartsong. She looked between the two troubled faces before her.

"If you haven't come to spring me out, which I assume you haven't, then you probably shouldn't be here. I know from experience that if the council suspects you of exposure to things they don't want you to know, your life will become a lot harder."

"I wasn't supposed to come inside the room or talk to you," Kaine admitted. "But I knew you couldn't be a violent criminal."

Marieke snorted over the bite of bread she'd just taken. "Hardly. Do you know what they're planning for me?"

Kaine shook his head. "We haven't been told anything."

"I need time to think," Solomon said, holding a hand to his head. Marieke sympathized with him—she remembered clearly how much the disillusionment had rattled her. "How can I help you, Mari? I suppose you want me to carry your news about Jade to the council, but—"

"No," Marieke cut him off quickly. "I would never expect that of you. That would embroil you in a way I'm sure you don't want to be. I fully intend to tell them myself. But I don't want to face Instructor Rafael alone." She thought for a moment. "Do you think Instructor Oriana would see me?" She gave him a hopeful look. "Do you think she might even come see me without telling the Head Instructor about it?"

"I can't speak for her on that," Solomon said. He pulled himself up with determination. "But I'm willing to ask her to come, and even to tell her you want her to hear you out before mentioning it to anyone."

"Thank you," said Marieke, recognizing that even this offer was uncomfortable territory for the rule-abiding academic. "I'm grateful."

The two men retreated, leaving Marieke to her thoughts. The chief object of these thoughts wasn't the visitors, or the danger from the council, or anything at all about her current circumstances. It was Zev. Had Veronica received her message? Had she managed to find Zev and talk him down from doing anything destructive in Tarandon that might bring attention to his family? Did they know where Marieke was now?

Zev would undoubtedly be furious. And afraid, which she hated to picture. Guilt lanced through Marieke as she remembered telling him that he was being ridiculous to worry about leaving her for a day, that she would be fine on the farm without him.

That had been optimistic.

To be fair, they'd both been concerned about Jade, and thankfully Marieke had seen no sign of the rogue singer. But being in the bowels of the council itself didn't feel like adequate protection, not when she was without her song. Word would quickly spread regarding her arrest, and the longer she was held, the more time Jade would have to come after her, knowing Marieke couldn't flee or even fight back effectively.

She was torn between wanting Zev to come to her rescue and worrying about the consequences to him if he did. In all honesty, she was surprised not to have seen him yet. She'd expected him to come after her straight away, and had been watching for him all the way north. Hopefully his absence didn't mean he was in trouble of his own. The thought made her feel chafed and helpless, locked away without access to magic.

Solomon obviously hadn't wasted time on his errand, because less than an hour had passed when the sound of footsteps once again reached Marieke's ears. She fixed her eyes warily on the little window in the door.

The round face that appeared there, only partially visible, wore a somber expression that didn't suit it.

"Instructor Oriana." Marieke moved forward eagerly. "You agreed to come."

"Somewhat against my better judgment," she said. "I'm not sure how Solomon gained access to this holding room without a council member's approval in order to receive the message in the first place."

"Never mind that," said Marieke, not wanting to get Kaine in trouble. "What did Solomon tell you?"

"That you wanted to speak to me privately, and he strongly believed I would wish to hear what you have to say," said Instructor Oriana. "I don't know if I was right to trust him, frankly. It's only my belief in Solomon's good sense that has me here."

"I'm not exactly a threat to you," Marieke pointed out. "I can't even access my song in here."

Instructor Oriana nodded. "Yes, I can sense that. The room is surrounded by a barrier that keeps magic from entering and thus prevents the occupant from reaching it. It's a sophisticated enchantment, and much less barbaric than silencing prisoners' voices altogether."

"I suppose so," Marieke said. "It feels more barbaric on this side of the barrier."

"It's intended for suspected criminals awaiting trial," Instructor Oriana pointed out. "You don't belong in a prison, child. What have you gotten yourself involved with?"

"I haven't done anything to deserve being locked up," Marieke said. "As far as I'm aware, I haven't even been formally accused of anything."

She waited for the older woman to contradict her, but Instructor Oriana just bit her lip. Clearly she was uneasy about the irregular process that had landed Marieke in the dungeon. Otherwise she wouldn't be there.

"I know you came for answers," Marieke said. "But I have some questions I've been dying to ask you myself, and I don't know when I'll get another chance."

"What questions?" Instructor Oriana sounded wary.

"About storytelling song," Marieke said. The instructor

didn't speak, so she pushed on. "Was the class really full when I applied?"

"I—Marieke, that's a complicated matter of—"

"No, it's not," Marieke cut her off brutally. Her heart sank at the instructor's manner. It seemed she had her answer. "It's actually a very simple question. Did I score well enough to continue, or not?"

She heard Instructor Oriana's sigh through the door. "Yes," she said softly. "You did. The class wasn't full."

"Then why?" demanded Marieke. "Why did you tell me it was? Why was I blocked from continuing?"

"It wasn't my decision," Instructor Oriana informed her. She winced. "Well, it was my decision to tell you that the class was full. It was a lie, and I regret it. But I only said it because I truly believed it would cause less pain and frustration than telling you that you were barred from studying storytelling song through no fault of your own."

"Why was I barred, though?" Marieke asked desperately. "I didn't think anyone had a problem with me back then. Even after I graduated, the Head Instructor personally selected me for the delegation to Aeltas!"

"No one had a problem with you at any point during your studies," the instructor assured her. "It wasn't a question of character or likability. It was purely a matter of aptitude." She drew in a breath. "Do you remember the introductory course you took?"

"Of course I do," said Marieke. "It was fascinating, and I was eager to continue."

The part of the instructor's face she could see was nodding. "Of course you were. You tested very high in aptitude, which almost always coincides with high interest in the subject."

"You're telling me my aptitude was *too* high to study story-telling song?" Marieke asked. "We both know that makes no sense." She pinned the older woman with a stare. "It wasn't the strength of my aptitude, was it? It was its direction. I showed signs of having the aptitude songcraft that we call questioning and the Aeltans call sifting, didn't I?"

Instructor Oriana stared at her. "How did you know that?"

"I figured it out," Marieke said, not caring that her tone was snarky. "Because apparently I have a knack for asking the right questions."

Instructor Oriana looked pained. "You do indeed. And it stung both personally and professionally not to be able to train you in the craft. So few students have the aptitude, and I used to love helping them develop it. They always made such engaged students, full of all the right questions, eager to pursue every lead. Well, you were that type of student in your other classes, weren't you?"

"So why wasn't I allowed to take storytelling song?" Marieke demanded. "If you love teaching questioning song, why didn't you want to teach it to me?"

"I *used* to love teaching it," Instructor Oriana corrected her. "And it wasn't a matter of what I wanted. Storytelling song is powerful and important in all its aspects. But questioning is a dangerous branch of it. After a rather disastrous experience with a former student, the difficult decision was made that we would no longer teach that branch of storytelling song at our academy. I'm afraid that displaying that particular aptitude in the testing disqualifies students from studying storytelling at all. It's a rare enough aptitude that very few students were affected in the years since then, but unfortunately you were one. It wasn't about you personally, Marieke. It's just the policy. And I preferred to tell you the class was full rather than give you cause for resentment. Perhaps that was cowardly."

Marieke sank onto the bed, her mind whirling as she took it all in. She hadn't expected such an honest answer. The instructor hadn't told her everything, of course, but little did she know how well Marieke could fill in the gaps. But she was still confused on one point.

"I assume from what I know that the Head Instructor is the one who insisted on that policy," she said, not bothering to ask Instructor Oriana to confirm it. "If he knew you'd applied that policy in order to stop my further studies, I'm surprised he was willing to send me to Aeltas at all. I would have thought he'd have marked me as dangerous in his mind."

"Well..." Instructor Oriana's discomfort was clear. "I didn't mention your aptitude to him. There was no need to. The rule is universal, and you weren't continuing in the discipline, so it wasn't relevant."

Marieke stared at her. "Why would you keep it to yourself?" But it took only a moment to realize she knew the answer. "Because you knew it as well as I do," she said, a hint of accusation in her voice. "You knew that he *would* have marked me as dangerous, and I would have faced prejudice in my other studies."

"No," said Instructor Oriana unconvincingly. "I just didn't want anyone to get the wrong idea about you."

"You didn't want anyone to think I was like Jade," Marieke said flatly. "She's the student you mentioned. She had the questioning aptitude as well."

"What do you know of Jade?" Instructor Oriana asked, clearly unnerved. "She was well before your time."

"We've met," Marieke said mildly. "She invited me to...what was her wording? To help her or be removed from her path."

The visible part of the instructor's face had gone pale. "Help her do what?"

"She didn't specify," Marieke said. "But given she was behind all those attacks on singers, and she's also behind all the disasters, I think I get the general idea."

"This is terrible," Instructor Oriana said hollowly. "It's just the sort of thing we've been afraid of." Her tone seemed to plead with Marieke. "Doesn't her behavior demonstrate why we decided it was too dangerous to keep teaching questioning song? Can't you see why we regretted losing track of her after we expelled her, and why everyone was alarmed when another student who'd shown the same type of defiance disappeared from under our noses, all in the midst of unexplained attacks and disasters?"

"The problem wasn't the desire to ask questions," Marieke retorted. "The problem was the answers those questions revealed."

"I agree in general that asking questions should be encouraged," Instructor Oriana said. "But Jade was a very angry young woman. She had a complicated background." The instructor sounded weary. "She was one of my best students, and I had hoped she would rise above her past to achieve great things, but..."

"What do you mean by a complicated background?" Marieke asked, distracted in spite of herself.

"She didn't come from a singing family," Instructor Oriana said. "Her parents were shopkeepers in a town about an hour from the capital, and I believe were surprised when she showed the singing aptitude."

Marieke said nothing. The story sounded eerily like her own thus far.

"She had a great deal of attitude when she arrived at the academy, and it took a while for me to learn why." Instructor Oriana sighed. "But I'd rarely seen a student with such raw capability, and I was motivated to try to reach her. So I made inquiries. It turned out that her father had been in constant conflict with the singer who served as the council's representative for the area. Nothing major, just regular clashes over trading regulations and the like."

"So she's conflicted about singers as a result of petty conflict between her father and a council singer?" Marieke asked, frowning.

She pictured the calm fury in Jade's eyes, and her chilling detachment when she spoke of the murders Gorgon had carried out on her orders. Surely there was more to the story.

"Not exactly." Instructor Oriana's voice was heavy. "There was an altercation one night. I think the council representative caught Jade's father receiving smuggled goods. Anyway, things turned violent, and her father ended up dead."

Marieke's eyes widened. "Dead?"

Instructor Oriana was silent for a moment. "It was a terrible tragedy. There was an inquiry, and it was ruled an accident. All of this was years before Jade started at the academy."

"And she didn't consider it an accident?" Marieke guessed. "She didn't feel her father had been given justice?"

"She did not. The troubling part was that she didn't say any of this. I wouldn't have known about any of it if I hadn't gone digging. When I raised it with her, she had plenty to say, however. She fully blamed the singer in question, and was highly critical of the process by which the matter had been investigated."

"Do you think she was right?" Marieke asked.

"It's not as simple as that," Instructor Oriana said. "I reviewed the matter myself, using my craft. Of course years had passed, so my inquiries were hampered. But I do believe that it was an accident, something Jade would never accept, I think. But that doesn't mean she was completely wrong. She made some points that were hard to argue with, regarding the power imbalance and bias inherent in an investigation by singers into the conduct of one of their own."

Marieke crossed her arms over her torso. "What about the singer? The one who fought with her father?"

"He died." Instructor Oriana said the words without inflection. "In a freak accident. Within a year of Jade's expulsion."

Marieke's eyes flew to the older woman's, and there was a moment of silence.

"She was once my most promising student," the instructor went on sadly. "I used to think it was a good thing that she challenged me. Not easy, but good. But she learned to use her questioning craft as a weapon, and she took it beyond my classroom. She pushed and poked at the leadership, using her aptitude to find every weak point, every uncertainty. She came to convince herself that anything less than perfection made those in leadership unworthy of power. When she first showed signs of willingness to use her magic to work against the authority of the academy, she was expelled."

"She was offended by anything less than perfection?" Marieke repeated skeptically. "Do you really not know that her questions uncovered more than just petty failures of leadership? Or is that the benign version you tell yourself to justify keeping the council's secrets?"

Once, she would never have imagined talking to an instructor so boldly. But now...there wasn't much she couldn't imagine. And Instructor Oriana's obvious discomfort validated her criticism.

"It's easy to make it sound simple from the outside, Marieke," the older woman said, shifting her weight so that her head bobbed in Marieke's limited vision. "But these things are never truly simple. Governing a country is complicated, and the council is doing the best that it can under less than perfect circumstances."

"I'll reserve the right to respectfully disagree on that," said Marieke, her tone admittedly not very respectful.

"Marieke, this isn't a helpful attitude," the instructor insisted. "You're talking like Jade used to talk. You're not going about it very wisely if you want to convince the council that you can be trusted with the privilege that comes from being an academy-trained singer."

"Who says I do want to convince them of that?" Marieke countered. "What's going to happen to me, Instructor? Am I going to stand trial? Will I have a chance to testify on my own behalf?"

"Well…" The other woman seemed reluctant to answer. "That's the normal way if you're charged with an offense. But I don't believe there are any formal charges. My understanding is that you're to be held for everyone's safety pending further investigation of the incidents you were involved with."

"I can't be left to rot in here without access to my magic," Marieke said. She didn't even bother to protest the suggestion that she'd had a hand in the fire or the other attacks and disasters, too consumed by alarm for her immediate situation. "I'm not safe in here."

"Of course you are," the instructor said, perplexed. "No one is going to attack you, Marieke. The council has process regarding accused criminals, you know."

"You just admitted that the council has neglected to formally charge me and has therefore found a convenient way to sidestep being bound by its own processes," Marieke reminded her.

"That's hardly what I said." Instructor Oriana sounded frustrated, but Marieke didn't give her the chance to defend her words.

"It doesn't matter, because it's not the council I'm worried about. You have to convince them to let me out, Instructor Oriana. I'm willing to face questioning, just don't leave me without my magic."

"Marieke, I really think you're overly concerned about—"

Her words were cut off by a splintering crash that sounded like the door at the top of the stairs had been thrown violently open. Marieke's heart soared as a familiar voice rang out with an authority that was indefinable but undeniable, even here in a country not his own.

"Marieke? Where is she?"

FOUR

Zev

Zev leaped down the stairs three steps at a time, his eyes fixed on the woman gaping up at him from the dungeon level and his veins coursing with energy. It had been a very trying journey to the Oleandan capital—one seemingly plagued with every delay that could make travel frustrating. Zev was exhausted and stressed, but he had no intention of laying his head down until Marieke was free from the prison she'd been thrown into.

"Marieke is fine," the stranger said crisply. "Who are you, and how did you get in here?"

Zev didn't answer her. No doubt the unconscious guard would be located soon enough—fortunately they'd only had to use force in one instance, Veronica managing to use her craft to clear the rest of the way into the dungeon for them. In fact, Zev had been impressed by her strength—she was hiding out of sight, so he couldn't congratulate her, but she'd overwhelmed the council's defenses with surprising ease.

"What is that?" The woman standing outside the cell frowned at the stairwell behind him. "Whose songcraft can I feel?"

Zev strode forward, again not answering. It would be too much to expect Veronica's unseen work to be undetectable to a trained singer. There was no time to waste. As soon as the presence of unauthorized strangers was realized, they would have the might of the Oleandan Council of Singers to deal with. He intended to have Marieke free and out of reach before then.

"Marieke?" he called again.

"Zev, I'm here!" Her cry sent a wave of relief over him. She must be inside the cell the woman was standing next to.

The woman opened her mouth, and recognizing impending songcraft, Zev raised his arms in an instinctive—albeit futile—defense. He lowered them with a start at the sound that came out of her mouth. It was like no song he'd heard before. Was it a more potent type of magic he didn't know?

"You're shielded." The woman's song dropped away in favor of normal speech as she stared at his clearly non-singer self, her brow furrowed. "Magically shielded."

Thank you, Veronica.

"What was that?!" Azai came thundering down the stairs behind Zev. He sounded outraged. "I can't believe you've been trying to tell me the Oleandans aren't barbaric, Zev. I'm guessing our council has a dungeon of its own, but even it isn't bad enough to literally torture the prisoners!"

"Azai?" Marieke's voice came from out of sight again. "No one's being tortured. That's just..." She cleared her throat. "Well, Instructor Oriana has an unusual singing voice."

"Never mind that," the older woman said, apparently untroubled by the fact that Azai had misinterpreted her song as the sounds of torture. "Who *are* you?"

"We're here for Marieke," Zev said, striding past her. He could feel Azai tailing him as he approached the door and peered through the tiny window cut into it. Marieke stood on the other side, looking travel-worn but mercifully unharmed. "Are you all right?"

She nodded. "I'm fine." A crooked grin crossed her face, lighting up her familiar features. "I did wonder what was taking you so long."

Zev smiled fiercely at her. "And here I thought you'd tell me I shouldn't have come. Why did you let them take you away like that, Mari?"

She sighed. "I didn't want it to come to a fight. I didn't know they were going to ship me straight across the border to my own council for them to throw me in prison." An anxious expression crossed her face. "Zev, they intend to keep me locked up down here indefinitely."

"No need to worry about that," Zev said shortly. "We're leaving."

"I hate to interrupt," the other woman said, sounding like she was unsure whether to be amused or outraged, "but none of you are leaving, least of all Marieke. She's in the custody of the Council of Singers for a reason."

"Yes," said Zev shortly. "That reason is that your council is corrupt."

"He's right, Instructor Oriana," Marieke chimed in. "My only crime is learning what Jade's questions uncovered. I can't believe I even have to say this, but unlike her, I didn't turn to violence in response. I didn't do anything except find things out that Instructor Rafael and the rest of the council don't want me to know." Her blue eyes were even more piercing than usual as they shifted over Zev's shoulder to fix on the woman behind him. "And I think you know that."

Zev turned his head, surprised to see the instructor hesitating, her expression conflicted.

"We'll fight you if we have to," he told the woman shortly. "But what we don't have time to do is stand around and talk."

"So let's get moving," Azai chimed in.

"I just can't believe you convinced Azai to come," Marieke said, sounding dazed.

Azai made a disgruntled noise from behind Zev. "It wasn't my idea. Apparently we're now part of your quest to save your country." He paused. "Although Zev is also going to burn the whole country down to save you, if necessary. I can't keep up with him, honestly."

Zev stepped back, shrugging as he studied the door to Marieke's cell. "I'm a complicated person."

Marieke's eyes once again shifted to the instructor, now that Zev was no longer blocking her limited view.

"He's really not," she told the other woman sagely. "He's a farmer. Very salt-of-the-earth."

Marieke's captor moved forward into Zev's line of sight. She looked hopelessly confused, and who was to blame her?

"Look, I still have very little idea what you all think you're doing, and I don't wish any harm to friends of Marieke's who are understandably concerned about her welfare. But I will not be allowing you to simply walk out of here. Marieke needs to stay where she is until—"

"Can you sing your way out of the room?" Zev cut her off, ignoring her words as he focused on Marieke. "The way out of the building is clear. For now."

"Listen here." The instructor was starting to get annoyed, but Marieke disregarded her as completely as Zev had done.

"I can't. I have my voice for speaking, as you can hear, but the magic is blocked from reaching me inside this room. I can't sing."

"Hm." Zev considered her words. "Magic has always responded differently to us, though, hasn't it?"

Marieke brightened. "Do you think...?"

Zev didn't wait for her to articulate the thought. He reached toward her, his hand slipping between the bars of the little window.

"That's enough."

The sharp words from the instructor were followed by an indrawn breath, as if she was gathering her voice for song. But instead of the horrid warble Zev had heard before, a gurgling splutter met his ears. He glanced back to see Azai grappling with the woman, blocking her songcraft with the good, old-fashioned method of covering her mouth with one hand while his other pinned her arms. The woman looked outraged, and she was doing her best to wrestle free. But however powerful a singer she might be, there could be no doubt that Azai was physically stronger.

"Sorry, Instructor Oriana." Marieke winced. "Kaine is right—we really should all be taught the basics of combat." She turned to Zev. "There's no time to waste."

He nodded agreement, holding out his hand in an insistent invitation. Her fingers were cold when she slipped them between his, but that didn't stop the heat from racing over his skin from the contact. Something in him relaxed at the rightness of being reunited with her. He'd felt all wrong since she was taken from him—hollow and tense, her absence like a splinter in his mind.

Marieke seemed to feel something even more substantial. As their fingers twined together around the thin bars, he saw her face shift into a look of concentration he'd learned to recognize. It was how she looked when she was gathering magic to her, ready to sing. The next moment, she let out a gasp, her eyes flying to his.

"The magic!"

"Is it pooling to you now?" Zev asked.

She shook her head. "Not exactly. I can feel the blockage that's stopping the magic from reaching me. But it's pooling to you out there, and I think…I think it's trying to break through the barrier."

Zev had no idea if anything he did would help, but he silently willed the magic to reach Marieke, to give her the power she needed to free herself.

"It's working," she breathed. "It's fighting the barrier enchantment!" Her eyes were awed as they found his. "Even here? Even in Oleand you have this kind of power?"

"This is our land," Zev said, the truth of it blazing into life inside him. "Yours and mine, all of it. Humans live and die by political borders, but do they mean anything at all to the power of the land?"

How could he ever have hidden behind the cowardly argument that Oleand's troubles weren't his problem? How could he ever have thought Aeltas unaffected by the blight now staining their continent?

"Zev!" Marieke's grip tightened on his hand. She didn't need to explain what she was feeling. Her cry turned smoothly into a song, the sound reverberating off the stone walls as magic flowed into her. They'd broken through the barrier.

Zev heard the startled splutter from the still-fighting instructor, but he didn't turn. His ears had also caught a crash in the distance, and he had a feeling their window of opportunity to flee rather than fight was closing quickly.

"Marieke," he said, his voice low and urgent. "We need to go. Are you versed in structural songcraft at all? Can you weaken the weakest points of the door? I imagine it'll be the hinges. Then I can lift it off."

Marieke looked impressed, but she didn't pause her song to comment. Instead she directed her gaze to the door's hinges, her hand gripping Zev's so tightly her knuckles were white as she put words to her song. Zev caught mention of breaking and shattering—it was an angrier type of song than any he'd heard from Marieke before. A moment later, he heard a splintering crunch, and several pins shattered from inside each hinge. Zev let go of Marieke's hand, drawing his quickly out of the window to steady the now-leaning door.

"Come on!" he shouted.

He could now hear yells from the direction of the stairs, another loud bang following close behind. The muscles in his arm shook as, with a grunt of effort, he shifted the heavy door out of the way, throwing it to the stone floor with a deafening clang that would be sure to bring any guards not already on the way.

Marieke darted backward to scoop up her pack, then catapulted through the doorway and into him so quickly she almost bowled him over. His arms tightened around her for a moment to steady them both before he released her, searching her face urgently as he seized one hand in his.

"Nicely done," he said. "You sure you're all right?"

She nodded. "Good tip about the hinges. I didn't know you even knew that structural song was a type of songcraft. Did I tell you that?"

"Actually," started Zev, "it wasn't you. We're here with—"

But the explanation was cut short as Marieke's hand tightened on his and her eyes flew to the door above.

"What was that?"

"What?" Zev asked, spinning around.

Even Azai's struggle had stilled, the instructor pausing her attempts to get free as her head whipped toward the staircase like Marieke's had done.

"Magic," said Marieke. "A strong surge of it—it feels like someone just blasted everyone and everything out of their path."

Zev and Azai exchanged a look. "Veronica came with us,"

Zev said uneasily. "She's hiding upstairs, providing shielding from a distance. Maybe she's run into trouble."

Marieke looked astonished at this mention of the Aeltan singer, but she pushed it aside. "Veronica's barely graduated. She didn't do what I just felt."

"I felt it, too." Instructor Oriana ripped free of Azai's slackened grasp, her voice quivering with anger and—unless Zev was mistaken—fear. "I don't know what exactly you're all mixed up in, but you listen to me. Every one of you is going to—"

With a crash that made them all jump, the door flew open at the top of the stairs, and a lone figure appeared—a figure that brought a tangled rush of fear and rage rising to fill Zev's mind, driving everything else out before it.

He practically threw Marieke behind him, his sword in his hand before the newcomer could take more than a step down the stairs.

"Jade!" The instructor was the one to gasp out the name, sounding like this development had shaken her more than everything else.

"Hello, Instructor Oriana," Jade said pleasantly, descending another step. "Have you missed me? I never did get to graduate your class, did I?"

"Jade, what have you done?" the instructor whispered. "Why are you here?"

"I have a promise to keep."

Jade's eyes glinted maliciously as they found Marieke behind Zev. His hand tightened angrily on the hilt of his sword.

"Stay away from her," he growled.

Her eyes returned to his face. "And you have a decision to make, I believe."

Zev didn't get a chance to reply. With a cry of fury, Azai

launched himself toward the stairs. Marieke's voice swelled behind Zev, the tone frantic as she threw together what he could only assume was a shielding song. Zev took a step forward, surprised when the instructor's voice joined Marieke's.

They seemed to be focusing their efforts on Azai, who was only a few steps from their father's murderer. But Jade didn't appear concerned with Azai. Her voice swelled the noise that already filled the confined space, and the step where Azai had just placed his foot changed shape, turning to a smooth slope that sent him slipping back down to land in a heap at Zev's feet.

"Don't be hasty, little warrior," Jade said, her condescending voice grating on Zev's ears, although she wasn't speaking to him. "Your ferocity can be put to better use than this if you'll just trust me."

"Trust you?" Azai roared, springing back to his feet.

"What are you doing here, Jade?" the instructor demanded over the top of his anger.

"The same as these fine gentlemen," Jade said flippantly. "I must say, Zevadiah, I'd hoped you had a better plan. I admit I was irked to learn that Marieke had been taken into the custody of our dear council, but imagine my delight when I realized you were on your way to break her out. It would have been much more convenient for me if you'd done so without my involvement and I could have caught up to you once you were on the road again. But this is a sadly disorganized rescue mission. You wouldn't have even made it in without my assistance, and you certainly weren't going to make it out. As it is, we'd best make our business quick. I didn't come prepared for a face-off with the might of the council. They'll break through my defenses soon."

Zev stood frozen, suddenly understanding the ease with which they'd breached the council. Veronica hadn't been the only one assisting them from out of sight. In fact, her efforts had likely had very little to do with it.

Jade turned her eyes to Marieke, rubbing her hands together briskly. "You've done more than enough damage to my cause."

"And I'm just getting started," Marieke spat, stepping around Zev to face Jade.

The other singer clucked her tongue. "Such misapplied determination. You could have been such an asset to me." She sighed. "But you're a risk I can't afford."

Her voice turned smoothly from speech to song, the transition so quick no one had warning before the ground under Marieke's feet erupted, shards of stone lancing upward from now-ruined slabs.

With a cry, Marieke jumped out of the way, the movement carrying her closer to Jade. Zev was at her side in a moment, putting his body between her and the murderous singer.

But Jade didn't need direct access to Marieke to do damage. Under her song, a metal bar from the tiny window of the nearest cell bent outward, the pole detaching from the wood with a crunch. Marieke's voice was raised now as well, her face screwed up in concentration as she stared at Jade. Zev didn't know what she was trying to do. All he knew was that she seemed unaware of the metal rod now angling toward her.

He leaped around her, his blade intercepting the pole as it flew straight at Marieke. The weapon sent the metal rod clanging to the floor, Zev's heart pounding with the awareness of how near a miss it had been. Marieke didn't appear to have even noticed. By the look of things, she was drawing every grain of loose dust she could take hold of, forming it into a smothering cloud that was closing in on Jade.

The ghastly sound of the instructor's voice added to the chaos as she also targeted her song at Jade. Zev could see no visible effect from her efforts, but the instructor's forehead was beading with sweat, her eyes widening a little at whatever she was experiencing.

Marieke's dust cloud enveloped Jade, and a moment later, her voice faltered in a cough. Zev felt a stab of pride in the simplicity and effectiveness of Marieke's attack.

"Come on!" he shouted. "We have to get out of here!" He grabbed Marieke's hand and started toward the stairs. But behind Jade's dust cloud he caught a glimpse of figures crowding the doorway, all of them in purple.

"Council members," Marieke gasped. "We can't get past them, Zev, there's no way." She spun wildly, then pulled him back toward the cell. "Come on, Azai!"

As soon as her song had stopped, the dust had begun to dissipate. Jade's screech of anger vied with Marieke's song, which seemed to speed out ahead of them. Before Zev's eyes, the stone wall of the cell shifted and buckled, a fissure opening underneath a tiny window.

The instructor's song had paused, but it started up again. A glance back showed her trying to intercept Jade, but the next second, the older woman was flung through the air into the open cell. She hit the wall and slid down it, her vision dazed.

"Instructor Oriana!" Marieke yelled, half turning from the escape route she'd made.

"Marieke, no!" Zev grabbed her around the waist, trying to pull her back toward safety.

"Don't run like a criminal." The instructor's pained murmur made Marieke relax in Zev's hold. The other woman was conscious and lucid.

"Can you really look me in the eye and tell me they won't find a way to blame all this on me?" Marieke said. She shook her head. "I'll be no one's prisoner willingly."

A wordless roar drew Zev's attention back to the dungeon

outside the cell. To his horror, he saw that Azai hadn't followed them. Instead, he'd taken the instructor's defeat as an opening to fling himself on Jade with his weapon raised. If his aim had been to distract the singer, it would have been effective— between keeping the council members from coming down the stairs and fending off his continued assaults, her songcraft seemed fully occupied. But he was clearly trying to kill her, showing every sign of being determined to fight until his last breath. Zev could tell at a glance that if Jade had wanted to kill his brother, Azai would already be dead. She obviously still believed the brothers were more use to her alive, but would that certainty withstand Azai's frenzied attacks? Even as he watched, an angry note entered her song, and Azai's blade began to glow. He dropped it with a cry, his hand burned.

"Azai!" Zev boosted a protesting Marieke up through the window, then flung himself back across the dungeon. He grabbed hold of his brother's shirt and forcibly dragged him away from the singer.

He was barely aware of Jade turning quickly toward the dungeon opening, his attention mostly captured with his struggling brother.

"You'll have your chance!" he shouted at Azai as, with a loud crash, Jade brought a section of ceiling down, blocking the stairway. "But today isn't it!"

He shoved his brother toward the window, where Marieke crouched, arm extended to help them clamber through. Azai gave up the fight, cradling his burned hand to his chest as he let Marieke grasp the other hand and tug while he climbed.

Zev followed, aware that Jade was close behind. With a metallic crunch, the rocks she'd piled over the stairway flew outward, many voices coming together in a chorus that quickly filled the room they'd just escaped.

Not that they were out of danger yet. He could hear Jade

scrabbling toward the window as he emerged into fresh air, and they were still within the council's complex. Jade's head was through the hole when a new figure came sprinting around the corner. Veronica was singing while she ran, causing the stone slabs that Marieke had shattered when opening up the entrance to re-stack themselves in front of Jade's face.

"This way!" Veronica yelled, beckoning to them. "It won't hold long!"

Zev didn't need telling twice, but to his frustration, Azai turned away from Veronica's direction.

"Give me your sword," he told Zev tersely, holding out a hand.

"No."

"Give it to me!" Azai insisted. "I lost mine in there!"

"Don't be a fool, Azai!" Zev yelled. "We have to get out of here before she—"

The rocks burst outward, once again revealing Jade's face. No weapon in hand, Azai strode toward her, apparently not daunted by the song building as she opened her mouth.

Marieke came flying out of nowhere, her fist colliding with Jade's head in a purely physical attack that caught everyone by surprise. It was undeniably a weak punch, so Zev didn't expect the sharp cry of pain that escaped Jade. He did expect the fury in her eyes as she pulled herself free of Veronica's makeshift wall, however, and he felt a flash of annoyance with Marieke for putting herself back in harm's way. As if he didn't have enough to do keeping Azai from getting himself killed.

"Come on!" he shouted, shoving his brother toward Veronica and grabbing Marieke's hand. At least she didn't fight him, sprinting at his side toward the high fence not far away.

He expected Jade to be hard on their heels, but although she cleared the building, a glance back showed her facing the hole into the dungeon, her voice raised in a rapid song. No doubt the council members had caught up with her. It was clear that she wasn't ready for a confrontation with the council. Zev had the impression she'd laid her plans carefully and wouldn't want to act ahead of them. With any luck, getting cleanly away herself would take all of her focus.

"I've made a hole in the fence," Veronica panted, running alongside them as they rounded a corner of the building so that Jade was no longer in their sight. "I'm sorry I wasn't more use. By the time I realized something had gone badly wrong, the way to you through the building was blocked. Here."

She stopped and gestured to the fence in question. Her work was much neater than Zev had expected. She hadn't blown a hole in it like Marieke had in the cell wall. Instead, a strip of bricks had been removed all the way from the ground to the top of the fence and stacked in piles nearby. How had she found time to deconstruct it so cleanly?

The obvious answer came after Veronica had ushered them all through the fence, following last. It wasn't time that was the key, it was magic. Zev watched, impressed, as she formed a quiet, steady song, the words along a theme of mending. Before his eyes, the fence knitted itself back together, the bricks flying into place in perfect formation, even the joining material filling the gaps. In moments, the fence was whole, showing no sign that the bricks had been out of place a moment before.

"That's..." Azai's dazed voice reminded Zev how much less his brother had seen of magic than he had.

"Like magic?" Veronica quipped, grinning. On their journey north, she'd formed quite the habit of ribbing Azai. She couldn't be blamed for taking this latest opportunity to continue it, given she hadn't witnessed Azai's confrontation with his father's killer. "Structural song is one of my areas of specialty, remember?"

"Structural song," Marieke repeated faintly, shaking her

head at Zev in amazement before turning back to Veronica. "You have some questions to answer, but there's no time now. We need to get away from here before Jade or the council or both come looking for us." She glanced around her. "I know where we are. Come on."

She sprinted down the street, the others following. Thankfully no one seemed to have witnessed their escape from the council compound, but they were attracting attention from passersby as they ran, and no one's expressions were very friendly. Marieke led them into a market square, then slowed.

"We should try to look less conspicuous," she panted. "No more running." She glanced around, and Zev frowned.

"What's wrong?" he asked.

"I don't know." Unease was written across Marieke's face. "I thought I knew this area, but..." She shrugged. "The market looks different. There used to be more stalls, and I don't remember any shopfronts being boarded up. And the whole air of the place feels—"

"Tense," Veronica finished for her. "So it's not usually like this?"

Marieke shook her head. "Not in the years I've lived in the capital."

"I don't think it's a good idea to hang around," Zev agreed.

He knew what the girls meant. He didn't say it aloud, not wanting to increase Marieke's distress, but the city had been the same all the way to the council building. The troubles plaguing Oleand's countryside were well and truly being felt in the capital now.

"We're not far from the stable yard my father orders supplies from," Marieke offered. "I've been there lots of times, it's always busy, with plenty of people browsing for horses and supplies. No one will think it odd if we take a long time wandering through, and I doubt the council would think to look for us there."

Once they'd caught their breath enough to move more casually, she left the market, taking the group through winding streets into a quieter part of town. The bustle picked back up again as they neared the stable yard, and Zev felt himself relax. It was much easier to blend in with a crowd than in an empty alleyway.

They'd barely gone inside the first building in the complex when Marieke stiffened. "Do you feel that?" she asked Veronica.

The other singer nodded. "Songcraft nearby."

"Not just nearby," Marieke said. "Above us. I think it's Jade. It feels like a seeking song traveling over the area." She let out a long exhale. "Still your senses. No singing—don't even think about songcraft. If you don't even draw any magic toward you, she shouldn't be able to identify us, right?"

"I think that's right." Veronica sounded nervous, and she closed her eyes as she let out a long breath like Marieke had done.

Azai stared at her for a moment before turning angrily to Marieke. "If Jade is out there, I don't want to hide in here! Where is this seeking enchantment or whatever coming from?"

"I'm not telling you that," Marieke said flatly.

"Why not?" he demanded.

"Because you're clearly not thinking straight," she said.

"I don't have the patience to argue with you." Azai's face was hard as he turned to Zev. "Give me your sword." He repeated his demand from earlier.

"You know I'm not going to do that," Zev said evenly. "Marieke is right."

"Of course you'd agree with her," Azai said, his temper rising fast. "But I'm not a coward like you are. I'm ready to fight!"

"Hey!" Marieke was getting angry now. "Don't call him a coward."

"It's all right," Zev said, raising a hand.

Unlike Azai, he wasn't in the grip of blind rage anymore, and he knew better than to take his brother's insults to heart. Zev wasn't really the target of Azai's anger. And as much as Zev appreciated Marieke's defense of him, she didn't understand what Azai was feeling, not like Zev did. She hadn't watched her father killed in front of her while powerless to stop it.

"It's not all right." Azai was still furious. "Why did you stop me back there, Zev?"

"Because you weren't going to be able to get to her," Zev said. "You were getting nowhere, you know it's true."

Veronica had opened her eyes again, her gaze wary as it passed between the brothers.

"All I know to be true is that she killed our father, and you stopped me from making her pay!" Azai's voice was raised enough to draw some attention. "Why?"

"Why?" Zev's patience was at last being tested as he caught the furtive glances around them. "Because I didn't want her to kill my brother as well, that's why."

Azai flung away from him, thankfully disappearing into the musty closeness of the nearest row of stalls rather than outside toward Jade's questing enchantment.

"He'll be all right," Zev said gruffly. "He just needs some space."

"Was that singer who was chasing you really the one who killed your father?" Veronica asked, her voice hushed and her eyes following Azai's disappearing form.

Zev nodded, his brow dark. "And Azai isn't wrong that she needs to pay. Today wasn't the day, but it's coming."

"We have to be strategic about it, though, Zev," Marieke said seriously. "I have a plan, but it will be seriously complicated if Azai can't get within five leagues of Jade without throwing himself at her and trying to take revenge that will obviously fail."

"You have a plan?" Zev demanded, staring at her. "Since when?"

"Since I saw an opportunity and grabbed it," Marieke said. "Literally."

"An opportunity to do what?" Zev asked.

She smiled grimly, holding up a fist to reveal the strands of long, dark hair gripped inside it.

"To get this."

Marieke

Marieke paced the floor of the bedchamber she was sharing with Veronica, trying to get control of her nerves. She really hoped she wasn't making a mistake. It would be awful if they all got caught because she'd been too trusting. A knock on the door made her look up, drawing magic through the ground toward her in readiness. It was an instinctive reaction.

"Come in," she said warily.

She'd expected an overzealous maid, sent by the innkeeper to clean the room, so she sagged with relief when Zev appeared.

"It's nearly time," Zev told her. "If we're going to be there before noon, we need to leave in a minute."

She nodded, but didn't move toward the door.

"Are you all right?" Zev looked concerned.

Marieke nodded again. "Just nervous." She tilted her head in an invitation. "Come in out of the hallway, you don't know who might be watching."

Zev cast a glance around the small bedchamber. "I don't think I should."

Marieke gave him a look. "Where are Veronica and Azai?"

"In mine and Azai's room next door," he said, nonplussed. "Why?"

"I'm just pointing out that they don't seem to have any objection to being in a room just the two of them in the middle of the day," Marieke said. "So I think you're being overly fastidious."

"It's not the same for them," Zev said, although he did step through the doorway.

"And why's that?" Marieke tucked her hands demurely behind her back, raising both eyebrows at him.

"Because," Zev told her, placing one strong finger under her chin and tilting her face up ever so slightly. "They don't have the problem I have, of wanting to kiss you senseless every time we're alone together."

Marieke felt her cheeks flush with pleasure. "It doesn't seem like a terrible problem to have," she informed him. "At least not from my perspective. And it might not be as easy a challenge as you think. I'm a very sensible person...you might have to kiss me very hard to make me senseless."

Zev made a gravelly noise in his throat at the provocative words. "Don't tempt me, Mari."

"It's all very disappointing," Marieke pressed, quite pleased with the results of her efforts. "Don't you realize that Jade wanted to kill me back there?"

All playfulness fell from Zev's face at once, his eyes taking on a now-familiar tension. "Of course I realize. Am I likely to forget?"

"I thought you might have," Marieke told him solemnly. "Because you didn't even kiss me. Usually after someone attacks me, you kiss me. Or at the very least, you *almost* kiss me."

Zev's forehead crinkled in confusion as he cast his memory

back. She could see the moment he realized she was right, as his expression transformed into one of exasperation.

"It's not an intentional pattern," he protested. "I'm more concerned about the fact that you've been attacked enough times for there to even be a pattern in my response to it!"

"Well, you should have other concerns, too," Marieke told him. "You've created certain expectations. And you risk hurting my feelings if you don't fulfill them."

"You're impossible," Zev said. "Do you really need my prompting to take threats to your life seriously?"

"I take them perfectly seriously," Marieke assured him. "That's part of my motivation. One of the key benefits of being alive—in spite of threats to the contrary—is being able to kiss you."

"You're ridiculous," Zev said. But his eyes were straying toward her lips.

"It's very possible Instructor Oriana is going to show up with a squad of council guards and throw us all in prison, you know," Marieke said, smoothing a wrinkle from his tunic with her hand. "Who knows when we'll have another chance to—"

Her words were cut off as Zev finally gave in and claimed her lips with his. Triumphant, Marieke snaked her hand around his neck, savoring his nearness.

The kiss was sweet and brief, Zev already pulling away before footsteps sounded in the corridor.

"Are we going?" Azai paused in the doorway, only by the slightest of grimaces acknowledging how close the pair were standing. "I thought Marieke's note said noon."

"It did." Marieke stepped back from Zev, clearing her throat. "And we're ready."

Veronica appeared behind Azai, looking determined. "I think the instructor is going to come," she said. "So we shouldn't be late."

Marieke nodded, lifting her pack from the floor. If all went well, they'd be back at the inn soon, but she wasn't inclined to leave her meager belongings behind, just in case. As they walked down the stairs and out of the building, she positioned herself alongside Veronica.

"You really think she's coming?"

Veronica nodded. "I hovered nearby after I delivered your note. She didn't see me, but I watched her read it. She looked...I don't know, not guilty exactly. More like chastened."

"Hm."

Marieke cast her mind over the contents of the note she'd written to Instructor Oriana. Veronica had been the one to deliver it, being the only member of the group who hadn't shown her face in the confrontation in the dungeon. Even so, Marieke had been nervous to see her friend put herself at risk of arrest or sanction. It had been a relief when Veronica returned, reporting that no one had questioned her when she'd strolled up to the academy's public reception area and delivered a letter for Instructor Oriana.

What Instructor Oriana had done with that letter remained to be seen. She would surely have been surprised to learn that Marieke and the others were still in Ondford. The council probably imagined they'd all fled the city, like Jade seemed to have done. It was entirely possible that Instructor Oriana had taken the note straight to Instructor Rafael, or one of the other council members.

Marieke wanted to believe she hadn't, though. She wanted so badly to have faith in the instructor who'd always seemed so kind and genuine. And her conversation with the instructor in the dungeon gave her hope. If Instructor Oriana had decided not to tell the Head Instructor about Marieke's aptitude for questioning, in order to protect her from prejudice, then some part of her had always known that the academy's so-called policies were wrong. Hopefully that part of her would take prominence on this occasion.

"What exactly did you say in the letter?" Veronica prompted.

"That we can't trust the council—for reasons she knows if she's honest with herself—but we're still determined to stop Jade, without their assistance if we have to. I said we need her help, and we'll be waiting in the main market square at noon today. But that if she brings anyone from the council with her, she won't see us." Marieke grinned crookedly at Veronica. "That last part was my attempt to make us sound more skilled than we are. I can't really guarantee we can get away unnoticed if there's a battalion of guards there looking for us."

"Give us more credit," Veronica said. "We make a pretty good team, with our songcraft and the boys' physical strength."

Marieke threw Veronica a sideways look, amused by the airy way the other girl said *the boys*. The cheerful Aeltan hadn't let the fact that she understood at most a third of what was going on stop her from throwing herself into their group with enthusiasm. Marieke had never dreamed that asking Veronica to intercept Zev in Tarandon would end with the graduate accompanying the brothers all the way to Ondford. She still felt guilty for indirectly embroiling her friend in their adventures without all the information, but she wasn't free to tell Veronica everything. Not when Zev and Azai's lineage was so central to all that was going on.

"I wish you could have seen our daring crossing over Sundering Canyon," Veronica went on cheerfully. "Highly illegal, might I add, since the bridge was blocked off. We had to go at night and climb along the bottom of it. I have no idea how the boys intended to manage if they hadn't had my songcraft to help."

"Zev often doesn't seem to have a plan ahead of time,"

Marieke commented. "He just goes in full of confidence and trusts that he'll figure something out. And in fairness to him, he usually does." Like in his mission to rescue her from the dungeon.

"You're right that we make a good team," she added, her voice more serious now. "But we're walking a dangerous line here, Veronica. I know all this feels far away and disconnected from your life back in Tarandon. I thought the same about my troubles here when I was in Aeltas. But they followed me, with a vengeance. And even without the risk from Jade, if this meeting gets us in trouble with the Oleandan council, that's likely to impact your future back in Aeltas. The fact that I got shipped back across the canyon shows that however independent each council might want to appear, they have plenty of communication between them. Dare I say it, even cooperation."

"Yes, quite inspiring, isn't it?" Veronica said lightly. "And here I thought the councils were too mired down in bureaucracy to work together effectively." She gave her friend a solemn look. "You underestimate me, Marieke. I realize how serious the situation is. I didn't insist that Zev and Azai let me come because I wanted an adventure." She paused. "I mean, it is an adventure, of course. I've never had the chance to use my songcraft for something that's actually real before. It's exhilarating, even though it's a little terrifying."

Marieke could understand that reaction. She'd felt the same way when she'd battled the fire back in Bull Creek. And Veronica had only just graduated, so everything would be even more fresh for her. Using songcraft in the unpredictable environment of the outside world was so different from using it in the academy.

"But adventure is the least important of the reasons I'm here," Veronica went on. "I know there's more you aren't telling me, but I know enough to understand that something big is going on." Her eyes strayed to where the brothers were walking ahead. "I want to know if what Azai says is true, that the council which just gave me the status of an accredited singer did so on stolen authority, using power based on murder and lies."

"Azai told you all that?" Marieke asked, stunned.

Veronica frowned. "Isn't it true? I thought that the council's dishonesty about the past was the loose thread you pulled on that made this whole situation unravel."

"No, it is," Marieke assured her friend. "I'm just surprised Azai told you. When Zev and I first met, he hinted at the true history regularly, but never came out and said it. And Azai is usually even less willing to share information than Zev, especially with singers. He seems to mainly communicate in snide asides."

"He's maddening, I agree," Veronica said cheerfully. "But he's actually not that complicated. He's quite easy to read if you figure out the right approach." She grinned suddenly. "Easy to read, and easy to goad into revealing far more than he intends to."

"Well." Marieke didn't quite know what to say. She supposed she'd never taken the time to learn how to navigate Azai's prickliness.

"Is it bad that I find it entertaining how much he can't stand me?" Veronica added.

Marieke laughed at that. "No. I think Azai can be absurd, to be honest, and you're entitled to feel amusement."

"Oh, he's not absurd," Veronica said. "Just conflicted."

Marieke once again didn't have a response, but she didn't need one. Zev had been leading the way, following the route of their earlier scouting trip to the market, but Marieke had still been paying attention to their surroundings. They were almost there. Just like the market in the other part of the city, the anxiety was palpable. So many people were arguing prices for the limited supplies available, and many of the vendors looked on edge, as if fearing thieves. Marieke suspected there would be plenty of pickpockets around—she even passed a few beggars, something that had been rare to see in that part of the city during her years at the academy.

"All right, like we discussed," she said, as the group slowed. "Azai and Veronica will take the rooftops, Zev and I will be on the ground."

"Keep your senses alive for my signal," Veronica said, all traces of their light conversation gone. "I'll send a slight breeze if I see your instructor."

With a nod, Marieke slipped into the stream of people heading into the market square, Zev at her side.

"I think we should change the plan slightly," Zev said once they were alone, his casual tone not fooling Marieke for a moment. "I think I should approach her if she shows up, and you should hang back and get a feel for the situation before you come out."

Marieke actually rolled her eyes at him. "We're not changing the plan at the last minute, Zev. *If* she's come, she's come to see me. She doesn't know you, and she won't trust you. This is a part of the mission you have to let me do." She gave him a pointed look. "And no hovering around me like a bodyguard, remember? You stay out of sight unless I signal to you."

Zev sighed, the resigned sound telling Marieke he hadn't really expected to get his way on this point. "I still don't like it," he muttered.

Marieke felt free to ignore the words, her focus on the crowd they were wending through. No one paid them much attention in their travel-crumpled clothes, rucksacks on their backs. Travelers were common enough in the Oleandan capital. In fact, she thought there were more than usual. Probably people from suffering rural areas coming in search of assistance which the capital couldn't offer.

As discussed with Veronica, Marieke resisted the urge to pool magic to herself, knowing that a skilled singer would be able to identify her presence from a distance if she did so. It took a lot of focus *not* to pull in magic when she was so on edge —she had to fight to keep a gathering hum inside her throat. Instead she put all her attention into her other senses, scanning the crowd for anyone familiar. She and Zev made their way to the alcove they'd previously scouted. It was the entrance to one of the many boarded up shops. The owners of this shop had taken more care than others, placing a large ceramic garden bed in front of the door to discourage market-goers from coming into the entrance area. It provided a convenient place for Zev and Marieke to linger, able to observe the crowd a little through the plants, but not easily visible to those going past.

Zev shifted from foot to foot as they waited, running his palm distractedly down his leg, next to where his sword was strapped on. Marieke knew that he didn't like the fact that their hiding place had only one way out. But they'd had little time to make their plans, and they'd had to take what they could find.

They drew back uneasily as a scuffle broke out only a few yards from them. Marieke didn't try to listen too carefully to the words being shouted. The scene was much like similar ones they'd witnessed when scouting the location the day before. There wasn't enough produce to meet the demand, and people were becoming afraid about the future. And that fear inevitably came out as anger.

Marieke stilled further as a pair of council guards came into view. Were they looking for her? Had Instructor Oriana reported her?

But the guards were focused fully on dealing with the disturbance. They were probably in the market to enforce the new buying limits placed on highly sought after resources. They moved on soon enough, and Marieke allowed herself to shift position slightly.

"Are you all right?" Zev asked, more attuned to her mood than she'd realized.

Marieke let out a breath. "It's just sobering," she said. "Things have gotten a lot worse in such a short time. The deterioration of the arable land isn't a future problem anymore. It's well and truly here. At this rate, they'll be rioting outside the council in no time."

Zev's expression was hard to read as he looked sideways at her.

"What?" she demanded.

"I don't know how good a look you got at the place as you arrived," he said. "Maybe you came through a more official entrance than we did. But when we broke into the council building, the situation outside was pretty close to rioting."

Marieke bit her lip, a weight dropping into her stomach. "No wonder they want someone to blame," she muttered.

"Using you as a scapegoat won't improve the situation," Zev reminded her. "It won't do anything whatsoever to stop what's happening."

"I know," she said, returning her attention to the crowd in the market. She hoped Instructor Oriana appeared soon. She was desperate to feel like she was doing something.

Thankfully it wasn't much longer before Marieke's senses picked up an active enchantment approaching. She stiffened, narrowing her eyes in focus as a breeze swept right into their alcove and lifted her hair briefly from her shoulders.

Just the one eddy of air swirled around her, falling still quickly. Marieke waited, but no more magic breezes followed. One swirl for one person, that was the signal. If Veronica and

Azai's observations were accurate, Instructor Oriana had come alone as requested.

"Did you feel that breeze?" she murmured to Zev. "She's in the market."

Marieke moved out of the alcove, her eyes searching the crowd. She probably wouldn't have to look too hard. She suspected that Instructor Oriana would have sensed the enchantment at work in that breeze, and would follow it to Marieke's hiding place.

Sure enough, the slightly rounded figure of Instructor Oriana came into view, making directly for their position. She was more conspicuous than Marieke would have liked, in her black instructor's robe with the purple edging and the insignia of a bird in flight embroidered in silver thread over her heart. But she was alone.

After a quick glance around to confirm that the guards from earlier were no longer nearby, Marieke stepped into the older woman's path.

"Instructor Oriana." She could sense Zev's gaze as he stayed back in the alcove. "You came."

"Yes." Instructor Oriana's normally cheerful face looked strained. "Perhaps foolishly."

Marieke shook her head quickly. "You truly have no reason to mistrust me."

The instructor didn't answer, and Marieke went on.

"Will you come back to my lodgings? We can't talk freely here, and it would draw too much attention for you to work an enchantment in the marketplace."

"Hold on." Instructor Oriana raised a hand, palm outward. "I haven't agreed to do any enchantments for you."

"I know," Marieke assured her. "But you came, which must mean you're at least willing to talk." She gave the older woman a shrewd look. "And I think it means you know something isn't right with the council."

"I don't want to comment on that until I hear what you have to say," the instructor said. "But I've come this far, and I didn't do it lightly. I'm willing to hear you out."

Marieke nodded, signaling to Zev with a tilt of the head. "Let's go, then."

Instructor Oriana followed her, starting as Zev appeared beside them. She clearly recognized the Aeltan who'd broken into the dungeon, but she didn't comment. When they exited the market and she realized they were being flanked by two others, she found her voice, however.

"Just how many of you are there?"

"This is it," Marieke told her. "We're not some army of rebels, and we're really no threat to Oleand. Quite the reverse." She glanced around at her companions. "My friends aren't even Oleandan, and they're still risking their own safety to try to save our country."

The instructor looked troubled, but she said no more until they reached the inn. She must have been perfectly aware, as Marieke was, of Veronica's quiet song of assessment questing through their immediate surrounds while they walked. If Instructor Oriana had companions following them at a distance, Veronica would hopefully learn about them before their final location was revealed.

Given Veronica remained silent, Marieke continued into the inn, leading the group straight up the stairs and into the room she and Veronica had slept in the night before. The five of them squeezed into the small space, Instructor Oriana warily taking the sole chair as directed.

Marieke sat on the bed, trying to make it seem less like they were all towering over the older woman.

"Thank you," she said by way of opening. "Thank you for trusting me enough to come."

The instructor's brow didn't lighten. "Like I told you at the council building, Marieke, you don't belong in a prison. At least, not based on anything I've ever seen or heard from you." She sighed. "But I've been wrong before."

Marieke leaned forward, her elbows on her knees. "You're talking about Jade."

Instructor Oriana nodded. "I've been able to think of nothing else since our last conversation. If it's true that Jade is behind the attacks on singers and the recent disasters, as you claim, then I feel culpable. She was my student more than any other instructor's—the storytelling discipline is so targeted and rare. I was too lenient with her when she first showed signs of aggression, and I advocated for expulsion rather than a more severe punishment."

"You're not responsible for Jade's actions," Marieke said, her tone not intended to comfort. "You're responsible for your own. And you've taken part in a countrywide deception."

She narrowed her eyes at the instructor. "Do you really feel responsible for not stopping Jade's misdemeanors? Or is that confession a handy way to seem like you're taking responsibility when in fact you're keeping the blame focused on Jade's conduct rather than your own secrets?"

"Oof." Instructor Oriana's expression was rueful, but there was a gleam of professional interest in her eyes. "Did you feel the magic respond just then? You might have as strong a questioning aptitude as Jade did, if you developed it properly."

"Well, I was denied that chance, wasn't I?" Marieke said. "But I don't want to talk about my education. Tell me honestly, Instructor. Do you know about what Jade discovered? That the singers behind the coup didn't exile the monarchs so much as slaughter them while they attempted to flee, and that they hid the truth from everyone afterward?"

The instructor pulled her robes more securely around herself in a gesture of discomfort. "I do."

"You're an instructor," Marieke protested, momentarily sidetracked. "Your whole purpose is to teach students the truth. How do you justify lying for your whole career?"

"I didn't lie for my whole career," the instructor said wearily. "I knew nothing of the deception until Jade uncovered it and threw it in my face."

CHAPTER
SIX

Marieke

"Wait...really?" Marieke straightened. "You didn't know the truth about the coup?"

"Most of the instructors don't know," Instructor Oriana confirmed. "I don't even know if everyone on the council knows."

"The Head Instructor does," Marieke said. "And Councilor Isabel. Half the reason I went looking for answers is because I overheard them talking about Jade and heartsong."

At her last word, Azai shifted uncomfortably in his position by the door, but Marieke didn't look at him. They'd discussed it and agreed that if they wanted Instructor Oriana's help, they'd have to talk to her about heartsong. It was too late to back out now.

"You know about heartsong as well, do you?" Instructor Oriana studied her. "You certainly have asked the right questions, it seems. That's another dark detail from our past that I didn't know until Jade learned it."

"So you claim," Zev murmured.

"I believe her," Marieke said. "Although I'm surprised."

"You shouldn't be," Instructor Oriana said. "Did you really

think everyone at the academy was part of some dark conspiracy? Our training doesn't include an induction into all the dirtiest secrets of councils past, you know."

"Honestly, I did think something like that," Marieke told her. "I assumed that the lies must be fully institutionalized to be so universally taught."

"I hate to say it, but they have been institutionalized," Instructor Oriana said. "To the extent that even the institutions believe them. Of course the original councils knew the truth, and I imagine that subsequent ones had some awareness for a little while. But it's not as though they made and kept secret records of their own atrocities, you know. Since Jade opened the issue, I've learned from the Head Instructor that there are a few surviving letters referencing what happened, but there are no official texts outlining the version of events Jade discovered."

Her tone had a note of entreaty. "I've seen the letters, and they give the impression that a few singers who were part of the original coup unleashed violence on the royals without necessarily having approval from the rest of the group. I can imagine how those circumstances might have all but forced the other conspirators to follow through at their sides. For all we know, the original intention of the coup was to be the bloodless transfer of power we were all told it was."

"But that isn't what happened," Marieke said.

"I know that now," Instructor Oriana said. "And I felt all the discomfort you could desire me to when I first found out. I don't want to think that my predecessors were murderers any more than you do. But what was done was done—there was nothing for the singers of the time to do but move forward. And as for now...well, we're left with a situation not of our making, and we have no choice in the matter, do we?"

"Yes, you do." Azai pushed off the wall, his face marred by a scowl. "You have the choice to tell the truth or to perpetrate lies, and you've chosen the latter. You choose it daily."

Marieke could see the conflict in Instructor Oriana's eyes as she looked up at the Aeltan. She knew he was right.

"Our whole system is based on the premise that singers have the naturally given aptitude to rule," Veronica said quietly. "At least in Aeltas, we're told that the land suffered under the monarchs but it thrives under the Council of Singers. It changes everything to learn that power was forcibly and violently wrested from the monarchs by the singers, and that they lied about it to everyone. It shows that the original singers were no more fit to rule than the monarchs they overthrew. No matter how uncomfortable that truth is, you can't deny it."

"And not every singer is as uncomfortable with the truth as you three." Zev's interjection surprised Marieke. "Your academy's Head Instructor, for example."

Instructor Oriana bit her lip. "I think Instructor Rafael already knew before Jade went looking," she acknowledged. "He's a great scholar, whatever his faults, and an expert at assessing primary documents. I doubt there's much about our history he hasn't learned throughout the course of his studies."

"I have a question." Azai moved to stand in Instructor Oriana's direct line of sight. "You referred to heartsong as a dark detail from the past. Why is it dark?"

She looked at him curiously.

"Who are you again?"

Marieke started slightly. Magic had undulated around Instructor Oriana when she spoke. It was so subtle that Marieke would never have noted it if she hadn't become accustomed to sensing the way magic could respond to questions. The instructor obviously had the questioning aptitude that Marieke and Jade shared. Marieke should have guessed it, given Instructor Oriana's position. What would she make of the magic's response to her asking Azai who he was? It was fascinating and alarming that it could be activated by such a simple question—Marieke was starting to understand why it had been marked as a dangerous skill.

"I'm Zev's brother," Azai said impatiently. "Azai."

"From Aeltas?" Instructor Oriana's face was crinkled in concentration, no doubt trying to understand why the magic had prompted her to pursue the line of inquiry further.

"Yes," Azai said.

"And you know what heartsong is?" Instructor Oriana pressed.

"You've just heard Marieke ask about it, so it stands to reason we've all heard of it in this group." Azai's surliness came to his aid in making the evasiveness of his non-answer less conspicuous. "Now answer the question. Why did you call heartsong dark?"

"I don't necessarily think heartsong was dark," Instructor Oriana said. "I referred to its existence as a dark secret because of the destruction the singers' coup caused when it unintentionally removed heartsong from the land by killing the royals."

"Unintentionally?" Zev repeated skeptically.

"Of course," she said. "The singers had no idea that killing the monarchs would physically harm the land. I don't think anyone knew. Heartsong was never well understood, even in the old days. I believe it was seen as myth rather than actual magical lore."

"I hate to display my ignorance," Veronica said, "but I still don't really understand what it is. Marieke's explanation left me confused—no offense, Marieke."

Marieke grimaced. It had been hard to explain the concept to her friend without revealing Zev and Azai's secrets, something they were all still trying to avoid.

"I'm no expert," she said. "But Jade definitely knows about it, so I'm doing my best to understand it."

"Yes, it fueled Jade's anger," Instructor Oriana sighed. "She saw it as physical evidence of the crime that so offended her."

"It's fueling more than just her anger," Marieke said. "That's why we wanted to speak to you, Instructor. We think, from some of the things Jade says, that she's actually found a way to *use* heartsong. We think that's how she's making the country physically deteriorate."

"How could she possibly do that?" Instructor Oriana asked blankly. "It's supposed to have been a subtle power that gave magical force to the connection between the royals and their land. Jade can't harness that. It was a blood force. Even if the theory is correct that the blood force was released destructively when so much royal blood was shed in the coup, that was long ago. That old power isn't active and capable of being manipulated, and with the bloodlines gone, no new power of heartsong is being unleashed."

"So we all thought," Marieke said, keeping her voice even. She'd already been nervous about saying the next part without revealing too much, and she was doubly so now that she'd seen Instructor Oriana's questioning aptitude in action. "But like I said, Jade said things that suggested something different. I think it's possible that someone in Oleand's royal bloodline survived the coup. If Jade found their descendants, and convinced them to harness their power *against* the country, don't you think we might see the kind of slow destruction we're witnessing?"

"It's conceivable," the instructor conceded slowly. "But it's quite a leap, Marieke. What exactly did Jade say that made you think that?"

Marieke could see the concentration on the older woman's face as she asked, and even caught the flicker of surprise that told her that Instructor Oriana had noted, as she had, that the magic didn't respond to her question. Marieke knew why—what Jade said wasn't the key to figuring out the mystery. It was what Zev had revealed. Marieke didn't want Instructor Oriana to have the opportunity to ask questions that would identify that fact, though.

"That's more detail than you need to know," Marieke told her bluntly. "I can't prove it to you—I'm only guessing myself. But whatever the vehicle, I'm confident that Jade is behind what's happening to Oleand. And that's why we need your help."

The instructor was shaking her head before Marieke finished speaking. "Don't ask me, Marieke. There's no use me getting involved. I know I've told you that I took a special interest in her, but Jade won't listen to me. The investment I felt in her went one way. And it's long gone."

"I'm not asking you to reason with Jade," Marieke said. "I'm just asking you to help us find her."

"Judging by how she came charging into the council itself to hunt you down, I don't think you'll have any trouble," the instructor said dryly. "Just put yourself out in the open, and she'll come."

"We don't want her to come to us," Zev said. "We want to track her back to where she came from."

Comprehension lit Instructor Oriana's eyes. "You think her trail will lead you to whoever she's working with? To the so-called royal descendants?"

"That's our hope," Marieke said. "We'd rather try reasoning with them than reasoning with Jade."

"Even supposing these people exist, what makes you think they'd listen to any of you?" the instructor asked dubiously.

"You never know," Marieke said lightly.

No need to explain that they had a resource no one else did

—the Aeltan counterparts, the only people who could possibly understand the position Jade's conspirators were in.

If, as Instructor Oriana said, these people even existed.

"So why do you think that I can help you find Jade?"

"I saw Jade use a sophisticated enchantment," Marieke said. "One that I believe has its origins in storytelling song. By casting it on Zev, she was able to follow his trail back the way he'd come, over days' worth of travel, including travel in vehicles where there was no possibility of leaving a literal trail or scent or anything like that."

The instructor looked thoughtful. "She managed that, did she? Obviously she didn't cease her studies when she left the academy. It's a complex enchantment, and you're right that it's connected to the storytelling discipline."

"And you're the only other person I know of who I'm confident would be capable of it," Marieke said.

"Which is why you asked me to meet you," the instructor commented.

"It's part of the reason," Marieke said. "The other part is that I trust you more than most council or academy members. At least, I want to trust you. I didn't want to believe you were part of something sinister."

"I've never wanted to be part of anything sinister," the instructor said sadly. "I never wanted things to be so complicated."

"Neither did Marieke," Zev cut in. "And the things she's learned have turned her life upside down. But she didn't try to hide from them or add her voice to the lies."

The instructor didn't answer, and Marieke sent Zev a look. She was grateful for the support, but she wasn't there to talk about herself. It was the instructor they needed to focus on.

"I do know how to do the enchantment you mentioned," Instructor Oriana said after an awkward silence. "But I'd need her to be present in order to craft it. If she's trying to kill you, it seems far too dangerous to draw her out just for that purpose."

"Does she have to be present?" Marieke asked. She reached into her pocket and carefully drew out the clump of hair. "Or is it enough that we have this?"

Instructor Oriana stared at the tuft. "Is that Jade's hair? Theoretically it's possible, but I'd be tracking where that specific clump had been. If you acquired it a while ago, it'll just lead you to where she'd been prior to when you extracted it."

Marieke shook her head. "I ripped it right off her head yesterday. If she came to the capital from wherever she currently lives, it should lead us there." She paused. "If you can craft the enchantment for us, that is."

"But...what will you do if you find Jade? I don't want to be part of anything violent."

"We're not planning to attack her," Marieke said quickly.

In her peripheral vision, she caught Azai's reflexive movement, and she also caught the restraining hand Veronica put on his arm. Marieke sent silent thanks to the other girl. She knew Azai was bent on making Jade pay for killing his father—she suspected Zev harbored the same intention, although he was more restrained about expressing it—but it was true that their plan didn't involve an altercation with Jade just yet. And there was no need for the instructor to know the depth of their grudge against Jade, not if it might make her less inclined to help them.

She drew in a breath, hoping that Instructor Oriana hadn't caught the silent exchange. "We just want to find where she's basing herself. If we're right about our guess regarding heartsong, that should lead us to the only people who really have the power to stop what's happening to Oleand."

The instructor leaned back, her round face creased in thought as she considered Marieke's words.

"I don't know...your theory is based on a great deal of conjecture. And unlike the lot of you," she cast her eyes around the group, "I'm too old to go trekking across the country on the slim chance of—"

"Oh no," Marieke cut in quickly. "We're not asking you to come with us. Just to do the enchantment to show us the way. We'll follow it, and you can stay here. In fact, we have another request of you once we're gone."

Her frown deepened. "What request?"

"Once we're clear of the capital, we want you to tell the council," Marieke said.

"Tell them what?"

"Everything," said Marieke simply. "That Jade is behind what's happening to the country, and that we think she's planning some kind of attack."

"You want to tell the council?" Instructor Oriana stared between them. "You're not trying to keep all this secret?"

"Of course we don't want to keep Jade's plot secret," Marieke said impatiently. "That's her aim, and our whole plan is to try to stop her. We don't trust the council, but we still recognize that they're the ones whose role it is to defend the country from threats. They need the information."

"Then why not tell them yourself?"

Zev made a derisive noise in his throat, and Marieke agreed with him.

"Yesterday, I was locked up in their dungeon," she reminded the older woman, trying to speak patiently. "Even then, they had no intention of giving me the chance to state my case or tell everyone what I know. And things have only gotten worse for me since then, right? Given how quick they were to suspect me of starting the fire I helped stop, I'd wager what little coins I have left that some at least are accusing me of being a conspirator in Jade's break in. Am I wrong?"

The instructor sighed. "You're not wrong. I've told them it was clear that Jade came to attack you rather than to help you, but I don't think the council is convinced. Some if not most of the members think I've been fooled and Jade actually came to break you out."

"Of course they do," Zev said contemptuously. "They don't even trust their own."

The instructor shrugged. "I'm not their own, not as much as you think. I'm not on the council, and I have no standing there. The Head Instructor has an automatic council position, but otherwise the council and academy operate separately for the most part."

"It's the council which needs to hear what we've learned, though," Marieke said. "They definitely won't listen to me, but they might listen to you if you have all the information this time. We're just not willing to pledge our freedom on the possibility, which is why we want you to approach them after we've left."

Instructor Oriana let out a long breath as she thought it over. "I'm willing to try."

"Thank you," said Marieke, relieved. "If you're interested in my advice, share the information as publicly as possible. Don't have a quiet conversation with the Head Instructor in his office. Tell the whole council, preferably the other instructors, as well."

Instructor Oriana didn't look like she relished the prospect, and Marieke didn't push it. She couldn't control what the older woman did. She would just have to hope Instructor Oriana succeeded where Marieke had failed.

"I think the council will want to send someone after you," Instructor Oriana said. "To find Jade. I'm sure they'd prefer someone go with you from the start." She gestured at the strands of hair Marieke was still holding. "To make the reverse tracking enchantment work on an inanimate object like this, you'll need to keep hold of the object. The enchantment will attach to the hair, and it will prompt you where to go. How about I retain some of it, to allow reinforcements to go after you?"

"Absolutely not," Marieke said flatly. The group was agreed on this point. "Like I said, we don't trust the council. We won't risk them sending someone to quietly eliminate Jade and whoever is working with her so that they can then continue to lie about what was really causing the country to suffer."

"Or, more likely, kill us as well, and claim that we were the ones behind everything that's happened to Oleand," Zev said darkly.

The shock on Instructor Oriana's face suggested that she hadn't thought of that possibility. And judging by the discomfort that followed, she acknowledged to herself that it wasn't altogether far-fetched. Hopefully she was starting to comprehend just how insidious were the lies she'd been part of.

"Will you work the enchantment now?" Marieke asked. "We don't want to waste more time."

The instructor drew in a deep breath, then nodded. "Hold out the hair."

Marieke did so, holding her palms flat with Jade's hair on top of them, ready to pull them back if the other woman tried to take the hair from her.

But she didn't. Instructor Oriana squinted at the dark strands, magic pooling noticeably to her as a hum started deep in her throat. She took her time before releasing a song, clearly preparing to craft what must be a complex enchantment.

Marieke was fascinated by the process, sensing the different streams of magic twisting themselves up from the ground below into the singer's form. She couldn't identify what they were each doing without the training, and it only made her more eager to study storytelling song.

When Instructor Oriana started to sing, Marieke saw the winces that crossed both Azai's and Zev's faces. Veronica, no doubt with broader experience of singing abilities, hid it better, but Marieke could still see her expression flicker.

She was used to the instructor's tuneless attempts at melody, so she didn't let it distract her from observing the actual songcraft. She was impressed. Instructor Oriana's song was precise and tight, powerful without being showy. Truly a master at work.

Just a master whose voice unfortunately sounded like a seagull's screech.

When Instructor Oriana's voice petered out, she was noticeably more weary. Her plump shoulders sagged a little, and she leaned back in her chair.

"Do you feel the enchantment?"

Marieke nodded, closing her fist over the hair. "It's heavy."

"That's good you can feel it." Instructor Oriana nodded. "You'll be able to follow the trail through its prompting. It will be useless to someone who can't sense magic, though."

"Thank you."

Marieke tucked the hair safely back into her pocket. It wasn't currently communicating with her, but she didn't doubt the instructor. She stood, the others doing the same as they grabbed their packs, ready for immediate departure. It would be wise to get a head start before the instructor had regained her energy. At the doorway, Marieke turned back to Instructor Oriana.

"I hope we meet again, Instructor. I know you're taking a risk by helping us."

"It's the least I can do," the instructor said faintly.

"Agreed." The caustic comment came from Azai, but it was

Zev whose commanding voice captured the older woman's attention.

"You seem capable of feeling shame."

"Not entirely," Azai muttered, perhaps thinking of the singing he'd just heard.

Zev ignored him, his focus still on Instructor Oriana. "I don't know if your council is, but I hope they feel it when you tell them that while they try to pretend everything is fine, and blame the country's problems on anyone but themselves, the only people actually trying to help Oleand are the graduate they've treated like refuse, and three Aeltans with nothing to gain from helping a country not their own."

He moved to Marieke's side, just within the doorway.

"And you should know that if they try to blame any of this on Marieke, or lock her up again, there's nothing I won't do to free her." Power swirled subtly around their feet as he slid his hand into Marieke's, and the instructor's confused expression suggested that she felt it, too. "And I have more power to keep them accountable than they think."

With the words, Zev strode from the room, pulling Marieke with him by their joined hands.

The four of them hurried from the inn, Zev having settled their account before proceeding upstairs. They were all in agreement that the sooner they left the capital, the better.

"Can you feel anything from the enchantment?" Veronica asked.

Marieke shook her head. "No. I guess Jade wasn't here, was she? We'll need to intersect with her path before it can start leading us back down her trail."

"But you grabbed that hair from her when we were inside the council complex," Zev said. "Surely it's too dangerous to go back there."

"Hopefully it won't be necessary to go right inside,"

Marieke said. "But unfortunately I don't think there's any way to find the trail without getting close to it."

"Does she always sing like that?" Azai asked, as they moved cautiously through the city toward the council building. "How did she gain a position as a teacher if so?"

"Don't be fooled," Marieke told him. "She's incredibly skilled, and her grasp of magic is powerful. She just...can't hold a tune very well. Or at all."

Azai didn't look as though this explanation told him much, but Veronica nodded. "I could feel the sophistication of her enchantment. I must say, the tunelessness is unfortunate."

Marieke shot her a grin. "Remember how I told you about choral class?"

Veronica nodded.

"Instructor Oriana has been at the academy for a long time. I have a feeling that the introduction of that class followed her appointment pretty closely."

Veronica stifled a chuckle. "Well, I'm glad she was willing to help us."

"So am I," Marieke said. They were entering the part of the city where the council building sat, and her eyes darted around as they moved carefully from street to street. "You know, this is probably a good time for you to peel away, Veronica. You should be safe enough if you travel back to Aeltas without us. I doubt either Jade or the council will be interested in you if you're not with our group anymore."

"Don't be silly," Veronica protested. "I'm not leaving. I want to see this through along with you all."

"But it's not your fight," Marieke said earnestly. "There's no reason for you to risk your safety to solve our problems. You're not even Oleandan."

"Neither are the boys," Veronica pointed out.

"I'm not letting Marieke out of my sight again," Zev said simply.

"And I'm not going back to Aeltas until Jade is dead." Azai's tone was just as unemotional as Zev's had been, but somehow it felt very different.

"Looks like you're stuck with all of us," said Veronica pleasantly. Seeing Marieke's uncertainty, she added, "I'm not here by accident, Marieke. I want the truth. The idea of just going home and looking for a graduate position, pretending I don't know about any of this, is inconceivable. Besides which, you sorely need another singer in your group."

Marieke sighed. "Well, that's true."

Veronica gave a tight nod. "So stop wasting energy trying to send me away. Let's focus on finding Jade's trail without getting caught by the council."

Luck was with them on that point. They didn't head toward the main entrance of the council complex, instead skirting around it toward the area where they'd escaped through the brick wall. They were still a couple of blocks away when Marieke felt magic tugging at her awareness.

"Did you feel that?" she asked Veronica.

The other singer shook her head. "Is it the enchantment on the hair? You must have to be holding it for it to communicate the trail."

"I think you're right." Marieke plunged her hand into her pocket, closing her fingers around the strands. Magic swirled through her senses, pulling her further from the council building. "This way," she said confidently, changing direction.

"Wait." Veronica's command brought them all to a stop. "Before we leave the city, we should double check that the instructor didn't put any locating enchantment on any of us, or anything like that."

"Good idea," Marieke said. "She's very skilled. I'm not

confident I would have noticed if she'd worked it into her song."

She stepped up to Veronica, scanning her form carefully, her extra sense on high alert. She could find no sign of any lingering enchantment, and Veronica said the same of her.

"Your turn," Veronica said, as they both swiveled to face the brothers.

"I'll check you, Zev," said Marieke, stepping up to him.

"I don't object," he murmured, a mischievous glint in his eyes as she ran her fingers carefully over his arm, her face scrunched in concentration.

"This is purely professional, Zev," she told him with dignity.

He leaned down as her hand moved across his chest to the other arm.

"If you say so."

His breath brushed her face, and the low words sent a pleasant shiver over her. But she refused to be sidetracked from her task, checking Zev with meticulous care. Thankfully she could find no sign of magic clinging to him. Satisfied, she turned to see that Veronica was having a hard time with her charge.

"What are you doing?" Azai demanded uneasily, twisting around as Veronica circled behind him to poke his back, the physical action assisting her to focus her magical sense.

"I'm checking for malignant enchantments, now stand straight and stop interrupting me," she told him severely, continuing her circuit back to stand in front of him.

"How do I know you're not putting a malignant enchant-ment *on* me?" Azai demanded.

Veronica rolled her eyes. "Do you hear me singing, you impossible dunce?"

"Oi." Azai tugged his arm from her grip in evident offense.

She reclaimed it, undeterred, pausing her assessment to

squint at his hand. "The burn is healing up nicely, at least. It wasn't as bad as it looked at first."

"It's fine." Azai pulled himself free again, clearly uncomfortable with her attention.

Veronica's tone became imperious. "Lean down. I want to check your head."

"I don't think I will," Azai said contrarily. "Who's to say you won't *start* singing?"

Zev sighed. "You are a dunce," he told Azai brutally. "She's not going to use magic on you without asking your permission. It's part of their code."

Azai didn't look convinced. "That didn't stop Jade."

"Jade is obviously a rogue singer and a criminal," Marieke said, also losing patience with the belligerent farmer. "Do you really think she's following any kind of singers' code?"

A look of determination crossed Veronica's face. "Happily, I didn't take any vow relating to physical force," she said. With lightning speed, her hand shot up, her fingers curling into Azai's hair and tugging his head down to the level of her face.

"OW!" Azai's outraged dignity—as he bent double in front of the slight form of the eighteen-year-old singer—had Marieke raising a hand to hide her laugh.

"He's clean," Veronica informed her cheerfully, adding insult to injury by giving Azai's hair an unnecessary extra tousle as she released it. "Could do with a haircut, though."

"I've been a little busy," Azai growled.

"Believe it or not, I can actually cut hair using songcraft," Veronica informed them all cheerfully. "It's one of the fun electives they offer over the summer in Tarandon."

"Wow." Marieke was impressed. "They don't offer anything like that here. It's all serious disciplines. More practical, everyday skills would be great."

"You are NOT cutting my hair with your song," Azai interjected, his tone comically horrified as he smoothed down the abused tufts. "There are some things magic has no place doing."

Veronica shrugged. "Suit yourself, if you prefer to be unkempt."

"Unkempt?" Azai spluttered, more outraged than ever.

"This could be a long journey," Marieke muttered to Zev over the bickering.

"Then we'd better waste no time in getting started," he replied. He glanced at her pocket, which her hand had slipped into again. "Which way is it saying?"

"That way." She pointed. "Which I think is west."

Zev nodded. "Let's go."

CHAPTER

SEVEN

Zev

Zev frowned at the trail ahead, winding its way up yet another rocky hill. "I think we might be getting close."

"Why do you say that?" Marieke asked, her gaze unfocused as it usually was when she was sensing the magic of Instructor Oriana's guiding enchantment.

"These hills." Zev gestured with an arm. "They don't seem quite natural, do they?"

"They're unnaturally annoying," Veronica panted, looking disheartened as she stared up at the rise. "All morning we've been climbing up just for the pleasure of climbing straight back down again."

Zev didn't answer, catching Azai's gaze instead. He saw comprehension light his brother's eyes. The hills might be harsher and more barren here—a lot more barren—but their presence was reminiscent of the undulating terrain that surrounded their own family's home. Had these hills also not been here back when monarchs ruled the land?

"Well, I don't know if we're getting close," Marieke said. "But we're definitely still on the right track."

"So the enchantment is still strong?" Veronica asked.

Marieke's face twisted in unease as her senses probed something Zev couldn't see.

"Strong is too generous. It's definitely weakening. We must be nearing the edge of its reach. I just hope we find Jade's base before it runs out altogether." She glanced up at the sun. It had passed its zenith, marking that their third day of travel out of the city was half over. "Maybe we should proceed more cautiously. Perhaps split up?"

Zev nodded. "I can scout ahead."

"I can do that with magic," said Veronica. "Then we can stay together."

"I prefer the old-fashioned method of gathering information," Zev informed her.

Marieke shook her head, a smile dancing on her lips. "You know, magic is as old as the land is, Zev. Doing everything without it isn't old-fashioned. It's just unnecessarily inefficient. But in this instance, I do think you're right that we shouldn't send any enchantments ahead of us. If Jade's base is nearby, she might sense the magic approaching."

"Good point," Veronica conceded. "I'll come with you, just in case you run into any trouble that magic might help you get out of."

"We all know Zev wants to stay with Marieke," said Azai in a long-suffering voice. "I'll go scouting."

"All right," Veronica said, shrugging.

Azai eyed her. "What was that look for? Let me guess, being a mighty singer, you don't need my inferior physical assistance?"

Zev could feel Marieke's impatience at this latest instance of Azai's churlishness, but as usual, Veronica seemed untroubled.

"Not at all," she said amicably. "There was no look. Naturally I appreciate the help. Two together are safer than one alone."

For reasons that surely did Azai no credit, this pleasant response seemed to agitate him more. But for once he held it in, just striding forward to join Veronica as she moved away from the group.

"Your brother is impossible," Marieke commented once they were alone. "Why is he so determined to pick a fight with Veronica? It's been endless."

She looked surprised when Zev chuckled. "He's trying to fight with her so he can stop fighting with himself."

"What do you mean?" she demanded.

"He wants singers to be unreasonable and heavy-handed," Zev said. "He'd be much more comfortable if the real-life singers he's spending time with were power-hungry and combative, as he expected them to be."

"Ah." Marieke's face suggested she was starting to comprehend. "And Veronica is proving impossible to bait."

"Exactly," Zev said. "Personally I find it highly entertaining how uninterested she is in fighting with him. I could hardly keep a straight face yesterday when she spent half an hour acting like she couldn't tell he was being sarcastic and taking his comments on her path-clearing song as genuinely complimentary."

Marieke grinned at that. "It was very satisfying," she acknowledged. "He looked a fool, didn't he? What could he do, correct her and tell her he didn't actually mean what he said and was in fact trying to insult her and everyone like her? He would have made himself even more ridiculous."

"I was impressed she kept it up so long and never cracked," Zev agreed. "She certainly knows how to handle him."

"Better her than me," Marieke said.

Zev shook his head. "Azai's not so bad, Mari. He's going through exactly the process I went through when we met. I just kept it inside."

"If you're trying to make me think better of your brother, then comparing him to you isn't the way to achieve it," Marieke told him. "You outshine him in every way."

"Well..." Zev grinned, a shot of warmth going up the back of his neck. "I won't pretend I don't like hearing that."

Marieke just laughed, the expression slowly easing into a more serious one as she looked around them. "It's worse here, isn't it?"

Zev also scanned the area. "Definitely. I doubt this area will see any harvest at all. It's gotten steadily worse the further we've gone from the capital."

Marieke nodded soberly. She was likely picturing the scenes they'd witnessed when leaving the capital. If this whole region had no harvest to speak of, the streams of people pouring into the city from the countryside would only grow in size. The worst of it was that they wouldn't find the relief they sought. As far as any of them knew, the council had no solution for the looming food crisis. The situation had intensified too suddenly for them to be adequately prepared.

"The magic feels different here, too," Marieke informed him, her eyes staring unseeingly in front of her. "It's still there, but it's not very responsive. I don't think it wants to work with me."

Zev shot her a look of amusement. "You realize it's not alive, right? It's not your pet dog you're talking about."

She just rolled her eyes at him. "If our theory about Oleand's heartsong is right, the increasing barrenness probably means we're getting close to the royal descendants. It seems our gamble might pay off. We're lucky Jade wasn't coming from somewhere else entirely when she pursued us to the capital."

Zev's reply was interrupted by a familiar whistle. His gaze darted to the nearest hill.

"That's Azai," he informed Marieke. "They must be coming back."

"Already?" Marieke's gaze followed his. "Does that mean they found something?"

They soon had their answer. Veronica had a spring in her step as she approached them, Azai following with a short, tense stride. Had they been fighting again? Or rather, had he been attempting unsuccessfully to fight with her?

"There's a town just over this section of hills," Veronica told them. "Not huge, but bigger than a village." She pointed. "Over there. Does that seem right?"

Marieke frowned. "It's not quite where the tracking magic is directing me."

"I think we should still check it out," Zev interjected. "If we really are close, we should take the chance to get information before charging into a possible confrontation."

"The aim is to *avoid* confrontation with Jade at this stage," Marieke said, a sharp note to her voice. "Remember, Azai?"

Zev's brother raised his palms in a gesture of defense. "I didn't say anything."

Marieke still looked wary, and Zev cleared his throat, eager to redirect the conversation. He wished Marieke had a better opinion of Azai, but he had to acknowledge that Azai hadn't been giving the best impression of himself.

"Let's see what we can learn in the town," Zev said. "Azai, you and me."

His brother nodded, moving away from Veronica to Zev's side.

"We should come, too," Marieke said. "We're perfectly capable, Zev, we don't need to hang back where you think we're safer."

"It's not that," Zev assured her. "I just think it's better for us to draw as little attention as possible."

"What do you mean?" Marieke demanded. "Why would we draw more attention than you would?"

Zev exchanged an amused look with Azai, who let out a chuckle.

"It's the way you carry yourselves," Azai informed her. "You may as well be wearing council robes." He glanced at Veronica. "Especially you. No offense."

For once he actually sounded like he meant it.

In her usual unruffled way, Veronica just let out a sigh. "I'm too much of a city dweller, am I? I suppose Mari at least grew up in a farming community."

"Don't feel bad," Zev said, as he pulled his jacket around him so the blade he was wearing on his back would be less conspicuous. "Mari has academy education written all over her as well."

Marieke looked like she was considering arguing further, but Zev didn't give her the chance.

"You two find somewhere sheltered to keep an eye on the path into town. We won't be gone long."

On the words, he strode in the direction Azai and Veronica had come from, his brother close behind.

"Aren't you worried about leaving Marieke exposed?" Azai asked. "I thought you were determined to protect her."

"We won't be gone long, and she won't be exposed," Zev said, wishing Azai's words didn't spark an anxiety that he knew was overblown. "She's sensible, she'll monitor the situation from somewhere defensible."

"If you say so." Azai's voice held definite judgment, and Zev sent him a look.

"Is it possible that it's not Marieke's safety you're worried about?"

"Don't be ridiculous!" The strength of Azai's response betrayed him. "I'm not worried about either of their safety."

"If you say so." Zev repeated his brother's words with a hint of sarcasm before putting the matter from his mind as the town came into view. "There's the road, look."

The two of them moved onto the path, entering the town not far behind an empty wagon. Zev generally knew what to expect from a farming town, but it took only a moment to realize that this wasn't like the towns he knew.

"The place is deserted," Azai said.

It was an exaggeration, but Zev knew what he meant. The bustle he'd expected was markedly absent. The whole place had a gloomy, desolate air about it. Oleand's troubles had hit this particular region hard.

"A lot of the residents have probably headed for larger cities," Zev said. "If there aren't many people here, then we'll stand out more than we were hoping."

Azai nodded. "We shouldn't linger."

"I don't plan to." Zev's eyes were resting on a boy of nine or ten who was sitting outside a nearby shop, repeatedly throwing a small and grubby ball against the wall.

"Hey," he said, drawing the child's attention. "You hungry?" He pulled an apple from his rucksack, and the boy's eyes lit up. No doubt he hadn't seen fresh produce in a while. As his gaze passed between the brothers, his expression became more suspicious.

"What do you want for it?"

Zev kept his expression calm, but his heart wrenched a little at the cynicism this boy had already learned in his short life.

"We just want you to tell us about the area. Times are pretty bad, huh?"

The boy shrugged. "I guess so. We're hungry most of the time. Me ma says it'll pick up, though."

"Why's that?" Azai asked, frowning.

The boy's eyes were on the apple. "She said the town had times like this when she was a girl, but it got better."

"But the whole country is falling apart this time," Azai said. "Not just this area."

"I dunno anything about the rest of the country," said their young informer, not sounding too concerned. "But anyone in this town'll tell you the same as me ma. We have the highest of highs and the lowest of lows around here—we're known for it. My grandparents say the same. In their day our town had the best harvest of the whole region for years straight. Then we were hit with a drought that almost killed the town." He shrugged. "That's life, isn't it? 'Least round here it is."

Zev exchanged a look with Azai, sure his brother was forming the same conclusions he was. Frowning, he turned the apple over in his hand.

"Do you ever get singers around town?"

"Singers?" the boy repeated incredulously. "Out here? Nah, I don't reckon."

"What about a tall woman with dark hair?" Azai pushed, as usual being less discreet than Zev would have liked. "Probably between thirty and thirty-five?"

The boy brightened. "Oh yeah, I think I know who you mean. She comes through all the time, buys stuff from the shop but never stays in town. I think she visits the lot at the manor house." He shivered. "I wouldn't be caught dead up there."

"What's the manor house?" Zev demanded. "And why wouldn't you go there?"

"Cursed, isn't it?" the boy answered matter-of-factly. "Not

that they welcome visitors, anyway. Like to keep to themselves. Think they're pretty fancy, living in that crumbling old building. Me ma says it's nothing more than an eyesore, with the way it's falling apart."

"Where is it?" Zev asked.

"Not far." The boy pointed southwest.

"Thanks."

Zev tossed him the apple, and the boy's eyes lit up. He was already biting into it when Azai threw in one last question.

"Have you seen that tall woman around lately?"

"Not for a week or two." The boy didn't look up, his attention fully on his prize.

"Come on," Zev said quietly. "I think we've learned what we need to know."

He could see a pair of men leaning against a building just over the road, arms crossed as they eyed the brothers. Azai followed Zev readily, his demeanor seeming relaxed, although Zev knew him well enough to realize it was an act.

"Did you see that?" Azai murmured out of the corner of his mouth.

Zev grunted acknowledgment. He hadn't missed the two men pushing off from the wall and strolling toward the boy as soon as he and Azai had left him. He risked a glance back when they neared a corner. The men must have been very brief in speaking to the boy, because they were now walking in the same direction Zev and Azai had taken.

"They're following," he said to Azai.

"Run or fight?" His brother sounded perfectly calm.

Zev considered it for only a second. "I think draw them further out of town, away from backup."

Azai nodded, matching as Zev increased his pace. "Then we fight. I agree—we don't want them following us all the way to this manor house. I assume we're leading them away from where the girls are waiting?"

"Yes."

But Zev didn't make for the opposite direction from where they'd left the girls, east of the town. Because that would take them too close to the manor house. Instead he went north, aware that the strangers were following them at a distance, and that their numbers had swelled to four.

Only once they'd cleared the last straggling buildings, and the town had disappeared behind a low hill, did they come to a stop. The two of them turned, standing shoulder to shoulder with arms crossed as they waited for their pursuers to appear.

The men had picked up the pace to match Zev and Azai, and two of them hurried around the corner before skidding to a stop. They obviously hadn't expected the strangers to be waiting motionless for them.

"Why are you following us?" Zev asked, his voice hard.

The man at the front of the group darted his gaze from one brother to the other. "What was your business in our town?"

"I don't see how that concerns you," Zev said.

"It's our town, isn't it?" The man lifted his chin, his eyes narrowed.

"We're not in it anymore."

"You left without paying the visitor's tax," the man said.

Azai snorted. "You might have the patience for a drawn-out pretense," he told Zev. "But I don't. Let's get it over with."

The strangers obviously felt the same way, because Azai's words acted like a signal. Two men sprang from behind a nearby hill, having circled around the brothers' backs while they spoke with the first pair. One had a knife in his hand, the other a raised club.

Without the need for discussion, Zev and Azai spun, pulling out their own blades as they took up a position back-to-back.

By the time Zev lunged out at the man with the knife, he could hear that the first pair had drawn weapons on Azai. He wasn't concerned for his brother. He'd spent more hours than he could count sparring with Azai throughout his life, and they were very evenly matched.

Which was to say, none of these untrained ruffians were any match for either one of them.

Zev's first opponent cried out as Zev's sword nicked his hand in the process of flicking the knife out of his grip. Zev could have done it without making contact, but he wanted to send a warning just as surely as he sent the knife spinning off out of reach.

He ducked as the man with the club took a wild swing at him, recovering himself in time to spare a glance for Azai. As expected, he wasn't in need of any assistance—one of his opponents was already out cold, and the other was wielding what looked like a meat cleaver. Not an ideal weapon against the sword Azai had acquired in Ondford. It wasn't as fine a blade as the one he'd lost in the rescue mission in the dungeon, but it was still superior to anything carried by their opponents.

Zev brought his attention back to his own fight in time to kick the club-wielder in the gut as hard as he could. The man dropped his weapon, clutching at his stomach as the wind was knocked out of him. The one with the knife had recovered himself sufficiently to make a wild grab at Zev's leg as he pulled it back from the kick. But Zev evaded him, maneuvering behind him as he changed his grip to allow him to bring the hilt of his sword down into the center of the man's back.

With another cry, the stranger dropped to his knees. Loath to kill an opponent he saw as little better than unarmed, Zev spun back to the advancing club-wielder without changing his grip, using the hilt of his sword for a carefully placed hit to the head. The man crumpled, unconscious. He wouldn't be out for long, and if Zev was as skilled as he thought he was, he should wake with nothing worse than a raging headache.

The other man was on the ground now, still clutching his back in pain, but Zev had underestimated him. As he turned, panting slightly, to check in with Azai, the stranger suddenly sprang into motion. Zev spun back, barely catching a glimpse of a dagger before Azai's form came between him and his attacker. With a crunch, Azai brought his foot down on the man's already injured hand. The stranger let out a scream of both anger and pain as the dagger fell from his grip. The scream was cut off as Azai knocked him out in just the way Zev had done to his fellow.

"Thanks," said Zev, glancing around to see that Azai's two opponents were also unconscious, one of them bleeding from the leg, but neither looking seriously injured.

"No problem." Azai checked his sword carefully before sliding it into the belt strapped onto his back. He slapped Zev amicably on the shoulder. "I got you, brother. Nothing reminds me that I do actually like you so well as fighting together. Nice to get a bit of exercise, too."

Zev laughed. "It's been too long," he agreed.

"Should we—" Azai cut off his own words, stiffening as a flash of movement caught both brothers' eyes. He spun, his hand halfway to his weapon again, before relaxing as he caught sight of the two figures watching open-mouthed from the top of a nearby hill. "Oh, it's just you."

"What are you doing over here?" Zev asked, frowning slightly at Marieke and Veronica. "You were supposed to be lying low."

"We were lying low." Marieke hurried down the hill toward him, her eyes concerned as they raked over his figure. "We explored the area, and we thought this was the best spot to watch people coming out of the town. Well, not right here. We climbed up those trees over there." She gestured vaguely behind her, her tension relaxing as she drew level with Zev and realized that he was uninjured.

"But when we saw you being set upon, we climbed down and came to help," Veronica added. Unlike Marieke, she remained taut, her expression stunned. "At least, I wanted to help. Mari told me we should leave you to it rather than risk complicating things by adding magic to the situation."

Azai nodded to Marieke with more politeness than usual. "Thank you. That showed excellent sense."

"You're welcome," Marieke said gravely, although her eyes danced. She met Zev's gaze, and her lips twitched slightly.

"We should move," Zev said. "None of them will be out for long."

Azai nodded. "And there's probably not much point worrying about whether we leave a trail. They probably already know from our conversation with that boy that we're headed to this manor place."

"What boy?" Marieke asked, as they all started walking.

Zev explained about their brief visit to the town as Azai led the group in a wide arc around the town, toward the south-west, where the boy had pointed.

"I hope he'll be all right," Azai interjected, glancing in the direction of the village, which was obscured by the low hills.

"Who?" Veronica asked.

"The boy," said Azai. "They saw us speak to him, and they'll undoubtedly ask him to repeat every word." His brow was lowered. "I hope he won't get into any kind of trouble for helping us. He couldn't have been more than nine years old. Just a kid."

Veronica didn't respond, and Zev noticed her looking sideways at Azai with an expression he couldn't quite read.

"I'm sure he'll be fine," said Zev.

"So you think this manor house is where we'll find the descendants we're looking for?" Marieke asked.

"It makes sense if that's where Jade has been going," Zev said. "If the boy is right about the constantly changing nature of the region's fortunes, it sounds like their family line has been here for a long time."

Marieke nodded thoughtfully. "During which time they haven't been steady and consistent like your family has."

"No, it sounds like their effect on the land has been sometimes good and sometimes bad," Azai agreed. "Depending on their own state, I imagine."

"Do you think it's true that Jade hasn't been in the area since we last saw her?" Veronica asked, finding her voice at last.

"No idea," said Zev. "The boy didn't say that, he just said he hadn't seen her. But it makes sense to me. She presumably doesn't have any idea Marieke took her hair, so I don't think she would expect us to have access to a backward tracking enchantment like the one she used on me when we were in the jungle. But she might have expected us—or the council—to try to track where she went when she left the city. So she probably didn't come straight back here."

Marieke nodded slowly. "This is our time to strike, then."

The boy in the town hadn't lied when he said the manor wasn't far. They'd only been walking for about fifteen minutes when a wide—albeit overgrown—road appeared. Following it, they soon found themselves looking up at crumbling stone gateposts, although the gate between them had long since fallen apart. Beyond, Zev could see a dilapidated building. It was larger than any country home he'd ever seen, but far short of anything like the old castle in Tarandon that the council now used as its headquarters.

"I see why there's local superstition around it," Azai commented. "It *looks* cursed."

Zev knew what he meant. At a glance, he would have called the structure ruins rather than a building. Time had not been kind to what had once been a grand dwelling. But looking more closely, he could see that those windows which were broken had been boarded up rather than left open to the elements, and there was even a thin curl of smoke rising up from what was probably the kitchen chimney.

"Smoke. Someone's home," he commented to Marieke.

She didn't respond, her eyes closed with the look he'd come to associate with her feeling for magic.

"It doesn't just look cursed," she said in reference to Azai's words. "It feels cursed. Or at least...unstable."

"I feel it, too," Veronica said. "The magic in this area is strong, but not very responsive to me. I wondered if it was because I'm Aeltan."

Marieke shook her head. "It's the same for me."

"Should we circle back, try to find an unobtrusive way in?" Azai suggested.

"No." Marieke seemed confident. "We won't achieve our purpose without making our presence known. I think I should risk some songcraft, to try to identify how many people are here."

"Yes, this is a good opportunity to practice!"

Veronica sounded enthusiastic, and Zev had to admit curiosity of his own as well. The two girls had been practicing the so-called storytelling song to the best of their ability during their journey west. It seemed they'd both only done the most rudimentary study on the subject, so their application was limited, but if Veronica was to be believed, Marieke's results were impressive for such sparse training.

Marieke cleared her throat, her lovely voice raised in a quiet, wordless note. The sound died out quickly, and she bit her lip.

"I wish the magic was more responsive," she murmured to no one in particular.

Zev stepped up, trying to be unobtrusive as he rested his hand on her lower back, not wanting Veronica to guess what he was doing. His skin tingled from Marieke's warmth, but he didn't let himself get distracted. They still didn't fully understand the bond that seemed to exist between Marieke's songcraft and his heartsong, and physical touch might not be necessary to activate it. But it surely wouldn't hurt. And it would be interesting to see if the same thing held true here as it had in the dungeon in Ondford—namely that the magic of the land didn't seem to care much that he'd crossed a political border and was no longer within his own country.

Apparently it did hold true. Marieke drew in a sharp breath, then raised her voice again, her song more confident this time. Zev didn't catch the words, too mesmerized by the pleasant intonation of her voice as it danced on the wind, seeming to reach invisible arms toward the building in front of them. When she let the sound die out, Veronica jumped in eagerly.

"That felt like fully formed songcraft. Did it work? Did it tell you what's happening in there?"

"I think so," Marieke said cautiously. "I mean, not with a great deal of detail. But I think there's only one person in the building. And maybe something smaller, like a cat or a dog or something."

"Huh." Veronica looked impressed. "I wouldn't have even thought to check for animals."

"It's worth knowing exactly what we're dealing with." Marieke shot Zev a smile, no doubt thinking of the time she'd used this type of songcraft to identify that they'd entered the hunting territory of a panther.

"And you don't think this one person is Jade?" he asked.

Marieke shook her head with confidence. "I really don't. I'd be surprised if this person was a singer. But I can't know for sure from out here." She turned her face to the empty gateway. "I'm done sneaking around. I'm going in."

She walked forward, Veronica hurrying to keep up. Zev exchanged a quick glance with Azai before, reassured by his brother's nod of readiness, he strode through the gate as well.

EIGHT

Marieke

Marieke felt strangely calm as she approached the run-down dwelling. It would be logical to feel afraid, but she didn't. Maybe she was putting too much faith in her fledgling storytelling abilities, but the presence she'd felt through her songcraft hadn't seemed intimidating to her. And it was such a relief to reach their destination before the tracking enchantment expired. She would be glad to be rid of the lock of Jade's hair. It had become distasteful to her, like an enemy presence in her pocket.

The carriage yard was big, and she had ample time to examine the building as she neared it. She'd never seen such a large home outside the capital. In Ondford, some of the wealthier and more influential singing families had dwellings as impressive as this. But in the country it was an oddity.

"Who do you think built such a big home?" Veronica asked.

"It's a manor house," Azai said. "The boy in town even called it that."

Veronica's expression showed that the word meant nothing to her, so Azai explained.

"Back when the country was run by a monarchy, there were

other levels of nobility below royalty. Most of those people would have had large, grand dwellings like this. And not just in the capital, but all over the country."

"Ah, the king's court." Veronica nodded. "Yes, we learned all about that corrupt system in history class."

Marieke caught Azai's scowl, and she wasn't surprised when Zev jumped in before his brother could say anything combative.

"In itself, the system was no more corrupt than the council system. The power of the court was of course open to abuse."

"As is the power of the council," Azai added.

Honestly, it was the mildest Marieke had ever heard him be on the topic, and it made his point seem reasonable rather than belligerent. She had the sense Veronica realized it as well, the other girl sneaking a sideways look at Azai.

"Well, whoever built this place is long dead, and it's far from grand now," Marieke said. Boldly, she walked up to the front door—a solid wooden affair that was still intact—and knocked.

They waited a couple of minutes, but no one answered. Undeterred, Marieke stepped back, scanning the building for the smoke Zev had mentioned before. It was off to the right, and she marched around the outside of the building in that direction. Once they rounded the side of the grand facade, they found themselves in a kitchen garden, one with surprisingly healthy plants growing. It looked like it had once been fenced in, but it was open now, and they were able to walk right between the rows of vegetables. Marieke watched with interest as a plump chicken strutted across their path. Apparently it had been too small to be picked up by her earlier song, unless this was the creature she'd guessed to be a cat or dog.

A simpler door was set into the stone wall of the building at one end of the garden, and Marieke approached it with renewed determination. This time, when she knocked, they only had to wait a few moments before the door was pulled open.

"Not trading today, we didn't get enough eggs to—"

The speaker—a young woman perhaps a couple of years older than Marieke, with curly, mouse-brown hair tied up in a kerchief—cut herself off, her eyes widening as she caught sight of the group standing in her garden.

"Who are you?"

"I'm Marieke," Marieke told her calmly. "I'm a singer, and I've come from Ondford."

"You're a singer?"

She didn't miss the way the other girl's eyes hardened, or the fact that one of her hands strayed out of sight behind the doorframe.

"I'm not here to hurt you," Marieke said quickly.

"Unless you try to hurt her," Zev interjected, his voice steady and commanding. "In which case our intentions would change very quickly."

The girl stared at him, her expression familiar as she examined him from head to toe. Marieke held in a sigh. Zev *was* inconveniently impressive. She'd felt it from the first moment of meeting him, so she couldn't blame other girls for having the same reaction.

"And who are you?" she asked.

"I'm Zevadiah," Zev said. "And I don't want to be your enemy any more than Marieke does."

"So what *do* you all want?" the girl asked warily.

"To help you, I hope," Marieke said. "But mainly to save Oleand. Can we come in?"

The girl's curiosity was definitely roused as she studied Marieke before letting her eyes flick back to Zev. "I don't think I should let you."

"Are you all alone here?" Veronica asked, her voice sympathetic. "We're not trying to scare you. If you'd prefer to talk out here, we can do that."

The girl let out a long sigh before muttering, "What do I have to lose?" She stepped back and vacated the doorway. "Come in then, if you must."

Marieke looked at Zev, who gave a silent shrug before preceding her into the building. Overprotective as ever, he scanned the room—a moderately sized kitchen—before taking up a position near the door, as if wanting to make sure no one could block their exit. Marieke sent him a quelling look. She didn't think they'd get anywhere by intimidating this girl.

"Sit down, I suppose." Their hostess gestured ungraciously toward a scrubbed wooden table boasting a few chairs. Marieke and Veronica both sat, but Zev stayed where he was, and Azai positioned himself by the room's other door, moving with a casual grace that surprised Marieke.

"What did you mean when you said you want to save Oleand?" the girl asked Marieke abruptly. She was also still standing, her arms wrapped around herself defensively.

"I assume you're aware that the country has been slowly deteriorating for a while now?" Marieke said.

She hesitated, then gave a curt nod.

"And that it's gotten drastically worse in recent weeks?" Marieke pressed.

The girl bit her lip, and Marieke leaned forward. She knew more than she was saying, but Marieke would be wise not to spook her.

"What's your name? I've told you mine, after all."

The girl let out a long breath, her eyes darting to each of her visitors in turn before she spoke.

"Tarenne."

"I'm Veronica, by the way," Veronica interjected. She

gestured to the remaining member of their group. "And this is Azai. How did you come to live here all alone, Tarenne?" Veronica's voice was gentle, and Marieke felt a swell of gratitude for her friend's presence. The Aeltan girl had a way of warming people to her, she'd noticed.

Tarenne shook her head. "I don't live here alone. This has always been my home, and my brother lives here, too. He's just not...not here right now."

"And your parents?" Veronica asked delicately.

"They died." Tarenne didn't show much emotion, although she looked particularly listless as she said it. "A few years ago."

"I'm sorry." Marieke paused, unsure what to say. "Tarenne, has your family lived here for a long time? Longer than your parents' lifetimes, I mean?"

The other girl's eyes held a definite hint of resentment as they rested on Marieke. "That's none of your business. None of this is. I don't know what makes you think you can come into my home and ask me all these questions."

"I'm sorry," Marieke said quickly. "I don't mean to offend." Acting on the impulse of the moment, she decided to be bold. "Like I told you, I'm just trying to help my country. The council is useless, they won't act until it's too late, if even then. My friends are the only ones helping me, even though none of them are even Oleandan." She held the other girl's gaze. "If you can honestly tell me that the history of your family has no relevance to saving Oleand, then I won't ask you any more questions, and I'll leave you in peace."

Tarenne's discomfort increased visibly, but she didn't respond to Marieke's challenge. Her eyes passed around the group again, and when she spoke, it was to Zev.

"None of you are from Oleand?"

He shook his head. "Azai, Veronica, and I are Aeltan. But we don't want to see your country fall apart. We don't want to see people starve."

"Because then they'll probably flee into your country, right?" Tarenne said cynically. "You don't want the problem to grow to the point that it affects you."

"Of course we don't," said Azai bluntly. "Is that a bad thing? Would you feel any differently if you were us?"

"I suppose not," she said cautiously.

"It's not just that," Veronica said. "We really do care, Tarenne. And it's a very strange and meandering road that brought us to your door in our mission to stop Oleand from falling apart."

"What *did* bring you to my door?" Tarenne demanded.

"Jade." Marieke watched Tarenne closely for her reaction as she gave the blunt answer. The girl started visibly, her eyes flying to Marieke's with a hunted look.

"Who?"

"No, don't play dumb." Marieke shook her head. "You know your reaction gave you away. And besides, we followed her trail right to this building. She's been here, hasn't she? Probably lots of times."

Tarenne swallowed, keeping her mouth shut.

"Where's your brother, Tarenne?" Zev asked. "Is he with her right now?"

She tightened her grip on her own arms. "That's none of your business. I don't have to tell you anything."

"You don't," Veronica agreed.

Her eyes found Marieke's, and Marieke knew what she was thinking. But she hesitated. Should she attempt to use story-telling song again, this time to paint a picture of what had passed rather than what was presently before her? Or would that just alienate Tarenne beyond reclaim? She caught a movement in the corner of her eyes, and looked over her shoulder at Zev. He was gesturing subtly to her.

"Excuse me," she said politely to Tarenne as she rose and went to Zev's side. Watched warily by their hostess, the two of them slipped out into the garden.

"You're considering using that storytelling song to find out what she's not telling us, aren't you?" Zev said at once.

Marieke nodded. "Considering it. What do you think?"

"I don't think songcraft will help us here. We didn't come because we have your singing ability. We came because we have another resource no one else has."

"You," Marieke finished. "Do you want me to distract Veronica somehow?"

Zev sighed. "I think we're beyond that. Do you think Tarenne and her brother are the ones we're looking for?"

"I do. I can't say it for certain, of course. But the magic responds to her. It doesn't pool like it would to a singer, but it's sort of...aware of her. I don't know how else to describe it. It's something I would never have noticed if I hadn't learned to look for it. But it interacts with her, even though she's not trying to harness it. And she clearly knows more than she's saying."

"That much is obvious," Zev agreed. He ran a hand through his hair, his expression tense. "All right."

Without another word he let himself back into the kitchen, Marieke close behind. It didn't look like Veronica and Azai had gotten anywhere in their absence.

"Naturally you're right that you don't have to tell us anything," Zev said abruptly. "But I think you want to. I think you let us in because whatever situation you've found yourself in, you don't *want* to stand in opposition to the goal of saving Oleand. And you might find relief in speaking openly with perhaps the only people who can understand your situation."

Tarenne made a noise in her throat. "I doubt any of you understand my situation."

"You'd be surprised," Zev said.

"A singer and a bunch of Aeltans?" There wasn't much mirth in Tarenne's dry laugh. "How would you understand my life?"

"Because you're descended from the Oleandan monarchs of the past," Zev said evenly. "My guess is that your absent brother is the heir, if such a position still has any meaning so long after your ancestors were deposed."

Tarenne had frozen in position, her eyes wide and her voice apparently silenced. Marieke got the sense she was trying to decide whether to deny it or whether opening her mouth at all was too great a risk.

"Don't look so shocked," Zev went on. "If Jade found you, it stands to reason others will, too. Did you already know about heartsong, or did Jade tell you? She's persuaded your brother to use his power over the land to harm it, hasn't she? That's why Oleand is in such trouble. But I don't think you're fully convinced of her plan. If you were, you wouldn't have even agreed to speak with us."

"I..." Tarenne's voice was a raspy whisper. "How do you..."

"How do I know all this?" Zev was still so calm. "Because I'm one of the few others alive who knows firsthand what heartsong is. As your brother is heir to the shattered throne of Oleand, so I am directly descended, father to son, from Aeltas's last crowned king."

Marieke

The ripple that went around the room with Zev's declaration was so tangible, Marieke almost misidentified it as an enchantment. And Tarenne's astonishment was the least remarkable reaction. Azai stiffened, his fist clenching on the bench where it rested and his face a mask of shock at his brother's exposure of the secret they'd lived by all their lives. Veronica's mouth actually fell open, her eyes bulging as they traveled from Zev to Marieke then, thoughtfully, on to Azai. Veronica was too smart not to realize at once that the news was no surprise to Marieke.

"It's true," Marieke said, her words directed at Tarenne, but meant for Veronica as well. "His family has documentation proving it, and I've felt the way his heartsong interacts with my songcraft. But his family have used their influence on the land to help it prosper, not to make it wither."

Tarenne gave no response to Marieke's words, her eyes fixed on Zev as she sank into a chair at last. A sleek, gray cat appeared from under a cupboard, startling Veronica as it slunk past her before leaping lightly onto Tarenne's lap. So Marieke's assessing song earlier hadn't been wrong.

Their hostess stroked the cat's back mechanically as she studied the self-proclaimed Aeltan heir. To her unease, Marieke realized there was something more than shock on the other girl's face. Marieke would almost call it hunger. Not greed or malice—it roused Marieke's sympathy more than her suspicion. But it also made her uncomfortable in a way she couldn't put into words.

"Where have you been all these years?" Tarenne asked hoarsely. "Your family line, I mean. All these generations."

"In Aeltas, where we belong," Zev said simply. "Our ancestor fled the massacre at Sundering Canyon as a child, and made a life in the northern part of our country. We're farmers. We work the land, and it thrives under our stewardship."

Tarenne ran her tongue over a dry corner of her lips, her fingers still moving rhythmically over the cat's fur. "Our ancestor escaped by boat, or tried to. He intended to sail to Providore to seek assistance from the monarchs of those kingdoms in reclaiming his throne. But the singers attacked the vessel before they could get into deep water. They no doubt thought they'd sunk it. But by hugging the coast, the group made it far enough to get their feet back on land further north. They hid and traveled by foot. It took weeks to reach the sanctuary of the estate of a loyal supporter, and by then the original owner of this house was either dead or exiled and the place was looted. We've lived here ever since." She shrugged. "Or so the story goes. I can't verify it. And I don't have documents proving who I am." Her face hardened. "I don't want them. I don't want to prove my identity—I wish I was anyone else."

"But you're not," Zev said. "You can't change who you are or what family you're born into. And you were born into a family with power—power that you're using to kill the land. Make no mistake, Tarenne, if you keep killing the land, you will be responsible for killing the people as well."

"I'm not the one—" Tarenne started defensively before cutting herself off. After a tense moment, she eyed Marieke. "You say your songcraft interacts with his heartsong. How?"

"I don't know how to explain it," Marieke said. "I access the magic in the normal way I was taught, and use it according to my training. But Zev's presence...more than that, his support...it amplifies it in a way that I'd never heard of before we met. It's like the land itself gives power to my song."

"That's a much nicer way than she phrased it," Tarenne said, her voice wistful. "She made it sound like the land was vindictive, and eager to turn on the magic of the singers if given permission to do so by the keeper of its heart."

"By she you mean Jade?" Marieke pressed.

Tarenne nodded. "Clancy—that's my brother—was captivated by the idea. He hated knowing that we should have power when we actually have none. Or at least, we thought we had none. We've sometimes suspected that we affected the land. My father was generally an even-tempered man, and the region did well in the years of his life. My grandfather was bitter and angry, and there were a series of bad harvests in the region when he was alive. It was subtle enough that it might be coincidence."

She sounded bitter herself. "And even if it wasn't, it was too abstract to bring Clancy any relief. What good was power he couldn't intentionally wield? Well, when Jade showed up, she told him there was a way for him to wield it. He just had to trust her to guide the details, and she would help him take vengeance for what the singers did to us." She looked suddenly much older. "I don't think my father would have been so easily convinced. But he and my mother had just died."

"Just?" Zev asked, frowning. "How soon before Jade showed up?"

"A matter of weeks." Tarenne eyed him. "Why?"

"How did they die?" Marieke asked, a sick feeling stealing over her.

"As best we could tell, my father died of a heart attack," Tarenne said dully. "My mother was with him, and it looked like she fell from the loft. Probably trying to get down to help him."

"As best you can tell?" Zev repeated. "You and your brother didn't witness it?"

Tarenne shook her head, apparently catching the look Zev and Azai were exchanging. "What is it? Why are you looking at each other like that?"

"Because our father—who was the keeper of our bloodline —died recently as well." Outwardly, Zev was calm, but there was a hardness in his voice that made Marieke's heart ache afresh for the rawness of his loss. "Jade killed him."

Tarenne had gone pale. The cat, unimpressed that she'd stopped stroking it, nudged her hand. Tarenne ignored the gesture, her face still unnaturally colorless.

"There must be a mistake," she said. "Jade can be unyielding, I'll admit, but she wouldn't do that."

"She did do it," Azai said harshly. "We saw it happen."

"Do you mean...do you mean it was an accident?" Tarenne demanded. "Or that she didn't know who he was? She wants to restore the power of the royal bloodlines. She would never—"

"It was no accident," Zev cut her off. "And she knew who he was. That's why she killed him. She doesn't care about our bloodlines. She hates singers for her own reasons as much as for what happened in the past, and she cares about making the councils pay. We're just the excuse she's told herself."

"How can she hate singers?" Tarenne protested. "She *is* a singer. I'm sorry about your father, but I don't think you can have understood what you saw."

"The fact that she's a singer makes her vendetta all the

more dangerous," Marieke said quietly. "She's conflicted, and more volatile because of it. I suspect she's directed so much hatred at the council partly to deflect any she might feel toward herself. Convincing herself that the real problem is singers in government is probably the only way she can live with her own prejudice. Knowing her history, I doubt she was excited when she learned of her songcraft."

"All of that is just speculation," Tarenne said stubbornly.

"Yes," Zev agreed. "But Jade's murder of our father isn't. My brother and I were there. She didn't intend for us to witness it, but when we realized what she was doing and tried to intervene, she showed no remorse. Right in front of us, she used her magic to pierce his heart without leaving a mark on him. If we hadn't run in when we did, we would probably have thought his heart had failed by itself."

Tarenne surged to her feet, the cat flying to the floor with a yowl. "What are you implying?"

"I'm not implying anything," Zev replied. "I'm just telling you what we experienced. I heard Jade call my father a traitor because he refused to turn on his land like she wanted him to. She told me I have a choice to make, and that she isn't afraid to wipe out my family's line if I make the wrong one."

Tarenne swallowed visibly, her tongue once again seeking to moisten her dry lips. For a long and painful moment there was silence.

"I don't know what you want me to say," she whispered.

"We want you to say that you're not going to let yourself be manipulated by Jade's hatred," Marieke urged. "We want you not to turn on your own country."

"It's not up to me," Tarenne said. "Jade has Clancy fully convinced." She shot a resentful look toward Zev. "You might have a prosperous life farming the land, but all we've ever known is hunger and frustration. Knowing about our lineage is a curse when it doesn't gain us anything. And," she added, her voice growing heated, "the council is made up of traitors and liars. Why shouldn't it be punished?"

"What Jade is doing isn't just punishing the council," Marieke said. "She's ready to destroy a whole country for the crimes of a few. She has no hesitation to sacrifice lives in her cause—including the life of Zev and Azai's father."

She didn't say the conclusion they'd all silently reached, that Jade had sacrificed the lives of Tarenne's parents as well. She suspected that Tarenne was still wrestling with the truth, and wouldn't take kindly to Marieke saying aloud that the woman to whom she and her brother had been giving their allegiance had murdered their parents to manipulate them. Clearly Jade considered the younger generation more malleable for her cause.

Well, Marieke thought with a flash of fierce pride, she might have been right with Clancy. But Zev was no one's puppet. He wouldn't be so easily corrupted. Her eyes slid to Azai, and her certainty wavered.

"I still don't know what you want from me," Tarenne said gruffly, her small frame stiff with tension. "I'm not saying I want to see Oleand suffer. But I don't know how I'm supposed to stop it."

"Can you tell us anything about Jade's plan?" Veronica asked gently. "How long has she been working with your brother?"

"A couple of years," Tarenne said. "At least, we met her a couple of years ago. I don't quite know when it changed from talking about the past and what should have been to actually planning revenge. It happened so gradually."

"I can imagine," said Marieke. "Jade is smart, and she seems to be very good at getting what she wants."

"Your brother is with Jade now, isn't he?" Zev asked. "Where are they?"

"I don't know," Tarenne said. "I was a little more reluctant than Clancy, and Jade's never pushed me to be involved. I thought she was respecting my space."

"More likely she was being careful with what information you had access to," Marieke said grimly.

She felt a familiar helplessness threatening to take hold. How many times had she chased answers and thought herself on the verge of finding them, only to come up empty yet again? Jade was always one step ahead.

But she shook off the exhaustion that threatened. They'd come so far—finding Tarenne was enormous, and the fact that she seemed willing to work with them even more so. She undoubtedly knew more about Jade's activities even than she realized.

"Has your brother been helping Jade with experiments or anything like that?" Zev asked.

Tarenne frowned. "I don't know what you mean by experiments. She told us from the start that the power was already ours. She told him that he had the right to shape Oleand's future, and if his wisdom said that it shouldn't thrive under the council, it would be so. I believe that later she started talking about specific ways she could enhance his impact using songcraft, but I never knew the details of that. I did go with them once, when she took Clancy to the top of a hill nearby. She had us say these phrases, calling on the land to rise up. It felt silly, honestly. But I don't think she made them up. They sounded historical."

"That reminds me of the invocations you say, Zev," Marieke said. "Like the one you spoke over me the first time we parted, that the land would be firm under my feet but gentle to my touch, something like that. I'm pretty sure it saved my life when the canyon edge collapsed as my group passed by it."

Zev stared at her, making her realize she'd never told him the details of that incident.

"That's a traditional Aeltan parting," Azai said. "Very old, not used anymore, except by us. I don't know if our words have power, but it's family tradition to act as though they do. Speaking words of blessing over the fields and the region is a daily part of life for us on our farm. We were taught to do it as small children."

"Something tells me the words Jade had Clancy say weren't words of blessing," said Marieke. Her eyes were back on Tarenne. "And Jade didn't overestimate the power of whatever she's encouraged your brother to do, since the whole country has been deteriorating. Was your brother involved in the attacks on singers a while back?"

Tarenne frowned. "Of course not. They were talked about a great deal in town, though. Weren't they eventually proven to be the work of renegades living in Sundering Canyon? Clancy was surprised when we learned that. And a little disappointed, even. Jade had thought it was the land finally turning on the singers, and I suppose Clancy liked that."

Marieke let out a snort. "She didn't think anything of the kind. It's interesting that she wanted your brother to think it, though. It seems she hasn't told him everything." Seeing Tarenne's confusion, she clarified. "The attacks were carried out by renegades from the canyon, like you said. But they were orchestrated by Jade. She enlisted a young, frustrated hothead from the canyon community—much like she enlisted your brother—and gave him talismans with magical power so he could launch attacks undetected and make people think it was the work of the destabilizing land."

Tarenne put a hand to her head. It was a lot for her to take in, and not knowing her at all, it was impossible for Marieke to tell if she was believing all they said, or still clinging to some loyalty to Jade.

"I did hear Clancy ask her about the fires and floods we've been hearing about," the other girl said faintly. "He asked if she was behind it and if he could help, but she told him not to worry about it. She said it was under control."

"Can't you see that she was never here to help with your cause?" Marieke said earnestly. "She's just using your brother to further her own plans."

"And he's walked right into it." Tarenne's voice was low and pained, and her eyes held a strange mixture of shame and defiance as she looked around the group. "I meant it when I said I don't know where they are now. But I do know they're planning something. Jade never used to seem hurried—she's always very calm. Many times I've heard her tell Clancy that a reckoning will come, but it seemed like she meant it would one day naturally happen. Then she showed up here a couple weeks ago and her whole demeanor had changed. She seemed...rattled."

"You can thank Marieke for that," Zev said. His tone was hard to read.

"I'm not taking sole credit," Marieke protested. "She's at least as worried about you."

"And yet," Zev's eyes lingered on her, troubled, "you're the one she keeps vowing to kill."

"From what Tarenne has just told us," Veronica interjected, "it seems likely that what worries her is the combination of the two of you. She knew before you did that heartsong and songcraft could be a powerful combination. She won't want that combination developing further—perhaps to the point where it could counter her plans."

Marieke nodded slowly, appreciating the speed with which her friend had grasped the situation.

"If that's what Jade is worried about, then that's exactly what we need to do," she said, determined. "I just wish I knew what exactly her plan is so we could figure out *how* to counter it."

"I don't know any specifics," Tarenne said. She sounded a touch defensive, although no one had demanded answers from her. "But she told us both the reckoning was closer than we'd thought. She told Clancy it was time, and he left with her. He told me to stay here. I didn't want to go with them, in any event. I just want to stay out of it."

"Stay out of what, though?" Zev asked.

Marieke could understand the sharp edge to his voice. Tarenne's account sounded as though Jade and Clancy had been building to something catastrophic. But given that they'd followed Jade's trail back here, she must have left with Clancy *before* she came to Ondford to attack Marieke in the dungeon. And she hadn't brought Clancy with her then. So where was Clancy now? Where was Jade? When was the blow going to fall, and how could they stop it?

"I've already told you, I don't know what they're planning." Tarenne's tone was evasive, and when she looked up to find Zev staring doggedly at her, she let out a breath. "But I know it's something. Something big. Clancy's been very..." She made a face. "Well, very smug about it. Whatever it is, he thinks it will change everything for us. Or at least, for him."

She stood up, walking to the small, grimy window. "It's already changed everything. Clancy wasn't always like this. I mean...he wasn't ever happy, really. We weren't taught how to be happy. We were only taught what was taken from us. Never allowed to forget who we are, never allowed to put it behind us. Never even allowed to leave and try to make a life for ourselves somewhere other than this barren corner of the country."

The bitterness in her voice made her seem suddenly much older. Then she let out a sigh, and her shoulders slumped.

"But all of that was normal to us. The fervor that's taken hold of Clancy since he threw his lot in with Jade...that's something else entirely." Her voice dropped. "It scares me sometimes."

Marieke felt a twinge of sympathy for the other girl. How could she not? But she still felt uneasy around Tarenne, unsure whether to trust her. However helpful she was being now, they couldn't assume her priorities aligned with theirs.

"I'm sorry," Zev said heavily. "Your life has been much harder than mine. I know what it is to wonder whether the weight of our secrets will crush me, and my parents didn't choose bitterness. I can imagine it was much worse for you and your brother."

His eyes were earnest and somber, and Marieke noted ruefully that they were having their inevitable effect. Zev likely wasn't even aware of how intensely he held Tarenne's focus, how unwavering her gaze had become as she watched him.

"But please," Zev continued. "Don't make the same choice yourself. Don't punish your land and your people for a history they can't change."

"What are you asking of me?" Tarenne asked, her voice little more than a whisper. "What is it you want me to do?"

"Help us find your brother and stop him," Zev said. "I hoped that if we could just get to him without Jade around, he might listen to me, given I understand better than anyone the position he's in. But if Jade has him under her thumb as much as you say, he might not be willing to even hear me. You, on the other hand—"

Tarenne cut him off with a bitter laugh. "He's not in the habit of listening to me. I don't know why he'd start now." She considered soberly for a moment before speaking again. "You're offering for me to come with you? To accompany you on a search for my brother?"

Marieke bit her lip, trying to hold in her frown as she exchanged a look with Veronica. The other singer looked as uncertain as Marieke felt. Was it wise to let Tarenne join their group? Sharing their journey would give her too much opportunity to help Jade attack them if she turned on them.

She could tell that Tarenne was going to agree before the other girl spoke. As always, Zev's manner was more commanding than he was aware of. He had a way of making people want to follow him.

"I'll come with you," Tarenne said abruptly, as if in confirmation of Marieke's thoughts. "But I'm not promising to do or say what you tell me to. If I can talk Clancy out of doing something destructive, I'll be glad. But I can't guarantee that." She paused. "And I'm bringing my cat."

"Bringing your cat?" From Azai's tone, you'd think Tarenne had suggested bringing a plague. "How do you propose to do that?"

"What I mean is, he'll follow me," Tarenne said. "I don't plan to stop him, and what's more, I won't come unless you all promise not to do him any mischief. Just leave him be and he'll look after himself."

"If you insist," Zev said mildly. "If he's anything like the cats on our farm, he'll go where he pleases, and it's not a matter of us allowing it or otherwise."

Tarenne nodded, looking pleased. "I see you understand cats. As much as anyone can, anyway." She stood. "I'll fix some food. Normally I'd say I don't have enough to feed so many, but if I'm leaving for an indefinite period, I may as well use up what I have. I don't think we should set off before getting a good night's sleep." She must have seen their uncertainty, because she added with a touch of impatience, "No one's going to attack you in your sleep. Jade and Clancy aren't coming back until they've done...whatever they've set out to do. If then."

Marieke didn't feel confident, but she supposed they had little choice but to take Tarenne's word for it. She would certainly welcome the prospect of sleeping in a real bed.

"Can you accommodate us?" Zev asked doubtfully.

Tarenne nodded. "It's not luxurious, but it's dry. You and your brother can sleep in Clancy's room. It's not like he's using it. And you," she looked at Marieke and Veronica, "can sleep in my room. I'll sleep in here." She waved off their polite protests. "It will be fine. I'll light a fire."

A couple of hours later, after a simple meal, she showed them to the rooms in question. As soon as Tarenne withdrew, Zev strode into the girls' room, examining it carefully. Knowing his protective ways, Marieke had expected him to do something of the kind. She was surprised, however, to see Azai checking the room over as well, with an equally severe brow.

"We're just on the other side of this wall," Zev told Marieke. "A knock will be enough to call us if you need help."

"We're not going to need help," Veronica pointed out matter-of-factly as she flopped to a seat on the bed. "We're singers. We'll set up a warding enchantment before going to sleep, won't we, Marieke?"

"Of course we will," Marieke agreed, sinking into a chair, only too glad to be off her feet.

"It would make more sense to split and have one singer and one non-singer in each room," Veronica went on.

Judging by the cheeky look she threw Marieke, she wasn't so much making a real suggestion as baiting. And Zev didn't disappoint.

"That's not a good idea," he said, frowning.

"It doesn't have to be you and Mari," Veronica said innocently. "If you don't trust yourself, Mari can share with Azai."

"That's not happening."

Zev was even less impressed by this suggestion, and Marieke felt her lips twitch. She had to acknowledge it must be entertaining from Veronica's viewpoint. Azai didn't even bother to comment, obviously finding the whole idea absurd. Marieke found his expression unusually hard to read as his eyes rested on Veronica.

"Is sleeping arrangements all you want to talk about?" he asked abruptly.

Veronica's face changed in an instant, and Marieke realized that Azai's question had been more astute than her own observations. How could she have forgotten the shock Veronica had just received?

"Yes," Veronica said shortly. "I'm too tired to talk about... everything else. Not tonight."

Azai nodded slowly, surprising Marieke once again by how readily he respected Veronica's desire for space. The look he shot at his brother suggested that Zev wasn't likely to be spared so easily. Once they were alone, Azai would probably have plenty to say about Zev taking it on himself to reveal the secret of their heritage.

Speaking of Zev making decisions alone...

"Why did you invite Tarenne to come with us?" she asked him suddenly. "I'm not sure I agree."

Zev looked faintly surprised for a moment, then he grimaced. "You're saying I should have consulted with you all. You're probably right. I confess I didn't think of it." His voice turned earnest. "I understand that there's risk. We don't know for certain if Tarenne is to be trusted. But to me, that's all the more reason. I'd rather have her with us where we can see what she's doing than out of our reach, especially now she has so much information about us."

"Hm." Marieke considered it. "You have a point there."

"Do we actually know our next move, though?" Veronica asked. "Where are we going? If Tarenne doesn't know where to find her brother and Jade..." She trailed off.

"Let's sleep on it," Marieke said quickly. She had thoughts, but she wasn't ready to share them. They weren't fully formed yet. "We can reconvene here in the morning, before we talk to Tarenne."

Everyone nodded their agreement, and the boys moved into their own room. When it was just the two singers, Marieke turned to her friend. She hardly knew whether to expect recriminations or just questions.

"I'm glad we have a safe place to sleep tonight," Veronica said, her smile unconvincing.

"Hopefully it is safe." Marieke glanced at the closed door, still not sure they were wise to trust Tarenne.

"Better than being out in the open," said Veronica, shrugging as she folded up her jacket for a pillow and placed it at the opposite end of the bed from where Marieke had thrown hers. "Those men who attacked the boys earlier meant business."

"Yes," Marieke agreed absently. "I don't think we can expect to be very popular around here."

Veronica nodded. Marieke paused to watch her friend, getting the sense Veronica had more to say.

"They were good, weren't they?" Veronica blurted out. "At fighting, I mean."

"The men from the town?" Marieke asked, surprised. "I didn't think so."

"No." Veronica sounded impatient. "Zev. And..." she hesitated, "even Azai."

"Oh, yes." Marieke nodded. "They have a training yard at their farm and everything. Part of their family's unusual education." She noted Veronica's thoughtful expression. "You said *even* Azai. Did you think his only skill was complaining?"

"Well..." Veronica suddenly grinned. "Maybe."

Marieke couldn't help laughing, but she grew more serious when Veronica spoke again.

"They could have killed the men. Easily. But they didn't. They went out of their way not to."

"They're good men," Marieke said simply. "And a good man doesn't take pleasure in killing. Or respond disproportionately to threats against him just because he's strong enough to."

Veronica nodded slowly, some invisible reordering of thoughts happening in her mind. Marieke would have loved to know what she was thinking, but she didn't pry.

"I'm sorry, Veronica," she said instead. "I never meant to embroil you in any of this, and doing it without you even understanding what you were mixed up in ..."

Veronica waved a hand. "I embroiled myself," she said. "It wasn't your doing. But...it's hard to take it in. Are Zev and Azai really descended from the royals?"

Marieke nodded. "Their mother showed me the ancestry records herself. And this strange power that ties them to the land, heartsong, is like nothing I've seen before. It's subtle, but it's strong. And they sense it in their own way, even if they can't wield it like we wield magic."

"I don't know what to make of it all," Veronica confessed.

Marieke gave a shaky laugh. "I don't think anyone does. Not even them. There's so much we don't know, Veronica. So much we weren't taught." Her mind strayed to the elves she wasn't allowed to mention. "So much of history that's been buried."

"I don't like it." Veronica looked as unmoored as Marieke had felt when she'd first learned all of this. "I don't know what to trust."

"I understand the feeling." Marieke gave her friend a hopeful smile. "You can trust me."

Veronica's answering smile was warm. "I do trust you,

Mari. And I don't regret joining you." She gave a wry laugh. "This adventure is undoubtedly more exciting than the apprenticeship with the structural singer that I was supposed to start last week."

Marieke gasped. "You abandoned an apprenticeship for this?"

"I did," said Veronica calmly. "To be fair, I didn't know I was abandoning it when I decided to come with Zev and Azai. I thought I might be back in Tarandon in time. But like I said, I don't regret it. It was part of a future I'm not sure I believe in anymore. My eventual goal was to be employed by the Council of Singers in structural songcraft, and I don't think I could do that now. Not knowing what I've learned."

Marieke didn't respond. She understood Veronica's view—she applauded it. But it still sat heavily on her to know how dramatically she'd disrupted the direction of her friend's life.

Beyond coordinating some basic songs of protection to cover their room and the boys' room, they didn't attempt further conversation. It wasn't long before they lay down, but it was a long time before Marieke actually succumbed to sleep. Her thoughts were too troubled, her mind too full of unanswerable questions about trust and the cost of her cause both to herself and to those she cared about.

TEN

Zev

"Good morning."

Zev started at the greeting, turning quickly to see Tarenne picking her way between the rows in the kitchen garden. He'd thought no one else was awake when he stepped outside at dawn for fresh air.

"Good morning," he said.

He was uncomfortably aware that Marieke had suggested they not approach Tarenne again until they'd all had a chance to discuss their plans. She'd called him out the day before for being heavy-handed—he hadn't meant to go over the heads of the rest of the group.

"I saw you crossing the yard, and I followed you," Tarenne went on.

There was a pause as Zev searched for a response to this announcement. "All right," he said at last.

"How are you so calm?" The words came abruptly from Tarenne. She was studying his face with an intensity that was hard to tolerate.

"Calm?"

"If you were raised on the tales of what you should have

had but don't, like we were, how are you not angrier? You seem so...settled. I don't think I've ever felt that way in my life. I know my brother hasn't."

Zev folded his arms, considering her. He could see the hint of desperation in her eyes, and sympathy flickered within him. Her lineage had been much more of a curse than his ever had.

"I suppose I don't spend my life thinking about what I supposedly should have had."

"But how?" she asked, inching toward him in her need to understand. "How do you stop yourself from thinking about it?"

"Well..." Zev was a little overwhelmed by the intensity of her plea, but he tried to give her a real answer. "I like the life I have. It's not perfect, but there are many good things in it. My family, my farm...I suppose I've chosen to be content with the life I have rather than focusing on what I don't have."

Tarenne sighed. "You make that sound so simple." She eyed him. "And I'm not sure I believe it. You're here, aren't you? If you were so content with your life back in Aeltas, why did you leave it?"

For Marieke. The answer rose in Zev's mind at once, but he didn't voice it. He didn't want to get so personal with this stranger.

"Being content doesn't mean you don't ever want anything to change," he pointed out. "You can still pursue something new. Sometimes I wonder if my ancestors should have pursued a change long before now. But who knows?" He shrugged. "Maybe it wasn't time. Maybe that was always going to be my job. In any event, my..." He paused as a lump rose to his throat, but he mastered himself before Tarenne's curious gaze. "My father showed me what it meant to live a contented life, and I'm grateful for it. If my life is going to change, so be it. But it won't be because I'm running away from something."

"I wish I was like you," Tarenne said wistfully. "Has anyone ever told you that you project strength, Zevadiah? I feel like if there was a gale-force wind, I could stand behind you and I wouldn't be blown away."

"I..." Zev trailed off, unsure how to respond to this...compliment? Was it a compliment? Her tone was too sad.

Thankfully a distraction appeared in the shape of the cat from the night before. It wended its way between plants before curling its sleek body around Tarenne's legs. She crouched down to absently run one of its ears between her fingers.

"How does it feel, working together?" she asked Zev, her eyes still on the cat.

"What do you mean?" Zev asked cautiously.

She looked up. "You and the singer. Marieke, isn't it? You're...sweethearts?"

She posed the word as a question, but Zev didn't feel an answer was necessary. After a moment of silence, Tarenne went on.

"She said your heartsong interacts with her songcraft. How does it feel?"

"I...I don't know," said Zev. "I don't feel the magic itself. Only singers can do that. When Marieke and I work together it feels right. I don't know how to explain it better than that."

And he didn't know if that had anything to do with the different types of power interacting, or if it was just a reflection of how he felt about Marieke. He'd be ready to undertake just about anything if he did it at her side.

"Stronger together," Tarenne mused. "It's not what we were taught growing up."

"Or us," Zev agreed. "Singers and royals were never supposed to mingle their power, even in the days of the monarchy."

"The idea of combining power for more strength makes

sense, though," Tarenne mused. She didn't really seem to be listening to him. "Less vulnerable that way. That's what the monarchs should have done. Combined with each other, I mean. Maybe then they would have been able to defend against the singers."

"I doubt it," said Zev. "From what we were taught, they faced an overwhelming assault. The singers of the two kingdoms combined forces to attack."

"Yes, they had the right idea," she said ruefully. She gave her head a little shake, returning her gaze to the cat still leaning against her leg. "Anyway, since Tommy and I have agreed to come with you, where are we going? What's your plan?"

"Tommy?" Zev asked, amused.

She shrugged. "He's a tomcat, isn't he?"

It seemed Tarenne and her brother weren't prone to sentiment.

"He's a little tamer than the cats on our farm," Zev commented.

"Yes, he's sociable when he feels like it," said Tarenne. "And heaven help anyone who tries to approach him when he *doesn't* feel like it."

Zev chuckled, and it elicited an almost-smile that softened Tarenne's usually tense features.

"To tell the truth, I don't really know if he's my pet or I'm his pet," she added.

"Do you really think he'll follow you?" Zev asked.

"I do." Tarenne said it matter-of-factly. "He's drawn to me. It was the same with our previous cat. Even the chickens seem to like me."

"Some people do have more of a way with animals," Zev observed.

"Yes." Tarenne hesitated, then went on in a rush, as if relieved to say it aloud. "I've sometimes wondered if it's more than that, though. I mean, Clancy doesn't have much patience for the animals, but he has a way of making the plants thrive, or he did back when he was actually willing to give attention to the garden. Sometimes it's seemed to me as though the way animals respond to me is my version of that."

"Interesting," Zev mused. "Azai is good with animals, too. And with growing crops, to be fair. I just never wondered whether successful animal husbandry might be one of the ways our heartsong recognizes our connection to the land."

"Not that Tommy has anything to do with animal husbandry," Tarenne said, amused.

Zev laughed. "I suppose not. But animals are aware of their environment, often much more than humans are. If the land responds favorably to you, that might draw him to stay nearby."

"Perhaps," Tarenne agreed. "I wouldn't hazard any coins on it, but it is true that when Tommy and I go into town, everyone assures me that he doesn't behave quite like a normal cat. And the man who trades for our eggs says it's unusual for chickens to lay as responsively as mine do." She let out a sigh, her gaze pinning Zev. "Never mind all that. You didn't answer my question earlier. Where are we going when we leave here?"

"Let's talk once everyone is up," Zev said. "I'll go and wake the others if necessary."

"All right." She didn't sound excited about it. "I don't know how secretive you want to be, but I should warn you that I'm expecting someone to bring milk for a trade within the next hour or two. So if you want to leave without being observed here or connected with me, we should go soon."

"Thank you for the information," Zev said politely.

Tarenne looked like she wanted to say more, but Zev didn't wait. He was already striding across the yard toward the door he'd come out of earlier. He dodged the kitchen, aware that Tarenne had used it as sleeping quarters.

To his relief, the others were already awake, the two girls having found their way into the room he and Azai had shared the night before. The three of them looked up as he opened the door, Marieke relaxing visibly.

"There you are!" Azai reproached him. "Where did you slip off to?"

"Sorry," said Zev. "I was just getting some air, and Tarenne approached me."

"What did she want?" Marieke asked, her expression hard to read.

"To know our plan, which is obviously a question I couldn't answer."

Zev strode past the chair Veronica was sitting in, lowering himself to sit on the bed beside Marieke. He wasn't quite sure what was in her mind, but he sensed that she needed reassurance, and her rebuke from the day before, however mild, still seemed to hang between them. Moving casually, he placed his hand over hers where she was leaning back on it, matching her posture so that he leaned back as well. He felt her hand stiffen in surprise, then relax again as she slid her slim fingers between his.

Yes, definitely stronger together. Zev felt some of his own tension ease at the rightness of Marieke's touch, and he sent her a swift smile which she returned a little shyly.

If either Azai or Veronica noticed the exchange, they didn't comment on it.

"Our plan is exactly what we were just talking about," Azai said. "Or rather, our lack of plan."

Zev nodded, passing on what Tarenne had said about leaving soon.

"Let's not delay, then," Marieke said. "I don't want a run in with the locals from the town."

"I agree," said Zev. "I half expected to be followed here by those men. We should leave as soon as practical."

"All right, but leave to go where?" Veronica asked. "Tarenne said she doesn't know where her brother and Jade went."

"No," said Marieke. "And I wish we did know, so we could intercept them earlier. But as it is, I think the only thing we can do is head for their final destination to make sure we're there to fight back against whatever they're planning. And I can't think of anywhere else they'd stage this supposed *reckoning* other than the capital."

Veronica frowned as she thought it over. "It makes sense," she agreed. "But you're still just guessing."

"I know." Marieke shrugged. "But do we have any other ideas?"

Zev eyed her, feeling her tension through their linked hands. "What is it, Mari? What aren't you saying?"

"Nothing nefarious," she said quickly. A little too quickly. "But we have new information now about the threat Jade is to Oleand. Credible information. Without a clear idea of where to go, I don't think we can just wander around looking for Jade without warning the capital."

Zev frowned. "How do you propose doing that?"

She didn't quite meet his eyes. "We can figure out our plan on the road. The point is, if we're agreed on our destination, there's no reason to delay leaving."

Not satisfied, Zev kept his eyes on her as the others debated it. What wasn't she saying? Was it something she didn't want the others to hear?

Without any better ideas, everyone soon reached the conclusion that Marieke was right. It was the work of a moment to gather their things and move into the kitchen area, where Tarenne was waiting for them. She was in the act of packing some food into a rucksack, and had laid out bread and cheese for their breakfast.

"Thank you," said Marieke, sending Tarenne a tentative smile that she didn't return.

"I assume we're leaving at once?" Tarenne said by way of response. "We don't want to walk on empty stomachs."

"Agreed." Veronica had already bitten into her cheese, by far the most cheerful of the group. "And yes, we're ready to go when you are."

Tarenne nodded. "We're ready. Aren't we, Tommy?"

The cat gave a plaintive mew from under the same cupboard it had appeared from the day before.

"Are you sure Tommy wants to come?" Zev asked skeptically.

Tarenne shrugged. "I guess we'll find out. So where are we going?"

"The capital," said Marieke.

"Ondford?" Tarenne frowned. "You think my brother and Jade went there?"

"Well..." Marieke exchanged a look with Zev before she answered. "Actually, we know that Jade went there. We tracked her from there back to here using magic."

"She broke into the council and tried to kill Marieke," Zev added flatly. "But your brother wasn't with her. At least, not that we saw. We don't know if she sent him somewhere else, or if he was just waiting for her nearby."

"Why did she try to kill you?" Tarenne asked Marieke.

Zev felt irked by how little emotion she displayed with the question.

"I suppose I know too much," Marieke said. "Jade's whole strategy is based on keeping people in the dark."

"I thought she was trying to expose the truth," Tarenne said.

"Yes," Azai agreed unexpectedly. "I have no love for Jade, but let's not forget who started all the lies. The councils are the ones responsible for keeping everyone in the dark."

"I know that," said Marieke patiently. "I just meant that Jade's plan—convincing Clancy to curse the land, convincing Gorgon to kill singers in apparent accidents, and using her own magic to create natural disasters—relies on people not knowing that she's behind it all. It's supposed to look like the land itself is turning on the council. She didn't want me telling everyone what I've learned about her."

"Hm." Tarenne didn't look convinced. "But you all know she's behind it. That doesn't explain why she's so determined to kill you specifically." Her eyes passed thoughtfully between Marieke and Zev. "I don't think it's just what you know. It's the unique power you have because of your connection with Zevadiah. That combination of heartsong and songcraft you were talking about earlier this morning."

The last words were clearly directed at Zev, and he saw Marieke's eyes flick to him uncertainly. He winced internally, wishing again that he hadn't accidentally managed a private rendezvous with Tarenne before speaking with the group.

"Maybe you're right," he said gruffly, not liking the topic. "But the reasons are immaterial. The point is that Jade wants to kill Marieke, and we're not going to give her the chance."

"But we're not going to retreat, either," said Marieke firmly. "We need to be ready for whatever she's planning. Because presently, no one else is doing anything useful about it."

"I suppose that's our cue to get going." Tarenne still seemed unmoved by the intensity of the stakes for their little group, but at least she'd agreed to come with them. From all she'd told them, Zev doubted they'd have much success changing Clancy's mind without her.

The group slipped out of the dilapidated manor house within minutes. As Tarenne had predicted, they hadn't made it far down the road from the main gate when Zev caught sight of the cat loping along the top of a nearby hill. It still looked disgruntled.

Zev and Azai walked at the front of the group, Azai seeming ill-at-ease. Speaking too quietly for the others to hear, Zev moved alongside his brother.

"You all right?"

Azai shot him a look before nodding. "I'm fine."

Zev hesitated. He'd expected to be more roundly criticized the night before. But their conversation regarding his unplanned disclosure to Tarenne and Veronica had been short and terse.

"If you're angry with me, I'd rather you just said it, Azai," he said. "It's not like you to hold back."

Azai let out a breath, his eyes staring unseeingly at the path ahead. They were approaching the first low hills near the manor house.

"I was angry when you spoke up," Azai admitted. "I wish you'd given me some warning at the very least. But that's not what's troubling me. The truth is I keep thinking that Father will be horrified when he learns, and trying to think how to break it to him that we've revealed our secret. Then I remember..."

Zev felt his fist clench as his brother trailed off. There was no need for Azai to finish the thought. Zev understood perfectly. He was constantly experiencing the same thing.

"So in reality," Azai continued, "you really do have the right to make these decisions."

"I'm not trying to cut you out," said Zev quickly. "I acted on the impulse of the moment, but Marieke was right that I've been too quick to make decisions without speaking to everyone. And that particular decision is one we should've made together."

Azai gave his head a little shake, his expression wry. "It's—"

He never finished the sentence. Under their feet, the path rounded a low hill, and two men sprang out in front of them. Caught up in the conversation with Azai, Zev was taken by surprise. He reached for his sword as he ducked a clumsy swing from the closest attacker, recognizing as he did so that it was one of the men he'd knocked out the day before.

To his dismay, he heard Azai give a grunt of pain, and caught sight of a flash of red on his brother's shirt. It seemed the other assailant was a little more skilled than Zev's one. With a growl, he sprang to his brother's defense, covering Azai while he extricated his weapon from where he wore it over his back.

"Not you again," Zev said impatiently, as he blocked another thrust from the man who'd slashed Azai's arm.

"Yes, us again," the stranger snarled, as three more men moved into view behind him. "And this time you won't find us so easy to—"

His voice was cut off by a fierce song, the melody issuing from behind Zev. Two voices mingled together, dancing beautifully around one another as they sent invisible power racing toward the men. Zev looked back and caught Marieke's eye. Her eyebrows were raised in a silent question, and he nodded his approval.

With renewed determination, he spun around, tossing his sword into his left hand as he lunged toward the man who'd first attacked him. His right fist moved with lightning speed, connecting with the man's head with enough power that Zev had to intentionally pull his punch so as not to risk killing the stranger.

The man went down hard. He was still conscious, but he was moaning and clutching his head in a way that suggested he wouldn't be getting up anytime soon. Zev turned his attention to the two men now rushing Azai. His brother's sword arm was the one that had been injured, and although he'd raised his weapon in readiness, Zev didn't like the sight of the blood running down it.

But he needn't have worried. The first blow aimed at Azai never made contact, bouncing off an invisible barrier. Zev turned to see Veronica's eyes narrowed in concentration as she sang, her focus on Azai. Marieke's voice was raised again as well, and Zev watched as roots twisted their way up through the earth to trip the approaching men.

"Come on," he called, as the men fell over themselves in confusion. They were crying out in terror, trying to get away from the magically driven plants. Clearly they had very little experience of songcraft. "Let's get out of here."

He had no desire to spend half an hour fighting these men, possibly killing one of them by accident.

The group edged past the mob, Azai staying at the front with Veronica's shield still around him. Once they were clear, they ran, Tarenne keeping pace with the other girls, Azai and Zev bringing up the rear and keeping watch for pursuit. The two singers didn't let their voices drop until they were well out of sight of the group, by which time they were panting for breath from the dual exertion of running and singing.

"Stop if you need to," Zev urged Marieke, coming alongside her. "Azai and I can defend the group the old-fashioned—" he caught her look and amended, "I mean the *non-magical* way if you need to rest your voice."

"Thanks," she gasped, bending over and putting her hands

on her knees. "This isn't the first time I've wished I did more physical training at the academy."

"You're doing great," Zev reassured her, running his hand over her back in a circular motion. His gaze flicked to his brother, whose arm was still bleeding, before he addressed Tarenne. "How far do you think they'll follow us?"

She shrugged, panting a little herself. "It depends how much the magic scared them. Maybe not at all, maybe further than this. But not for days or anything."

"I think we can afford to slow down," Zev said. "But it would be good if we could obscure our tracks."

"I can do that," said Marieke, lifting her head. "As soon as I catch my breath."

She turned toward the path behind them, pausing as a lone figure ambled along it toward them. A lone, small, feline figure. Tarenne's cat had disappeared as soon as the men from the village had challenged them, but he reinserted himself into their group now, winding his way between Tarenne's legs before settling on the grass to clean his paws.

"A hound would have been much more useful," Zev heard Marieke mutter between breaths.

"We need to...stop that...bleeding," panted Veronica. She seemed uninterested in the cat, her eyes fixed on Azai.

"It's fine," Azai said dismissively. He pulled his sleeve up to examine the wound. "It's not too deep."

"Actually, it's quite deep," Veronica said in a scolding tone. She glanced at the empty road down which they'd just run, and up which Tommy had ambled. "We'll just have to take the time to treat it. You can't travel on like that."

Azai protested, but she ignored him. She led the way off the path behind the shelter of a nearby hill, the others following her. Zev had forgotten that Veronica was trained in healing song, but she was showing it now. She'd suddenly adopted very much the manner of the healing singer who'd checked on his leg after Marieke healed it. A touch bossy. In fact, Marieke herself had become quite similar when she was tending to the wound. It must be part of the training, he reflected ruefully.

Zev positioned himself so he could keep an eye on the road, throwing a look back at his brother.

"You all right, Az?"

"I'm fine," Azai insisted impatiently, as Veronica pulled up his sleeve with a firm hand. "We're wasting time."

"We're not," Veronica contradicted. "Healing is always time well spent." She rubbed her hands together in a businesslike fashion, eyed uneasily by Azai.

"What are you doing? What kind of magic is that?"

"It's not magic," she said in exasperation. "I'm trying to warm up my hands. Unless you want my freezing fingers all over your skin."

"I don't want anyone's freezing fingers on me," Azai complained. "This is all unnecessary. The wound will heal fine on its own."

"Don't be difficult," Veronica said. She turned Azai's arm in her hands, examining it with a clinical eye. "It could be worse," she announced. "Now." She looked expectantly up at him. "Do I have your permission to attempt a healing song on you?"

"What?" Azai looked bewildered.

"It's standard practice not to use magic on someone without their permission," she said impatiently. "Now do I have it?"

"That didn't stop you back there," said Azai skeptically.

Veronica blew hair out of her eyes in exasperation. "Firstly, yes it did. If you were paying attention, you would have noticed that neither Marieke nor I used magic directly on those men. Secondly, even if we had, defending yourself or someone else against physical attack is an exception."

"What are the other exceptions?" Tarenne asked curiously.

"One of them is to save someone's life," Veronica said, her usually cheerful face crinkled in a forbidding expression that was honestly comical. "So if you're going to be difficult, I can always just make your injury worse, so that it really is life-threatening."

"That seems like it would be against your precious singers' code," Azai pointed out.

"Not if I did it with non-magical means," Veronica said sweetly. "Then it would just be against, you know," she gestured vaguely, "other laws."

"I don't know how either one of you can accuse the other of wasting time," Marieke interjected, peering over Zev's shoulder to watch the road. "You're as bad as each other."

"She's right," said Veronica. With her fingers still curled around an uninjured section of Azai's arm, she looked up into his eyes. "Azai. Do I have your permission to heal your wound?"

The silence was so charged, Zev couldn't help looking fully away from the road to watch his brother's reaction. Azai stared down into Veronica's eyes for a long moment, his expression hard to read even for Zev, who'd known him all his life.

"Yes," Azai said at last, his voice gruff. "All right."

"Thank you."

Pleased, Veronica set about her task at once. Zev exchanged a look with Marieke, who clearly shared his surprise. He'd expected Azai to continue being difficult.

"Is this your first time accessing healing magic?" Veronica asked Azai.

He nodded. "Of course."

"Normally, I'd talk through everything I'm doing for a first-timer," she told him. "Just so you understand what's happening to you." She paused. "And because it's fascinating. But in the interests of time, I'll just get on with it. The short version is that

I'm not going to do anything wild or unnatural. I'm just going to speed up the natural processes of your body so that the wound heals faster."

"Like I did to you that time," Marieke said to Zev, sounding pleased. She grinned. "I didn't do healing song, so I wasn't sure if I was doing it right."

"Reassuring," Zev retorted with a grin of his own.

Veronica ignored them both, starting to sing over Azai's arm. Her voice was lower in pitch than Marieke's, but no less melodious. Even Tommy appeared to approve, the feline leaving Tarenne to come and lie on Veronica's feet as she sang. The words were quiet enough that Zev couldn't catch them, but they were obviously the right ones, because before his eyes, Azai's wound closed up. Azai didn't quite manage to hold in his gasp, his eyes wide as they passed from Veronica's face to his arm. When she stopped, the gash wasn't fully healed, but it looked like it had been several weeks since the stabbing instead of a matter of minutes.

"There," she said, her voice faint but pleased. "I think that's enough for now." She looked down, apparently surprised to discover a cat stretched across her feet.

Azai was silent for a moment, his hand moving slowly over his arm. Then his gaze passed to Veronica, and he frowned.

"Are you all right?"

"Of course," she said cheerfully. "I just need to catch my breath."

Zev looked up the road in concern. He'd forgotten how much healing song had taken from Marieke when she'd done it for him, and Veronica had undertaken it just after using defensive songcraft and then sprinting. She would be exhausted, but they couldn't afford to wait for her to recover.

"We have to keep moving," Tarenne said, unemotionally

saying what Zev had been thinking. "Unless we want to fight them."

"We don't," Azai said. He held out his arm to Veronica, his voice still gruffer than usual. "You can lean on me for support as we go. I'm perfectly recovered now."

She flashed him a smile. "Perfectly is an exaggeration, but I'll take the compliment to my craft."

Zev had expected her to decline, but she accepted the offer of assistance readily. Once she'd shaken off a protesting Tommy, she leaned on Azai's arm as they started to move. She was genuinely exhausted, that much was clear. Unfortunate so early in what would be a full day of travel.

"You're a natural, Veronica," Marieke said admiringly. "So much quicker and more precise than my attempts have been. I'm surprised you were pursuing a structural apprenticeship rather than a healing one."

"Oh, well." Veronica's voice was light. "I probably would prefer to do healing song, to be honest. But my parents are of the view that structural song has more potential as a career. They're perfectly right, and I do enjoy it as well, so…"

She trailed off, conserving her energy.

"You should do what you prefer to do," Azai said, not looking at her. "And we should pick up the pace."

Conversation ceased then, as they sped up to put distance between them and any pursuers who might be rallying. Thankfully, Veronica's ministrations hadn't taken long, and they were soon far enough from the town that Zev felt himself relax.

The next couple of days were much more difficult than the journey west had been. They were all tense, knowing that Jade and Clancy were somewhere out there, and they still had very little idea of their plans against Oleand. And the introduction of Tarenne to their group had everyone a little more on guard. She was hard to read and always listening. More than once Zev thought he was having a private conversation with one or other of the group, only to look up and realize that Tarenne had heard it all. In fact, she seemed adept at catching him in quiet moments. She never openly followed him, but he often turned around to find that she was there. On those occasions, like when they'd been in the kitchen garden back at the manor house, she seemed to want to say something more. But whatever it was, she never actually said it.

Perhaps the new dynamic was why Marieke seemed subdued. Zev had the feeling something was bothering her, but they had very little opportunity for private speech.

They were still a day out of Ondford when Zev found himself in a rare moment alone with his brother. They'd made camp for the night rather than going into an inn, and Tarenne was resting on a boulder nearby while Marieke and Veronica were building a fire, watched by a wary Tommy. They were using songcraft, of course. Their voices, punctuated with the occasional laughter, carried across the clearing they'd selected.

"You seem worried." Azai's voice pulled Zev's gaze from the girls, and he turned to see his brother watching him.

He shrugged. "Do I?"

"Yes. You're getting more tense as we get closer to the capital."

"I don't like not having a plan," Zev said.

Azai raised an eyebrow. "That doesn't usually bother you. Usually you say you'll work it out, and somehow you do."

Azai knew him too well.

"All right," Zev acknowledged with a sigh. "I'm worried because I have the feeling that Marieke has a plan, she's just not telling me."

"I thought you told each other everything," Azai quipped.

Zev shot him an irritated look, and he raised his hands in a placating gesture.

"I didn't mean offense. She's not so bad, Marieke."

"High praise, coming from you." Zev almost smiled.

"I'm not saying I understand why you abandoned your family for her," Azai said. "Just that she's not so bad."

Zev threw a bedroll at him. "I didn't abandon anyone."

Azai ducked the missile effortlessly. "Maybe abandon is too strong. But your priorities have changed. A lot."

"Yes, I suppose they have." Zev considered it as he stole Azai's bedroll to replace the one he'd thrown, and rolled it out. "But that's not a bad thing."

"Not bad for who?" There was a hard note in Azai's voice. He might have warmed a little to Marieke, but he was a long way from actual warmth.

"For everyone," Zev said. "No really," he added, over Azai's quiet snort. "It was such a wrestle back before she knew the truth. I remember thinking I couldn't possibly do right by both the family—who wanted me to make sure she didn't learn about heartsong—and by her—who wanted me to help her figure out what was happening to Oleand."

"And you chose her," Azai said.

Zev shook his head. "I said I *thought* I couldn't do both. But the deeper in I got, the closer I came to finding out something much bigger than the choice I thought I had to make. Things started to make more sense when I began to understand how heartsong and her songcraft flowed together and became more powerful than they were separately. It was never one over the other. They didn't have to be separate like we were taught. The answer was always to come together."

Azai frowned, clearly not convinced.

"Think about it, Azai," said Zev earnestly. "The effects of my heartsong connection to the land became more concrete and specific when I opened myself to songcraft."

Still Azai said nothing, but he looked like he was thinking

about it, even if his brow remained furrowed. His eyes had strayed to where the girls were stoking the fire, only Veronica singing now. He watched her for a long moment before looking back around and realizing that he was being watched as well.

"What?" he asked Zev defensively.

"For someone so critical of me embracing magic, you seem fascinated by it. I could almost accuse you of enjoying the sound of Veronica's voice right now."

Azai turned his back on the fire, where Veronica's song had just died out. "Accuse me?" he repeated dryly.

Zev shrugged. "Well, you were pretty vocal about the evils of all songcraft not too long ago."

Azai rescued the abused bedroll and laid it out, not looking at Zev. "I have every reason to think songcraft is evil," he said belligerently. "And you know it."

"I know my brother," Zev said, unimpressed. "And I know when you're being difficult because you don't want to admit you're wrong."

Azai looked up, surprising Zev with his sigh of surrender.

"All right," he said. "I am surprised by how pleasant the singing is on the ear. It's..."

"Captivating," Zev finished.

"I didn't say that," Azai protested quickly.

"I know. I said it for you."

Azai scowled, predictably becoming reactive. "I didn't notice it before Veronica healed me. I'm not convinced it's natural."

Zev stared at him. "What do you mean?"

"I mean that I wonder if it was a mistake to give permission for her to use her magic on me directly. What if there's an impact we don't understand? What if singers are taught in their academy to use their voices to, I don't know, ensnare people?"

"Excuse me?"

The icy voice made them both turn, Zev cursing his own distraction for not noticing that Marieke and Veronica had left the fire and were approaching. From the half-defiant, half-ashamed look on Azai's face, he was cursing himself as well.

"I heal your injury, and you accuse me of ensnaring people?" Veronica demanded. It seemed she was capable of losing her cool after all. "I'm not a *siren*!"

"What's a siren?" Azai asked blankly.

"They're creatures from stories," Marieke supplied helpfully. "Like mermaids. They lure men to a watery death. They're not real. Although..."

She trailed off, but Zev understood the unspoken thought. If elves were real after all, were mermaids, too? Who knew, at this stage?

"I don't lure anyone to anything." Veronica radiated disdain as she glared at Azai. "And even if I did, do you really think I have any interest in ensnaring you? A grouchy, unreasonable farmer who thinks he's better than everyone else?"

With a flounce, she turned away, leaving the rest of the group standing in awkward silence.

"Ouch," said Zev at last. "She's not wrong, but...ouch."

"Whose side are you on?" Azai protested, his face red with either anger or embarrassment. Maybe both.

"Hers," said Zev promptly. "You know I have your back when it counts, Azai, but to put it simply, you're an idiot. No one's bewitched you." Honestly, only Azai could think that if he was learning he'd been wrong and slowly having his mind changed, it must be the work of evil magic.

"You wouldn't know, would you?" Azai said angrily. "You don't know what you really think anymore, because a singer has you too wrapped around her finger."

"Hey!" Anger flared in Zev at this unjust attack against Marieke. He knew Azai's embarrassment was bringing out the worst in him, but it didn't make Zev any more willing to let his brother speak about Marieke that way. "Don't be more of an idiot than you can help, Azai."

"I'm not an idiot just because I don't blindly agree with every decision you make," Azai spat. "Generations our family has kept our lineage secret. And within months, you've revealed it to singers from both countries!"

"I thought you didn't have a problem with my decision," Zev said, feeling his body tense. He couldn't tell whether Azai's anger was driving him to say things he didn't really mean, or whether Azai had been holding this view under the surface all along.

"Well it looks like I do have a problem with it," Azai growled.

Zev frowned at him. "I'm sorry you had no warning, Azai, I really am. But we are where we are. We can't turn back time and return to the peaceful hiding of our fathers. I thought we agreed when Father died that we didn't want to."

"Don't talk to me about Father."

There was a dangerous edge to Azai's voice, and Zev could tell it wasn't the time to push. He raised a hand in surrender, the gesture barely complete before Azai turned away, striding between the trees to wrestle with his disillusionment.

Zev could do nothing but watch him go, his heart heavy. He'd thought in recent weeks that he and Azai were almost back to the easy camaraderie that had characterized most of their lives. Now he was left wondering whether the relationship with his brother was too broken to be fixed after all.

CHAPTER
ELEVEN

Marieke

Marieke woke to the sound of birds singing in the trees above, and she lay there for a moment listening to them. Their song was uncomplicated, non-magical.

Unlike everything else.

She sat up, thinking she was probably the first to wake. Her eyes flew immediately to where Zev had been sleeping, her heart still hurting on his behalf over the scene between him and Azai the night before. But the bedroll was empty, and with a glance around the clearing she realized that Tarenne's was as well.

Marieke frowned. Were they together somewhere? The other girl seemed to be pulling Zev aside constantly, and Marieke could tell that he wasn't entirely at ease with it. It was strange, honestly. Marieke rose, moving quietly as she passed between tree trunks toward the tiny stream nearby. She was almost there when she heard a familiar voice and pulled up short.

Through the trees she could see Zev, and by moving slightly to the side, she was able to observe that Tarenne was with him. Tommy was there, too. He really was a strange feline. She'd never seen a cat follow his owner across great distances like Tommy did for Tarenne. As Marieke watched, he batted at his reflection in the stream, then let out a yowl of disapproval at discovering that his paw was wet.

He licked it with a disgruntled air until he was distracted by his reflection...upon which he promptly repeated the whole performance. This time he streaked to the humans when he realized his paw had again been attacked by the water, wending between their legs with a disapproving mewl.

Marieke would have found Tommy's foolishness amusing in other circumstances. But as it was, while neither Tarenne nor Zev seemed particularly aware of the cat, his behavior gave the scene an intimate feel that increased Marieke's discomfort as Zev spoke.

"I don't...that's not something that..."

Zev trailed off, and Marieke frowned in consternation. Curiosity raged inside her, battling with guilt over her eaves-dropping. She'd rarely seen Zev so discomposed. As she watched, he drew a deep breath.

"I understand what you're thinking," he said more calmly. "But that's not a serious option."

"Of course it is." Tarenne's matter-of-fact answer seemed a poor match for Zev's tone. It also allowed Marieke to move forward naturally, pretending she hadn't been listening in on a hushed, charged conversation.

Zev looked up at the noise, a strange expression flitting across his face when he saw Marieke. Her stomach dropped. She hated feeling like she'd interrupted him doing something secretive.

"Marieke." Tarenne nodded to her. "Good morning."

"Good morning," Marieke said, trying to speak naturally.

"I'll see you back at the clearing." Tarenne strode off, disappearing between the trees at once, Tommy ambling casually after her.

Marieke turned slowly to Zev, her gaze wary. "What was that about?"

"Nothing," he said, his face softening as his eyes met hers. "Something silly. Nothing to take seriously."

Marieke frowned, not satisfied with the non-answer, but the next moment, Zev stepped toward her. Her thoughts became jumbled as he ran a finger gently under her chin, coaxing her face up toward him.

"I've missed you," he said, his voice low.

She swallowed. "We've been traveling together all this time."

He shook his head, a smile dancing on his lips that made her heart skip a beat. "Surrounded by other people every step. It's not the same."

"It's not, is it?" Marieke closed her eyes, relishing his touch as his hand moved to cup her cheek. She leaned into it, for a moment giving in to the exhaustion that tugged at her. "I wish we were back in your orchard, with no one there but us."

"Mm." Zev's free arm snaked behind her back, pulling her close as his voice hummed in his throat. "Pretend that we are."

Marieke placed her hands on his chest, shamelessly feeling the firmness of his muscles through his tunic.

"I don't know how," she murmured. "It feels so far away. Everything is so complicated."

"This isn't complicated." Zev's whisper danced around her as he lowered his forehead onto hers. "And I'm not far away. I'm right here."

All of a sudden, warmth rushed through Marieke, driving out all her worries before it. She tilted her head, too impatient to wait for Zev to make the first move. Her lips found his, and immediately his arms tightened around her. She let her hands travel over his shoulders to clasp behind his neck, abandoning herself to the sensation of his lips moving against hers. For a moment she really could let go of everything and imagine that she was back in the stillness of his orchard, safe and at peace.

But of course she wasn't there, and the stolen moment was all too short. The sound of a heavy tread caused them to break reluctantly apart, just as Azai's voice broke into their peaceful bubble.

"Please." He still sounded irritable, but it was definitely an improvement on the rage of the night before. "I can't deal with this kind of thing before breakfast."

Zev made a noise that could arguably be called a growl as he released Marieke. "Go eat breakfast, then."

"I will once I've washed my face," Azai said shortly. "But you'll have to move out of the way for that."

Still grumbling, Zev took Marieke's hand, tugging her way from the stream and back toward the clearing.

"To be fair," she said, unable to help smiling at his grouchy demeanor, "Azai could also interrupt us if we really were in your orchard."

"He wouldn't dare," growled Zev, making her smile grow.

"Don't think I've forgotten that you didn't answer my question," she told him. "What was Tarenne talking to you about? I thought we didn't keep secrets from each other."

Zev gave her a challenging look. "So you're not keeping anything from me over this journey?"

Marieke felt her cheeks heat. Blast. He knew her too well.

"That's what I thought," Zev said, frowning. "What's going on, Marieke?"

"I'm about to raise it with the group," she told him. "It's just my thoughts about what to do next."

"All right." Zev sounded wary, and she didn't let him get

anything more out of her until they'd all gathered in the clearing.

"So we're within reach of Ondford now," Marieke said, once all eyes were on her. "If travel is smooth, we could reach the capital today."

They all nodded.

"Which means it's time to discuss our plan for what to do once we get there."

"Past time," Veronica agreed. "What's our objective?"

"Well, finding Jade and Clancy would be ideal," Marieke said. "But we don't have any leads on them at the moment. Personally, I feel that our other priority needs to be getting the new information we've gained into the hands of people who can actually use it to protect the city."

"Well, if they're even vaguely doing their job, the council members are the ones best placed to do that," said Veronica skeptically. "But last I checked, they're trying to arrest you. In fact, I think we have to assume they'll be on the lookout for us after the breakout. You three in particular." Her gaze encompassed Zev and Azai as well as Marieke. "We may not be able to just walk freely into the city."

"I agree, and I have a plan about that," Marieke said. She drew a breath, and her eyes flicked to Zev. "But you're not going to like it."

"What do you mean?" he asked, his tone ominous.

"I think I should turn myself in," Marieke said in a rush. "Just me, on my own, while the rest of you take the opportunity to get into the city while they're distracted. I think I should let them capture me and lock me up again."

There was a moment of silence. Zev looked like he was waiting for her to laugh and declare the plan a joke. With each passing second where she didn't, his brows drew closer together.

"You're right," he said at last, his voice deceptively calm. "I don't like it. I don't like it at all."

"No, hear me out," Marieke insisted. "We need to be strategic. Jade is always a step ahead, and we can't let it stay that way, or we won't stop her plans in time. We have to think unemotionally." Her eyes bored into Zev's. "You're too focused on protecting me, Zev. While I obviously appreciate that on a personal level, it's not the most strategic use of our resources. I'm not the valuable one—you are."

"Of course you're valuable," Zev protested in indignation. He saw that she was about to challenge him, and he added smoothly, "Even thinking unemotionally, it's still true. If Jade didn't see you as a threat, she wouldn't be targeting you."

Marieke shook her head. "Tarenne is right. Jade's only targeting me because of my connection to you. Without you, I'm nothing powerful."

Zev started to argue again, but Marieke silenced him by means of raising her hand and talking more loudly.

"In fact, I'm far *less* powerful than any of the singers who hold positions in the council or the academy. It's the simple truth, and I'm perfectly comfortable with it, no need to be sentimental about it."

"Don't undervalue yourself, Marieke," Veronica said seriously. "You have an aptitude for storytelling song that's rare."

"Maybe." Marieke shrugged, wishing she could get them to understand how little her vanity had to do with any of it. "But it's undeveloped. It's not a threat to Jade's plans. Zev and Azai are a much greater threat, because of who they are and the unique power they hold. They're the ones we should be protecting."

She cast a serious look around the group. "All of which is why I'm the only one who should take the risk and approach the council with what we know. And the surest way to do that is to let them take me in. Meanwhile, you can search for any sign that Jade or Clancy have put their plans for Ondford into action."

"No." Zev's voice was firm. "There's nothing admirable about making noble sacrifices if they won't gain anything. Last time they didn't give you the chance to speak to the council. Letting them arrest you will just land you back in a locked room, with less chance than ever to tell everyone what they need to know."

"Maybe," said Marieke. "But I'm more optimistic than that. Things have changed since last time."

"What things?" Veronica challenged.

"A lot more people know my version of events. Solomon and Kaine both have faith in my intentions, and Instructor Oriana knows just about everything. For all we know, she's convinced the council to change their approach since we left."

The look Zev gave her was so deeply incredulous, she had to smile.

"All right, that's not likely. But I refuse to assume she's been fully corrupted by lies since last we spoke. I think her desire is to do the right thing, and she's not the only one. I know something is broken very deep within my country's leadership. I know the power of the council is built on lies and violence, and I know that those lies are what sent Jade down such a dark path. But I studied at the Academy of Song in Ondford. Unlike the rest of you, I know it really well. And the more I think about it, the more I can't believe that most of the instructors and students are corrupt. I *don't* believe it. I have more faith in the academy than that. And the academy and the council stand hand in hand. There are enough people I trust not to let those who want to silence me do so without accountability."

Tarenne scoffed quietly at her mention of trust, although she raised no objection to the plan. Zev looked equally unconvinced, a furrow appearing on his brow and showing every sign of being there to stay. Veronica, on the other hand, was nodding.

"I applaud your desire to trust those who trained you, Marieke. Song preserve me, it would make me so happy to believe that my own academy wasn't corrupted to its core. I would explore every other option before accepting that they were all liars and frauds. But I don't want to see you get hurt."

"I don't want to get hurt, either," Marieke informed her seriously. "I'm obviously gambling on the belief that they won't hurt me out of hand. But we can take precautions to make it harder for them to do that."

"Precautions like me going with you?" Zev suggested, the hopeful lilt to his voice making Marieke smile.

"That wouldn't help anything, Zev. You're too prone to losing your head when you think I'm in danger. And I need you to be free so that if things go badly and I need help from outside, you're able to give it. Besides, no offense, but your sword wouldn't do me much good against the might of the whole council in preventing my arrest."

"If you'd learned to use your heartsong aggressively, like Clancy has, it might," Tarenne chimed in unexpectedly.

Marieke frowned slightly at her. "My plan isn't to do anything aggressively. Turning myself in is a defensive move."

"One based on incredible naivety, if you ask me." Tarenne shrugged. "But no one did ask me, and it's not my affair."

"It might be your affair," Azai said bluntly. "If Marieke plans to tell the council about you."

Tarenne's brows drew together, and Marieke hastened to speak.

"I'll have to tell them about Clancy working with Jade if there's any hope of them defending against the attack. But I won't mention you if I can help it. You might think I'm naive, but I'm not foolish enough to simply trust the council. I don't want to give them the chance to hunt you down if they're inclined to see you as a threat to be eliminated."

Tarenne said nothing, her demeanor hard to read. She generally seemed to exude an air of having nothing to lose and not caring much about anything. But Marieke knew she should assume that the other girl would fight hard to protect herself if she thought the group had become a danger to her.

"The council is only one concern," Zev said, his voice tight. "Last time you were locked up, Jade came for you, remember?"

"I most definitely do remember," Marieke said. "And that's part of why I think it will be different this time. Surely they won't lock me in that dungeon or anywhere else exposed. Surely they'll have tightened their defenses."

"Which won't help us if we have to break you out again," Zev pointed out. His brows were lowered, making his face more severe than usual. "What are these precautions you propose using? I can't imagine them being strong enough to make me agree to this plan."

Marieke gave him a hard look, albeit one laced with sympathy. "You don't have to agree, Zev. I'd rather you were behind the plan, but unless you have a better idea, I'll be doing it with or without your support." She hurried on to forestall the argument Zev was clearly itching to make. "And as for precautions, I think I should make my arrest as public an affair as possible. That makes it harder for them to just bury me away again. It's possible that no one will care or remember me even if they witness my arrest. But it's worth trying. And I have a friend among the council guards. He's actually a singer. If I can orchestrate it so he's involved in my arrest, they won't be able to do anything sinister like killing me then claiming it was done in defense."

Veronica's eyes were wide. "Would they really do that? Are they so corrupt?"

Marieke shrugged. "I don't know. I don't think most of them are, but I don't want to find out with my life."

"I can't speak for most of them, but the Head Instructor is absolutely capable of that kind of underhanded violence," Zev added. "He was watching from behind the bushes when Gorgon tried to kill Marieke. He could easily have intervened, and chose not to. If I hadn't been there, he would have watched Marieke being killed, then deplored it as a terrible crime."

Marieke stared at him. "You never told me that."

"Yes, I did," Zev contradicted. "I told you to be especially careful of him."

"What?" She raised her hands in exasperation. "Only you would think that kind of cryptic hint constitutes *telling* me anything!"

"Well," he said, his tone one of concession, "perhaps I was overly cautious at the time. I didn't want you to know that I'd been listening in as well, and had heard your whole discussion with Gorgon about heartsong."

Marieke just shook her head. "It doesn't matter now anyway."

"No, what matters is having a solid plan for when we get to Ondford," mused Veronica. "I think we should try to involve Instructor Oriana. I know she's not on the council, but she must have some influence as an instructor at the academy."

"Yes," Marieke agreed. "Maybe Kaine would take me to her first, or get a message to her somehow."

"We need to plan this rather than just rush into the city," Veronica said decisively. "As far as we know, I'm still not recognized or connected with the rest of you in any way. I think I should go in first and set things up. I'll speak to this Kaine. Will they know him if I ask at the guardhouse?"

Marieke nodded. "They will. But that plan puts too much risk on you, Veronica. It isn't supposed to be your neck on the line."

"Nonsense," she said dismissively. "I'll be fine." Her pleasant face crinkled in a grin. "We're all taking risks, and I refuse to be left out."

Azai didn't sound convinced, either. "Too much risk of you being arrested, and then where will we be? Don't you think it'll be suspicious if you go around asking for Kaine when you don't know him at all?"

"No," said Veronica tartly.

Since the awkward confrontation the night before, her light and unconcerned manner had disappeared entirely where Azai was concerned. Far from being impossible to bait, she was proving extremely reactive to him.

"I don't think it will be suspicious at all," she went on. "Because I'm not an idiot, and I'm not going to go about it in a suspicious way."

"How will you go about it?" Azai persisted stubbornly. Bizarrely, Veronica's change in demeanor had led to one in him as well. He no longer seemed to want to pick a fight with her.

Veronica flicked her hair behind her shoulder, looking pointedly away from him. "I'll pretend to be his sweetheart."

"That's smart," said Marieke, nodding. "Anything suspicious about your approach will take on a different meaning, and no one will guess the real reason for being clandestine."

"It doesn't seem smart to me," Azai frowned, his tone still far from its usual combative state. "Won't people who know him realize it's not true? Won't they call you out if you go around claiming to be his sweetheart?"

Veronica rolled her eyes, her own voice pitying. "You really are dense, aren't you? I won't be claiming anything. I'm not going to walk around saying I'm his sweetheart. I'll be much more subtle than that."

Azai looked to his brother, his expression blank. "I'm lost."

Zev shrugged, and Marieke had to fight back a laugh.

"Just trust us," she said. "A giggle here, a certain way of casting your eyes down when asking if Kaine is in, an overly earnest explanation that you're just a friend of his passing by…" She smiled. "This is one of those times when being indirect communicates much better than saying something outright. Veronica will figure it out."

"It all sounds diabolical to me," said Azai, looking alarmed at the news that girls apparently had a universal language of unspoken communication. "Is that part of your training at the academy?"

Veronica and Marieke both laughed at that.

"I mean, in a way," said Marieke, grinning. "But not from any classes."

Zev eyed her. "Manipulated many handsome young singers, did you?"

Marieke was still chuckling. "Not me. I kept my head down. I was a nobody from a mostly song-less farming region. The only boys who showed interest in me thought that I would reward their egos by falling all over myself to vie for their attention." She shrugged. "They soon learned I had a better use of my time than that. I was there to learn songcraft."

Zev seemed pleased with this answer, and Marieke had to roll her eyes.

"I, on the other hand," Veronica's light tone sounded off, "was studying something else entirely. I was learning how to *ensnare* people. Maybe I'll use it on Kaine."

There was an awkward silence during which Marieke could have sworn she saw color creep up Azai's neck. She cleared her throat quickly.

"We've strayed from the point. If we want to reach the city today, we should start moving. We can discuss how exactly we'll carry out the plan while we're on the road." She looked earnestly around the group. "This can work, it really can. Ondford has been my home for years. I lived at the academy, which is closely connected to the council. I understand the system there like none of you can. Whatever you think, the council does have rules and regulations, and they care about keeping order. I just need to use those rules to my advantage."

Judging by their expressions, her listeners still had some doubts about the plan, but everyone dispersed to prepare for departure, with one exception.

Marieke turned to Zev, bracing herself for more arguments.

"I know you don't want me in danger, Zev."

"I don't."

"And I know you won't like being separated, but—"

"I'll hate it," he corrected her. "I swore to myself I wouldn't let you out of my sight again, and last time I did it against my better judgment, you were snatched from my own home and locked up in a foreign country."

"Not foreign to me," Marieke pointed out in a weak attempt to soften what was unfortunately an accurate description.

Zev ignored it. "And now you want to intentionally hand yourself back over to them?"

"I don't exactly want to," she said. "I'm just trying to do the right thing, Zev. I'm trying to do what has to be done."

Zev stepped closer, cupping the back of her head with one hand as his eyes captured hers with an intensity that threatened to rob her of breath. "Maybe I don't want to do the right thing if it means losing you."

Marieke closed her eyes and leaned against his touch. "I know what you mean," she murmured. "But I also know you don't mean that."

He didn't reply, apparently not so sure. After a long moment, his voice broke the silence, its clipped tone causing Marieke to open her eyes.

"There's something I need to say."

Marieke searched his face, silently signaling for him to go on.

"There's another reason I didn't tell you that the Head Instructor and I were both listening when Gorgon attacked you. The truth is, I hesitated when I realized you were onto heart-song. I hesitated, even though your life was on the line. If I hadn't come out of my stupor quickly enough, you would have been killed. I was—I still am—ashamed. I didn't want to admit it to you."

Marieke laid her hand against his cheek, feeling the roughness from days on the road without shaving. "You never have to be ashamed with me," she whispered. "You owed me nothing, and you still endangered your own life to save mine. We've been through so much since then. I don't doubt you for a moment. You shouldn't doubt yourself."

Zev pulled her close, his voice gruff as he rested his chin on her head.

"Don't doubt me when I tell you this, then. If they hurt you, forget whatever Jade is planning. I'll destroy the whole council myself."

CHAPTER

TWELVE

Zev

Zev pulled the hood of his traveling cloak further around his face as he kept step with Marieke. The city gate was in view ahead, and he didn't intend to leave her side until the last minute. He wouldn't be leaving her side then either if it was all up to him.

He could feel Marieke's tension beside him, and he slipped a hand into hers in an inconspicuous movement. She responded to the pressure, squeezing his hand tightly. Her fingers were cold.

"You don't have to do this," he murmured to her.

"I'm allowed to feel nervous without it meaning I want to abandon the plan," she told him sternly. "Don't get distracted."

"Hard not to." Zev's mutter wasn't really directed at anyone in particular.

His gaze flicked up to the large posters affixed to poles on either side of the city gate. Whoever had drawn them obviously knew Marieke from her time at the academy, because the likeness of her was very good. His and Azai's not so much.

"Let's hope Tarenne doesn't want to make some quick gold," Marieke said lightly, her eyes following his.

Zev gave her hand one more squeeze before releasing it. "I doubt she'd choose to put herself forward to collect it. She has too much to lose from becoming visible."

"You should go now, Zev," Marieke said. "If you leave it any later, you'll be conspicuous."

With reluctance, Zev had to acknowledge she was right. So far, they were blending into the huge stream of people moving into the capital. But once they got to the gate, where there was a bottleneck caused by the guards checking everyone's faces to see if they could spot the fugitives, they wouldn't be able to escape notice so easily.

"It's convenient, really," Marieke said, clearly trying to remain positive. "We didn't know how hard it might be to orchestrate a public arrest. Turns out it's not difficult at all. I'm glad Azai scouted ahead so we knew how big the crowds at the gate consistently are."

"Yes." Zev was unenthusiastic. "I don't think you needed to worry about no one caring about or remembering your arrest."

Judging by the wanted posters that had appeared several towns ago, the whole city would know of the rogue singer's capture within hours.

"Things are going to plan," Marieke reassured him, her eyes moving to the gate where two guards were visible. "Go find Tarenne."

Zev stared into her eyes for a moment, hating the impending separation with every fiber of his being. There was so much he wanted to say, and nothing at all that would be helpful right now.

"Be careful," he settled for, as he moved away from her and was consumed into the crowd.

He'd thought himself aware of his surroundings, so he almost jumped when Tarenne appeared at his elbow out of nowhere. She'd obviously been paying attention, ready to move into position. Since the posters suggested the guards were looking for Marieke and two male companions, they'd decided their best way to get into the city after Marieke's arrest would be to travel in pairs, Zev and Tarenne followed by Azai and Veronica. Hopefully Kaine would do his best to provide some cover. But even though Marieke assured Zev that the tall, young man who'd recently arrived at the gate was indeed Kaine, there was only so much the guard could do to prevent his fellows from seeing Zev and the others.

Zev watched tensely as Marieke reached the gate. He saw recognition light Kaine's eyes, and the young guard raised his voice.

"Halt." Marieke stopped as instructed. "Lower your hood."

Something in the guard's tone caught the attention of those nearest, and the whisper spread quickly through the crowd that someone was in trouble up front. People pushed and shoved, straining to see the action. Zev, his pack slung over the front to better protect it from opportunistic thieves in the crush, kept his elbows rigid, maintaining his position against the flow. It took all his resolve not to move to Marieke's side as Kaine's fellow guard gave a shout.

"That's her! Don't move!"

"I'm not moving." Marieke's voice seemed to carry clearly even through the bustle, but that may have just been because its cadence was so familiar to Zev. The crowd watched, agog, as she raised her hands before her, fists together. "I'm not resisting. I'm willing to be taken to the council."

"Not another word," the second guard said, frowning as Kaine moved forward to bind Marieke's hands. "We'd best gag her so she can't sing."

"Relax," Kaine said, master of the situation as he tied up Marieke's hands. Zev had to clench his own hand into a fist in his effort to stay in place. "I'm a singer, remember? I'll be able to tell if she tries to gather magic to herself. She's not doing anything."

"Ah yes." The guard sounded pleased as he eyed the epaulet that distinguished Kaine's uniform from his non-singing fellow guards. "That's convenient."

Kaine nodded absently. "Yes, it is. Let's get this one to the council at once."

Zev knew the reason for the guard's hurry. When Veronica had entered the city the day before, she'd had no trouble finding Kaine, and he'd proved as willing to help as Marieke had predicted. And he'd been as good as his word in finding his way onto a shift at the gate when he'd told them he would. It seemed she was right that some at least in the sphere of the council could be trusted.

However, Kaine hadn't been sure it was safe to bring Instructor Oriana into their confidence. Nevertheless, he had been able to learn her schedule sufficiently to allow him to time the arrest so that the instructor would be almost certain to see him taking Marieke to the council. They had to hope that if the instructor was sympathetic to their cause, she would involve herself at that point.

Kaine and his companion called for reinforcements from the guardhouse, the crowd eagerly watching the drama unfold as the new guards took up their positions at the gate. In the few minutes it took for the changeover to happen, Zev could see that Marieke was determinedly avoiding scanning the crowd for him. She probably feared giving their position away, and he knew she was wise to be cautious. But he found himself desperate for one more look, one more silent reassurance that she knew what she was doing and wouldn't take any more risks than her already risky plan required.

His wish wasn't granted. Her eyes remained averted until the guards led her into the city and out of sight, hands tied in front of her and head held high. Zev let out a long, slow breath. He felt like he'd just watched part of himself leaving. He couldn't imagine he would feel whole again until Marieke was safely back in his reach.

The arrest had caused predictable excitement, and for a short while after the new guards took up their post, they had their work cut out for them just to stop the crowd from rushing the gate to follow the captive and her guards. By the time things had settled enough for them to start letting people through again, they were flustered and dealing with an enormous backlog of people. Zev and Tarenne moved through unhindered amidst the crush, Azai and Veronica following shortly after.

Only once they were several blocks into the city did the four of them meet. Well, five of them if Tommy was to be counted. Zev hadn't seen the cat since the day before, and he certainly hadn't observed him anywhere near the gate crossing. But somehow he appeared at Tarenne's ankles, mewing his displeasure over the new environment.

To be fair, they did seem to be in a particularly dirty part of the city. It wasn't the same gate they'd left through when they followed Jade's trail, so it was hard to tell if it had gotten worse since they were last in the city. But Zev suspected so. The hordes of people leaving the barren farmlands for the capital had taken their toll. Too many people were crowded into the space, inns overflowing and rubbish piled against buildings on all sides. They could barely walk down any street without seeing a beggar doing his best to solicit mercy from the crowd. They even had to dodge a brawl that was spilling out of a nearby tavern, despite the fact that it wasn't yet noon.

"Do you want me to show you the room I secured?" Veronica asked. "It's not the most reputable inn, but I think we were lucky to find anything. The four of us will have to share the space, but it's not really different from sleeping out on the road."

"No, I want to head for the council building," said Zev. "I want to make sure she's taken there as planned, if we're not too late to catch up."

"We can try," said Veronica. "It's this way, come on."

They followed her through the streets, the rumor of the arrest swirling all around them. They passed more wanted posters in market squares, and Zev and Azai kept their hoods pulled low. Zev knew it was good that the crowd were all talking about Marieke—it had been part of their plan to be conspicuous. But it still made him uneasy to hear her name whispered on all sides. Had the council spread lies about her that might prevent people from caring enough about her fate to keep them accountable? The posters only said they were wanted for questioning rather than accusing them of any crime, but he didn't put much faith in that.

With the generous use of their elbows, they made quick progress through the curious crowd. Even so, by the time they reached the gates of the council building, a large crowd had gathered there. They split up, so as to be less conspicuous as they watched. To Zev's disappointment, there was no sign of Marieke.

"What's going on?" he asked the nearest bystander, feigning ignorance.

"They've arrested the girl from the posters," the man said eagerly. "She was caught trying to sneak in the northern gate."

"Not what I heard," another man cut in. "I heard she handed herself in."

The first one snorted. "Why would she hand herself in?"

"I saw her go past," announced a young girl proudly. "Just now, bound and with guards and everything! She looked just like her poster."

Zev peered over the heads of the crowd. The kerfuffle had caused the council gates to be closed, but through the bars, he thought he caught a glimpse of a trio moving away from the gates on the other side. His heart lifted when he recognized Marieke's dark braid. She'd made it that far. Hopefully Kaine would protect her until her status was more certain.

Zev's fists curled at his sides. How he hated not being able to protect her himself! Nothing had ever felt more wrong in his life than watching passively as she was arrested and taken away.

He pushed further through the crowd, approaching almost right to the gate. A figure had appeared from the academy building, hurrying toward Marieke and the guards. With relief, Zev recognized Instructor Oriana. She looked tense, but at least she was there.

Quite suddenly, the instructor swung her head around toward him, her expression confused. Zev lowered his head quickly, letting his hood fall more fully over his eyes. Had she seen him? He waited another moment before looking up. The instructor had turned away again, and as he watched, she preceded Marieke and the guards into the building and out of his sight.

For a full minute, Zev stared after them, feeling helpless and restless. Then, to his surprise, he heard himself hailed by name.

"Hello Zevadiah. Nice to see you again."

He spun quickly, his hand flying instinctively to his back and closing over the hilt of his sword. But he released it in astonishment as he caught sight of the grinning, young face looking up at him.

"Do you remember me?"

"Trina?" he asked cautiously.

"Yep, that's me!"

The teenage girl looked delighted that he remembered her

name, but Zev could only stare. How was she in Ondford, so far from her home among the monarchists in Sundering Canyon?

"What are you doing here?" he demanded.

"Looking for you," she said, still sounding enormously pleased. "It was very convenient for me that a crowd was gathered all in one place for me to search for you."

Zev blinked. All in one place? There were crowds all over the city.

"Well, in the one place I knew you'd be," Trina amended, as if she could guess his thoughts. "From what I heard on my way in, they've just arrested Marieke, yes? I'm sure there's a story there. The posters aren't a very good likeness of you, are they? And who's the other man?"

"Keep your voice down," Zev hissed, alarmed at this flow of words. His eyes scanned those standing close to them, relieved that no one seemed to be focused on their conversation. Everyone was still gossiping excitedly about the arrest.

"Right, sorry," said Trina brightly. "It's just all so exciting— this city is enormous! I was supposed to be inconspicuous, but it's hard to keep it all in. You should have seen the market we passed through back that way!"

She jerked a thumb over one shoulder, shaking her head in wonder at the indescribable delights of a city market. Zev could imagine it would all be overwhelming and incredible to someone who'd lived in a tiny, isolated, underground community all her life, but he didn't have much emotion to spare for Trina at that moment.

"What was I saying?" she said. "Ah yes. We were hoping to speak to you *and* Marieke, but as soon as we reached the city, we heard that she'd been arrested. When we realized what the crowd was gathered for, we thought that if you were anywhere, you'd be nearby." She frowned at him. "Why did you let her get arrested, by the way? It seems unlike you."

"You said *we*," Zev said, ignoring the uncomfortable question and looking around warily. "Who else is with you?"

"Oh, of course." Trina stepped to the side to reveal a child sticking close to her legs, swathed in an oversized traveling cloak. Zev couldn't see the child's face. "This is my little sister. She's traveled with me from the canyon."

"But why?" Zev asked blankly.

Trina cast a conspiratorial look around. "Is there somewhere more private we can talk?"

Zev let out a sigh, feeling like he'd strayed from the nightmare of Marieke's arrest straight into an even more bizarre dream.

"Come on," he said. "I have a room." He waded through the crowd, pausing to make sure Trina was following. After attempting to push her way through, she scooped up her sister and carried her to more easily traverse the throng. The child looked heavy, though. Trina was soon puffing.

"Do you want me to take her?" Zev asked, frowning slightly as he looked at the little girl. He caught a glimpse of pale skin and a straight nose, but the child didn't seem eager to show her face.

"Thanks, but I don't think she'd like that," Trina said. "We're almost through the worst of the crowd, then she can walk. Her legs are so much littler than mine, you see." Her matter-of-fact tone added to the feeling that Zev was in a dream, but he walked on without protest.

As they left the square, the others appeared, each of them staring at his companions.

"Who's this?" Azai demanded.

"An old acquaintance," Zev said, resigned. "She's coming with us, so I'll tell you more once we're back at the inn."

The journey felt interminable, Trina's wide-eyed fascination with everything she saw making it very difficult to blend in. But at last they reached the grubby little inn near the gate they'd come through, looking just as disreputable as Veronica had said. They squeezed through the crowded public room and up the stairs, cramming the whole group—now six instead of four—into the small bedroom.

"Everyone, this is Trina," Zev said. "She's from the group of monarchists who live hidden in Sundering Canyon."

"Hello." Trina smiled and gave the group a wave, as if this was a perfectly ordinary introduction and as if they weren't all staring at her with open mouths.

"Trina, this is my brother Azai," Zev said. "And some friends. You don't need to know who they are. But you do need to tell us what in the world you're doing here."

"Like I said, we came looking for you and Marieke," Trina said. Her face became serious for the first time. "We have a warning."

"Who exactly is *we*?" Azai asked, frowning at Trina's companion.

Trina looked down, her manner odd, as if she was looking to her little sister for a decision. The child stepped forward, raising pale, thin-fingered hands to drop her hood and reveal a face that drew gasps from everyone in the room but Trina.

"Kiarana!" Zev stared at the little elf, whose tapered ears wobbled as she inclined her head in acknowledgment.

"Zevadiah. Well met."

Zev just stared at her. Elves had been nothing more than legend to humans for generations, and intentionally so on their part. How and why was the leader-in-training of the elf community that was hidden deep in the southern Aeltan jungle standing here in this dingy inn all the way in Ondford?

"What is that?" Veronica whispered, sounding terrified.

"That is a rude way to express yourself," Kiarana pointed out, although she didn't look offended.

"Careful," Zev said quickly. "Careful how you speak. Elves are shrewd, and bargains with them have power whether you intend them to or not."

Kiarana nodded. "Unscrupulous, humans used to call us. Or so I'm told." She studied Zev. "I'm glad that seeking enchantment worked in the crowd. It was a damaged talisman, and I didn't know if it would be effective."

"You used a talisman to find me in the crowd?" Zev frowned as he remembered Instructor Oriana looking up and right at him. She must have felt the release of the magic. "You almost got me caught."

"But we didn't, so never mind that," Trina said. She bit her lip. "Zevadiah, have you heard anything from home since you left?"

"From home?" Zev stiffened. "What do you know about my mother?"

She shook her head. "No, no, not your actual home. I mean Aeltas."

"No, we haven't." It was Azai who answered, his voice sharp. "Why?"

Trina sighed, looking at Kiarana before returning her gaze to them.

"In that case, it looks like I'll be the bearer of the bad news."

THIRTEEN

Marieke

Marieke let out a long, slow breath between her dry lips as she followed Instructor Oriana into the council building. Her hands were still tied in front of her, but they weren't uncomfortable. Kaine hadn't made the knots tight. In fact, his grip on her arm had been reassuring rather than restrictive all the way through the city. She wished she could thank him for taking the risk of secretly helping her, but she didn't think it wise to say it aloud. From what Veronica said, he'd been eager to help, and perfectly willing to do so openly. But Veronica had told him that the group felt it would be more effective in achieving their goal of drawing the right kind of attention if he played the part of a loyal guard.

What she had probably been tactful enough not to say was that Marieke wanted to protect him from himself. She didn't want friendship with her to cost him his livelihood or his standing.

Instructor Oriana glanced back at her as they walked into the council's large entranceway. Marieke sent her a muted smile, feeling her tension ease a little. Kaine had timed things perfectly for them to arrive at the council as the instructor was due to attend something there herself. Marieke didn't know the details, but she'd been relieved to see Instructor Oriana appear from the academy building as soon as they passed through the complex's gateway.

"I'll fetch someone," said the guard whose name Marieke didn't know.

Kaine nodded. "I'll watch her." His voice was calm and confident, and he kept a hand around Marieke's arm.

The first guard strode off, leaving the trio waiting amidst the stares and whispers of everyone in the vicinity. The council seemed particularly busy, and Marieke had to remind herself that she'd done this voluntarily and there was no reason to feel humiliated.

"Oh Marieke." Instructor Oriana sounded distressed. "What's happened? What fresh disaster are you in?"

"No disaster," Marieke said evenly. "I turned myself in willingly, as the guards can testify."

Kaine nodded. "It's true."

"But why?" The instructor's round face looked much more drawn than the last time Marieke had seen her. "I'm afraid you won't get a kind reception here. Things have gotten so much worse since you left."

"Have they?" Marieke turned her head to properly look at the instructor, interested. "I've been wondering about that. Have there been any more natural disasters since I was last in the city?"

"Well…" Instructor Oriana frowned in realization. "No, actually. Not that I've heard about, anyway."

Marieke had suspected as much. Jade had been otherwise occupied.

"So I guess having me on the loose wasn't the danger the council feared."

The instructor sighed. "I wouldn't count on proving that to

them, Marieke. Not when the general deterioration of things has worsened. People are scared, and it makes them angry. The council is in a tight spot."

"Then surely at least some of them genuinely want the help I can offer in getting out of that tight spot."

"Some, perhaps." Instructor Oriana looked weary. "But they don't have the loudest voices."

The sound of a door opening at the far end of the entranceway made Marieke look up. With a lurch of her stomach she saw the Head Instructor striding toward her, another council member by his side. The other guard was with them. Turning back to Instructor Oriana, she spoke quickly and low.

"Then we need to do what we can to make sure the loudest voices aren't the only ones heard. I can't do this alone, Instructor."

Instructor Oriana stared back at her, still worrying her lip. Her eyes passed slowly to the pair approaching, and she stepped back slightly from Marieke.

"Oriana." Instructor Rafael addressed himself first to his colleague, his brows drawn together. "Do I understand that you've been meeting with fugitives again?"

"Hardly." She frowned. "I was walking here from the academy—as expected—when I saw Marieke being brought through the front gate."

The Head Instructor didn't look entirely satisfied. "Yes, well. I've just come from the hearing room, of course."

"Where are the rest of the panel?" Instructor Oriana asked with a frown.

"Never mind that," said Instructor Rafael. "Given this development, your hearing will be rescheduled. You can go about your business."

Hearing? Marieke looked between the two instructors in

confusion. Instructor Oriana was watching the Head Instructor through narrowed eyes. For a moment, Marieke was hopeful that she would protest, but after another moment, the older woman turned abruptly and strode away.

Marieke felt herself deflate. Her task would be much harder without support. She forced herself to meet the Head Instructor's gaze. She vaguely recognized the man with him as another council member, but didn't know his name. He wasn't from the academy—Instructor Rafael was the only one who was both an instructor and a councilor, his role as Head Instructor earning him a place as council member.

"Marieke." Instructor Rafael's tone was somber as he addressed her, but Marieke could swear she saw a spark in his eyes. He was glad to have her under his control again. "It grieves me that you've come to this pass. If you'd been cooperative when the council generously showed you grace on your previous arrest, it would not have been necessary to hunt and capture you like a criminal."

"She wasn't captured, sir," Kaine interjected. "She handed herself in."

His voice carried throughout the entranceway, where every person present had stopped to watch the spectacle. They weren't all wearing council uniforms, either. The gates to the complex may have been closed behind them, but plenty of members of the public were already inside the council building.

Heartened, Marieke spoke up, also projecting her voice. "That's right. I turned myself in because I want to help the council solve the crisis befalling our country. And I don't remember much grace on my previous arrest—unless you call hiding me away in a dungeon with no trial date grace."

The Head Instructor frowned, his eyes flicking quickly around before he answered. He didn't like the public nature of the conversation.

"Well, we can discuss the matter further," he said, his voice much lower than theirs. "Guards, it will be best if you take her to—"

"Hold on." Instructor Oriana's voice carried into the conversation.

She'd reappeared from the doorway behind the Head Instructor, half a dozen more people with her. Four of them wore the robes of council members, the other two of academy instructors.

Marieke caught the flash of annoyance that passed over the Head Instructor's face, but her own heart was soaring. Instructor Oriana hadn't abandoned her.

"Rafael." One of the council members nodded to him. "What have we missed?"

"The matter is under control, Councilor Bernard," Instructor Rafael said. "There's no need for the whole panel to be disrupted."

"Well, our hearing is disrupted anyway, isn't it?" the councilor pointed out. "Instructor Oriana suggested that the matter was of sufficient importance for the whole panel to be involved. She said that the renegade student handed herself in because she has information to share."

"The details are yet to be examined," Instructor Rafael said smoothly. "But as she's my student, I will take responsibility for—"

"I'm not your student," Marieke interrupted. "I graduated some time ago. And Instructor Oriana is right, I did hand myself in because I want to help. The information I have should be heard by the whole council, not just Instructor Rafael."

"Any testimony of Instructor Oriana's is suspect," said the Head Instructor tartly. "Given she's known to have colluded with you and your accomplices before now."

"Hold on, Rafael," said another of the councilors. "Her

conduct in that matter is still to be considered by the council." She frowned. "And perhaps you are too close to the matter to sit on the panel. I understand that as she is under your instruction, you may feel strongly about her decision to take action without consulting you. But—"

"Nonsense," said Instructor Rafael sharply. "As a member of both the academy and the council, I'm ideally placed to head the panel regarding Instructor Oriana. And that's not the issue in question right now."

"No," interrupted Marieke, "the question is what to do with me. And if you're interested in my opinion, what you should do is listen to me."

"I don't think we are interested in the opinion of a wanted criminal, actually," said Instructor Rafael. He nodded to Kaine. "Why don't you take her to the holding cell while we discuss—"

"The holding cell is still under repair," Instructor Oriana interrupted dryly.

"From a breakout that *you* allowed," the Head Instructor retorted.

"It wasn't her fault," said Marieke. "She had nothing to do with that. But I don't see what choice I had but to escape, since the council clearly wasn't capable of protecting me from Jade, and you weren't making any move to charge me with anything or let me testify on my own behalf." She raised her voice a little. "I certainly hope you don't intend to repeat that breach of regulations this time. You wouldn't want to erode faith in the institution of the council at a time when tensions in the city are already so high."

"There is no need for a display," said one of the newly arrived councilors mildly, clearly recognizing her intent in laying out the situation publicly. "Of course proper process will be followed."

"And proper process for criminals is locking them up while their fate is discussed," Instructor Rafael added quickly.

"*Am* I a criminal?" Marieke countered. "The posters didn't accuse me of a crime. They said I was wanted for questioning, and I'm here to answer questions. I have information that can help stop the impending famine."

"Then share it," said one of the academy members who'd accompanied the group from the hearing room. There was an edge of desperation to her voice. "None of us want to see the country starve."

"Hold on," said Instructor Rafael. "We can't trust this renegade. She can't be allowed to spew whatever misinformation she wishes in a public forum."

One of the other councilors frowned at Instructor Rafael. "You seem very eager to prevent her from speaking to the council, Rafael. Why is that?"

"I'm simply trying to ensure proper process is followed, as we've been exhorted to do," he said with dignity. He passed his eyes meaningfully around the busy entranceway. "There is a time and a place for her claims to be examined, and this is not it."

The councilor studied his face for another second before nodding. "You are right. We need to notify the full council of this development."

Instructor Rafael relaxed. "Indeed. In the meantime, I am willing to take responsibility for holding Marieke in—"

"No." Marieke cut in firmly. "I don't want to be left in Instructor Rafael's power."

"It's not a matter of what you want, child," said one of the councilors sternly. "You may have handed yourself in rather than being captured, but you still handed yourself in. You are within the jurisdiction of the council now."

"I accept that," Marieke assured her. "I don't have any

requests about where I'm taken or who is responsible for me. My only request is that the Head Instructor *not* be given charge of me." She could see she was about to be scolded again, so she hurried on, her voice carrying more clearly. "I have reason to think he's corrupt, and I fear for my safety in his care."

Gasps went around the room, the expressions of the panel ranging from shock to disapproval. Instructor Rafael had gone pale with rage, but she ignored him.

"That's a very serious accusation to make," said one of the councilors whom Instructor Oriana had fetched.

"I know it is," said Marieke seriously. "I have testimony to back up my accusation, which I'm willing to bring to the council. But until that time, surely the council can't in good faith hand me over to the man who is the subject of my allegations."

"How dare you?" Instructor Rafael spluttered. "You are under investigation, not me. You don't get to order your own imprisonment to suit your preferences, and you certainly don't get to smear my good name in the process. You will be silent, and you will submit to—"

"Rafael," interrupted the more reasonable councilor. "I understand your distress, but take a moment to consider your words. Wisdom should tell you that it is not in your interests to be given charge of a prisoner who has made such allegations against you." He returned his gaze to Marieke, his expression thoughtful. "I am willing to take responsibility for the prisoner's welfare and containment while the council decides on a way forward. She is unknown to me, and I to her." He looked round the group. "Unless anyone objects?"

Most of the group shook their heads, any who didn't like it apparently deciding not to speak up. Instructor Rafael also said nothing, presumably realizing it would look suspicious to keep pushing. He looked very displeased with the decision, however, which gave Marieke hope that it was a good outcome for her.

"Where will you take her?" asked the councilor who'd come into the entranceway at Instructor Rafael's side. He also didn't look happy.

"She will be kept secure and under guard," said the councilor in a tone that discouraged further questions. He nodded to Kaine and the other guard. "Follow me."

Kaine led Marieke forward, the trio following the councilor into the bowels of the academy. They went to a part of the building she'd never seen before, ending in a corridor lined with polished wooden doors.

The councilor stopped in front of one of those doors.

"This is where I propose to keep you while the council deliberates," he told her. "As you see, it's not a prison cell."

Marieke nodded cautiously.

"However, you're not free to leave," the councilor went on. "I will place enchantments on the room, and lock the door. It will be guarded at all times by a singer, and one of the enchantments will act to notify that singer of any attempt by you to engage in songcraft. Any such attempt will lead to proper imprisonment. In the event that a singer cannot be found to guard the door, you will be gagged for the duration of that shift. Do you accept these conditions?"

"I do," Marieke said readily. "They sound very reasonable to me."

The councilor nodded. "Good. I am Councilor Bernard, by the way. My area of expertise and responsibility is agriculture." He paused. "So you can imagine that I am extremely eager to identify and lift the blight on our land."

"Yes, sir," said Marieke. "So am I."

He studied her. "We shall see." Leaning around her, he opened the door to reveal a small but pleasant guest room, furnished comfortably. "I will arrange for someone to bring you food and other necessities. I'm afraid I will need to gag you in my absence, until a singer can be located to guard the door."

"He's a singer," the other guard piped up, pointing to Kaine.

"Is that so?" Councilor Bernard examined Kaine's epaulet with interest. "How long have you been on shift? Are you willing to take the first rotation?"

"Certainly, sir," said Kaine. "I only started about an hour ago, so I'm fresh as a daisy."

The councilor's lips twitched. "Very well. Thank you. That simplifies matters."

He left the two guards to watch Marieke while he stepped into the room. She didn't try too hard to follow as he sang in what her choral instructor would call a pleasant baritone, setting up the enchantments he'd described. He seemed to be the ringleader of the group of councilors Instructor Oriana had called to join the scene in the entranceway, and that in itself made Marieke trust him. She didn't doubt he was only doing what he'd said he would.

When he was done, he was noticeably more tired, from which she deduced that the enchantments were powerful ones. Not that she intended to test them.

"All right," the councilor told her, stepping back out into the corridor. "You may enter. I will make the full council aware both of your arrival and of your accusations." His face became severe. "Just know that if your allegations against the Head Instructor were motivated by self-interest or part of an attempt to deflect blame, I will be the first to push for the harshest of penalties."

"I understand, Councilor," Marieke said. "In fact, I'm well positioned to understand both how valuable and how fragile reputation is. You may have noticed the posters with my face plastered all over the city." Seeing that his expression hadn't softened, she added, "My accusation was made in good faith and for the sake of Oleand. I hope to convince you of that when given the chance."

He gave a curt nod, then retreated without another word, closing the door behind him.

Marieke looked around her, well pleased with her situation. Relieved to be alone, she sank into a high-backed chair. These accommodations were the most comfortable she'd had since leaving Zev's farm. Things could have gone very badly if Instructor Rafael had been given his way, but Instructor Oriana's intervention had salvaged the situation. And what had followed had only bolstered Marieke's belief that not all the council and academy were corrupt. There was hope yet.

She spared a thought for Zev, who would no doubt be restless and impatient at being separated from her, with no way to know her state. She could ask Kaine to get a message to him, but it seemed like an unwise risk. She would be well pleased if Kaine was one of her regular guards, and she didn't want to jeopardize that.

No, the plan had so far worked as well as could be hoped, and the next step was out of their hands. Zev, like Marieke, would just have to await events.

Marieke was left to her own devices for about two hours, before a knock on the door pulled her from her thoughts.

"Yes?" she asked cautiously.

She heard the click of a lock, and the door swung open just enough for Kaine to pop his head through.

"Some food has arrived for you," he said.

"Oh." Marieke stood. "Thank you."

"You need to move behind the bed," Kaine instructed.

She nodded, doing as she was told then watching as a maid

brought in a tray of food. Her spirits lifted just at the sight of it. Again, the best fare she'd had since leaving Zev's farm.

The maid withdrew, but Kaine remained in the doorway as her steps receded down the hall.

"It's just me here now," he said, once it was quiet outside. "The other guard is gone, and I'll be on solo shift for a while. Are you all right?"

Marieke nodded. "I'm better than all right. I think Councilor Bernard taking responsibility for me is a lucky turn of events."

"Seems that way," Kaine agreed. "I think he'll take you seriously. Is there anything you want me to do?"

"No." She shook her head. "What you're doing is more than enough. Thank you so much, Kaine."

He waved a hand in protest. "All I've done so far is do my job with integrity instead of blind loyalty to questionable masters. I hope no one ever has to thank me for that."

She nodded. "Did I understand correctly that the reason Instructor Oriana was coming to the council building was because she was supposed to face a hearing?"

"Yes," Kaine confirmed. "It's the talk of the academy. She's been under investigation, something to do with letting you all go."

"That's my fault," Marieke sighed. "We asked her to take a message to the council, and it looks like she did it, at her own cost."

"The cost isn't yet clear," Kaine said. "The council hasn't decided whether to censure her. Gossip says that Instructor Rafael is pushing for it, but not everyone on the council agrees. I don't know the details of what she told them, though. No one does. The council has kept it under wraps."

"Of course they have." Marieke frowned.

If the council told everyone Instructor Oriana's revelations regarding the source of the blight, they'd have to tell everyone what they were going to do about it. And apparently those who'd been actively hiding the truth about heartsong remained determined to protect their lies, even if exposing them might save the country.

"It's not just the council that's split," Kaine added. "The academy is in uproar over it. The Head Instructor's decision to stand Instructor Oriana down from her classes was wildly unpopular."

"She's not allowed to teach?" Marieke asked, aghast.

"For the moment at least. Word is that the Head Instructor is contemplating discontinuing the storytelling discipline altogether, but he'll have a battle on his hands if he does that. Even the temporary suspension has made a lot of people angry. She's very beloved. And," Kaine grinned, "her particular students have a knack of sniffing out exactly what's going on, even when the leadership is trying to keep it confidential."

Marieke gave a satisfied grunt. "Storytelling song, of course. I'm guessing the Head Instructor doesn't like the stories being told as his decisions are analyzed."

"Frankly, the academy is like a bonfire waiting to be lit," Kaine confirmed. "Getting Instructor Oriana on your side was a strategic move. No instructor is better liked or less believably paintable as a villain."

"I just approached the instructor I thought I could most trust," Marieke said. "The fact that she's the best liked gives me hope that whatever the state of the council, the whole academy isn't rotten." She sighed. "You should go back into the corridor now. If you're caught in here, you won't be allowed to guard me anymore."

"And that would be a shame," laughed Kaine, as he backed away. "I love standing for hours in an empty corridor guarding a prisoner who's not trying to escape. It's why I became a guard, after all."

Marieke winced. "Sorry."

"Don't be." He waved it off. "It might be boring right now, but being part of whatever you've started is probably the most important thing I'll do in my role as a guard."

"No pressure," Marieke muttered as he withdrew.

Other than another meal being delivered, no one else approached the guest room for the rest of the day. Marieke slept solidly in the comfortable bed, waking the following morning with a sense of anticipation. She was nervous but determined, and ready to face whatever came.

It was amazing what a solid night of sleep could do.

Her eagerness had waned a little by the time there was a knock on the door, just after noon. She was starting to become restless.

When the door opened, Councilor Bernard appeared, along with three others in the robes of council members. One of them was the man who'd stood beside the Head Instructor the day before, although Instructor Rafael himself wasn't there. Two guards, neither one Kaine, entered as well and moved to flank the doorway.

Marieke folded her hands in her skirts, trying to look poised and trustworthy.

"Marieke," Councilor Bernard greeted her. "The guards on duty report that you've made no attempt to use your songcraft."

"As instructed," she acknowledged.

Councilor Bernard nodded. "I'll be frank, Marieke. The country is in a state of crisis, and the council is already over-whelmed with matters requiring its attention. You have conduct to answer for, and we also take your allegations against a member of the council seriously. However, we feel it would be in everyone's best interests for these matters to be resolved expeditiously and with a minimum of fuss."

"What does that mean?" Marieke asked cautiously.

"We would like you to submit to informal questioning by a panel of council members. No formal charge would be entered, and if the panel is satisfied that you were not involved in the natural disasters or the blight on the land, nothing would go on your record." His eyes were earnest as they met hers. "I volunteered to head the panel, and I give you my word that we would hear you out fairly. Are you willing to cooperate with an informal inquiry?"

For just a moment, Marieke wavered. It was a much less intimidating option, and perhaps telling this seemingly trustworthy councilor would be enough. Perhaps he'd know what action was best to take with the information she'd learned.

But no. It left too much in the hands of someone she didn't know. She needed to stick to the plan.

"No, I'm not willing to cooperate. Respectfully, I don't agree that it's in everyone's best interests."

She could see the frustration in his eyes, whereas she thought the councilor who was a friend of Instructor Rafael's looked pleased.

"I urge you to reconsider, Marieke," Councilor Bernard said. "You have yourself pointed out that holding you without any charge is contrary to our usual processes. If this matter is not resolved expeditiously via some informal means, we will have no choice but to charge you with a formal offense."

"That's a matter for you," said Marieke.

"This attitude won't endear you to anyone at the council," he warned her. "Hearing a formal charge requires significant manpower at a time when the council is already stretched. And you should know that if you're found guilty of any part of the charges, you will be marked permanently as a criminal. That will affect your whole life."

"I understand," Marieke said. "But if the country is ravaged by famine, I won't have very good employment prospects anyway."

One of the other councilors scowled. "You're in no position to be flippant, young lady."

"I'm not being flippant," she assured him. "I meant it seriously."

"We know that you forcefully broke out of a holding cell, destroying council property in the process," another councilor said incredulously. "How do you expect to avoid being found guilty of any charge?"

"I didn't say I expect that," Marieke said. "But you can't assume I'm guilty before I've stood trial. No one can."

There was a challenge in her voice, and Councilor Bernard raised a placating hand.

"No one is assuming anything. But for what it's worth, I strongly advise you against the course you're taking."

"I understand," Marieke said again. "But my mind is made up."

He nodded, looking weary. "Very well. The council will meet once again. I consider it highly likely that you will be formally charged by the end of the day."

Marieke nodded, and the group withdrew. One of the guards went with them, leaving a single guard to lock and watch the door.

"If you want my opinion," the guard said, his hand on the doorknob, ready to pull it closed, "that was foolish. You were just offered a rescue, and you scorned it."

"I didn't mean to scorn anyone," Marieke said evenly. "But I'm not in need of a rescue. I wasn't hunted down and caught. I came here willingly."

"If you say so." The guard shook his head, returning to the corridor and pulling the door shut behind him.

Marieke had several more hours to wonder whether he was right and she was being a fool. But when Councilor Bernard returned, this time with only the councilor who'd ranged himself with Instructor Rafael, her patience was rewarded.

"Marieke of Oleand, I hereby notify you that you have been charged with the following offenses: escaping lawful custody, damage to public property, collusion with enemies of Oleand, sedition, treachery, and public nuisance."

It was a heavy list, but Marieke found herself fighting a smile. Success.

"I understand," she said solemnly. "I assume I'll have the chance to give testimony in my defense?"

"Of course." Councilor Bernard inclined his head. "Due process will be followed at all times. Your matter will be heard in three days' time before a select panel of the council."

"Hold on." Marieke raised a hand. "I want a full hearing in front of the entire council."

"It's not for you to dictate the manner of your hearing," said the other councilor dryly.

"No," Marieke agreed. "It's dictated by our laws. And if I recall correctly, anyone charged with public offenses has the right to select a public hearing before the full council. Since you've assured me that due process will be followed."

There was a moment of silence, during which Councilor Bernard looked surprised and the other councilor furious.

"You did say public nuisance and damage to public property, didn't you?" Marieke pressed innocently. "Those would qualify, I believe."

"Those can be dropped from the charges," the other councilor said darkly, earning him a frown from Councilor Bernard.

"No, they can't. Not at our whim, and certainly not as a

stunt to frustrate the accused's lawful request. The charges have been formally laid, they must be answered."

Marieke nodded, feeling elated. Had they forgotten that the academy required all students to undertake one governance class during their first year? Most of her peers hadn't been very interested in the topic, except for those few who already had ambitions of becoming councilors. But being from the country and unfamiliar with the details of the system, she'd been particularly curious. She still remembered feeling dissatisfied with how little opportunity non-singers like her parents had for their needs to be represented.

"A public hearing is a different matter," Councilor Bernard said. "I imagine it will take longer to coordinate. You will be advised of the date of your hearing once arrangements can be made."

She inclined her head.

The pair turned to go, the other councilor still looking irate, but at the doorway, Councilor Bernard paused.

"I understand that you entered the city through the northern gate," he said.

"That's right." Marieke spoke warily. Were they going to try to retrace her steps? She didn't want to expose Tarenne if she didn't have to.

"Am I to take it that during your absence from the capital, you didn't travel south and out of Oleand?"

"Out of Oleand?" Marieke frowned. "No, of course not."

Councilor Bernard gave the other councilor a pointed look, but all it earned was a scornful noise in his throat.

"You can't take her word for it. There are plenty of ways to expedite travel. She might have doubled around to enter the city from the north. She could still be responsible."

"Responsible for what?" Marieke asked. "What are you talking about?"

Councilor Bernard looked back at her, seeming reluctant to answer. "Instructor Oriana has argued on your behalf that the lack of disasters after your escape suggests that you were never behind them. But another possible explanation is that you instead took your activities over the border."

"I don't understand," Marieke said blankly.

"We've just received word that the Aeltan capital has been hit with a hailstorm more destructive than any before recorded," Councilor Bernard said. "Apparently whole neighborhoods were flattened. It seems unlikely it was natural."

Marieke's mouth fell open in horror. Jade. It had to be. After failing to eliminate Marieke and clear the way for an attack on an Ondford that was still unsuspecting, she'd taken Clancy into Aeltas. That's why they hadn't returned to Clancy's home, and why there was no sign of their activity either in Ondford or elsewhere in the country.

But why?

"In any event, you'll understand why the council won't welcome your request for a full public hearing at a time when so many other urgent matters require attention."

"It wasn't a request," said Marieke flatly. If he thought she would capitulate now, he was sorely mistaken. "It was an exercise of my rights under law. Unless we no longer operate within our own laws."

"There's no need to throw around accusations," the councilor said, sounding irritated. "As I said, we will notify you of the time of your hearing."

The pair withdrew at last, leaving Marieke to her thoughts. They were anything but peaceful. Councilor Bernard's annoyance she was able to brush off. She suspected that he reacted so much to her suggestions that the council might not follow process because some part of him feared there was truth in the accusations. Creating that discomfort in him was the main reason she kept bringing it up.

The information about Aeltas was much more distressing. She already wrestled with the loss she'd brought on Zev and his family. Had she brought disaster on his whole country now? And how would he react when he heard? Surely he would want to go to the aid of his homeland. And where would that leave their plan?

She passed a much less settled night. Where the day before she'd been impatient for someone to come for her, the new dawn found her glad of her solitude.

She was therefore flustered when a firm knock sounded on the door minutes after her breakfast tray had been left.

"Come in," she said, her voice wobbling slightly.

The door swung wide to reveal a welcome sight.

"Kaine," she said, moving forward. She paused, lowering her voice. "Is it just you on duty?"

"Yes and no," Kaine said cheerfully. "I'm the only guard here, but someone else has come to see you."

He moved out of the way to allow another figure to edge past him into the room.

"Instructor Oriana!" Marieke said.

She gave a strained smile. "Good morning. Are you well?"

"I'm all right," said Marieke quickly. "What about you? I heard about your suspension. I'm sorry I've brought trouble on you."

"I'm not," she said. "It's been a hard time, I won't deny, but I've slept better than I have in years. I should never have agreed to lie for the Head Instructor. And I should never have let him close down part of my discipline without a fight." She brushed her hands together in a businesslike manner. "That's why I'm here, incidentally."

"What's why you're here?" Marieke asked blankly.

"My discipline," said Instructor Oriana. "Storytelling song. Better yet, the questioning branch of it." She gave Marieke a smile that was too fierce for her kind face. "Well done for securing yourself a public hearing, Marieke. That was a master stroke. News is already spreading around the city, and I imagine the hearing room will be overflowing."

"Wow." Marieke felt a little dazed. "I expected the council to keep it quiet as long as they could."

Kaine grinned from the doorway. "There may have been some leaks in the flow of information. Let's just say that your friends helped the information find its way through the gate."

Instructor Oriana nodded. "You should have seen Solomon trying to be nonchalant about starting rumors in the dining hall. He's so serious usually, I don't think the students could get past the fact that he was initiating gossip enough to actually *hear* the gossip."

"I don't know what to say," said Marieke faintly.

"The main thing is, they won't be able to get away with canceling your hearing, or even deferring it too long, without backlash," Instructor Oriana said. "We can leave the rumor mills to do their bit. We should be focusing on your hearing."

Kaine nodded. "Anytime I'm on duty, Instructor Oriana will come. The enchantments on the room will notify me of the use of songcraft, but naturally I won't report it."

"What use of songcraft?" Marieke asked, still in the dark.

"Ours," said Instructor Oriana. "If you're going to make the most of the public hearing you've orchestrated, you need some training. It's years later than it ought to have been, but Marieke...it's time for me to teach you storytelling song. Let's put that aptitude for questioning craft to good use."

CHAPTER

FOURTEEN

Zev

Zev drew a deep breath, summoning patience from his position leaning against the doorframe of the little bedchamber. Trina was sitting on the bed, Kiarana on one side of her and Veronica on the other. The monarchist girl's declaration had consumed Zev's attention, and he was impatient to hear the rest of what she had to say.

But he had to acknowledge that it was perfectly reasonable for Veronica and Tarenne to be distracted by the sudden appearance of a mythical creature they'd never heard of. Even Azai, who knew elves existed, was staring at the alabaster-skinned, green-eyed, pointy-eared oddity. Seeing an elf in real life was very different from hearing about them.

"That's a good summary of our relationship with elves," Trina was finishing, clearly enjoying being the center of attention. "Don't expect more information from Kiarana here—she won't give anything away for free. But I'm happy to answer any more questions you have."

"How about instead you tell us what you meant about bad news from home?" Zev cut in, seeing that Veronica was poised to speak.

212

Trina opened her mouth, but Kiarana put a spindly hand on the girl's arm. "Don't be so hasty, child. We agreed that we would be judicious in the trade of information. We know things they wish to know, and they have answers we desire. We can surely reach a mutually beneficial arrangement."

"Oh yes." Trina nodded, sending Zev an apologetic look that he found unconvincing. "I did agree to that. We made the agreement down in the canyon, where the chaotic magic prevents it from being a binding bargain, but still...I think I should honor my word."

"Certainly you should honor your word," Kiarana said calmly. "What use is a creature whose word can't be trusted?"

"Are you threatening to harm her?" Veronica asked, frowning. She seemed to have taken a liking to the precocious teenager. "Because I'll have something to say about that."

The elf raised an eyebrow, apparently fascinated. "And what would you have to say?"

But Trina spoke before Veronica could answer. "No, no, she's not threatening me. She was simply making an observation. Elves don't have subtle undertones the way humans do. If she was threatening me, she'd come out and say it."

Veronica didn't look entirely reassured, but Zev felt it was time to take charge of the conversation.

"Will you answer the question about what's happening in Aeltas, or not?"

Kiarana's gaze was calm as she gave the predictable answer. "In exchange for what?"

Zev almost growled. "You're putting on a lot of dignity for someone who was being carried around like a child a short time ago. I would have thought the deception was beneath you."

Kiarana stared at him. "Why in the realm would you think that? Is it shameful to be a child in your culture?"

"Well, no, not exactly shameful," said Zev, annoyed with himself for going even more off topic.

"I do not put on my dignity, Zevadiah of Aeltas," the elf said, a dangerous edge to her voice. "I carry it as part of me at all times. I do not care if my means of staying hidden seem undignified to you or others of your kind, because I do not care what any human thinks of me. It is completely immaterial to my well-being."

"There's something to be said for that," Veronica said, sounding amused. She looked between Zev and Kiarana. "I'm still so confused. Did you meet in Sundering Canyon?"

Zev shook his head. "No, in the southern jungle."

"The southern jungle?" Veronica raised her eyebrows in surprise. "I've heard all kinds of tales about that place. They say if you stray from the path, you'll surely die."

"Well, I strayed from the path, and I didn't die," Zev said shortly. "You shouldn't believe every tale you hear."

"That tale has truth to it," Kiarana commented. "The magic of the jungle has grown thick to the point of being wild. Humans who stray in too deep will be crushed from the inside out by the magic's attempts to encroach on their body." She paused. "Except singers, of course, whose bodies are actually capable of channeling the magic."

Zev frowned. He remembered the Imperator, Kiarana's grandmother who was a leader of sorts among the elves, saying something about that. "I remember the pressure on my chest. But I wasn't crushed. And I'm no singer."

"Indeed." Kiarana nodded. "It was one proof of your lineage. Royal blood carries a protection of its own against wild magic. It's an expression of what you humans call heartsong."

"Really?" Azai sounded intrigued, but Zev felt they were straying further from the point.

"What is it you want to know from us in order to answer

our questions about what's happening in Aeltas?" he asked Kiarana flatly.

She considered for a moment. "A comprehensive update of what you've discovered in your attempt to stop the blight from consuming Oleand."

"And in exchange for that, you'll tell us what's amiss in Aeltas?" Zev asked. Another thought occurring to him, he added quickly, "And an honest answer as to why you came here?"

"Hm." Kiarana's thin lips curved in a smile. "You are a shrewd bargainer. Agreed."

Zev nodded, satisfied. He wished Marieke was with them—her new skill might have helped guide their questions—but he'd done his best.

Speaking slowly so as not to miss anything that would require him to double back, he recounted to Kiarana their discovery of Tarenne, and what they'd learned about Jade's manipulation of Clancy and intention to destroy Oleand from within.

"Did I miss anything?" he asked the group.

Veronica tilted her head to the side. "I think Jade's attack on Marieke is relevant. She obviously thinks that Marieke—or at least, Marieke's connection with you—can disrupt her plan, and that in itself tells us something about her plan."

"True," Zev agreed. He told Kiarana and Trina about Jade's attempt to kill Marieke during her imprisonment.

"That puzzles me," Kiarana confessed. "This vendetta Jade has. Why is she so fixated on Marieke as a threat? Simply because she's a singer? As she herself has demonstrated with this Clancy, your heartsong could interact with any singer to great effect, with the right effort. What does she hope to achieve by killing Marieke? She won't protect herself from your potential to counteract her plans. You could just embroil yourself with any singer in Marieke's place." She gestured at Veronica. "You could tie yourself to this one instead, for example."

"No." The answer came from Zev and Azai at the same time, in identical, unimpressed tones.

Zev raised his eyebrow at Azai, surprised to hear his brother coming to Marieke's defense as well.

"What?" Azai raised a shoulder defensively at Zev's look. "I'm on your side."

"Do I get a say?" Veronica asked wryly.

"I imagine so, but why would you say no to being paired with Zev?" Trina asked, grinning mischievously. "Look at him."

"Zev's trail is positively scattered with admirers, it seems," Azai said, a hint of acid in his tone.

Veronica's voice was cold as she replied. "Perhaps because he treats everyone he meets with basic courtesy, unlike some others in the room."

"I'm sorry, I didn't realize I was addressing one of his admirers," Azai shot back.

"Enough," said Zev. "Not all of us are enjoying this conversation as much as you appear to be," he added brutally, the words directed at Veronica. He turned to Kiarana. "We've fulfilled our side of the bargain."

She nodded slowly. "The first question you had is what's amiss in Aeltas. I will let Trina answer that, if she is willing."

"Sure!" Trina bounced a little in her excitement at being called on, before remembering the topic at hand. Her face fell comically. "It's not good news, I'm afraid. I don't know if you know this, but Svetlana has eyes and ears in both capitals. She keeps fairly well updated. And she learned some days back that Tarandon had been hit by an enormous, unnatural hail storm. There was a lot of destruction."

"What?" Azai exchanged a look with Zev, who could read a

reflection of his own alarm. "How do you know it was unnatural?"

"Well, for one thing, it came without any warning whatsoever. The storm was so large, it even took out some farmland surrounding the city. I believe one of the city's main storehouses was ripped open, and the grain inside was ruined by rain."

Veronica had gone pale, and Zev suddenly remembered that she lived in the capital. "Did people die?"

Trina shrugged, her expression sympathetic. "I don't know the details, but to be honest, I'd assume so."

"But who would do that?" Veronica demanded.

Tarenne, who so far had stayed quiet and still showed little interest in the fate of the southern kingdom, made a noise in her throat. "It's obvious who, surely."

Comprehension crossed Veronica's face. "Jade." Her expression took on an accusing edge. "Jade and your brother."

Tarenne nodded. "From what she told us of heartsong previously, I wouldn't have thought Clancy would be any use to her across the border. But your account of her attack on Marieke in the capital here changes that." She looked at Zev. "If she saw you do what you described, and use your heartsong to empower Marieke's magic even here in Oleand, she must have realized Clancy could do the same in Aeltas."

Zev's jaw worked as he tried to keep his anger in check. Tarenne was sharp, he'd give her that. She might not say much, but she was taking everything in, and her mind jumped quickly to conclusions everyone else was slower to see.

"But why would she do it?" Veronica cried.

"That's obvious, isn't it?" Azai's voice was hard. "She did it to punish us. Zev in particular." He turned his eyes on Zev, their expression making it clear that at least some of his anger was directed at his brother. "Zev couldn't leave her plans in Oleand alone, so she's taking the fight to our own land."

Zev ignored the accusatory note in Azai's voice, trying to think. "It's not just about revenge. Jade is more strategic than that. She tried to eliminate Marieke before striking her final blow so that our connection couldn't threaten whatever her big plan is. But that didn't work, so she's trying something else. She's trying to manipulate me. If I rush back to Aeltas, Marieke is no longer a threat to her, at least according to her estimation."

"She might even hope to drive a wedge between the two of you," Veronica added.

Zev clenched his fist. "Leaving the way clear for her to attack Ondford."

"Which isn't our problem," said Azai swiftly.

"Yes it is," Zev disagreed. "We've made it our problem, Azai. A problem we've been dedicating ourselves to solving for weeks."

"That was before," said Azai. "Zev, this changes everything. Allowing the threat to move into Aeltas was never part of the deal." He swept his hand toward the city outside. "You've seen what Jade's vendetta has done to Oleand. Do you want that to happen in Aeltas? Do you want Tarandon to be flooded with beggars and the countryside emptied?"

"Of course I don't," said Zev, stung. "And that's not what we're talking about. The storm sounds bad, I don't mean it isn't. But Oleand's deterioration is the work of heartsong. Surely Clancy can't do that to Aeltas, not with our own power counteracting it."

"But our power isn't counteracting it!" Azai cried. "Because we're not there! Our father is dead, and the power of our family's lineage rests with you and me. We've abandoned our own land to fight for someone else's! And Aeltas is suffering as a result!"

Zev clenched his hand so tightly the knuckles went white. He hated that Azai had a point.

"We have to leave right away," Azai said. "We have to return to Aeltas, and bring our power with us."

"That's exactly what she wants," Zev protested. "That's exactly the outcome Jade is trying to manipulate."

"Then she's played her hand well," Azai said, his voice rising. "Because I refuse to save Oleand at the cost of Aeltas. You should be ashamed to even consider it, Zev."

"Calm down," Veronica said, her voice steady even though her hands shook a little in her lap. "My family actually lives in Tarandon, and even I am keeping my head better than you two. A single storm, however catastrophic, is not enough to destroy a whole country."

"Do you really think Jade will stop at one storm?" Azai demanded. "This is just the beginning. She's showed us what she's capable of in Oleand. And if she's determined to target farmland, where do you think she'll focus her efforts first?"

Zev drew in a breath, again aware that his brother was right. They'd already lost their father to Jade's bitterness, they couldn't lose their mother as well. The thought of her under attack, with her husband gone forever and her sons both far away, was unbearable. But the thought of going back on the plan they'd agreed on with Marieke and abandoning her in captivity was unthinkable.

"I need to think," he said, putting his hands to his head. "I need time."

"There's no time," Azai said angrily. "It will take days to get back to Aeltas, even if we leave right away. Who knows how much damage Jade might do in that time?"

"An hour won't change anything," Zev snapped at his

brother. His eyes searched the room, looking for a solution. They settled on Kiarana, watching him out of beady, emerald eyes. "There's more," he realized suddenly. "More to our bargain. You said you'd give an honest answer as to why you came here. I doubt it was to tell us about a storm."

"It was in part for that purpose," Kiarana said. "But you're right that there is more to my motivations. I discovered something regarding Jade's plans which made me discontent. After careful deliberation, I decided to do something with that discontentment. I decided to communicate to you the threat she poses."

"Why would you help us?" Zev asked suspiciously.

"For the only reason an elf would ever help a human," Kiarana said simply. "Because it serves my own purposes. I do not want Jade to succeed. I believe it is time for my people to come out of hiding, and I do not believe we should do so if the kingdoms are in a state of anarchy."

"I feel the same way," Trina chimed in. "I want everyone in our community to have the chance to live on the surface if that's the life they choose. And if the countries are in ruins, it wouldn't be much of a life. Not to mention that Svetlana would never allow it."

"The difference," Kiarana said, "is that unlike among the monarchists, the leaders of my community are interested in emerging. Me being one of them. There have been rumblings about doing so for many years. But among us there are different ideas about how to achieve that purpose. Rissin, for example, has relished working with Jade. He believes that it would be to our benefit for the human structures of leadership to be substantially weakened before we make our presence known. He believes that our kind would acquire greater power that way. I do not agree that the elves would benefit in this event. I have no interest in having power in the governance of humans.

Our ancestors prospered from trading with the wealthy among the humans. There would be few in a position to pay handsomely for our craftsmanship if the countries as we know them fall." She folded her pale hands. "I have spent a decade convincing my grandmother that the time is approaching for our isolation to end. I do not wish to see the efforts of elves like Rissin destroy all that I have built."

"Surely Rissin must realize that as well." Zev's voice was dark as he remembered the vindictive elf who'd attacked him and Marieke numerous times, determined to capture them and study the way their connection affected the magic around them. "Are you sure he isn't just helping Jade because he wants revenge on the councils for their role in driving the elves underground?"

Kiarana sighed. "I'm sure." She considered Zev for a long moment. "I am of the view that this information is not required in satisfaction of our bargain. I offer it to you as a gift freely given, as a gesture of goodwill."

Zev inclined his head. "So received."

The little elf nodded. "The events surrounding our decision to withdraw from interactions with humans are not what you believe them to be. You have been led to think that the councils tried to hunt us to extinction because they wanted a monopoly on access to magic." Her emerald eyes sparkled. "That isn't *untrue*, exactly. I believe they would have been glad of that outcome. I certainly believe the first councils wanted to be the sole trustees of the power that comes with magic. But there's more to it. The elves were not mere bystanders to the coup that overthrew the human monarchs. They assisted the singers."

"I didn't know that," said Trina, eyes wide.

"Nor did I." Zev frowned. "Why would elves help the singers overthrow the monarchs?"

"For the same reason elves do anything," Kiarana said,

sounding impatient. "The reason I've already given, namely that they perceive it to be to their own benefit. The excesses of the monarchs had become problematic to our trade. They were regulating it heavily, and taxing our sales to a crippling extent. It was becoming harder for anyone but the royals and their inner circles to afford talismans, which was exactly their intention. My forebears wished to ease the stranglehold on our markets."

"And they thought slaughtering the monarchs, unleashing wild and angry magic that would splinter the land in two, and installing corrupt ruling councils would achieve that?" Azai asked sarcastically.

He was as tense as Zev had ever seen him, flexing his fingers and tapping his foot in his eagerness to return to Aeltas and fight for the country he loved. If the cramped room had allowed, he would no doubt be pacing.

"No," Kiarana said. "That was not the plan the elves agreed to. In fact, the original form of the coup was conceived by the elves. But it didn't involve slaughtering the monarchs. Had that idea been suggested, I have no doubt the elves would have told the singers that doing so could have dire and unpredictable consequences on the magic of the land. But it wasn't suggested. The initial agreement didn't even involve exiling the monarchs. That was a later decision made by the singers who carried out the coup."

Zev frowned. "What was the original plan, then?"

"To set up a council, similar to the one that exists today," Kiarana said. "But the council would have co-existed with the monarchy. They would have been there to provide advice and accountability. I've seen the original proposal—the elves remember it, even if the singers do not. It was detailed and viable. There were appropriate checks on both seats of power, and authority was spread in a way that was intended to counteract the monarchs' bent toward corruption."

"The monarchs of the time would never have agreed to that," Zev said. "The tales might be exaggerated, but they're not completely untrue. There is reason to believe they were power-hungry and beginning to oppress their critics."

"You are likely right," Kiarana acknowledged. "It is even possible that the singers who carried out the coup did as they initially intended and proposed that structure to the monarchs when they stormed the castle. The subsequent flight and slaughter may have been part of the monarchs' refusal to yield. But that I don't know, and can only speculate on."

"That...changes things, doesn't it?" Veronica said quietly.

"Not really." Azai frowned. "It doesn't change what actually happened."

"I suppose not." She didn't sound convinced. "But it changes how I feel about it. Not the murder or the centuries of lies," she added quickly, seeing Azai's expression. "But the original intent. Honestly, that system sounds like a good one."

Zev silently agreed with her. He didn't say so, though. He could see from Kiarana's demeanor that she wasn't finished.

"There's more, isn't there?" he prompted her. "You still haven't said what you learned about Jade's plans that sent you looking for us."

Kiarana inclined her head. "You are astute. What I learned is that Rissin has been working on something significant for Jade." She frowned, the tips of her long ears wobbling as they seemed to do when she felt strong emotion. "Something that ought not to have been traded outside our community. It is a new innovation, and my grandmother was not pleased when she learned of the deal he'd made."

"What's the new innovation?" Veronica asked.

"An enchantment, naturally contained within a talisman, which can transform matter," Kiarana said.

"What does that mean?" Azai asked.

She looked at him pityingly. "It means if a talisman crafted with this enchantment touches something, it changes that item into an entirely different type of matter from its original form."

"What does it change it to?" Zev asked.

"That depends on how the talisman was crafted," Kiarana said. "The nature of the transformation is determined at the time the talisman is created."

"That's complex magic," Veronica said. Judging by her tone, Zev should be impressed. "It's not supposed to be possible to change the actual nature of matter."

"We are always making new advancements in our craft." There was definite smugness in the elf's voice.

"It might be complex, but I don't understand how it's so dangerous," Tarenne chimed in. "Changing one object is a very limited attack."

"Ah, but that's the sophistication of this enchantment," Kiarana said. "It's not just one object. It's all of a type of matter, provided it's connected." She pointed to the floor. "This building is mainly wooden. If I touched a talisman of this nature to the floorboards, not only would they change substance, but any wood connected with them in an unbroken structure would do so as well."

Veronica raised an eyebrow. "The whole building could change?"

"If the talisman were strong enough," Kiarana said. "Now imagine that the substance of choice is water. What would become of this inn?"

The mention of water sparked Zev's memory. "We've seen the effects of this magic, haven't we?" he said. "When we were in the elf city, Marieke and I saw what looked like a forest spring, but it was glass where water should be."

Kiarana nodded proudly. "We have been experimenting with the effect for some time. It works."

"And Rissin has provided Jade with a strong talisman of this type?" Veronica asked.

"A very strong one," Kiarana confirmed. "Strong enough to change something much larger than this inn."

"Something much—" Veronica's eyes widened as she reached the same conclusion Zev just had.

"Her target is the castle," he said grimly. "Or rather, the council and academy complex. It's all stone, even the flagstones between the buildings. The whole thing could potentially come down if the talisman touched the structure itself."

"Do you know what the talisman would turn the stone into?" Veronica asked.

"I do." Kiarana looked like she had to fight her natural instincts to keep giving them information. But she must have decided it was still part of her original bargain, because she spoke again. "It would turn whatever it touched to the most difficult element of all to manipulate. Fire."

Zev's eyes widened, and he could see from his companions' faces that they were picturing the scene as surely as he was. If the very walls of the council and academy turned into an inferno, everyone inside would die. Horrible deaths they would be, too. The casualties would likely include almost the entire council, as well as the instructors and students at the academy. He was inclined to think Jade was right that such an attack would strike a blow at the structure of the country's government from which it would never recover.

His stomach clenched. And Marieke was in that building.

"We can't let it get that far," he said, determined. "We have to stop Jade and Clancy before they reach their target."

"Yes." Azai's agreement came as a surprise until Zev saw the hard look in his eyes. "Let's stop them all the way back in Aeltas."

Zev shook his head. "We can't leave now. It's too great a risk. What if Jade and Clancy are already on their way here? What if the strike on Tarandon was just a single warning shot, and they're already back in Oleand? They could be almost upon us for all we know."

"Or, they could be wreaking havoc across the Aeltan countryside," Azai argued. "They could have decided to use the talisman in Tarandon instead, where no one is standing in their way." He stared his brother down. "Are you truly not going to return to your own country to defend it from enemies *you* brought down on it?"

Zev wrestled with himself. He hated that there was any doubt about his answer to that question. A year ago, he would have had no hesitation. But so much had changed since a year ago. Everything had changed.

"I can't." The words burst from him in anguished defeat. "Not when it means abandoning Marieke when we've promised her aid. Not when she could be burned alive if we do nothing."

Azai made a disgusted noise in his throat. "Well, I'm going," he said. "I'll leave today."

Zev felt hollow, but he pushed emotion aside. There wasn't time for it. "That's a good idea," he said. "We should split up. We both carry the power of our bloodline inside us. Your return to Aeltas should help protect it. And you can warn the council of the threat that's coming against them."

"The council won't be my priority," Azai said curtly.

Zev drew a breath. "I won't try to tell you what to do," he said. "Your wisdom is no less than mine. I'm sure you can navigate whatever situation you find."

Azai hesitated for a moment, then gave a curt nod. He still didn't look happy, but he wasn't arguing outright. Zev noticed that Veronica looked doubtful about the whole thing, distress in her eyes at this fracturing of their group.

"What about you?" Azai asked her, apparently also noticing her dismay. "Tarandon is your home. Don't you want to come back with me?"

Veronica bit a dry lip. "Part of me wants to," she said. "But I can't abandon Marieke when our plan is already in motion. And I think it's more likely that Jade and Clancy will come back here. Oleand is the target they've spent months, perhaps years, weakening for an attack. It's in our interest to stop them. If they succeed here, not only will Aeltas be flooded with desperate Oleandans, but our country will be their next victim."

"I'll come with you," Trina said unexpectedly. "At least as far as the border. I agreed to help Kiarana bring you the message hopefully without being detected as an elf. But I don't think I'm much use here. I want to convince Svetlana to help. Or at least to give us all the right to choose whether we want to help."

"Thank you," said Zev. "We could use all the help we can get."

"Hold on." Azai was frowning. "I didn't say you can come with me. Presumably you don't know how to ride if you've lived in the canyon all your life. You'll slow me down too much."

"I don't think I will, actually," Trina said. "Perhaps taking a vehicle instead of riding will cost you time on the road. But how were you planning to get across Sundering Canyon? The bridge is still closed."

"And you won't have my songcraft to help this time," Veronica added.

Trina went on, "We have secret ways down into and up out of the canyon on both sides. I can get you across without detection, which will save you a lot of time compared to going around by the coast."

Azai considered it for a moment, then let out a breath. "All right," he said, not very graciously. "But we're leaving today."

Kiarana nodded. "This is a good plan. I will accompany Trina for now. But we have not met for the last time, Zevadiah of Aeltas." She gave him a searching look. "And I have not forgotten our bargain."

Zev hadn't forgotten it either, but it was far from his first priority. He was relieved when Kiarana made no more mention of it during the whirlwind of activity that followed the travelers' decision.

Before Zev knew it, Azai had sold his spare knife—a beautiful piece of craftsmanship worth more than the entire stall of the merchant who acquired it—and organized a vehicle. The trio was ready to depart, Azai stony-faced and Trina regretful. Kiarana showed no particular emotion.

"I'm sad I don't have more time to explore the city," Trina said.

"Let's hope you get another chance," Veronica said kindly.

"Yes, let's," Trina agreed. "Please say hello to Marieke for me." She sent a cheeky grin at Zev. "Tell her to hang on to that man of hers."

Zev didn't dignify the sally with a response. He was too focused on his brother. He strode up to Azai and put a hand on his shoulder.

"May the ground fly swiftly under your feet," he said quietly.

Azai hesitated, his face hard to read. "And may your labors prosper," he said at last. The words were familiar, but the tone was off. Zev wasn't sure his brother truly meant the blessing. But there was no time for more. Trina and her "little sister" climbed into the carriage, and Azai took the reins. With a backward glance that seemed to encompass the girls more than Zev, he urged the horses forward and disappeared down the cobbled street.

"And we're down to three," Tarenne commented, not seeming especially troubled.

"Four," Zev corrected flatly. "Marieke is still in the city, doing her part of the plan exactly as discussed."

"We hope so." Tarenne shrugged.

"One of us should really find out," Veronica said. "She needs to be warned about the talisman Jade has her hands on. Maybe I can try to speak to Kaine again."

Zev frowned. "I don't know. You were lucky to get away with it once, it seems like tempting fate to do it again. What if someone recognizes you from when you took a message to Instructor Oriana last time?"

"It is a risk," Veronica acknowledged.

"I can go," Tarenne said unexpectedly. "I've never been to the council complex. No one will recognize me. I could find this Kaine and see if he can sneak me in to see Marieke wherever they're holding her."

Zev and Veronica exchanged a look, the singer looking as suspicious as Zev felt about this offer from Tarenne. She didn't usually put herself forward to help with anything.

"Surely given your identity, it's too dangerous for you to go anywhere near the council," said Veronica cautiously.

"I don't see why." Tarenne's reply was matter-of-fact. "There's no reason whatsoever for anyone to guess who I am from looking at me. Especially since, as far as we know, they're not even aware I exist."

"True," said Zev slowly.

The whole thing made him uneasy. He'd been avoiding Tarenne as much as he could since she'd spoken to him their last morning on the road, when she'd made her outrageous suggestion. A suggestion he didn't believe would work. Or rather, he didn't want to believe it could work.

But in this instance, he didn't have a better suggestion. He certainly couldn't wander into the council complex, and he was reluctant to send Veronica into danger.

"All right," he said. "Let's try."

FIFTEEN

Marieke

Marieke paced her room impatiently, casting yet another glance at the small patch of sky that showed through her window. Surely it must be close to noon. Would the guard change never come?

It had been several days since Instructor Oriana offered to teach her storytelling song, and the few lessons they'd managed had been fascinating. Marieke felt like a whole new world of magic was opening up to her, and she could see the instructor coming alive as well. She must miss her classes since her suspension. And even when she was still teaching, she hadn't been allowed to include the questioning aptitude. She claimed she was rusty on the topic, but to Marieke, she seemed a wealth of knowledge.

The only trouble was, Marieke couldn't practice what she was learning unless Kaine was on shift. He was doing all he could to make himself available, but there was still a limit to how many hours of a day he could guard her door. And they didn't want him to push too hard and make the head guard suspicious.

Still, he'd told her the day before that he was fairly sure he'd be able to take the following afternoon shift. And with any luck, he'd bring Instructor Oriana with him.

Marieke paced back across the room, running over their last session in her mind. She'd been surprised by how relevant her agricultural songcraft had been. Instructor Oriana really was an excellent teacher—she'd explained that she liked to try to frame her lessons in the context of her students' existing areas of specialty. And the skills Marieke already had in assessing the contours of the land could be used in coaxing that land to communicate to her both its current state and its recent experiences.

It was fascinating, and she was certainly glad of the distraction. She'd still heard nothing about a hearing date, and there was only so long she could stay in one room without information or activity and not lose her mind.

Not that she was entirely without activity. Solomon had undertaken some study for her regarding the normal procedure at hearings, and had used Kaine's assistance to get notes to Marieke detailing the information he thought she might most need to know. Comprehending and committing to memory the contents of those notes had occupied many idle hours.

But those notes were far less captivating than Instructor Oriana's training, especially now that she'd announced that from now on, they would narrow their studies to the questioning craft. Like Solomon, her priority was preparing Marieke for the hearing. The decision suited Marieke just fine, given that questioning craft was the skill she most wanted to cultivate.

She glanced out the window again. When would Kaine arrive? If only she could tell Zev about all she was learning. He was constantly in her thoughts, their separation as big a source of anxiety as the looming hearing. It just felt wrong to be apart, like part of her was missing. Did Zev know about the attack on Tarandon? She could only imagine his distress if he did. And it only made her feel worse to know that he was almost certainly worrying about her. She felt guilty that he was likely picturing her locked in a dungeon—and torturing himself over it—when she was actually in a comfortable guest suite.

And what kind of conditions were he and the others facing? Had they even been able to find somewhere safe to sleep in the city? Things had looked pretty bad as she'd been marched through. Not to mention none of them had expected it to take this long for her to be tried. Zev and Azai had brought considerable resources from home, but they'd been on the road so long. Their supply of coins must be dwindling sadly by now, if they were paying for lodging all this time.

A knock at the door brought Marieke out of these thoughts, and she hurried forward.

"Yes?"

"It's me." Kaine's voice sounded strange. "There's someone here to see you."

"Excellent." Marieke folded her hands together, eager to start the lesson with Instructor Oriana. "I'm expecting her, send her in."

The door swung open, revealing an uncertain Kaine.

"What is it?" Marieke asked, realizing at once that something was off.

"It's not Instructor Oriana," Kaine said. Whoever he was talking about was out of sight in the corridor.

"Who is it?" Marieke asked, her tension returning. If it wasn't the instructor, why was he speaking so freely?

Before he could answer her question, a soft meow had both of them looking down in surprise as Tommy slunk around Kaine's legs and into Marieke's room.

"This is my visitor?" Marieke wasn't sure whether to laugh. How in the world had Tommy found her here?

"No, of course not," said Kaine, nonplussed. "Where did it come from?"

"He's usually not far away," came a voice from out of sight. "Even if you can't always see him."

"Tarenne?" Marieke moved closer to the door, her change in angle bringing the other girl into view. "What are you doing here?"

"I came to speak with you," Tarenne said, as if the question was foolish. "Are you going to let me in?"

"I hope I didn't err in bringing her here," Kaine said to Marieke. "She approached me when I was on patrol in the city, and your friend Veronica was with her. They said they needed to get access to you."

"Thank you," said Marieke quickly. "You did right as far as I'm concerned. She's part of our traveling group."

Tarenne gave a nod that was barely polite, obviously not interested in pleasantries with the guard. "So I can come in?"

"Yes, of course." Marieke stepped back to allow Tarenne to enter. Kaine shut the door behind them, remaining in the corridor.

For a moment, there was an awkward silence.

"Is it safe for you to be here?" Marieke asked at last.

Tarenne shrugged. "Is any of what we're doing safe? No one knows who I am."

Marieke nodded. "Well, it's very rare that anyone comes except for the guards, and Kaine has only just started his shift, so we should be all right. But it's possible of course that someone might come to notify me of a hearing time."

"I'll keep it quick, then, and then we'll leave the complex straight away."

She'd lowered herself into a chair, and Tommy took it as an invitation to leap lightly onto her lap.

"You weren't questioned coming into the complex?"

Marieke asked curiously, sitting down on the bed so she was opposite Tarenne.

The other girl shook her head. "The courtyard is open to the public again. I attached myself to a group coming in for the daily audience with a council member—an opportunity to air grievances which is, as far as I can tell, completely pointless as it leads to nothing whatsoever—and peeled off to meet Kaine at the agreed-upon place. He brought me in a back door and straight here. Coming in was the easy part. The hard part was finding Kaine. Veronica and I have been watching for a week, waiting to catch him outside the council complex to set this up. But he almost never leaves."

"Yes, he's been doing his utmost to get assigned to guard me," Marieke said. "I suppose that as a result he's on external duties much less frequently."

Tarenne grunted as she looked around the room.

"You seem perfectly comfortable."

There was a hint of accusation in the observation, and Marieke felt her cheeks heat. "I'm definitely better off than I expected," she agreed. "I'm not allowed to leave the room or use songcraft, but I've been made comfortable and fed well."

"I'm sure the others will be glad to hear it," Tarenne said.

Her choice of words left Marieke with the impression that she personally wasn't particularly glad. But perhaps Marieke was being too sensitive.

"Is everyone all right?" Marieke asked. "Are you all safe?"

"Zev and Veronica were safe enough when I left," Tarenne said.

"Not Azai?" Marieke frowned.

"He left," said Tarenne. She leaned forward. "This is the update I'm supposed to give you."

Marieke matched her posture, her heart sinking. Had Azai had a dire enough falling out with the rest of the group to actually leave them? Perhaps she shouldn't be surprised. He'd been cantankerous since Veronica overheard his embarrassing suspicion about being ensnared.

"A week ago, the day you were arrested," Tarenne started, "Zev was approached outside the council gate by a girl called Trina."

"Trina?" Marieke repeated, astonished. "From the rebels living in Sundering Canyon?"

Tarenne nodded. "So you do remember her. Yes, that's the one. She was accompanied by someone she called her little sister, but when we took them back to the inn, the small one identified herself as an elf."

She paused, leaning back a little and scratching behind Tommy's ear.

"That was...a surprise."

"I can imagine," said Marieke, her eyes wide. "What was an elf doing all the way out here in Ondford?"

"She came with a warning for us," Tarenne said. "She's some kind of leader, or leader's apprentice."

"It was Kiarana?" Marieke guessed.

Tarenne nodded. "That's the one. She doesn't want Jade to succeed, and I guess she thought you and Zev were her likeliest way to stop her. So she came to warn you that Jade has gotten her hands on a talisman from another elf. They've been working on a development that can turn one type of matter into another with a touch from a talisman. Zev said you saw it in their city, with glass of some kind."

"Yes," said Marieke, struggling to keep up with all the implications of the matter-of-fact account. "Water turned into glass, or at least that's what it looked like."

"Well, the one Jade has can turn whatever it touches into fire. Our best guess is she plans to use it on the council and academy complex of buildings."

Marieke stared at her. "She can set it all on fire with one touch of a talisman?"

"No." Tarenne shook her head. "Not set it on fire. Turn the stone *into* fire. There would be no structure left, or at least no stone structure left. The volume of the fire would be unbelievable, and anyone inside would be instantly trapped inside a raging inferno."

Marieke looked slowly from the stone floor to the stone walls of her room. "That would be a horrific disaster."

"Yes." Tarenne spoke in her usual unemotional way. "I doubt anyone actually in the building at the time would survive it."

"But that's so many people," Marieke said. She ran a hand through her hair. "We have to warn the council."

"Do you think?" Tarenne asked skeptically. "Would they believe you? And even if they did, would you trust them to respond appropriately to the risk? They haven't shown themselves very capable in that area so far."

"We can't just do nothing," Marieke said. "You said you learned this a week ago? Who knows when it will be too late to stop it?"

"Well, the consensus of the group seems to be that we should try to stop Jade and Clancy before they reach the city," Tarenne said. "But we don't know where they are now."

"Actually." Marieke bit her lip. "There's something the others should know. I think Jade's in Aeltas. Apparently there was a terrible storm, and—"

"We know about that," Tarenne cut her off. "Trina told us. That's why Azai left, to go and try to help Aeltas. But Veronica and Zev both seem to think that Ondford is still Jade's real target."

"I have no doubt it is," said Marieke heavily.

"In fact," Tarenne went on calmly, "we all think that the

only reason Jade attacked Tarandon was to try to lure Zev back there, away from you and your quest to help Oleand. We think she was trying to make the interests of the two countries conflict so that Zev would have to choose."

"The same thought occurred to me as well," Marieke said, her voice little more than a miserable whisper.

"Well, Azai chose Aeltas without hesitation, and left at once," Tarenne said. "Zev and Veronica stayed here because they think we shouldn't accept the game Jade is playing. But *I* think we should beat her at it. I think instead of pitting the countries against each other, we should combine the power of the two."

"Yes, I agree," said Marieke. "That's always been our—"

"No, I don't think you understand what I'm saying," Tarenne said, once again cutting her off. "I don't just mean working together. I mean an actual, unarguable alliance, that will literally and symbolically combine the power—by which I mean the heartsong—of the two countries. I think that would be stronger than what Jade has taught Clancy to do with his."

Marieke frowned. "I don't understand. What are you suggesting?"

"A marriage alliance," Tarenne said simply. "Between the two royal bloodlines."

"You...you mean..."

"Specifically, between Zev and myself, yes," Tarenne confirmed.

Marieke stared at the other girl, her ears ringing as the floor seemed to fall out from beneath her.

"I...I don't think Zev will agree to that."

"He hasn't yet," Tarenne said. "But he should. I can tell he knows he should. Think about it, Marieke. In the past, the royals and singers didn't intermarry. They kept their power separate, and with good reason. Our current system shows that it's not good for one group to have all the power. By having the monarchs and the singers separate, they could balance each other out."

Marieke frowned. But they hadn't balanced each other out, not well. Tarenne didn't give her a chance to object, however.

"Political alliances, on the other hand, were common. And effective. When the coup happened, the monarchs should have worked together to stop it. They likely would have if the singers hadn't been one step ahead in combining their own forces across the border."

Marieke raised a hand to her head as Tarenne went relentlessly on.

"I know you and Zev care for each other, but what future do you envision? Your whole focus is saving Oleand, and whatever he's telling himself to the contrary, his place is and will always be in Aeltas."

"You're from Oleand, same as me," Marieke pointed out.

Tarenne nodded. "I know I am. But I'm a younger sibling. Traditionally, they often married outside their kingdoms and left their own land to form an alliance. If Zev and I committed our lives to one another, my heartsong would enhance his. The natural power of both countries would be combined, and we could use it to save both Aeltas and Oleand. And not just today. Jade won't be the last threat the countries face. Power like I'm describing would be potent, in a way marriage alliances of the past never were, because they didn't know what we know now about activating our heartsong."

"I...I don't know enough about heartsong to know whether what you're saying makes sense," Marieke said.

"It does make sense." Tarenne certainly sounded confident. "It's not about romance or attraction, Marieke. It's about strength."

"But Zev and I are stronger together." Marieke's arguments

felt weak, like she was trying to convince herself rather than Tarenne. "We both feel it."

"I'm not denying the power of combining your songcraft and his heartsong," Tarenne said. "But you can still do that. Jade has proved with Clancy that a romantic relationship isn't necessary in order for heartsong to enhance a singer's magic. Imagine if we had both types of power at our disposal. If you really care about saving our country, you'll want all the forces possible available to us."

"Of course I care," said Marieke. "It's just…"

"You care about your own happiness more?" Tarenne asked brutally.

Marieke fell silent, mutiny and guilt warring within her. She couldn't give Zev up. It was unthinkable. But was Tarenne right?

"Zev is reluctant," Tarenne said. "And I understand why. It doesn't bother me, which should prove that it's not about romance for me. It's about a secure future."

"For you or for Oleand?" Marieke shot back.

"Both," shrugged Tarenne. "But Zev isn't going to agree unless you give him permission to think clearly. Otherwise, he'll be conflicted forever. I saw it when Azai left. Zev knew that Azai was right, that his first duty should be to his own country. But he couldn't let himself leave to defend Aeltas because he'd be letting you down. My proposal is the same. He needs to know that you'll support him doing what he has to, even if it's not what you would choose in other circumstances."

Marieke was silent.

"He's not happy," Tarenne pressed. "He's been ill-at-ease since Azai left. The cost of being away from Aeltas is high for him now that Aeltas is in trouble, too. I often see him staring off into the distance, always southward, obviously questioning if he made the right choice."

"All right." Marieke held up a hand. "You've said enough. Let me think through it all."

Tarenne nodded. "Think quickly. We don't know what tomorrow will bring." She stood. "I'll tell the others that you're safe and comfortable. We've heard that there's to be a public hearing. We're watching to see when it's announced. If we can get in, we'll be there."

Marieke nodded, barely hearing her. There was probably more she wanted Tarenne to tell Zev and Veronica, but she couldn't focus on anything but the other girl's startling proposal. She waited only until Kaine had closed and locked the door behind Tarenne before she lowered her head into her hands.

Was Tarenne telling the truth? Was an alliance between her and Zev the best way to protect both countries? If Marieke stood against it, would she be putting her own heart above Oleand and everyone whose lives might be destroyed by Jade?

Marieke's thoughts were still in turmoil when Instructor Oriana arrived half an hour later.

"Marieke." The instructor looked somber as she took in Marieke's demeanor. "So you've heard? Are you nervous?"

"Heard what?" Marieke asked, dazed.

"The hearing is set for tomorrow."

That got Marieke's attention. "Tomorrow? So soon?"

The instructor nodded. "I think they want to give people as little time as possible in the hope that it's not too crowded an event."

"Yes," said Marieke distractedly. "There's something to be said for that." It was one weight off her mind, at least. She'd been worried that when the public hearing was officially announced, the news might reach her parents. Now they definitely wouldn't have time to travel to the capital for her hearing, which was a relief. She didn't want them to see her tried like a criminal.

She looked up to see Instructor Oriana frowning at her. "If you didn't know about the hearing, what had you looking so anxious?"

"Nothing," said Marieke quickly. "A personal matter. No, wait!" Memory came back. "There is something. Instructor, I've learned something about Jade's plan. Something really bad."

"How did you learn it?" Instructor Oriana asked, confused.

"Never mind that," said Marieke. She told the instructor what Tarenne had said about the matter-transforming talisman.

"But how is it possible for her to have such a powerful talisman? None have been made in generations. We've lost the skill."

"Not everyone has lost the skill," Marieke said. "Just trust me, it's possible." She searched the instructor's worried face. "What should we do? Do we tell the council?"

"I think you should tell everyone," said Instructor Oriana. "Tomorrow."

"At the hearing?" Marieke considered it. "As long as it's not too dangerous to wait that long."

"You're unlikely to get an audience with the council before then even if you asked," the instructor pointed out.

Marieke nodded. "What about you? Will you be at the hearing?"

"Of course," said Instructor Oriana. "And I won't be there alone. I've been doing my utmost to spread the word among anyone at the academy who's sympathetic. I expect a huge academy presence at the hearing, and most of them will be on your side, Mari."

"Thank you," said Marieke, a lump in her throat. It meant a great deal that the instructor was championing her.

"I don't recall there ever being such tension between the council and the academy," Instructor Oriana commented. "It's sad, but given the state of the council, it's necessary. We should never have let any force or interest compromise our duty to teach the truth in our classes. And any good scholar will agree with that position."

Marieke remembered what Kaine had said, about the academy being like a bonfire waiting to be lit. Would her hearing be the spark that lit it? Was it possible that if things came to a fight, some at the academy would have her back? There was a lot of combined power of songcraft in that institution.

"This will be our last session before your hearing," Instructor Oriana said. "So apply yourself, Marieke. Who knows what might depend on your ability to ask the right questions when you get your chance?"

Marieke nodded nervously, rolling up her sleeves. Tarenne's plans for Zev were still in the back of her mind, screaming for her attention, but she tried not to let them distract her. Too much was at stake.

Which was exactly Tarenne's point.

How had it come to this, with everything seeming to depend on her making the right choices? If only she knew the right path to take.

SIXTEEN

Zev

"Zev." Veronica's hiss came from the side. "Pull your hood further over your eyes. Your posters are still up."

Swallowing his frustration, Zev did as instructed, not breaking stride as they moved through the crowded streets. It went against every inclination to be hiding like this. Today Marieke faced a host of serious criminal allegations, and he was expected to stand by while she was accused, hidden in the crowd as if he wanted to escape whatever fate was decided for her?

They'd only found out the time of the hearing early that morning. The council had fulfilled its obligations about notice for the hearing to the bare minimum. Clearly they didn't want it to be well attended.

Zev didn't know about the rest of the jostling crowd, but for his part, if they wanted to keep him out, they would have to strike him down altogether.

He cast a glance at Tarenne as they approached the council and academy complex. She'd been her usual unconcerned self since her return from the council the day before. She claimed to have spoken to Marieke and found her well and safe, but she'd been maddeningly reluctant to give details. Zev was sure she was being intentionally uncommunicative, and he felt uneasy every time he thought about it. What exactly had she said to Marieke?

Worrying about Tarenne was the last thing he needed on his mind. The last week had been near unbearable as it was. He didn't handle idleness well, and there had been nothing for him to do but wait. At least Veronica and Tarenne had spent time each day trying to intercept Kaine. He'd been lying low, gaining nothing but the occasional gossip he gleaned from the market.

And worse than the idleness was the worry. Worry about Marieke taking on criminal charges, worry about Azai, who must have crossed the border days ago, worry about Aeltas, now the target of Jade's malice due to his own actions. The worry went hand in hand with guilt as well. He woke in the morning feeling guilty as he wondered whether Azai was right about Zev's priorities, and went to bed feeling guilty about refusing to talk to Tarenne about her ideas. Her constant, subtle campaign to convince him they needed an alliance of their heartsong was overwhelming.

And, he thought dryly, as something brushed against his leg with a touch too gentle for the jumble of the crowd, he'd been worried Tommy would give their position away, coming and going from the dilapidated inn at all hours. Apparently he'd even accompanied Tarenne on her visit to Marieke.

At least he didn't have to worry about being found now. One way or another, the hearing would bring everything to a head. No more hiding, and what a relief it would be.

The throng trying to push their way through the gates of the council complex was intense. Zev leaped lightly up onto the row of stone from which the iron bars of the fence protruded, to better see over their heads.

"It looks like the hearing is set up in the open space

between the council and academy buildings," he said. "It's a raised platform, and there are barriers set up from the gate to that area, to channel everyone toward the hearing and keep them from overwhelming the rest of the complex."

Veronica nodded. "Makes sense. With so many people interested, they wouldn't want to hold it inside the building. They'd be risking a riot."

"The public gallery is full," a council employee was calling over the crowd. "No more space."

Protests sounded on all sides, and Zev and his companions weren't the only ones who continued to press forward in defiance of instructions.

"We want to see the culprit brought to justice!" someone called from behind them.

"End the blight!" another agreed.

"The council are the culprits," grumbled someone just next to Zev, not loud enough for the council employee to hear. "They're not doing anything about it, are they?"

"Reckon they'll use this girl as a scapegoat?" the man's companion asked.

"Maybe."

"Not while I'm breathing," Zev muttered. He caught Veronica's attention with a jerk of his head. "Come on."

Taking advantage of an argument between the council employee and another member of the public, they pushed around the side of the group and into the straight path between the barriers. A drop of rain fell onto Zev's arm as he pushed his way through the crowd.

He glanced up to see that the sky, which had been a tranquil blue when he'd risen that morning, was filling with dark clouds.

"Not ideal weather for an outdoor hearing, is it?" Veronica commented.

Zev just grunted. "Are you ready?" he asked her.

She nodded. "Like we've discussed. I'll watch for your signal. But don't be hasty, Zev. If we try to break her free, we'll only have one chance at it. This is the council's own building, there are many more powerful singers here than me. As soon as I use my songcraft, they'll be on me."

"I understand," Zev said. "I won't start anything unless I'm sure it's necessary."

"There she is."

Tarenne broke into their discussion, and Zev spun to see a trio of figures approaching the platform. Marieke looked small and vulnerable between the two guards, and Zev had to fight an impulse to run to her side. Her hands were bound in front of her like a true criminal, and her face was pale. She was poised, though, and as they drew closer, he realized with relief that one of the guards was Kaine.

To his anger, he heard many in the crowd heckling. Clearly there were plenty who believed the story the council had tried to sell by use of the wanted posters, and blamed Marieke for the blight on the land.

Marieke didn't seem to have spotted them, but Zev saw her eyes dart across the crowd before she relaxed slightly. He followed her gaze to see Instructor Oriana standing at the center of a sea of others in robes of the same design as hers. Others from the academy, then. He noticed that they all looked alert and ready for action, unlike the curious, staring crowd. What exactly were they ready for?

Marieke was led to a wooden chair which had been placed at the center of the dais. It faced three rows of elevated chairs where it looked like the full Council of Singers had gathered.

"Marieke of Oleand." One of the councilors stood as soon as Marieke sat in her chair. "Please rise."

She did so.

"You have been summoned to answer the following charges: escaping lawful custody, damage to public property, collusion with enemies of Oleand, sedition, treachery, and public nuisance."

"It's quite the list, isn't it?" Veronica murmured.

Zev said nothing. He wasn't happy with their position. He could barely hear what was happening, they were so far back in the standing mob that formed the public gallery. And he wanted Marieke to be able to see them, to know that they were there. Not caring about the muted protests of those he pushed past, he started shuffling forward through the press, Veronica and Tarenne doing their best to follow in his wake.

"Do you understand the charges?" the councilor asked.

"Yes," said Marieke, and Zev felt a surge of pride at how confidently her voice carried.

"And it is at your invocation that the matter is to be decided at a public hearing."

"That's correct," Marieke agreed.

The councilor then turned and addressed the crowd. "It is the right of the accused to be tried publicly. That does not mean that members of the public have the right to interfere with the hearing. You are present as witnesses—any disruptive behavior will cause the person responsible to be removed."

Glancing around, Zev saw that the employees at the gate had succeeded in stopping more people from attending, and guards had now moved into position to surround the entire hearing. There were a lot of them, too, and they were clearly at the ready to step in if anyone caused trouble.

"My name is Councilor Bernard," the councilor went on, "and I will be conducting this hearing." His gaze returned to Marieke. "Do you accept the charges?"

"I do not," said Marieke.

"None of them?" Another councilor stood, and Zev realized with a flash of anger that it was the Head Instructor.

Councilor Bernard didn't look pleased at the interruption. Perhaps the Head Instructor had known that forcing himself in was the only way he'd be allowed to speak.

"You deny even that you're guilty of escaping custody and damaging public property in the process?" Instructor Rafael challenged.

Marieke stood with straight back. "I deny that I committed a punishable offense, given I acted in reasonable defense of my life, which creates an exception to most crimes."

His brow darkened. "Reasonable defense? You were lawfully detained, and you forcefully broke your way out in defiance of the council."

"For what crime was I detained, Instructor?" Marieke asked.

"You are not asking the questions," the instructor said angrily.

"But surely it's not a difficult question to answer," Marieke insisted. "At least, if the detention was lawful, as you claim."

Zev felt Veronica shift beside him, and he noticed muttering passing through the group surrounding Instructor Oriana as well.

"What is it?" he murmured to Veronica.

She just shook her head, her gaze rapt as she focused on Marieke.

"If Councilor Rafael will resume his seat," Councilor Bernard said shortly, "we can proceed with our hearing."

He shot the Head Instructor a warning look.

"He didn't deserve to be rescued," Zev muttered in annoyance. "He was cornered."

"It doesn't matter," Veronica said encouragingly. "It was clear that he had no answer to the question. It's a good start."

Zev didn't reply, tightening his hand over the hilt of the dagger hidden in his belt as he listened to Councilor Bernard resume his address.

"You have indicated that you do not accept the charge of escaping lawful custody," he went on. "I have here witness accounts from multiple council employees, all of which corroborate the allegation that you forcefully escaped the council's holding rooms with the assistance of two Aeltan men who did not appear to have singing abilities."

Zev's eyes flew to Marieke, whose face remained calm as the councilor read out the time and date of their escape, and offered her the chance to testify in her own defense. How would she answer? Would she explain all about Jade, and the reason she'd had to escape to save her life?

But Marieke took a different approach altogether, one that made Zev think she'd been studying carefully during her isolation.

"I beg your pardon," Marieke said, her voice perfectly polite. "But is escaping lawful custody the first matter to be heard today? I understood that standard practice was to address the most severe offense first. Surely an offense such as sedition or treachery would be considered more severe than escaping lawful custody."

The crowd's murmuring increased at this unexpected reply. The rain was falling harder now, but it didn't seem to deter anyone. The public gallery remained as packed as ever.

"It is not for you to order the conduct of this hearing."

Instructor Rafael was once again on his feet, and once again he was reprimanded by Councilor Bernard.

"I have the hearing in hand, Councilor." Councilor Bernard spoke loudly to be heard over the rain. His voice was commanding, but his frown was troubled to Zev's eye. Had he realized he was departing from procedure in the order of offenses prior to Marieke's challenge?

Unlike Councilor Bernard, Marieke looked pleased by the interruption.

"It's not my intention to order the hearing, Instructor. Is it not my right to have due process followed? Am I in some way exempt from normal regulations? Is that why I was detained on that previous occasion—lawfully, you claim—without any charge or suggestion of a hearing? Can you give me any reason why I would be exempt?"

Her words caused a ripple through the crowd, and Zev noticed that it was most pronounced among the group surrounding Instructor Oriana. Veronica also made a satisfied noise next to him.

"That was strong. She's improved since we last practiced. I think she's learning to follow the thread of the magic and build, question to question."

"What are you talking about?" Zev asked, frowning.

But he had his answer from the stands above him. This time, Instructor Rafael seemed to be speaking through another councilor, the man next to him standing with a subtle push from the Head Instructor.

"She's using magic, Councilor!" he said sharply, gesturing at Marieke. "I'm sure I'm not the only one who felt it. It is a serious offense for an accused to use magic during a hearing!"

"I beg your pardon," Marieke repeated her earlier words, although her polite tone had an edge to it now. "But every single person present can attest to the fact that each word from my mouth was spoken. Unless I'm mistaken," her tone told Zev that she knew she wasn't, "the law states that it is prohibited for an accused to *sing* during the course of a hearing."

"That's true," Councilor Bernard said slowly. "I did,

however, feel the movement of the magic to which the councilor refers." He scanned the crowd, raising his voice still further to be heard over the growing downpour. "If any member of the public present today is colluding with the accused and singing on her behalf, you will be found and charges brought against you."

"No one's singing for me," said Marieke. "The magic moved because I was asking questions, and I have the questioning aptitude."

Comprehension came over Councilor Bernard's face, but it was nothing to the horror that had entered Instructor Rafael's expression. Marieke hurried to pursue her advantage.

"That particular aptitude craft is a well-known part of the storytelling discipline, even if it is rare. Can the Head Instructor explain why it's not familiar to everyone? Why was this important discipline discontinued as an area of study?"

"Ooh, the magic liked that question," Veronica said beside Zev.

Councilor Bernard apparently didn't like the question as much. "Marieke," he said, frowning, "I must remind you that you are here to answer questions, not ask them. And while you are correct that technically only singing is prohibited, if you insist on interacting with magic during your testimony, you are not obeying the spirit of the law."

"Would you say the spirit of the law has been obeyed in how I've been treated?" Marieke asked. She let the question hang in the air for a moment—a moment that was charged with magic for those who could sense it, judging by Veronica's palpable delight—then went on. "I can't help that I have the questioning aptitude. It's simply something I was born with. I'm entitled to speak in my own defense. If the magic responds to reasonable questions that are an appropriate part of my defense, how can I help that?"

"The Head Instructor should answer the original question!"

The shout came from someone standing near Instructor Oriana. "Why is the questioning craft not taught? Why did he censor our studies?"

Instructor Rafael's face was red with anger, and perhaps something else. "Are you going to allow this?" he demanded of Councilor Bernard. "You said you had the hearing in hand!"

"Disruption from the crowd will not be tolerated," Councilor Bernard called in the direction of the academy group. "This is your last warning." He turned to Marieke. "No one is claiming that you are to be blamed or punished for having this questioning aptitude."

"Are you sure no one claims that?"

Marieke's pointed gaze was directed at the Head Instructor. Judging by Veronica's gleeful chuckle and the jeers of the group from the academy, the question was as pertinent as previous ones had been.

"I've never experienced it like this before," Veronica murmured. "No one in my cohort had the questioning aptitude, it's really rare. This is incredible to witness, I wish you could feel how the magic is growing, guiding every word she says."

"Enough," said Councilor Bernard, trying valiantly to keep the hearing from descending into a spectacle. His tone said that he'd had enough of playacting. "No more posturing, Marieke. You can speak in your own defense without posing questions."

"Very well." Marieke nodded, and Zev recognized the hint of steel in her frame as she straightened. "I won't ask questions. I'll make statements. Such as this one: the Head Instructor struck the questioning craft from the storytelling discipline after a former student named Jade used it to discover that he was embroiled in multiple and egregious lies that threaten the very fabric of our society."

Instructor Rafael rose to his feet, but his furious protest was cut off by a roar from the academy group. The rain was hammering them all now, but somehow Marieke's voice rose at an impossible volume, her words still clearly audible.

"These lies weren't of his making, but he perpetuated them. Him and others on the council. The lies call into question the very legitimacy of the council, and they are the reason our land is dying. Some at least in the council know this, and they refuse to act to protect Oleand because doing so would expose them."

"Look!" Veronica pointed to where Instructor Oriana stood. Her mouth was open in what was clearly a song, although the sound was lost in the growing storm—probably for the best, in Instructor Oriana's case. "She's ignoring the warning and using songcraft to amplify Marieke's voice."

Veronica was right. Zev had been too focused on Marieke to see the scale of the drama unfolding in the crowd, but now he looked, he saw that the instructor's defiance hadn't gone unnoticed. Council guards were attempting to get to her, and the rest of the students and instructors who'd accompanied her—one of whom he recognized as Solomon—had formed a protective square around her. Their mouths were also wide in songs he couldn't hear as they openly battled the guards. As he watched, their numbers seemed to swell, Instructor Oriana soon at the center of a small army of defiant academy members.

"It's all falling apart," Veronica said, dazed. "The academy is turning against the council. Both institutions have a lot of magical power at their disposal—I just hope this doesn't turn into a bloodbath."

Zev pulled out his blade, holding it against his body where it was inconspicuous but ready. "So far I don't see any of the rebels actually inflicting much injury. They're mainly just keeping the guards back from Instructor Oriana."

Veronica nodded, her eyes on Marieke. "They're scholars,

not soldiers. But the council will regret it if they underestimate them. Keep going, Marieke. Don't stop now."

Marieke didn't seem to have any intention of stopping. She'd continued over the top of their quiet conversation, and she continued still.

"We've all been lied to about the past. The singers' coup wasn't bloodless. The monarchs were slaughtered as they attempted to flee to Providore. The signs of the massacre are still visible in Port Taran—that's how Sundering Canyon was formed. And when they were killed, a curse was unleashed. That curse has been activated against Oleand by Jade, the very student the Head Instructor expelled for threatening to expose his lies."

"A nice summary, really," Veronica said approvingly.

Guards had converged on Marieke by now as well, but none of them seemed able to get to her. Apparently Instructor Oriana was doing more than just amplifying Marieke's voice. Zev realized that she looked pale and drawn, and wondered how much longer her energy would last. She must be wielding incredibly powerful magic, because some of the guards were singing as well, and their efforts still hadn't broken through her defense of Marieke.

Zev moved through the crowd, which was in uproar, Veronica and Tarenne close behind him. As he drew nearer the action, he realized that Kaine was part of the group of guards.

"Kaine's magic is fighting theirs!" Veronica gasped. "I don't think they've even realized it, look how confused they are." She closed her eyes for a moment. "It all feels chaotic, I don't think he's the only one secretly fighting against his fellows."

"The council has claimed it has left no stone unturned in trying to solve the blight," Marieke was calling, ignoring the chaos around her, "but one thing they've refused to try is the truth. Oleand deserves better. Oleand deserves the truth, and I intend to tell it, even if that makes me a criminal."

Councilor Bernard had stopped trying to intervene. He stood on the dais, watching on with a stunned expression, apparently unsure what to do. Zev had the impression he wasn't one of the council members who'd known about the lies. It seemed Instructor Oriana was right that not everyone had knowingly participated in the deception.

Zev had almost reached Marieke, and his passage through the crowd suddenly became easier. A painful blow to the head made him realize why. The rain had turned to hailstones, and they were larger than any he'd ever seen. Many in the public gallery were running for cover, shouting in alarm.

Marieke raised her arms—hands still bound—over her head in protection, but otherwise continued speaking unchecked.

"Jade might be the evil mind behind what Oleand is suffering, but the council handed her the weapons to destroy us. Some of the royals survived, and their power over the land remains. She found a way to harness that power to turn Oleand against itself."

Zev heard Tarenne draw in a quick breath, and he saw a few shocked faces. But most people weren't listening anymore. The scene had descended into complete disarray.

Suddenly a small figure barreled through the empty space left by the fleeing crowd, leaping up onto the dais and racing toward Marieke before bouncing off the invisible barrier Instructor Oriana was still maintaining.

"Ouch!"

Zev was close enough to the dais now to hear the cry, and with a start, he recognized the speaker.

"Trina?" he shouted over the battering hail.

"Yes, we've come to warn you all!" Trina cried, swiveling to find him in the crowd. "You have to get ready!"

We? Had the elf heir returned as well? Zev wasn't sure the crowd could handle another shocking revelation of that magnitude.

But the other woman who fought her way to the edge of the dais was very much human.

"Who's that?" Veronica called beside him.

"Svetlana." Zev could hardly believe it. "She's the leader of the monarchist group." What had brought her out of hiding and back to Ondford with Trina?

He pushed to Svetlana's side, grabbing her shoulder roughly.

"What are you doing here?" he shouted, his other arm over his head in an attempt to keep off the hail. A hailstone struck his forearm, large enough to make him wince. "Do you have more news about Aeltas? Has Jade done another attack?"

Svetlana shook her head. "It's not Aeltas you need to worry about. This storm is barely beginning. It's going to get much worse."

"This storm..." Zev's eyes widened. How had he let himself get so immersed in the drama of the trial that he'd failed to recognize the significance of the hail storm? His grip on Svetlana's shoulder tightened. "You're saying Jade is here?"

"If what Trina told me is right, she will be any minute," Svetlana said. "We've been traveling as fast as we could and staying only just in front of the storm all the way from the border." She shook her head. "I think we're going to find that it's left a trail of destruction."

"Zev!" Veronica and Tarenne had stayed further back, but they wrestled to him now, wading through hailstones. "This storm isn't natural. I can feel the magic fueling it. I think it's—"

"Jade," Zev finished grimly.

His eyes flew to Marieke, still at the center of the dais, several guards still attempting to reach her. Zev had to get to her side before Jade arrived. Of course Jade would choose this moment. It was perfect for her. Maximum people gathered in the vicinity—she'd probably expected them to be in the building rather than alongside it, but that wouldn't prevent a lot of people from dying. And the council gathered together so they could see her, and know she was the architect of their destruction. It wouldn't even matter that she'd doused the area with the rain beforehand, because she wasn't planning to set the building on fire. She was planning to turn the building *into* fire.

Zev grabbed the edge of the dais, ready to vault up, when Tarenne's scream made him pause.

"Clancy!"

He followed her gaze, freezing at the unnatural sight before him. No wonder she'd screamed. Jade had arrived, but she wasn't walking through the gates, or even striding across the roof of the building for dramatic effect. She was moving through the air, carried by a billowing wind that seemed to be fueled by her voice.

And she wasn't alone. She was flanked, on one side by a dark-haired man Zev had never seen before, and on the other...

Zev's heart lurched with sick horror as he recognized a form he knew almost as well as his own.

Azai.

CHAPTER

SEVENTEEN

Marieke

Marieke felt the moment when Instructor Oriana's protective enchantment gave out. Her eyes flew to the older woman, concerned to see her collapsing into the arms of some of her companions. At least she was being looked after. Marieke just hoped she hadn't paid too high a price for coming to Marieke's aid.

A hailstone smashed onto the dais by Marieke's foot, this one much bigger than any she'd seen before. She needed to find shelter like the rest of the crowd, or she'd be in real danger. But would the guards let her?

She spun around to see that in spite of the barrier disappearing, the guards weren't rushing her. Kaine was moving toward her, but slowly, his eyes fixed on the sky like the rest of the guards.

Marieke followed his gaze, fear rippling through her as she caught sight of what—or rather, who—was floating impossibly above her. Jade had come. And her eyes were on Marieke, their gaze piercing and malicious as the wind, driven by her song, brought her to rest on the top of the council building's battlement.

Marieke could read the silent message.

The reckoning had come.

"Marieke!"

Zev appeared beside her, grabbing her hand and tugging her off the dais. They ran a short distance across the courtyard, stopping once they reached the dubious shelter to be found against the academy's wall.

Zev's arms closed around her, and he pulled her against his body, as if trying to shelter her both from the storm and from Jade's malice.

"You were amazing, Mari." His breath was warm in her ear as he murmured the message.

She let herself relax against him for a moment, her shelter in the storm that threatened to engulf them and everything they loved. Even in the midst of the melee, some part of her was at rest once again, complete now she was back in Zev's arms. But she couldn't afford to dwell in that feeling.

"It's not over, Zev," she said, raising her face to his. "Why did she have to come now? They were listening to me, Zev! They were starting to understand."

"I know, love," he said, the endearment sending a thrill through her, even though it was spoken with aching sadness.

"Did you see how the academy was turning against the Head Instructor?" she went on. "They were standing up against the council! I said I had more faith in the academy than the council, didn't I?" She met Zev's eyes earnestly. "I know you want to protect me, Zev, but I'm not going to run or hide. We've been doing that for too long. This is what it was all for. This is the confrontation we can't escape."

"I know," Zev told her, his voice deep and as strong as the arms that enfolded her.

She searched his features, trying to understand what she was seeing. If he wasn't looking for a way around the coming fight, why did he look so conflicted? Where was the determination she'd expected to see blazing in his eyes when his chance to face off against Jade finally came?

"What is it?" she asked.

He didn't answer, but his eyes left hers, moving slowly cross the courtyard. Marieke followed his gaze up the battlements of the council building where Jade still waited, watching the chaos her storm had unleashed. Marieke squinted through the rain, trying to make out who was with Jade.

The man standing on one side of Jade was tall, with dark hair and straight features. He must be Clancy, but Marieke was surprised at his appearance. He was older than she'd expected. The gap in age between him and Tarenne must be considerably greater than that between Zev and his brother. She couldn't make out much at the distance, but his posture was rigid and his bearing proud as he stared down at the courtyard, one foot up on the battlement edge.

He had the presence of an avenging king.

Marieke's eyes flicked to the other man, and she let out a strangled cry. It was Azai! And he was no hostage. He stood tall beside Jade, his hand on the hilt of his sword as he towered above the chaos.

"No," she whispered.

"I guess he managed to find Jade in Aeltas," Zev said. His flat, lifeless voice cut Marieke to the heart.

"He wouldn't," she whispered. "He can't."

But Zev must have heard the lack of conviction in her voice. She knew how much he'd wanted her to like Azai, but the younger Aeltan had never made his friendship available to Marieke. He'd always held himself back. Still, angry as she knew he was, she never could have believed him capable of this level of betrayal.

"We can't think about Azai right now," Zev said gruffly.

"We have to focus on Jade. Marieke, I don't know if Tarenne warned you, but—"

"The talisman," Marieke gasped, her eyes flying to Jade. "Yes, she told me. Why hasn't Jade used it yet?"

"I don't know," said Zev. "But my best guess would be that she's not done making her big statement. I've never seen anyone as driven as she is by her vendetta. She'll want the council to know that she's the one wreaking their destruction. And half of them fled inside before she even arrived."

"She may not realize that we know about the talisman," Marieke said. "She won't think there's any haste to use it if she thinks it's a secret. Although," she glanced at Zev, "I suppose Azai will have told her."

"Maybe." Zev's face didn't communicate much. "The fact is she hasn't used it yet, and we have to try to stop her."

Marieke nodded. "Come on."

Taking Zev's hand, she ran out from the shelter of the building. They had to break their grip on each other to shield their heads with their arms as they ran, the hail still pelting down. Marieke raised a simple protective song as she ran, encompassing both her and Zev. She didn't want to waste her energy before they reached Jade, but some of the hailstones were big enough to kill if they hit her head directly. She could already see a bruise blossoming on Zev's arm, where his sleeves were rolled back to allow greater freedom of movement.

A glance toward the gate showed that the hail was falling on much more of the city than just the council complex. Marieke could see collapsed roofs on the closest building, and piles of rubble on the cobblestones. The destruction was enormous, and it was only beginning.

Jade must have built unprecedented endurance to have successfully harnessed enough power for such a strong perpetual enchantment. Because while she seemed to be periodically encouraging the storm with her magic, it wasn't fully dependent on her efforts. Marieke didn't know exactly what enchantment Jade was using but, even from so far away, she could feel the intensity of the magic that flowed up from the ground into Jade at every moment. It was like no songcraft she'd witnessed before.

Just how far had Jade and Clancy explored the connection between heartsong and songcraft? They'd done much more than the simple rituals Tarenne had witnessed. And now Azai had joined as well, meaning Jade potentially had the power of two lands behind her. If only there had been more time for Marieke and Zev to experiment with it. Marieke felt hopelessly outmatched.

But they had to try.

The courtyard was almost deserted, but when they neared the council building, Veronica and Tarenne peeled off from the wall to meet them. They'd obviously run the opposite way for shelter when Zev pulled Marieke toward the academy building.

"Are you all right?" Veronica called, catapulting herself into Marieke and enclosing her in a bear hug.

"I'm fine," said Marieke. "You?" She searched her friend's eyes. "Did you see...?"

"I saw." Veronica's face was as hard as Zev's had been. "Let's not talk about it."

"Stop acting like he's died," Tarenne said, her anger representing more emotion than Marieke had seen in her throughout most of their acquaintance. "It's not so inconceivable that he'd want to help Jade. Clancy made the same decision, and he had his reasons."

"Jade murdered my father," Zev said harshly. "And your parents, whether you want to admit it or not. Anyone who joins with her is as good as dead to me."

Marieke bit her lip, exchanging a look with Veronica. The

fight against Jade was going to be hard enough already. Azai's defection would make it a hundred times harder. Veronica's eyes were dull, giving her a look nothing like her usual self.

"We don't have time to argue," said Marieke. "We need to reach Jade before she does something we can't undo."

"You want to go up there?" Tarenne protested. "When the whole building might become an inferno at any second?"

"Do you have any other ideas for how to stop Jade?" Marieke shot at her. "Go and find shelter if you want to stay out of it. But your brother is up there!"

Something small and gray streaked past Marieke and into the building, and it took her a moment to realize what she'd seen.

"How is your cat here?" she demanded, incredulous. "*Why* is your cat here?"

"Tommy!" Tarenne let out an exasperated growl. "Looks like I am coming with you."

Marieke didn't stay to comment on Tarenne apparently caring more about her cat than her brother. She ran through the open doorway Tommy had disappeared into. It was an employee entrance, and it took her a few wrong turns to get her bearings. It would have been much easier if Jade had planted herself on top of the academy building. Marieke knew that one like the back of her hand.

"I don't know if there's a way up onto the top level roof," she called over her shoulder, where the others were following her. "But I've been onto a terrace on the second story before. There might be a service ladder between the two."

They passed lots of hysterical people taking shelter from the storm on the first floor, and a few council guards even yelled for them to halt as they passed. But there was no clear leadership directing the chaos, and no one actually accosted them. Once they mounted a flight of stairs, the crowd thinned.

Within a few minutes, they were bursting through a doorway onto the terrace roof Marieke had mentioned. They raced across it to a decorative archway over which plants trailed. It wasn't full shelter from the hail, but it was better than nothing.

"Did you see the meeting room on the second floor?" Veronica asked, panting as she drew alongside Marieke.

"Meeting room?" Marieke shook her head. "I was too focused on finding the route."

"There were a lot of people in robes, talking over each other," said Veronica. "I think it was the council trying to make a plan of defense."

"Were the robes all the same color?" Marieke asked.

"No. Two different colors."

"Some from the council and some from the academy, then," Marieke said. "I'm glad they're doing *something*, but why are they staying in the building? Don't they realize—" She cut herself off, her eyes widening. "Of course not. They don't realize the danger! Thanks to the storm and Jade actually arriving, I never got as far as telling everyone about the talisman!"

Zev appeared at her side. "I don't see any ladders, Marieke. I can see them up there, but I don't see a way to reach them."

"We might have to climb," said Marieke, determined. "But who knows how long it might take?" She grabbed her friend's arm. "Veronica, you have to go back inside. Warn the council— if they won't listen to you, try the instructors. The students if all else fails! Get them to evacuate the building, and the academy too. Anyone who's not needed for the evacuation can come and help us take down Jade."

Veronica hesitated for a moment, clearly reluctant to leave them at such a crucial moment.

"There are so many people sheltering inside the complex, Veronica," Marieke pushed her. "None of them realize how much more danger they're in if they stay inside than if they brave the hail."

"You're right," Veronica said. She gave Marieke a fierce look. "But I'll be back as soon as I can. Don't die before then."

Marieke couldn't help laughing, in spite of the seriousness of the situation. "I'll try my best."

Veronica turned to Tarenne. "Are you coming with me?"

Tarenne didn't look very happy about her decision, but she shook her head. "No, I'd better go after my brother. And I don't see Tommy, which means he's probably placed himself in the most inconvenient location possible. I wouldn't be surprised if he's found a way up to the top battlements, although why he wants to go there is beyond me."

From what she'd seen of the cat, Marieke wouldn't be surprised either. But she wasn't especially interested in Tommy's location.

"Do you see a good place for climbing?" she asked Zev.

"Not really," he said. "Marieke, I know we have to hurry, but it might be wise to make a plan before we get there. How are we going to stop her?"

"I don't know." Marieke bit her lip. "Her songcraft is superior to mine, there's no question about that. I can't beat her in a straight-on battle. We have to find another way to outsmart her."

"It's not about outsmarting," Tarenne cut in. "It's about raw strength, plain and simple."

"She has that, too," Marieke said heavily. "I can't even describe what I'm feeling from her, Zev. She's stronger than the last time we encountered her. Much stronger. With Clancy and...and Azai by her side, the potency of the magic she's accessing is dizzying."

"We'll find a way," Zev said firmly.

"We've already found it," Tarenne said. "You just have to be willing to take it."

"Not now, Tarenne," said Zev sharply. "This isn't the time for—"

"This is exactly the time," she contradicted him. "What Marieke is sensing is exactly what I told you. The combined strength of the two kingdoms is formidable. I know you've felt it, Zev. My heartsong is drawn to yours. It must be the same for you."

"It's not," Zev said shortly. "I've given you my answer, Tarenne."

"We could be just as strong as they are," Tarenne insisted. "Stronger, because if you commit yourself to me, it will be much more than Jade ever did for Clancy." She spared a glance for Marieke. "And we could still lend our power to Marieke's songcraft, like Clancy does for Jade's. The three of us could be even more powerful than the trio up there." Her eyes were relentless, staring Zev down. "It will take nothing less than that to stop them. But it can't be based on false promises. The magic will know. You have to swear it."

A sick feeling had enveloped Marieke, and she felt a paralysis creeping over her as Tarenne reached her hand out toward Zev. Whatever the other girl had claimed about romance and attraction playing no role in her proposal, Marieke could see a longing in Tarenne's eyes. On her normally inexpressive features, it almost looked like desperation. She didn't love Zev—she didn't know him well enough to love him. But she loved the idea of him. She'd fallen for the stability and safety she saw in a future with him.

But that didn't mean she was lying or wrong in her argument. What if she was right that combining her heartsong with Zev's through a formal alliance of the two lands would open up the level of power they needed to beat Jade? If that was what it took to save both Oleand and Aeltas, were she and Zev being unforgivably selfish to put themselves first?

Marieke brought her gaze reluctantly to Zev's face. He must be feeling the same doubt she was. She knew how deeply he loved Aeltas, and how heavy a burden he carried for the country of his fathers. Would he take the hand Tarenne was still stretching out to him? *Should* he take it?

Zev must have sensed her eyes on his, because his own ones, as gray as the storm clouds above them, shifted to meet them. As their gazes locked, she read the reflection of every thought that had just flown through her anguished mind.

Then all at once, certainty blazed into Zev's eyes. He turned away from Tarenne and reached for Marieke's hand. When his strong fingers closed around hers, she could have sworn her heart actually sang. At least, she had no other language for the joy and rightness that saturated every fiber of her being. In spite of everything happening around them, she felt peace wrap itself around her for the briefest of moments. Her mouth was still closed, but she could almost hear a song within her, one that seemed to pour from her very heart. Magic clamored at her feet, eager to bend itself to her will, making her feel almost as though she had no choice but to sing.

She raised her voice, and a song like none she'd sung before was released. She had no plans, she chose no words, she formed no enchantment. And yet magic surged from the ground and into her with overwhelming power. Without her prompting, it formed a mighty wind that swept her and Zev off their feet at once, catapulting them upward and away from the terrace roof where Tarenne still stood.

The moment Marieke's feet touched stone, the unnatural wind died away. She blinked, her hand still grasped firmly in Zev's, and the scene before her came into focus.

They were on the battlement, Jade and her two henchmen

staring at them with varying levels of surprise. They stood on a large square of stone, the trio on the far side of it. Curiously enough, no hail fell up there.

"Well." Jade's voice was a purr. "You've learned some new tricks since we last met, I see. But how convenient of you to come to me."

"Azai." Zev ignored Jade, his eyes only for his brother. "How could you join with her? How could you be part of this destruction?"

"Your brother has more vision than you, Zevadiah," Jade said.

"Better destruction in Oleand than in Aeltas," Azai said defiantly. "She's agreed to leave Aeltas alone, Zev. It was never her target."

"Do you hear yourself?" Marieke asked incredulously. "Do you really think you can negotiate with her?"

Azai's attention stayed focused on Zev. "I didn't claim it's a perfect solution. But she's the only one doing something! Generations our fathers have sat in the shadows, bewailing the councils' crimes but doing nothing to punish them."

"Am I doing nothing?" Zev demanded furiously.

Azai was just as angry as he was. "You're the first to take action, and what do you choose to do? To help the councils! To stop the only one willing to make them answer for what they've done. How can you fight for the ones who destroyed everything for us?" His eyes passed to Marieke, their gaze hard. "You don't get to tell me what to do now, Zev. You had your chance to come to Aeltas with me. And you refused. When it came down to your family or her, you chose her. Well, I choose us."

Marieke's stomach twisted, every fear about what she'd done to Zev's life taking shape before her.

But Zev was far from chastened. "Who is *us*?" he raged.

"You talk about our family, but not a single one of them would want this! No one would want you to side with the woman who murd—"

"You don't speak for all of us," Azai cut him off savagely, turning away. "You should give up now, Zev. You won't beat us. We're too strong now that we bring the combined power of both kingdoms."

It was the same phrase Tarenne had used, its unfamiliar cadence impossible to miss. It had been generations since the crowns had held power in either Aeltas or Oleand, and no one called them kingdoms anymore—no one but the lost royals.

No, it was singers who'd ruled the Sovereign Realms for hundreds of years, and with a craft Marieke carried within her. Better yet, her song wasn't like the stolen power of the councils. It had the blessing of a surviving royal, and with it, she was more powerful than Jade wanted her to believe.

All of that came to Marieke in a flash of comprehension. It was time to stop seeing Jade as an all-powerful enemy, and see her instead for what she was. An angry, bitter singer who'd been expelled from the academy and therefore sought the darkest ways to increase her knowledge of her craft.

"What's your plan, Jade?" Marieke asked. "Everyone knows about your role now. What's the point in wreaking destruction on the country when you can't keep selling the lie that the land itself is behind everything you've done?"

"But the land is behind me," Jade said gleefully. She spread her hands wide, indicating the two young men surrounding her. "Both lands."

"You have enough blood on your hands," Marieke insisted. "What do you hope to gain?"

"It's not about gaining." Jade's hiss was venomous. "It's about the councils losing what they should never have had in the first place." She narrowed her eyes. "Blame yourself if you don't like what you see. I would have achieved a more gradual destabilization if the two of you hadn't forced my hand by figuring out that I was pulling the strings." She grinned suddenly, the sight unnerving. "I don't mind bringing the fight into the open. Especially not once you inspired me by the unique combination of your power. Clancy and I have come a long way since I first caught a glimpse of your..." her lips curled into a sneer as her eyes passed between them, "connection."

"Don't you see that you've become so much worse than what you claim to hate?" Marieke cried. "You've been trying to convince the whole country of a lie, and for what? To uncover the lies of the council? You want to destroy all this," she gestured at the council complex below them, "but what will take its place? At least the singers' coup had a plan for who would rule once the monarchy was gone."

"You are a true child of the academy," Jade spat. "I had such high hopes when I learned of your quest for answers. But you've been duped into taking their side."

"I haven't been duped by them, and I don't intend to be duped by you," said Marieke. "What you want is anarchy, and it's not good enough. My country deserves better."

"Don't waste your breath, Marieke," Zev said, his hand tightening on hers and his eyes hard as they rested, not on Jade, but on Azai. "You'll never persuade her to change her course."

"You should listen to your sweetheart," Jade said. "He's right. And don't let Oleand's fate worry you. You won't be here to see it." She strode forward, leaving the two men some distance behind as she came halfway across the flat surface toward Zev and Marieke. "You can't be allowed to warp Zevadiah's power further than you already have."

"The only one warping anything is you," Zev spat at her.

She shook her head. "You don't even comprehend your own power, Zevadiah. You could be an incredible force. But you've let a puppet of the council fool you into thinking you should use it to strengthen a corrupt and broken land that should be shattered, not saved." She looked at Azai. "Your brother understands what I've learned to be true—heartsong is strongest when it's angry. He's been doing good work since he left you, using that anger to turn your country against itself, and when all this is done, no one will go back to how it was."

"Azai, what have you done?" Zev said sharply.

Azai didn't answer, and Jade's focus had already shifted to Marieke. "I've waited too long for this, Marieke. But it will be all the sweeter for the wait. When Zevadiah watches you die in front of him, we'll see how well he holds on to his sweet little plans for peace. He'll help me destroy the Sovereign Realms without trying to. His bitterness will eat the land from underneath him."

"You'll never touch her." Zev stepped in front of Marieke, his blade suddenly in his hand.

Sensing that there would be no more stalling, Marieke raised her voice. She drew on the new potency of the magic she and Zev had unlocked to summon power from the ground far below them. The magic rushed eagerly into her, and she formed it into a sharp, angry song that made the stones under Jade's feet crack and splinter.

But Jade was ready for her. Her own voice sounded across the battlement, and Marieke felt something curl around her throat. She grabbed at it, realizing with alarm that the laces of her own gown were attempting to strangle her. They tightened enough that her voice became a croak, limiting her access to the magic that longed to course through her.

"Finish her off," Jade barked to her two followers. "I want to know she's dealt with before our final strike."

Clancy moved forward readily, Azai a step behind.

"AZAI!" Zev let out a furious cry, although he kept his eyes on Jade, his sword held out in front of him. "If you kill her, you kill me, too."

"So dramatic," said Jade, disgusted. "I think you'll find Azai has grown beyond mere brotherly loyalty."

Clancy was stalking past Jade as she spoke, and Azai had almost reached her. Jade's eyes remained focused maliciously on Zev, eager to watch him suffer the loss of what he loved, and she didn't seem to catch the swift movement. Even Marieke, facing them, almost missed the sudden lunge of Azai's hand.

Jade obviously felt it even if she didn't see it, however. With a shriek, she swirled, her hand flying out in anger. But she was too late. Azai had already thrown himself out of her reach, something closed in his fist.

Jade lunged at him, but Marieke was ready. Jade's distraction had caused the band around her throat to loosen, and she let out a raspy song at once, pouring every bit of her newly harnessed power into a shielding song that blossomed around Azai.

"Give it back!" Jade screamed, trying in vain to penetrate the shield. It was so much stronger than anything Marieke had created before. "You traitor!"

CHAPTER
EIGHTEEN

Zev

Zev's heart soared as Azai let out a furious laugh.

"A traitor, am I?" His brother sneered in Jade's face as he scrambled to his feet. "You don't like betrayal so much when you're the one being betrayed, do you?"

He walked backwards toward them, keeping his eyes on Jade. Judging by her unsuccessful attempts to reach him, he was still encased in whatever protective enchantment Marieke had fashioned.

"You're an arrogant fool," Azai told Jade. "I will never *grow beyond* loyalty to my brother. Did you really think you could twist me to your will with a few stirring speeches? You destroyed any chance of manipulating me when you murdered my unarmed father, you foul, cowardly worm."

Zev had the sense he'd been longing to say those words for some time. Azai ranged himself shoulder to shoulder with Zev, stowing the talisman into a pocket Zev hoped was secure, and drawing his blade before him.

Lightness blazed through Zev, more like release than true relief. With it came the realization that he'd never truly believed

Azai had turned on him. It was unthinkable. Of course Azai had been fighting for them all the time. Of course he hadn't told Jade they knew about the talisman. She'd obviously had no fear of him stealing it, probably believing Azai ignorant of its existence.

Clancy, on the other hand, seemed genuinely shocked by Azai's defection. He pulled up short, abandoning his advance on Marieke and letting out a yell of anger in Azai's direction.

"We are not the same," Azai told him coldly, making Zev wonder what had passed between them. "You've let your bitterness consume you. I won't make the same choice."

"He took something we need!" Jade screamed. "Kill him!"

Clancy bared his teeth, his straight features taking on a feral look as he sprang suddenly toward Azai, a blade appearing in his hand. Azai's own weapon was up in flash, steel clashing against steel as Zev paused, his eyes darting frantically between his brother's fight and Jade—she was too smart not to use the opening if Zev allowed himself to become fully distracted by Azai's situation.

As he'd feared, Jade's eyes were on Marieke now, although she was keeping track of the fight at the same time. Marieke had moved to his other side when Azai joined them. She'd been singing the whole time, her voice steady and loud, and she must be getting tired. She seemed to be maintaining the shield, but they couldn't just defend. If they wanted to eliminate Jade, they would have to attack.

"I've got this, Zev!" Azai shouted, somehow reading his brother's thoughts even in the midst of his own battle. "Take Jade out!"

It was all the permission Zev needed. Azai could handle himself against an opponent without songcraft. He drew alongside Marieke, raising his voice over the sounds of the duel now dancing dangerously close to the battlement's edge.

"How far can your shield protect me? Can I reach her without leaving it?"

Marieke shook her head, unable to answer his question without breaking her song. He could see sweat beading on her forehead.

"The shield is a physical area rather than attached to me?" He guessed. "We'd risk bringing Jade inside it?"

She nodded. Zev saw the gesture in the corner of his eyes, his main focus still on Jade, whose attention was divided thanks to the nearby fight. She obviously wanted the talisman back desperately, and her impatience was growing visibly as Clancy failed to overpower Azai.

Marieke was gesturing wildly, forcing Zev to take his eyes from the fight. She was pointing to herself and then to Jade, and Zev frowned. Was she saying she'd have to be the one to attack? Her songcraft rather than his blade?

"I can see I'll have to deal with this myself," Jade snarled suddenly. Her eyes shifted to Marieke. "But first I have a score to settle with you."

Marieke's song abruptly cut off as she put her mimed plan into action. She swiftly raised it again, and Zev could feel the difference in the tone of the melody as Marieke went on the attack. She thrust out her hands as if encouraging her song forward, and Zev leaped to her side, hoping his heartsong could give her magic the power it needed.

But Jade was far too quick and far too skilled for their poorly planned assault. The moment Marieke's shield enchantment dropped, Jade's voice seemed to slice through Zev's awareness. He heard shattering, and suddenly shards of glass came pouring over the edge of the parapet and speeding toward them.

Zev threw himself over Marieke, bringing them both crashing to the stone as glass fragments from different directions met in the air above them. Broken shards showered down onto them, fortunately propelled only by gravity now rather than Jade's magic.

Through the tinkling, deadly rain, Jade's song had continued unchecked. A cry of pain from Marieke made Zev clamber up, horrified to find that the stone of the parapet beneath them was jutting up, trying to impale her where she was trapped between his body and the surface.

"Marieke!" he shouted.

"I'm all right," she gasped, wiping a trickle of blood from one arm. "Don't take your eyes off her!"

With the words, she started to sing again, her voice creating a wind that pulled broken rubble from the ground and sent it swirling around Jade, the pieces doing their utmost to strike the other singer's head.

Jade rebuffed them all, showing no sign of fear or fatigue as she sent a chunk of rock flying back at them. Zev deflected it with his sword, moving to place his body between Marieke and Jade.

Marieke's song became more like a scream, the tune continuing but the words she was singing changing to be a message for Zev. Her eyes were unfocused, as if it cost all of her concentration to make her song do what she wanted it to do while her words abandoned the role of guiding the magic to instead communicate with Zev.

"She's sending magic straight at you," she sang. *"I think she's trying to pierce your heart like she did to your father. I can't attack. I have to focus on shielding you."*

"I'll have to get close enough to attack her with my sword," Zev said.

It was all he could do to keep his focus on Jade's attack. He could hear the grunts and shouts from Azai's fight growing in intensity, the two men now fighting inches from a side of the battlement where the stone wall had been blown apart by Jade's and Marieke's enchantments.

"Zev! Marieke!"

The faint shout from below sounded like Veronica. She must be back on the terrace roof, hopefully with reinforcements. But by the time they found a means—magical or otherwise—of reaching the fighters on the battlement above, it might be too late.

Fear tried to take hold of Zev, and he beat it back. He couldn't afford to become distracted.

"Just focus on shielding me," he cried to Marieke. "We'll have to hope the shield doesn't attach to her."

Marieke didn't look confident, but she nodded. Zev moved forward, unease sweeping over him as he caught a glint in Jade's eyes. She was pleased with their change in strategy. Why?

A gurgle behind Zev made him turn his head, fear ripping through him as Marieke's song faltered. She was trying valiantly to keep singing, but she clutched at her chest, her voice clearly communicating pain.

"NO!"

In a flash, Zev understood Jade's malicious look. She'd never wanted to kill him—she wanted to use his heartsong to destroy Aeltas in its turn. Marieke was the one she wanted to eliminate. She'd wanted Marieke to think Zev was her target so Marieke would put all her magic into shielding him and keep none for her own protection, and they'd played right into her hands.

There was no time for a complicated plan. Zev threw himself physically onto Jade, his blade aiming for her heart.

Her song turned to a shriek as she redirected it rapidly, an invisible force vying with the strength of Zev's hand as it attempted to move his blade in a different direction. She didn't stop his body, though, and Zev's tackle sent her sprawling across the stones. He was on her in a moment, still wrestling with his blade. The tip had almost reached her skin when a scream issued from her, eerily melodic as it unleashed a torrent of destructive power.

The stones from beneath Zev's feet exploded upward, throwing him into the air. Before he could fully comprehend what was happening, he was plummeting downward, other bodies falling beside him.

A powerful melody erupted at his side, sweeter in note but no less dangerous than Jade's. His eyes closed involuntarily against the gale-force wind that swept up at him from the ground, cushioning his fall. A moment later, he landed face first on something wooden, falling with no more force than if he'd rolled off his bed in his sleep.

Zev jumped to his feet, trying frantically to get his bearings. He was on the wooden dais where Marieke's hearing had commenced what felt like a week ago. The hail had stopped, and the courtyard below the dais was deserted. Marieke was lying beside him, and nearby, Azai and Clancy were both stirring. They'd obviously all been thrown from the top of the battlement by Jade's attack, and somehow Marieke had found the voice while falling to summon a wind strong enough to break everyone's fall. There was no sign of Jade.

Zev fell on his knees beside Marieke, pulling her into his arms.

"Marieke! Talk to me!"

She opened her eyes, one hand massaging her chest. "I'm all right," she told him faintly. "She was aiming for my heart, but you disrupted her song before it could get inside me. I don't know what magic that is—it's nothing we ever learned at the academy."

Zev clutched her against him in relief, allowing himself a

moment to press his face to her hair. His heart was pounding so frenetically, she must be able to feel it, with her cheek against his chest as it was.

He pulled back, his breaths coming unsteadily. "You're amazing, Mari, how did you act so quickly when we were falling?"

She gave him a wan smile. "The instinct to protect what we love goes deep."

Her eyes flew to something over Zev's shoulder, and they widened. "Zev...Azai!"

Zev jumped to his feet, one hand stabilizing Marieke as she struggled up, his eyes searching the dais. He hadn't noticed at first, but Azai looked injured. Judging from his position, he'd landed on the chair Marieke had sat in so briefly, before he'd rolled off onto the wooden base. He was still prone, clutching one arm, as Clancy advanced on him.

Zev had lost his sword in the fall, but he still had a dagger in his belt. He pulled it out as he sprinted across the platform, aware of Marieke following. Zev threw himself in front of Azai just in time to block Clancy's death blow. His dagger was a poor match for the other man's blade, and it was all he could do to keep himself alive while Azai, finally realizing the danger, clambered to his feet.

Zev heard the clattering sound of Azai picking up a sword, then his brother appeared at his shoulder, his sword extended in one hand while the other curled in to his chest.

The two of them against only Clancy should have been child's play, but Zev knew they were in real danger. His dagger was little use against a sword, and Azai was fighting with his non-dominant hand. They'd sparred that way for fun many times, back on the farm. But that had been against an opponent doing the same, and no one's life had been on the line.

Somewhere in the back of his awareness, Zev wondered

why Marieke wasn't helping with her songcraft, but most of his focus was on holding Clancy back. He wasn't as well trained as Zev and Azai, but he clearly wasn't entirely new to a blade.

"Why are you fighting for her?" Azai shouted, as he blocked Clancy's attempt to swipe across Zev's chest. "Why are you destroying your own land?"

"It hasn't been my land for a long time!" Clancy snarled, stepping back and running an arm across his brow, panting. "Not since it was stolen from me. I should be a king in a castle, not a peasant in a crumbling ruin. And I will be again."

"Better no king at all than a king who would destroy his own land out of spite!" Zev shot back. "A king would want to see his country prosper."

"You have no power in Oleand!" Clancy's features were once again twisted in a feral snarl. "This is *my* land, not yours. It's mine to curse or bless, and I'll curse it if I choose! I'd rather see it burn than bow to the treasonous singers."

He lunged forward again, his attack aimed at Azai. Zev took advantage of the move to slam himself against Clancy, shoulder first.

A splintering crack reached his ears, but he couldn't afford to investigate because Clancy had recovered quickly and spun to face him.

"It's not for you to say whether we have power over this land!" Zev yelled. "Your blood doesn't make you invincible, and it won't stop us fighting you if that's what it takes to save Oleand!"

He leaped forward as he spoke, his smaller blade sneaking under Clancy's guard and slashing at his ribs before the Oleandan managed to intercept it.

Red soaked through Clancy's tunic, the blood dripping to the ground.

The splintering sounded again, and Zev turned his head in confusion.

It was a mistake. Azai's cry brought his head whipping back around, to see that Clancy had succeeded in inflicting a long gash on the arm wielding Azai's sword. He was injured on both sides now, and he was flagging. His blood was staining the wood at their feet, and he seemed distracted from defending himself. Zev suddenly realized why Azai was clutching at his jacket instead of fighting. The talisman!

Zev threw himself forward, but as the three of them clashed once again, the air was suddenly filled with a deafening crack that seemed to go on and on. The ground moved beneath his feet, making him lose his balance and fall to the ground. Before his eyes, the dais cracked open, the earth beneath it doing likewise. The fissure spread out from where they stood, the nearest building splitting and tottering as its foundations began to fall into the ravine opening below it.

For a moment everyone froze, trying to comprehend what they were seeing.

The fight between the two royal bloodlines was causing Oleand to be sundered by a new canyon.

Screams rent the air on all sides, and Zev looked around properly for the first time since he'd raced to Azai's aid. His heart almost left his body when he realized that Jade had descended from the battlement unnoticed by him, and was throwing song after song at Marieke, who'd only made it halfway to the dais.

People had poured from the buildings at some stage during his fight. Most of them were watching on in disarray, but several academy-robed singers had come to Marieke's aid, which was likely the only reason she was still standing against Jade's targeted malice.

A high-pitched scream sounded above the others. The gorge

had only stretched out in one direction, and the fighters had been able to dive out of its way. Others hadn't been so lucky, however—a number of people had fallen into the new canyon a short distance away. From his angle, he could see a young girl clinging to the side of the rock several feet down, and she wasn't the only one.

Meanwhile, Clancy had recovered quickly from his shock, and Azai was barely standing as he tried desperately to defend with two injured arms against the other man's renewed attack.

For a heartbeat, Zev stood frozen in indecision, too many crises paralyzing him from attending to any.

Then a block of gray appeared at the edge of his vision, and he turned to see Svetlana a short distance away. It wasn't only Trina with her, either. There was a whole group of gray-clad monarchists with pale but determined faces.

"We've got them," Svetlana told Zev firmly. "That cliff face is more passable than it looks, if you know how to navigate it."

Zev didn't question her, gratitude washing over him as the canyon-dwellers sprinted toward the trapped people. That was one thing off his shoulders, but he was still in the impossible situation of choosing between defending his brother and defending Marieke.

The thought had barely run through his mind when a voice called him.

"Go to Mari, Zev!" Veronica didn't break stride as she ran past him. "Azai needs songcraft, not another blade!"

Zev didn't stay to watch, turning to sprint toward Marieke. He'd almost reached her when a wind swept around the court-yard, its circular motion dislodging a damaged pillar from the council building and sending it flying toward Marieke. The wind flattened everything before it, including the clump of singers whose voices were creating a chorus around Marieke. Zev suspected that Jade had intentionally dodged her with the wind, because Marieke now stood alone, her arms over her face to protect her from the gale but in the process stopping her from seeing the stone projectile that was heading straight for her.

Zev threw himself forward with a cry of warning. His body collided with Marieke's, her gasp changing to a song as he pushed her down. He felt a strange pressure at his back, as if someone had pressed a cushion against him, then everything went still.

He swiveled his head to see that the pillar rested on top of them, held back by an invisible shield that seemed to be costing Marieke everything she had, judging by her weakening song.

Zev shuffled to the side, dragging her with him until they were clear of the impossibly suspended pillar.

The moment it was safe to do so, Marieke released her song with a weary exhale of her breath. They lay for a moment, warmth emanating from her body into his as she lay cradled beneath him, her chest rising and falling rapidly.

"We really need to stop almost getting ourselves killed trying to save each other," she said weakly.

If there was a later, Zev would probably laugh about the comment then. But for now his terror at her near miss was still too fresh.

"I will never make that promise while I'm still breathing," he said gruffly. "Come on."

He pushed himself up, looking around for Jade. The threat was far from over.

To his amazement, he saw that not only was Jade nearby, but at her command, missiles were flying toward them in a constant stream. Yet nothing was touching them. As he watched, a chunk of masonry approached—judging by the gnarled iron bar projecting lethally from it, it had originated from the fence—and bounced harmlessly away. Zev stared from it to Marieke. She wasn't singing.

"Did you make it perpetual?" he asked, trying to remember all she'd told him about enchantments.

She was staring at the invisible shield as well, her eyes glazed as they passed to Zev.

"I didn't. I mean, not intentionally. It's not me powering it. Or at least, not just me. The magic is responding to you, like your presence is perpetually drawing magic from the land. It's maintaining the songcraft I did before, of its own accord."

Jade's frustrated scream brought their attention to her, but Zev's sense of urgency was gone. It seemed that, for the moment at least, she couldn't touch them. They'd done exactly what she'd feared and somehow unlocked new layers of the potential that came from mingling his heartsong with Marieke's songcraft. Not just combining it like she'd done with Clancy, although that was powerful enough. They'd mingled their very hearts' cores, and Marieke hadn't even needed to try to call on Zev's heartsong to enhance her magic. It had risen up to do it like an instinct.

"What happened over there?" Marieke gasped, her eyes drawn to where Veronica was facing off against Clancy, Azai attempting to help in spite of his injuries, but mainly just looking spellbound as he watched the singer at work.

Ensnared, one might even say.

"There's a new canyon," said Zev. "It broke open beneath our feet."

"I heard it," said Marieke. "It's—"

Her words cut off in a gasp, and Zev realized that Jade had seen the direction of their gaze and formed a new plan. She was striding toward Azai and Veronica, obviously planning to lure Marieke and Zev out by targeting their friends.

A plan destined to work. Zev took hold of Marieke's hand as

the two of them ran toward the others. They were faster than Jade, who'd seen their movements and slowed her own steps, her face curled in a chilling smile as she prepared.

"She's drawing magic to herself," Marieke warned Zev. "A lot of it."

She opened her mouth to call a warning to their friends, but as they drew close to the fighters, Tarenne appeared, for the first time since they'd left her on the terrace roof.

"Clancy!" Her voice had a note of pleading.

"Tarenne?" Clancy hesitated as he caught sight of his sister. "What are you doing here?"

"Clancy, you have to stop now," Tarenne said. "Please."

"Marieke, do you feel that?" Veronica took advantage of Clancy's distraction to throw a warning to the only other singer present. "Jade's building something."

"I know," Marieke said grimly.

"She's going to use the talisman, we have to stop her!"

Azai went to lay a reassuring hand on her arm then stopped himself when he saw that his hand was covered with blood from his wound.

"She doesn't have the talisman. I took it from her."

"You did?" Veronica gasped. "Be careful with it, Clancy! It's dangerous!"

"I know," he assured her. "I have it secure. It's safe in a specially designed case that stops it from being activated."

Zev saw Tarenne look around sharply as Azai patted his pocket, but a moment later the Oleandan girl was trying once again to talk her brother down.

"It's not too late to change sides, Clancy. They'll protect us."

"I don't want their protection!" Clancy cried. "I don't need it! Don't you understand, Tarenne? Once the council is gone, we'll have power again. Without their songcraft, ours will be the strongest power in Oleand."

"Songcraft isn't going anywhere," Tarenne said impatiently. "What about all the other singers?"

"Jade is stronger than all of them," Clancy insisted. "And she'll be at my right hand, protecting me."

Azai gave a snort of disbelief. "You really believe that? She won't serve you. She won't even defend you. She's just using you for her own coup. She doesn't believe in your right to rule. She just wanted the power of your heartsong. You've seen her idea of honor. You know I'm right."

"Enough, children." Jade had at last stopped her slow advance, and her high voice broke into their conversation. "It's time to end this."

Clancy moved toward her, but his eyes were narrowed.

"Tell him, Jade," Marieke called out. "What role do you plan for Clancy in the anarchy you wish to create? Or does his role end when you're done exploiting his power to overthrow the council?"

Zev couldn't feel the magic of the questioning craft any more than Clancy could, but even he could tell that the question struck right at the heart of the situation.

"Clancy will choose his own destiny," Jade said smoothly. "I'm sure he will find his place."

"They're right, aren't they?" breathed Clancy. "You think I'm expendable." His brow darkened. "You'll learn your mistake."

"Mistake?" Jade laughed mockingly. "You *are* expendable. You've done your part, but take heart, Oleand will thank you for it one day. You can live with dignity knowing you avenged your ancestors."

"Live with dignity?" Clancy repeated, outraged. "I'm not going to dwindle away—I deserve to rule!"

Jade's laugh was even more insulting. "You don't have what it takes to rule."

Clancy's gaze was alight with rage now. "I won't let my throne be stolen from me by a singer a second time!" he cried.

Before any of them saw it coming, he launched himself at Jade, blade drawn. Zev couldn't imagine what made him think he'd be able to reach her so easily—he must have taken a false sense of safety from her never using her magic against him before.

But this time, she didn't hesitate.

Her song was quick and sharp, and before he even touched her, before any of them could blink, Clancy lay dead at her feet, not a mark on him.

Tarenne let out a scream, the ground beneath them shaking as a sound like shattering glass accompanied a new section of canyon, splintering out from the first one right to their feet. They had to step back hastily to avoid falling into it, and Zev and Marieke somehow ended up on the opposite side from everyone else, although it would be only the work of a moment to run around the outside edge.

"A waste," said Jade unemotionally. "Now, on to more important things."

Jade drew in a deep breath, but Marieke was already singing. The song was by now familiar to Zev, and he could imagine he saw the shield blossoming out from her, creating a barrier between Jade and the rest of them. Jade's eyes narrowed in frustration, and she hesitated. She no longer had the power of heartsong at her disposal, and Zev could tell she didn't want to waste her song trying to battle through Marieke's shield. Marieke didn't even have to keep singing. As before, her shield maintained its form after her song stopped, presumably fueled by the heartsong that Zev both controlled and didn't control at all.

Everyone was still focused on Jade when Tarenne moved with lightning speed. Jade raised an arm, ready for a physical attack, but everyone was taken by surprise when Tarenne lunged instead at Azai. She didn't even have a weapon.

"I would have helped him if I could," Azai grunted, discarding his blade and holding off Tarenne's haphazard attack with his arms, one of which was still bleeding freely. "Please, I don't want to hurt you," Azai insisted, but Tarenne wrestled blindly on. "He was beyond my help, there was nothing I could—"

At first, Zev didn't realize what made Azai cut off his words. He'd taken half a step along the canyon's edge when he saw Tarenne spin away from his brother and toward Jade. There was something in her hand.

Jade's eyes widened as Tarenne lifted the little case high. The singer wanted the talisman inside it, desperately. She let out a song at the same moment as Tarenne did something none of them expected. In a swift movement, she wrenched the case open and slung her arm forward, the case remaining in her hand as the talisman hurled through the air.

Jade's magical attack was unable to reach Tarenne thanks to Marieke's shield, but the same protection didn't apply the other way. Tarenne's aim was true, and the talisman flew straight through the invisible barrier and struck Jade in the chest.

Marieke let out a gasp as she clutched at Zev's arm. She and Veronica wore identical winces.

If the talisman had truly carried enough magic to change the form of the entire complex, it was completely wasted on Tarenne's chosen target. The talisman hadn't hit Jade's actual body, just her clothes. Jade's thick, practical gown disappeared in a blinding inferno, the flames ferocious as they engulfed her.

There was nothing melodic about the scream that ripped from Jade's throat, splitting the air. She staggered backward, a blazing figure, just as something small streaked behind her.

Jade tripped over Tommy the cat, toppling over the uneven ground and straight into the new canyon.

Her scream cut off abruptly, and for a moment Zev expected it to turn to song, for her to save herself with a wind as Marieke had done earlier. But no song came—her flaming form plummeted silently into the darkness below.

NINETEEN

Marieke

Marieke turned her face away from the horrifying sight as the bright blaze receded into the chasm. Zev had started to move along the edge of the ravine, and she hurried to follow him and join the rest of the group on the other side.

"I thought she'd sing herself out," Veronica said, sounding queasy.

A shudder went over Marieke. Jade's gruesome end was too reminiscent of her own fall into Sundering Canyon.

"I think the canyon may have taken her voice," she said softly.

"She's gone now, anyway," said Tarenne hollowly. She was staring down at her brother's body with a lifeless expression. "I hope there's nothing left of her to even bury."

No one said anything, the rest of them exchanging helpless looks. What was there to say?

Zev moved to Marieke's side, his hand enveloping hers in a hold that made her feel truly safe for the first time in a long time. It was over.

"Is this still dangerous?" Azai asked at last, nudging the talisman with his boot where it had fallen on the ground.

Veronica shook her head, beating Marieke to the answer. "There's no more magic in it. At least, none that I can feel. It was obviously designed to change the first thing it touched, without the nuance to save some power if that item was something small."

Marieke nodded. "I'm pretty sure it released everything it had. Did you feel the torrent of magic when it touched Jade's clothes? It was overwhelming."

"I did," Veronica confirmed. "For a moment, I could barely breathe."

There was another moment of silence as they all looked at the gaping canyon that stretched out from their feet. It had ravaged the courtyard—not much of the once-wide empty space was left. The council building stood on one side of it, the academy on the other. Svetlana and the other monarchists could be seen further down, apparently tending to the wounds of various members of the public. Marieke realized that among the gray clothes of the canyon-dwellers, she could see the robes of council singers. Ones trained in healing, presumably.

In fact, lots of singers were emerging from the council and academy buildings, some just staring wide-eyed at the destruction, others already springing into action to start restoring order. She saw no sign of the Head Instructor, but Councilor Bernard was prominent, in discussion with a group of others at the entrance to the council building.

Marieke's eyes were drawn reluctantly to Clancy's body. He looked surprisingly peaceful in death. At least his end had been quick. Jade hadn't drawn it out like she'd done for Zev's father.

Tarenne knelt beside her brother's body, straightening his limbs and folding his arms across his chest in a posture of final rest. Then she sat down beside him, her arms on her knees and her head resting on top of them as she stared unseeing into the canyon. Her legs formed a tent of sorts, under which Tommy wriggled his way and curled up.

Marieke looked at Zev, feeling helpless. She had no idea how to comfort Tarenne, or if Tarenne would even welcome an attempt. The other girl had never really let any of them in.

"I'm sorry," Marieke said, keeping it simple.

Tarenne looked slowly up at her, then gave a nod of acknowledgment.

"Thank you. It's a hard loss. He was all the family I had left." She swallowed. "But I'll survive."

Marieke bit her lip, sure that such an impassive response wasn't even beginning to convey what Tarenne was feeling.

"If there's anything we can—"

"Some space," Tarenne cut her off. "That's what I need right now."

Marieke nodded quickly. "Of course."

She moved some distance away down the courtyard, the others following her lead. For a couple of minutes they stood in somber stillness, no one quite sure what to say.

It was Azai who broke the silence.

"Thank you." His low voice was gruffer than usual. "For coming to save me."

Marieke looked up to see that he was addressing Veronica. The Aeltan girl gave a dismissive shrug, but the pink tinge to her cheeks betrayed her.

"We were all doing our part." She eyed him sideways. "I'm glad you came to your senses. I know you're not as bright as those of us who are *educated*, but it would have been unforgivably stupid of you to be a traitor in the end."

"Actually, Zev and Azai received an extensive education from their family," Marieke said, her lips twitching.

"I meant academy educated," said Veronica airily. "In songcraft." Apparently she was still inclined to cling to her newly transformed personality where Azai was concerned—the one where she was critical and easy to offend.

"I didn't come to my senses," Azai told her, also sticking to his new role of patient and un-baitable. The complete switch of the two of them was so marked, it was comical. "I never lost my senses. Well," the lightest of grins crossed his face, "I may have lost my senses a little when it came to you, Veronica."

She raised her eyebrows. "You mean you were *ensnared?*"

"Maybe," Azai said brazenly. "But maybe I liked being ensnared."

The pink on Veronica's cheeks was pronounced now, but Azai didn't press her. Instead, his voice turned more serious.

"I honestly didn't lose my senses where Jade was concerned. I was never helping her, it was always an act." His eyes found Zev's. "I'm honest enough to admit I fell into her trap when I encountered her in Aeltas. Not that it was hard to find her—I just had to follow the trail of the destructive storm. But I raced in without a plan, and I was quickly at her mercy." He drew a breath. "You said you had faith in my wisdom to navigate whatever situation I found." He shrugged. "Well, this was the best solution I could think of. I would have been a fool not to realize that I couldn't beat her on my own. And since she had no idea I was aware of her plan with the talisman, I had an advantage. I just had to wait for the right moment." He frowned. "It took a frustratingly long time to present itself, though."

"What did she mean about you doing *good work* and using your anger to turn Aeltas against itself?" Zev asked him.

"Oh that." A flash of defiance crossed Azai's face. "I didn't travel with her the whole time. She wanted to start in Aeltas what she started here a long time ago, and spread discontent among the people toward the council. That was part of my role."

"So you helped weaken our own country?" Veronica asked, unimpressed.

Azai shrugged. "As for whether what I did leads to weakening or strengthening, I suppose time will tell."

"What exactly did you do?" Zev asked.

"I spread the word about the council's lies. I started in the capital, and continued all along my route to the border. I told everyone who I was, that I can prove my ancestry, and that the council had lied about the coup. I didn't actually give strangers any information that would lead them to our farm," he added quickly, seeing Zev's face. "I just planted the seed of our existence. People were rattled by the storm that caused so much destruction in Tarandon, and by the farmland that was destroyed in the region. Everyone was worried that a blight like Oleand's was imminent. A rumor that the council is responsible for our country's vulnerability to a curse is the type of thing that will spread very quickly."

"I still can't quite believe you were willing to do what Jade wanted you to do," Marieke said.

Azai was unabashed. "Jade was never using me," he said. "She thought she was, but I knew the whole time that I was using her. When her interests temporarily aligned with what I myself wanted to achieve, why would I shy away from it? Besides, I don't think my approach was what she would have chosen to do in my place. She would never have been so open. She preferred to move in the shadows."

"Like all liars do," Marieke agreed simply.

"Come on," Veronica said to Azai. "We need to get those arms treated. Looks like there's an impromptu healing clinic being set up over there."

"Can't you just do it?" Azai asked. "I thought you were trained in healing song."

"Oh, so now you *want* me to use my magic on you?" Veronica quipped.

Azai nodded innocently. "Yes, I do. You have such a lovely voice."

Veronica opened and closed her mouth a few times, apparently searching for a response. Azai just regarded her steadily until she gave up, throwing her arms in the air.

"You're hopeless," she declared. "And I'm not taking responsibility for your healing. Come on." Dodging his injured arms, she put her hands on his back and pushed him toward the healing station, the sound of her scolding drifting back as they went.

Marieke closed her eyes, drawing a deep breath as she tried to take in the reality of the fact that the crisis had passed. A deep weariness crept over her as she thought back to every lie that she'd uncovered—some willingly, some unintentionally—and how drastically they'd changed her life forever.

A strong arm slid around her waist, pulling her against a solid form she'd know anywhere. A smile curved Marieke's lips. Not that she would change it if she could. She'd never choose to go back to the existence she'd known before that life-shattering fall into Sundering Canyon.

She turned against him, not even opening her eyes before she pressed herself into him. His arms closed all the way around her, holding her close against his chest.

"You did it, Marieke. Oleand is safe." She could feel Zev's lips moving as he murmured against her hair. "And so are you."

"For now," she said, laughing unsteadily. "I might still end up in a prison cell."

"No." Zev laid his head on top of hers. "There's no way I'll let that happen. I won't let anyone hurt you, Marieke. I swear it."

"We were strong enough together," she said, her hands

creeping up so that her fingers tangled in his tunic. "We didn't need any other alliance but us."

Zev's arms tightened in a convulsive movement as Marieke went on.

"Do you think Tarenne was right about the strength a marriage alliance would have created? Was she just saying it to get what she wanted, or would it really have made it easier to defeat Jade and Clancy?"

"I doubt even she knows," Zev said. "On some level, she had to have been just guessing. This whole area of heartsong is so untested. But it doesn't matter, anyway. Because I was never going to agree to her proposal. I'm not willing to give you up, Marieke. I can't. It would kill me."

"What comes next, then?" she asked, feeling suddenly shy. "I know you'll be eager to return to Aeltas."

"I am," Zev confessed. "I have responsibilities there that I don't want to neglect. Possibly some new ones depending on whether Azai's actions have made a mess. But I won't leave straight away. Not until I'm completely confident you'll be safe without me. And I'll be back as soon as I can. I don't want to be apart from you any longer than—"

"Zev." Marieke cut him off, laying the tips of her fingers on his lips. "Stop. You misunderstood me. I don't expect you to come back here."

Zev searched her eyes. His hand closed around hers, and he pressed a kiss to her fingers before lowering them. "You don't? You don't want me to stay?"

"No." She almost laughed at the wounded look in his eyes. "No, I would never expect that of you." She looked around. "I love Oleand, and I always will. I could never have left for good while it was still under attack. But it can never be for me the uncomplicated home of my childhood." She felt tension ease from her shoulders with the words. "When I look at this place, I see my own disillusionment. And even if the council does decide to pardon me and forget everything that's led to this point, there will always be people who see me as a criminal. I can't just forget that my face has been plastered on wanted posters all over the city I once called home."

Zev's touch was light in spite of his labor-roughened fingers as he stroked her cheek. "I'm sorry. It's not fair that all you were ever trying to do was save your country, and doing it cost you your home."

"Not fair, maybe," Marieke said. "But not necessarily a disaster." She looked hopefully up at him, only to be met with a confused expression.

"Oh, Zev." She had to fight back laughter. He was trying so hard to be sympathetic and was completely missing what she was trying to say. "Being cryptic doesn't come naturally to me like it does to you. I would much rather just come out and say it."

"Say what?" Zev asked, perplexed.

"That I want to make a new home," Marieke said, flushing.

At long last, comprehension blazed into Zev's eyes. "A new home," he repeated. "You mean with me?"

"Yes, with you," Marieke said, trying not to sound exasperated. "But you're so cryptic, I can't tell if you want—"

Her words were cut off as, abruptly, Zev tugged her back against him, pressing her much closer to his body this time. One of his hands cupped the back of her head, holding her in place as he tilted his head toward her until his lips were right next to her ear. Marieke's heart pounded delightfully in her chest as his voice, low and husky, filled her senses.

"My apologies for making you come out and say it," he rumbled into her ear. "I thought my need for you was so known it didn't have to be said. It's the beating core of my heart, after all." His voice lowered even further. "You are my heart's song, Marieke."

There was room in Marieke's mind for nothing but Zev as he pressed the lightest of kisses to her ear. His lips moved across her cheek, leaving a tingling trail of heat on her skin until they claimed her lips at last.

She wrapped her arms around his neck as she returned the kiss, her heart thrilling with the rightness of finally being together, no more obstacles in their way.

If only they were alone in his orchard, where the kiss would never have to end. But they weren't. They were in a public courtyard—or the ravaged remains of it—surrounded by friends and enemies alike. After an endless moment that was still much too short, Marieke pulled back.

"I can't believe you almost forgot our post-near-death-experience tradition," she scolded Zev, her words broken as she tried to catch her breath.

Zev's laugh was throaty, his breathing also unsteady. "It would be a shame to break tradition." His eyes searched hers. "Do you really want to make a new life with me in Aeltas?"

"I really do," she assured him.

His gaze held her in its thrall. "As my wife?"

Marieke flushed with pleasure, her hands clasping more tightly where they rested around his neck.

"Yes," she whispered.

Zev's gray eyes gleamed, but they weren't to be left to enjoy their moment. Seeing over Zev's shoulder that a group was approaching, Marieke released her hold and stepped quickly back.

Reluctantly, Zev turned, and they both watched as Councilor Bernard approached, accompanied by a pale but conscious Instructor Oriana. More than half a dozen others followed, all wearing the robes of either the council or the academy.

"Marieke." Councilor Bernard came to a stop in front of the pair. "You're still here."

"Did you expect me to run away as soon as I got the chance?" Marieke asked, amused. "Do I need to remind you again that I wasn't captured? I turned myself in. And I did it because I thought it was my best hope of telling the truth to as many people as possible, and warning those who actually wanted to hear it that Jade was coming." She waved a hand vaguely. "Like so."

"Yes, well." The councilor seemed at a loss for words, and she didn't really blame him. "There's a great deal to consider."

"Let me take the chance to thank you for giving me a fair hearing," Marieke said seriously. "Or at least, attempting to. I gambled my freedom on the belief that Instructor Oriana couldn't be the only one in the council and academy leadership who wasn't corrupt. And I'm glad I was right."

Councilor Bernard looked taken aback. "I trust the corruption you allege is the exception rather than the prevailing—"

"Then you're taking trust too far," Zev cut in dryly.

The councilor raised an eyebrow at him. "And who are you?"

Zev didn't blink. "I am Zevadiah of Aeltas, descended father to son from the last king of the southern kingdom. I carry the blood of my forefathers, and the land recognizes the power of my heartsong. Marieke is my chosen wife, and I disagree in the strongest terms with the charges brought against her. I would take it as a sign of goodwill between our lands if the Oleandan Council of Singers were to drop any further action in relation to charges that can only be described as attempts by corrupt officials to silence someone seeking to expose their crimes."

"I...that is...well..."

Councilor Bernard trailed off inarticulately. It was

Instructor Oriana, her eyes round with both astonishment and excitement, who gave Zev an answer.

"Of course the charges against Marieke won't be pursued now the truth has come to light. I can give testimony as to the unethical conduct of the Head Instructor in bringing those charges to the council."

The councilor's shoulders sagged as he at last dropped his attempt at formality. He waved a hand. "Of course you're free to go, Marieke. I doubt anyone would try to stop you, anyway. We'll have more than we can handle trying to set all this to rights as it is."

"I would like to help if I can," Zev said. "We've learned that the power that connects us to the land doesn't stop at the border between countries. My brother and I may be able to assist in restoring blessing to Oleand, along with a young woman who traveled with us, who I believe to be descended from Oleand's own ancient royal line."

Councilor Bernard looked like he'd ceased to be capable of surprise. "Our country is certainly in need of whatever help it can get. I can't imagine anyone would reject your offer."

"Then, to be frank Bernard, you lack imagination," Instructor Oriana said. "I know many who would reject it outright. But their motivations for doing so are selfish and not in the interests of our country. It will be up to us to silence any voices that do not seek the prosperity of Oleand."

"I will certainly lend myself to that task," he said gravely.

"Starting with the Head Instructor," Instructor Oriana added grimly. "I should have reported him to the council the moment he instructed me to lie to our students about our history. And I should have refused outright when he told me to disqualify from my discipline anyone who showed an aptitude for questioning craft."

"I will certainly be pushing for his removal from office,"

Councilor Bernard said harshly. "And if criminal charges are in order, I will do all I can to make sure no one intervenes on his behalf in defiance of proper regulation."

"Where is the Head Instructor?" Marieke asked cautiously.

"Hiding in the basement," said Instructor Oriana flatly. "Along with a number of other councilors. Apparently they didn't see fit to use their considerable magical ability to help defend our city or our people."

"Conduct unbefitting the leader of an institution as important as the Academy of Song," Councilor Bernard said. "In this mayhem, we must minimize the disrepute that may attach to the academy from the council's failings. A new Head Instructor should be appointed as soon as practical."

From the sideways look he threw at Instructor Oriana, Marieke had a feeling she knew who he would nominate for consideration, and she wholeheartedly approved. No one was better suited for the job of leading the academy through the tumultuous time that was inevitably coming.

She felt almost guilty for how relieved she was to think that she wouldn't have to be a central part of that process. The idea of instead building a new life with Zev in Aeltas was nothing short of blissful.

"The concept of heartsong is a very new discovery for me," Councilor Bernard said to Zev. "I don't know how it works, or to what extent it might be possible to heal our land. Do you think your efforts could close this canyon?" He gestured at the gorge that had rent the courtyard in two.

"I doubt it," Zev said frankly. "The land can heal. One bad harvest isn't the end of a farm. But conflict leaves scars. Nothing can erase our history." He paused, his voice dry as he added, "Nothing *should* erase our history."

Instructor Oriana's gaze passed heavily over the shattered

courtyard. "The events of today won't be easily erased from our memory."

"I'm sure that's what my ancestors thought," Zev said bluntly. "It's up to whoever emerges with the power to make sure the truth is preserved."

"Yes," Instructor Oriana agreed. "Many of the catastrophes that have brought us to this point have been of our own making."

"I don't know," said Marieke. "I agree that the council—both the original one and its later versions—wronged the country with its deception. But that doesn't mean that there was no way forward but violence. Zev's family suffered the same betrayal as Clancy's, but they made very different choices about how to use heartsong."

"And Marieke made the same discoveries Jade did, without ever dreaming of using them to justify murder," Zev added.

"Very insightful." Instructor Oriana smiled at Zev. "It's our choices that decide the future. And now," she cast her eyes out over the chaos that was the heart of Ondford, "we have many choices to make."

TWENTY

Zev

Zev crested a small hill, a strange mixture of emotions sweeping through him as he caught sight of the huge gates up ahead. The last time he was in Tarandon, he was in pursuit of Marieke after she'd been snatched from his farm.

Honestly, all he wanted was to return to the farm and sleep for a week. But he knew that this visit to the Aeltan capital needed to happen first. As it was, they'd stayed much longer in Ondford than he'd wanted. But it wasn't a simple matter to just leave, not when the city was in such havoc. Not that he'd spent a great deal of time in the actual capital. Marieke had been the one stuck in endless conferences and hearings, usually with Veronica to keep her company.

Zev's role had been exhausting in its own way, but much more tolerable. He, Azai, and Tarenne had accompanied a group of singers through the immediate surroundings, assessing the damage and speaking blessings over the land while they were at it. Time would tell whether it made a difference, but Zev was encouraged. Even on the journey south to the border, they saw the first signs that the blight was easing. Skies were seasonably clear, springs were bubbling again, and many a gnarled tree showed the tiny green sprouts of new life.

Jade would never again have power to attack singers or bring disasters on the countryside. And Clancy was gone, his heartsong along with him. No insidious force was at work to curse the land.

Oleand was still in a state of turmoil, no question. It would be too generous to say that order had begun to emerge—that was still far off. It could perhaps be said that the hint of a future order was starting to be visible.

By the looks of things, it would be a substantially different order from the one that had come before. The Council of Singers was in the process of a complete overhaul. In fact, it would likely no longer be known by that name. Each region had been invited to send representatives to discuss a new council, one that would be much more representative, with singers allowed to fill no more than half the seats and council members to be drawn from all parts of the country.

The Academy of Song had survived the uproar much more intact. In fact, classes had resumed within a week of Marieke's interrupted hearing. The main changes had been the separation of the academy leadership from the council, so that the educational institution had full authority over its own processes, and the appointment of Instructor Oriana as the new Head Instructor.

The former Head Instructor was one of a number of council members living under house arrest within the council building —in comfortable guest suites bounded by a sophisticated enchantment that kept magic from being pulled from the ground—until the new council had enough structure to justly hear their cases.

All the time Zev and the others had been assisting in Ondford, his heart had been back in Aeltas. He had only Azai's description of the damage Tarandon had sustained, and although Veronica had managed to exchange a letter with her parents and reassure herself that they'd survived the storm in Tarandon unscathed, they hadn't shared information regarding the wider state of the city. None of them had any idea how the Aeltan Council of Singers was responding to the dramatic events that had swept across the Sovereign Realms in recent weeks.

So, when Zev received a personal summons from the Aeltan council, using not only his name but referencing his claimed lineage, he was eager to respond. Azai felt the same way, and to Zev's relief, Marieke had felt she'd done enough to depart from Ondford without feeling she was abandoning it. Veronica, of course, had been eager to return home, and even Tarenne had requested to join them.

The journey south had been uneventful, even the crossing going smoothly. The bridge over Sundering Canyon wasn't technically open yet, but repairs were progressing well, and Zev felt confident that the ground wasn't going to shift beneath them and make it suddenly less stable. He'd demanded they be allowed to ride across and had simply refused to take no for an answer. Whether the change was the result of rumors spreading ahead of him or some increase to the power of his heartsong, people seemed to increasingly bow to his authority lately.

And now, at long last, they'd reached Tarandon. The gate was close enough that he could see some damage to one side of it, but it appeared structurally intact, at least.

He glanced behind him at the rest of the party. Marieke rode at his side, Azai and Veronica side by side behind them. Azai was also leading an empty horse.

"Where's Tarenne?" Zev asked Marieke.

She glanced back as well. "Oh, at the last stop she decided

to take a break from riding. She's in the carriage with Trina and the Oleandan representatives." She sounded doubtful. "I hope she doesn't regret coming with us. I hope no one tries to punish her for whatever part Clancy played in the destruction here. I thought for sure she'd want to stay in Ondford."

"She did seem surprisingly well occupied there," Zev said. "We had to practically drag her out when we did our scouting rides."

Marieke nodded. "Yes, I never would have predicted that the academy librarian would take Tarenne under her wing like she did. Personally, I've always found her a bit terrifying."

Picturing the elderly woman who'd questioned him about his ancestry records in a manner more interrogatory than Marieke's hearing had been, Zev had to agree.

"But I suppose she and Tarenne each had a great deal of information of interest to the other," Marieke went on. "It's easy to forget how little Tarenne knows of the country outside the corner of it that her family holed themselves up in. Plus, Tarenne is so severe and unemotional herself, I suppose she and the librarian understood one another."

"I suspect Tarenne also benefited from having something to occupy her mind," Zev said, thinking of the state he'd been in immediately following his father's death. "Idleness and grief are a poor combination for some of us."

"Yes," Marieke agreed softly.

The city gates loomed above them now, and Azai and Veronica drew their horses up closer.

"Are we ready?" Veronica asked, sounding excited. She'd been away from her home and family for a long time.

"Yes." Zev drew a breath. He was ready to return to his own land, his own complicated mess to sort out.

Before they could actually reach the gates, a cry went up from the city wall. To Zev's surprise, a trumpet sounded as they rode through the gateway. A guard stepped out onto the road, looking solemn.

"Welcome, lords and ladies," he said.

Marieke threw a bemused look at Zev. "Uhh, we're not…"

She trailed off as the guard gestured toward the main road that ran from the gate all the way to the council complex.

"You're expected."

Zev said nothing, just raising an eyebrow at Marieke as they nudged their horses forward again. People started to flock to the spectacle, lining the road and shouting to each other as the group passed. Zev could see many of them glancing curiously between him and Azai, muttering to each other. Some even threw flowers onto the road beneath their horses' hooves.

"Just how widely did you spread your tale through the population in the short time you were with Jade?" Zev asked Azai.

His brother shrugged. "We grew up being constantly drilled on how to not share information we didn't want people to have. It stands to reason that I'm extremely familiar with all the ways in which information might spread if I'm not careful." He grinned. "And I was very much not careful."

Veronica chuckled beside him. Since the dramatic events of Jade's attack, she and Azai seemed to be moving slowly but steadily away from the dynamic of taking turns being hostile. In fact, more often than not Zev caught them in the shocking act of both being kind to the other. It made for a less entertaining but far more peaceful journey.

They hadn't made it far into the city when an escort of half a dozen mounted guards appeared from the direction of the council complex, flanking them the rest of the way. Zev was heartened to see as they rode that while there was evidence on all sides of the damage caused by Jade's attack, it seemed to be mostly under repair. There was certainly nothing as dramatic as a new canyon right through the heart of the city.

Most of the onlookers lining the streets were falling in behind the group as they passed, and by the time they reached the council building, they'd amassed a significant crowd. Zev drew his horse to a stop in the courtyard, keeping his face impassive as he studied the huge blue banner on the front turret of the building, a large budding tree embroidered onto it in bronze.

His opinion of the Aeltan Council of Singers was much more complicated now than it had been before he met Marieke. It was too simplistic—indulgently so—to paint them as nothing but villains. But he still retained the view he'd held all his life— that somewhere, deep down in his being, he didn't answer to them. If they'd summoned him here to call him to account in any way, he didn't intend to take it meekly.

A group of council members awaited them on the steps of the building, looking somber and, frankly, pompous. Zev dismounted in an unhurried way, turning to assist Marieke down from her horse. They would face this together.

The crowd pressed its way through the open gates, forming an excited half-ring around the new arrivals. Half the city seemed to have arrived, and judging by the attire of those watching, the wealthy and the humble alike were eager to share the spectacle. Zev even caught sight of a group of unaccompanied children sitting on a garden wall within the council gates, legs swinging in the air as they watched the scene unfold.

"Welcome."

One of the councilors spoke, and with a flicker of resignation, Zev recognized him. He was the man who'd struck Zev as smug when he delivered Marieke to the capital back when they first met, after he'd pulled her from the edge of Sundering Canyon.

"Greetings." Zev inclined his head. "I am Zevadiah. I believe we have met before."

"We have indeed." The man seemed pleased to be remembered, and he also inclined his head. "Please come inside."

"Hold on," said Zev, speaking loudly and clearly. "Before I do so, I want it understood that although I have returned at your request from a sojourn in Oleand, I did so under my own power. If your summons was the precursor to any kind of charge against me or my companions, or intended to—"

"No, no," the councilor cut him off.

He looked alarmed at Zev's terse words, and hearing the affronted murmurs of the crowd, Zev could understand why. The council was clearly eager to avoid the people turning against them as had happened in Oleand. And if they were treading so carefully, they must perceive that it was a real and imminent threat.

"You misunderstand," the councilor went on. "The council does not wish to be your enemy, Zevadiah." He straightened his back. "We will of course defend our country against any threat, but we do not accuse you of anything. We would prefer to work together for the good of Aeltas." The councilor made a stately gesture, once again inviting Zev and his companions inside.

But Zev stood his ground. He had no doubt the council would prefer all discussion to be private, but that wasn't necessarily in his interests, or in the interests of all the rest of the Aeltans.

"Working together is my desire also," he said steadily. He looked around at the crowd, sensing that if he let this opportunity slip past, he may never get another like it. He let his voice ring out clearly. "I am aware that rumor has spread regarding me and my lineage. I am indeed descended father to son from the last king of Aeltas. I have records to prove it, and the land responds to the power in my bloodline."

The crowd's excited murmurs were growing in volume, but Zev wasn't done.

"My family has remained in hiding for many generations for our own protection. But we have not been idle. With our hands we have worked the land, and with our hearts we have blessed it. We have always wished only to see Aeltas prosper. And we wish it still. I have seen with my eyes the destruction that can be brought on a land when its royal line turns against it, and I swear I will never use my power over Aeltas to harm the land or its people."

Cheers broke out, and Zev restrained a smile at the council members' restless shifting. They'd decided to lean into popular excitement for the rumor of a lost monarch rather than trying to quell it, and Zev applauded them for it. But he wasn't naive. He knew that the decision had been made strategically, designed to protect the council from complete upheaval. They had clearly hoped that by responding swiftly and amicably to the news of a royal bloodline, they could distance themselves from any accusation of having benefited from and lied about the slaughter of the monarchs so long ago, and from sharing blame in the recent attack on the city. But he had no doubt that they'd also hoped that by making the first move, they would be able to control how the scene played out.

He didn't blame them. It was a logical strategy for them to adopt. But while he meant what he said, that it was his desire to work together with the council rather than to move against it, he also wanted to make it clear to everyone from the very beginning that he would be no one's puppet. He wasn't interested in playing a role they'd selected for him in the narrative they were trying to create.

Zev met the councilors' eyes, his gaze moving one by one down the line.

"It's not only a monarch whose malice can harm a land. I have also seen the devastation created when a ruling council seeks to suppress the truth and silence dissenters, even when those voices seek only to warn of the disasters brought about by the council's own crimes."

More murmuring. Of course everyone understood he was talking about Oleand.

"It is my fervent hope that it's not too late for us to avoid such corruption and damage in Aeltas," he finished.

"Our aims are aligned." The spokesman for the council had lost some of his grand manner, but he was still trying valiantly to present an image of benevolence. "If you and your party will come inside, we can discuss how best to achieve those aims for the good of all Aeltas."

Zev looked around at his party. Those in the carriage had opted to stay in the vehicle, perhaps wishing to avoid being part of the spectacle, but the others were grouped around Zev in support.

"I think you covered the main points," Azai said lightly.

"I'm ready," Veronica agreed. She was scanning the crowd, probably hoping to spot her family.

"We're with you, Zev," Marieke told him softly. She slipped her hand into his and squeezed, her touch anchoring him.

"We will be glad to do so," Zev said to the council members.

The four of them moved forward, but before they could actually ascend the steps, there was a flurry of movement from the front of the crowd, followed by a fresh surge of chatter.

Marieke's gasp was what made Zev look around, and he blinked in astonishment as the group of children he'd seen earlier leaped nimbly down from the garden wall. Some threw back their hoods and others pulled off hats, revealing their features to be those, not of children, but of fully grown elves.

One of them moved to the front of the group, trotting all the way up to Zev before inclining her head in a respectful gesture. The council members she ignored.

"Zevadiah."

"Kiarana." Zev blinked at her. "Why are you always where you're least expected?"

"I'm not always where I'm least expected," she said reasonably. "Most of the time I'm precisely where you'd expect me to be. Those occasions are merely not memorable enough to draw comment from you."

"I...I suppose that's true," Zev said blankly.

She nodded in approval. "As for why I'm here, you should not need to be reminded. We made a bargain, you and I. You would be very unwise to forget a bargain you'd made with an elf."

Their conversation wasn't loud enough to carry to the crowd, but it was certainly within the hearing of the council members. Zev heard some sharp intakes of breath at the word *elf*.

"I haven't forgotten our bargain," he assured Kiarana. "But the bargain was for me to assist the elves to come out of hiding safely only if and when I came into a position of power and influence over Aeltas."

"That's correct," Kiarana agreed. "And we've decided that we do wish to come out of hiding."

Zev couldn't help feeling amused. "So I ascertain. But don't you think you're a little premature in deciding that I've come into a position of power and influence?"

"Not at all," Kiarana said. "You handled your own emergence from hiding masterfully. You have secured yourself a place in the public imagination that ought not to be underestimated. You would still wield considerable power and influence even if the council were to decide to reject your claim to any formal position and try to deny your authority—in fact, perhaps even more so. I imagine you could stage a successful coup should you wish to do so, provided you approached it strategically from this point forward."

"No one is suggesting a coup," one of the council members said sharply. "And I will thank you not to jump to conclusions about the council's response to Zevadiah's claim. I don't know who you are, but this matter doesn't concern you."

"I am Kiarana, granddaughter and heir of the Imperator of the Elves of the Sovereign Realms," Kiarana said calmly. "And I wasn't jumping to conclusions, I was merely speculating upon possible outcomes of today's significant events. As for whether the impending change to the structure of power in Aeltas concerns me, I do not accept that you are qualified to discern that information."

"Will you *please* come inside so we can discuss these matters appropriately?" The councilor must have realized he'd started to sound like a nagging parent, but he apparently didn't care.

"We are ready to come," Zev said. "I think we would be wise to include Kiarana in our discussions. There is a great deal you don't know, and the elves will have insight that could benefit us all."

"We have more than just insight," Kiarana said. She pulled a roll of parchment from inside her garment. "I brought with me copies of the original proposal for the structure of government that the elves and the singers behind the first coup drew up together, detailing how power could be shared effectively between a singers' council and a monarch. I think you will find it sophisticated and compelling. And we come ready to bargain with the information."

"I..." The councilor looked taken aback, and a glance at his companions showed that he wasn't the only one who was reeling from the onslaught of information. No one was forthcoming with advice, however, and after a moment, he released an irritated breath. "Very well, you may join the discussion if Zevadiah wishes it. But we *must* take this conversation inside."

"Of course," said Zev with dignity. "I would be glad to once again enter the ancestral home of my line."

The councilor looked harassed, but he said no more, turning and preceding them into the building.

"You said that last bit just to be provocative, didn't you?" Marieke murmured as they followed the other councilors inside.

Zev shot her a sideways grin. "Maybe."

With stifled laughter, the four of them followed the councilors into the building. They would need to be focused and resolved, Zev knew. The events that had rocked the Sovereign Realms had changed everything—neither country had the option of things remaining as they'd been. The violence had passed, and with it the sense of crisis. But if Aeltas was to weather the changes ahead as unscathed as it had so far, there was much work still to be done.

And Zev had a feeling that at the end of it, his life would be as unrecognizable as everything else.

EPILOGUE
SIX MONTHS LATER

Marieke

Marieke moved through the wheat field, enjoying the quiet moment of solitude. Most of Zev's family had arrived the day before, and the farm had been a bustle of activity since then. When she'd heard someone mention that they'd seen Zev heading for the private cemetery at the back of the farm, she'd decided to steal away and snatch a moment with him.

Her shortcut brought her out right by the picket fence that surrounded the burial plot, and she paused to look over it. Strange to think that this simple, unassuming cemetery contained the remains of every carrier of the royal bloodline from the time of the coup to the present day.

Voices carried to her ears, and she looked up to realize that Zev wasn't alone as she'd assumed. Azai was with him. She hesitated, but the brothers had seen her, and Zev waved her over. Azai didn't even look irritated by the interruption. His demeanor toward Marieke had undergone a complete change. Coinciding, as it happened, with the disappearance of hostility between him and Veronica.

Marieke slipped in beside Zev, leaning against him as he put an arm around her waist.

"Do you know," Zev was saying to Azai, "they offered for me to move Father's remains to the capital when I go?"

"Really?" Azai looked at him sharply. "What did you say?"

"No, of course." Zev's eyes stayed on the simple headstone. "He should rest here, where his home was."

Azai nodded, looking relieved.

"He'd be so glad to know you're taking over the farm, Azai," Zev said. "There's truly no one better to run it than you."

"I'll see if I can't keep it alive," Azai said lightly. He shoved Zev's shoulder with his own. "I'll even give your orchard the occasional bit of attention, if I happen to be in the mood."

Zev grunted. "My orchard is the biggest thing that made me question whether I should forget about the whole idea."

Marieke let out a chuckle. "That sounds like my Zev. On the one hand, being officially crowned as king over the country you love, reinstating the royal line of your forefathers and ushering Aeltas into a new era of governance. Not to mention being entrusted with the challenge of pioneering an unprecedented relationship where a hereditary monarchy—supported by non-singing advisors—has oversight of a fully functional singers' council." She gave him a long-suffering look. "On the other hand, your orchard."

"A difficult decision," Zev agreed gravely.

"He's not joking," Azai informed her. "It seems like he is, but he's not."

That finally drew a smile from Zev. "I'm not second-guessing my decision," he assured them. "I love this place, but I think some part of me always knew my task was something different."

"Father knew it, too," Azai said. "I didn't understand it, and I hated that he wasn't restraining you from a course I thought would bring disaster. But he could see things I couldn't, and he was right."

"I don't know." Zev's voice was heavy now. "You were right, too. My course did bring disaster for Father."

"He wouldn't see it that way," said Azai. "And you shouldn't carry the blame, Zev. Jade was the murderer, not you."

There was a moment of silence, Marieke hoping her presence provided comfort to Zev rather than just intruding on the moment. The loss of Gideon was still so raw it was hard to believe he was actually gone. They'd all half expected him to reappear when they'd finally returned to the farm, the threats that had sent them out from it vanquished.

"I wanted to kill her myself," Zev said. "I didn't say it aloud, I tried to seem like I had it under control. But inside, I got through it by swearing to myself that I would be the one to cut her down."

"So did I," said Azai. He gave a wry smile. "Although I didn't really try to hide it, did I?"

Marieke caught the glance Zev threw at his brother. "No, you didn't," Zev agreed. "And you didn't get your wish. Will you be all right?"

"Yes." Azai's answer was immediate. "Wanting to kill her was selfish, no matter what I told myself. What I did was better. I stopped her. When I took the talisman, I was so tempted to plunge a blade into her instead. Traveling with her, being forced to pretend I was helping her, gave me a hatred of her I can't even put into words. But if I'd stabbed her on that rooftop, I couldn't be sure I'd be able to do it cleanly. And if I wounded her enough to take her down but not kill her instantly, she would have used the talisman with her dying breath, purely out of spite. Getting it off her was more important." He drew a deep breath. "And now it's all over, I can see that it's better this way. I don't want our line to be steeped in violence. It's not who we are. It was never the choice we made."

"You're right," Zev said. "You sound nothing like my little brother, but you're right."

Azai shouldered him again, this time harder, and the three of them turned away from the grave.

"You know," Azai commented as they walked, "I never would have thought in the past that it was realistic to have both a monarchy and a council. But I have to admit that the plan the elves brought forward is pretty well-conceived. It might actually work."

"It's not the elves' plan, remember?" Zev said, his face expressionless. "It's a plan formed between the council and me, lightly inspired by the information provided by the elves."

Marieke laughed, and Azai rolled his eyes.

"The worst part is most people will probably buy that story," he said. "It was almost comical, wasn't it, how endlessly they debated every single point only to arrive at precisely the elves' starting point on almost all of them?"

"Ah, but the debate was necessary," Marieke said in mock solemnity. "The painstaking process of debating and deciding every last thing is how they can legitimately claim that it's their own plan, not at all the elves' plan."

"I don't know how either of you will stand all the posturing and the tedious formalities," Azai said frankly. "I think it would drive me to insanity within a month."

"I suppose it remains to be seen whether we'll retain our sanity or not," Marieke said cheerfully. "We'll do our best."

"Either way, a lot of things are about to change," Zev observed, as they crossed back through the wheat field. "I wonder when we'll be able to catch our breath."

"I definitely won't relax until this big state wedding busi-ness is over," Marieke sighed. "I wish the private one we're having here was enough to satisfy everyone."

"Me too," Zev told her. "But I can understand why a big

event like that is strategic as we embark on the next stage. Agreeing to it was a good chance to show goodwill to the council, since I don't intend to say yes to everything. I have a feeling it will be a regular battle against forces trying to push me into a purely ceremonial role. It's a battle I plan to win."

"I don't doubt you," said Marieke. She smiled up at him. "Not everything is going to change—I have very good reason to know that you pride yourself on being under no one's control but your own."

Zev chuckled at the old comment of his. "I was overly confident when we first met, wasn't I? I hope I have changed in that way." He put his arm around her as Azai peeled off to cross the yard ahead of them, giving her a squeeze. "This is what won't change, even when everything else does."

Marieke's heart swelled, and she was just thinking that they might manage a private moment when they saw a vehicle pulling up outside the gate of the farm.

The gate no longer stood wide, as it always had when Marieke first knew the place. The Council of Singers had insisted on certain security measures while Zev was back on the farm, as evidenced by the guards posted on either side of the closed farm gate.

They watched as someone alighted from the carriage, exchanging a look of surprise when they recognized Tarenne.

"We'd better tell them to let her in," Zev said, linking Marieke's arm through his as he moved across the yard.

As it happened, it wasn't necessary. Tarenne paused when she saw them, apparently happy to lean on the fence rather than entering. The ubiquitous Tommy must have been in the carriage, too, because he leaped lightly onto the railing beside her.

"This is a pleasant surprise, Tarenne," Marieke said kindly.

"We didn't expect you, but we're glad you can be present for tomorrow's ceremony."

Tarenne shook her head. "I'm not staying," she said. "I'm passing through on my way back to Oleand."

"You're going back?"

Marieke raised her eyebrows. She knew Tarenne had been lying low in Tarandon until she received word that the bridge was officially cleared for passage. Marieke suspected that she was also giving things time to settle in the northern country, in case the chaos allowed for anyone so inclined to take revenge on her for Clancy's actions.

"I am," Tarenne confirmed. "It's time. Past time."

She looked thoughtfully across the farmyard, her eyes taking in every detail.

"This is where you grew up." It was a statement rather than a question, and Zev didn't respond. Not that Tarenne seemed to expect an answer. "Humble prosperity rather than ruins of grandeur." She sighed as she looked up at Zev. "Everyone in Tarandon is very excited about your coronation. I hope the reality can live up to the expectation."

"It won't," said Zev simply. "But things will settle. We will learn to re-establish expectations. It will take a long time to find our feet in this new endeavor. Years. Maybe a generation. But we'll get there."

"I envy your confidence," Tarenne told him. "And I'm glad I don't have need of it. It's a responsibility I don't want."

"You may need to consider what responsibility you will have," Marieke reminded her. "You can't change the blood you carry. The new council may offer you a position of your own."

Tarenne made a noise in her throat. "The sister of the one who spent years systematically eroding the health of the country? I doubt it." She shook her head. "I'm sure Clancy would have a different opinion, but it makes sense to me that the two countries are to have such different structures. We couldn't have the same result after such different choices were made by those carrying the royal blood." She sighed. "I've learned a great deal during my time in Tarandon. We were never taught that our ancestors played a role in their own downfall. I knew nothing of the greed and corruption that came before the coup, only the greed and corruption that followed it." Her expression was hard to read as her gaze passed over Zev's farm. "We were never good stewards of the power we had, so it would make no sense for us to lead the country forward. I wouldn't take any kind of official role even if it was offered to me. I'm not suited for a public life, and I don't want it."

"They may not be willing for you to just return to your old life," Zev told her. "For better or worse, you carry power. You might not want to use it to acquire a position of authority, but what if your children do? Or your grandchildren or great-grandchildren? What if they turn their heartsong against the land again, in an attempt to gain control? If the new council is wise, they won't want to lose track of your line again."

"I intend to make it simple for them," said Tarenne. "I've given it great thought, and I don't intend to have children. In fact, I'm resolved not to."

Zev frowned, perhaps feeling the same discomfort that was swirling through Marieke. They were getting everything they'd ever wanted. She felt guilty to see Zev's Oleandan counterpart bereft instead.

"You don't have to make that sacrifice," Zev told her.

"I know I don't," Tarenne said without heat. "No one is forcing a sacrifice on me. I'm not even forcing it on myself. It's possible I'll change my mind. But I don't think I will. And I certainly don't need your pity. I was there when Jade attacked Ondford, and I saw you fight." Her gaze flicked momentarily to Marieke. "You were willing to sacrifice your life for someone you love. If I choose to make a personal sacrifice on behalf of my country, that's no less valuable. I do care about Oleand, you know. I'm just less…flowery in expressing my love for my country than you both are."

"It's your choice," Marieke said respectfully. "You have our support, for what it's worth, if you pursue your current course, or if you change your mind."

Tarenne nodded. "Thank you." She cast another glance at the farm behind them. "I suppose it's possible I might change my mind when I'm older. Maybe if I can prove to myself that I'm capable of a different kind of life, one where I'm not driven by bitterness like my forefathers were, I might feel differently about producing and raising children who would share my bloodline and the inherent power that comes with it. I suppose time will tell. I'm not in any hurry to prove anything, to myself or to anyone else."

"You certainly have no need to prove anything to us," Zev assured her.

Her lips curved in a rare smile. "Good. Because right now, changing my mind seems unlikely. And I don't feel pitiable. I can live a full and happy life without having children—in fact, regardless, I *expect* to live a much happier life than I did before all this started. If I do choose to let my line die with me, it would be a peaceful passing, and I hope its absence wouldn't harm the land. I've spoken extensively with the scholars at your academy, and they don't think it will. It's a very different situation from being violently killed because of my bloodline. If I die peacefully and no one inherits my heartsong, it will likely fade into itself. It will be a new era for Oleand no less than for Aeltas."

"I respect your decision," Zev told her seriously. "And we will do our best to support our neighbor as it heals and rebuilds. But in the meantime, you should come in, have something to eat before you leave."

Tarenne shook her head. "I don't want to stop. No offense. It's a pleasant place, but it's not pleasant for me to see what we could have been."

She must have seen their uncertainty, because she went on, gesturing at the guards.

"Not all the fuss, I mean. Not the power, or the position. Everything else. Everything that came before. I don't envy the kings of the past, but I do envy you, and the simple, useful life your family chose. Our line chose violence and bitterness instead of contentment and service. And our country bears the consequences."

She was silent for a moment, during which they all surely pictured the gaping new canyon marring the city of Ondford.

"Even I have blood on my hands," Tarenne said. "Jade may have deserved to die, but strangely enough, that doesn't make her death sit lightly on me. Or so I'm finding." She shrugged. "Maybe I should be staying in the capital and using the power in my blood to help make things strong again, but I don't want to. I don't have any interest in governance." She gave a decisive nod. "Whatever happens, I will do all I can to ensure that the power in my blood isn't abused. But I'll do it from the background, not from a throne. I see a certain beauty in redeeming my bloodline in this way—if the best way my family line can contribute to Oleand's future is to permanently step back from a position of power, then so be it. I'll do it gladly, not under threats. I'm going to settle somewhere far away from the city. Not near my old home, somewhere new. I think might like to grow pumpkins. Or perhaps learn to fish along the shore."

Tommy mewed at this last suggestion, and Tarenne smiled again.

"Yes, you'd like that idea, wouldn't you? But it's not up to you, I'll decide for myself, thanks. Come on, then."

The cat jumped into her arms. It really was the most curious feline Marieke had ever encountered.

"Well, we wish you all the best," said Marieke. "And you will always be welcome to seek us out if you want any support."

"Thank you," said Tarenne. "But I don't anticipate it." She pushed off the fence, nodding in farewell before climbing back into the carriage, Tommy under one arm.

"I don't feel I ever figured her out," Marieke commented as the vehicle started to move.

"I'm not sure she's had the opportunity to do that herself yet," Zev replied. "At least she'll have time now."

"Marieke!" Veronica's voice carried across the yard. She'd emerged onto the broad porch and was waving them down. "The mothers want you. Something about ribbons for tomorrow."

"I've been summoned," Marieke told Zev, as they walked toward the house. "Do you remember me telling you that my parents would love you? I wasn't wrong. They're so overjoyed I'm marrying a farmer from a down-to-earth family. My mother and yours are as thick as thieves—I've barely seen them apart since my parents arrived."

Zev grinned. "Well, you shouldn't keep them waiting. Ribbons sound important."

They'd reached the porch steps, and Marieke looked wistfully up at him. She'd so hoped for a moment alone.

"What will you be doing?"

"I think I'll milk the cows," Zev said prosaically. "Very exciting."

"Really?" Veronica leaned on the porch railing, eyes wide with eagerness. "Will you teach me? I've been dying to learn!"

Zev laughed. "If you like."

"Great!" Veronica grabbed Marieke's arm and hauled her up the steps. "I'll just deliver her as promised, then I'll be right back."

She practically pushed Marieke through the front door, following her down the hall and up the stairs.

"Here she is," she announced, as they entered the guest room that had been turned into a wedding preparation space.

Both of Marieke's parents were there, as well as Zev's mother, fussing over flowers. Even Azai had somehow been pulled in and was writing out place cards with a long-suffering expression and a surprisingly neat hand.

"Do you need me?" Veronica asked the two mothers. "Because if not, Zev's promised to teach me to milk a cow!"

Narelle eyed her in bemusement. "And that excites you?"

Veronica nodded. "It's fascinating. I like it here, there's always so much happening."

She ducked back out of the room, but Marieke wasn't going to let her get away so easily. She slipped through the door as well, catching Veronica by the arm before she could get more than a few steps into the corridor.

"You like it here, do you?" Marieke gave her a sly jab in the ribs. "Enough to want to spend the rest of your life here?"

Veronica's face went pink, and she stole a glance through the doorway at Azai, who was finishing a name with a flourish. To Marieke's surprise, Veronica didn't dodge the question.

"Maybe."

"Veronica!" Marieke's eyes were shining. "You've been keeping me in the dark."

Veronica laughed. "No I haven't. It's more that I've been finding my own way so slowly, I didn't know where I was going until I was almost there."

"When did this happen?" Marieke insisted, delighted with the turn of events. If Veronica had softened this much, she had no doubt of the outcome. She'd been confident for some time that Azai was head over heels for her friend.

Veronica shot a careful look through the doorway before answering.

"It's been building for a while, I think. If you'd told me I'd feel this way when I first knew Azai, back when he was always trying to pick a fight with me, I would have laughed in your face. Not that I minded him trying to fight. It didn't bother me, because I didn't care at all what he thought of me when I thought poorly of him. But when I heard him talking about me trying to ensnare him like it would be a terrible fate to fall into my trap, I did care. I was really upset. Which made no sense if I didn't care what he thought. It was my own reaction to him thinking badly of me that gave me my first clue that I'd started to think better of him."

"I'm happy for you, Veronica," said Marieke, giving her a squeeze. "Selfishly, I wish you were going to be living in Tarandon with me, of course."

"I'm not sure I could handle the pressure of the life you're going to live," Veronica told her frankly. "I still can't believe you're going to be a queen!"

Marieke shook her head. "We won't be like the royals before the coup. It will be a different, less exalted role."

"But still a very public life," Veronica pointed out. "And with a great deal more power to bring about change than a random farmer has."

"I know," Marieke acknowledged. "And to tell the truth, I still can't believe it either."

"I think a rural life would suit me better," Veronica said. "Did you know there are no singers in the whole neighborhood? I was talking to Azai's neighbor, a man called Leonard, and he thought there would be a lot of interest in a healing clinic. That would keep me busy."

"It certainly would," Marieke agreed. "It's an excellent idea." She chivvied her friend toward the stairs. "You'd better go if you want Zev to wait for you."

Veronica ran obediently down the stairs, leaving Marieke to return to the spare room. She walked in to hear Narelle speaking to her mother.

"I just can't believe it, to tell you the truth. I keep asking myself, where did I go wrong that *both* of my boys brought home singers?"

"Mother!" Azai's protest was scandalized, but Marieke's mother was laughing.

"A sad turn of events, to be sure."

"Oh, Marieke, there you are." Narelle smiled at her. "You know I don't mean any malice, don't you? I'm well pleased with Zev's choice."

"I know." Marieke grinned. "And I think you'll be just as pleased with Azai's."

She sent him a sly grin, and he dropped his latest card in exasperation.

"I don't have to stand here and take this," he said, aggrieved. "You can write your own place cards."

His dignified exit was made less impressive by his mother's scolding. "Where are you off to, Azai?"

"My guess would be to help milk the cow," said Marieke, unable to resist baiting him.

Azai didn't answer, retreating in disorder amidst the laughter of all three women.

"Apparently I'm supposed to help with ribbons?" Marieke prompted them, once their mirth had passed.

"Not help," her mother said, smiling fondly at her. "Just submit to our fussing."

The session that followed was excellent practice for the next morning, when Marieke once again found herself sitting before a looking glass while her mother braided a white ribbon into her dark hair.

"You are a beautiful bride," Narelle told her as she tied a matching ribbon around a bunch of simple flowers picked from the property. "I'm glad you're humoring the family with this private ceremony before all the fuss there's sure to be in the capital."

"We're not humoring anyone," Marieke assured her, admiring her simple, ivory gown in her reflection. It had been her mother's wedding gown. Not grand enough for a state wedding in Tarandon. Perfect for a simple exchange of promises on a farm. "This is what we want to do. We would both be delighted for this to be the official wedding."

"Ah well, you won't be able to suit your preferences in lots of things going forward," her mother told her. "This is good practice, I suppose." She went quiet as she wrestled with a tricky strand of hair, then continued. "By the way, did I tell you about the elves in Ondford?"

"The elves?" Marieke frowned. "No."

"A group of them have expressed their intention to take up residence in the city. Specifically down in the new canyon. Apparently the magic down there is unusual and they want to mine it? Something like that."

"Huh." Marieke hadn't heard that detail yet. "If the council handles the transaction well, they could make a very beneficial deal with the elves, I imagine."

Her mother wasn't listening, too focused on the hair.

"There."

She stepped back, admiring her handiwork.

Marieke's deep, blue eyes twinkled back at her as she took in her attire. Her cheeks were pink with pleasure. She wouldn't be officially married until next week, but in a few hours, she would be promised to Zev before their friends and family, and it was a moment she'd treasure forever.

Her joy was doubled when she met Zev a short time later and saw it reflected back in his eyes. Naturally they'd chosen the orchard for the simple promise ceremony, and Marieke had never felt the magic of the place more. The morning was cool enough that the slightest curl of mist rose from the ground between the tree trunks. And as she walked toward where Zev waited for her, she felt the magic of the land respond to her passage, a gentle movement that seemed to welcome her approach as she wended her way through the group of family members and close friends who'd gathered under the trees.

Zev reached out eagerly, taking her hands in his as they stood before the great-uncle who'd offered to officiate for them. The man's deep voice spoke a few sincere words that Marieke barely took in, too lost in Zev's gaze.

"You're beautiful," he breathed, the simple declaration taking Marieke's breath away.

Prompted by Zev's great-uncle, they each spoke words of promise, sweet and heartfelt tastes of the forever that was hurrying toward them. Then, moved by a sudden impulse, Marieke raised her voice in a song. Zev's eyes shone back at her, his hands tightening around hers as her voice swelled. She didn't even try to guide the magic as she sang about love, just drawing it up into herself and releasing it for the sheer joy of it.

The magic of the land surged beneath her feet, bursting out of the ground and wrapping around her and Zev, forming an encompassing wave that she could feel even if not see. She could have sworn their souls were bound together in that motion, with a power nothing could ever break.

Overwhelmed by the beauty of the moment, she let her voice drop, melting into Zev as he took his opening and pressed his lips immediately to hers.

Their little audience clapped and cheered, and Marieke's heart sang with them as she kissed Zev under the embracing branches of his orchard.

They'd first been brought together by chance, then tied to one another's paths by powers they didn't understand, and now bound together forever by a love that was deeper and more powerful than any magic.

The songs of their hearts were entwined now, and with that kind of strength, they could face anything.

Turn the page for a bonus scene which takes place about a week after the end of the book.

A SHATTERED REIGN
BONUS SCENE

Marieke

Marieke carried the moment in the orchard in her heart as they navigated the overwhelming fanfare that accompanied their arrival in Tarandon. Between councilors and regional representatives and even elven ambassadors, she could barely keep track of who she was supposed to be meeting at any given time.

Zev had it even worse, moved from meeting to meeting as everyone wanted to discuss their most treasured policy areas with him. Only very occasionally was the topic of enough interest that he actually chose to give Marieke all the details later.

One such meeting had been requested by an enterprising shipwright who wished for support to expand his activities. He wanted to build open sea vessels large enough to reopen trade routes with Providore.

"Do you think it's possible?" Marieke asked, when Zev recounted the request to her. "At the academy we were taught that the kingdoms of Providore cut us off at the time of the coup with the threat of armed conflict if we attempted communication."

"That's my understanding as well," Zev said. "I suppose the monarchs of Providore's kingdoms didn't want to risk their people getting any ideas. But the shipwright thought that with a reinstated monarchy, we might be received differently."

"It's an interesting idea," Marieke said. "It would be fascinating to renew communication and trade with all those kingdoms."

"It might help us learn more about heartsong, as well," Zev said. "It could be very beneficial to compare the experiences of the two continents. The shipwright had done his research. Apparently he's been haunting the academy library learning all he can about Providore. He brought a scholar from the academy to support his cause."

Zev gave a wry smile. "Although, I think the scholar was actually more interested in the opportunity to pursue his own area of interest, which is heartsong."

"Yes, I understand that it's fast becoming a new favorite area of research," said Marieke. She grinned. "Lucky you snagged a position of authority when you did, or we might end up with the humans inflicting the fate on us that Rissin wanted, and I don't like the idea of becoming the subject of endless experiments."

"No, I have better things to do with my time," Zev agreed. "But I did find the scholar's comments interesting. He said he thinks heartsong is probably much less developed on Providore because—as far as we know—the royals haven't been separated from their rule. His theory is that ruling the country is the simplest and most natural outworking of the heart power that connects a royal bloodline to the land, and it was only the removal of that avenue that caused heartsong to take on an entirely different life. But he's only speculating. Communication with Providore would give us more insight."

In light of that conversation, nothing could have been

greater than their amazement the following day when they were approached by a flustered-looking council employee. Marieke could see her own annoyance at the interruption reflected in Zev's eyes. It was the one moment in the entire day they'd managed to spend in each other's company, and they'd been very fortunate to manage even that, given the bustle and chaos of preparation for the following day's wedding and coronation ceremonies.

The man bobbed an awkward bow before addressing them. "Your Majesties."

"Not until tomorrow," Marieke pointed out.

"But go on," Zev encouraged him.

"We've just received a contingent of guards from Port Taran," he said. "The head guard asked to see you."

"Certainly," said Zev, following the employee back the way he'd come.

Intrigued, Marieke kept pace with them. They stopped when they reached the entranceway to the former castle turned council building. Half a dozen guards were standing in the space, forming a loose circle around another two people.

"Sir." One of the guards stepped forward and bowed to Zev.

"What's going on?" Zev asked.

The man cleared his throat. "These two individuals were just intercepted arriving by boat in Port Taran."

"Yes?" Zev prompted, when the man paused.

"Yes." He shifted his weight from one foot to the other. "Reports are that they came up the coast from a southward direction, and that they appeared to both be using songcraft to locate the landing point."

"So they're both singers," Zev said. "Is there a reason their presence is being reported directly to me?"

"Yes, Sir." The guard's expression was stoic. "They were in a type of vessel none of us have ever seen before. They claim to have come from Providore."

Marieke let out a small gasp, her eyes flying to Zev's. He looked down at her, startled.

"We sailed from the kingdom of Vadolis specifically," chimed in a cheerful, feminine voice. "Although I'm guessing that doesn't mean much to you."

Marieke leaned around the head guard, curious for a better look at the pair in question. They were young, not much older than her and Zev by the look of them. The girl had fiery red hair, a freckled face, and skin as pale as her companion's was dark. They were a couple, most definitely. There was no mistaking the watchful look in the man's eyes, or the way he shifted his weight when the woman moved, placing himself always in a position to defend her if necessary. Besides which, closer inspection showed wedding bands on their fingers.

That didn't fully explain the curious magic that seemed to connect them, however. Marieke had never felt anything quite like it. Subtle but pervasive. They were linked together magically in a way that she couldn't decipher.

"The name Vadolis doesn't mean anything to me, I acknowledge."

Zev's voice was deep and calm, but Marieke could detect the undercurrent of excitement. This was too fortuitous. Had the task of reopening communication with Providore just come within their reach? What new possibilities and prosperity might be about to come to Aeltas through it?

"Understandable," the woman went on. "We don't even know the name of this country."

"It's Aeltas," said Marieke numbly. "You're in Aeltas."

"Thank you," the other young woman replied.

Her companion was frowning between Zev and Marieke.

"What is your position in Aeltas? We asked to speak to whoever is in charge."

Marieke hid a smile. They'd undoubtedly expected someone older and more impressive.

"You are speaking to King Zevadiah and Queen Marieke, the first in the line of the royal house of Heartsong," said the head guard severely. "And you will address them with respect."

The title sat strangely in Marieke's ears. King Zevadiah had a ring of rightness to it, but she wondered if she would ever get used to hearing herself referred to as queen. And she wasn't the only one taken aback by the guard's words.

"King and queen?" The redheaded woman's eyes widened in shock. "I thought...we understood that the kingdoms—that is, countries—of the Reviled Lands no longer had monarchs."

"The what lands?" The head guard was clearly affronted. "You are intruders in the Sovereign Realms, and in your tenuous position, I would advise you against insulting language."

"And I would advise you against threatening my wife." The stranger's tone was mild, but the warning in his low, rumbling voice was clear.

"It's fine." His companion waved him down, her face bright with excitement and no sign of either fear or offense visible. "This is no time to bring out the boar, he's quite right to correct me."

Marieke exchanged a look with Zev. Bring out the boar? Who in the world were these two travelers, and what were they talking about?

The woman turned to the two of them. "I meant no offense."

"We would be unreasonable to take offense," Marieke assured her. "Your understanding was correct—it technically still is correct until tomorrow. Aeltas has had no monarch on the throne since the time our lands ceased contact with yours. The royal line is only very recently reinstated. And Oleand—the country to the north—remains without a monarch or any intention of having one."

It was time for the other couple to exchange glances, clearly fascinated by this flow of information. It was once again the woman who spoke.

"I can only imagine that we have a great deal to learn from each other, if we're all interested."

She bobbed a curtsey that was graceful enough to make Marieke wonder if she'd brushed shoulders with royalty before.

"King Zevadiah and Queen Marieke, we are glad to meet you and grateful to be received into your country. My name is Ember, and this is my husband, Haiden. We've been waiting a long time to come and find you."

For Ember and Haiden's story, check out *Island of Secrets and Sacrifice*, a standalone YA fantasy romance that takes a sweet and light approach to the maiden-sacrificed-to-a-monster theme.

And if you've yet to discover the fairy tale adventures of the land of Providore, check out *The Singer Tales*, a completed series of six interconnected standalone fairy tale retellings featuring the magic of singers.

NOTE FROM THE AUTHOR

Thank you for reading *A Shattered Reign*. I hope you enjoyed returning to the world of the Sovereign Realms for the completion of Zev and Marieke's story. I would be so grateful if you would consider leaving a review on Amazon—it would really make a difference!

Just a reminder that if you want to read Ember and Haiden's story, and discover why they've been eager to reach the Sovereign Realms, you can check out no-spice fantasy romance *Island of Secrets and Sacrifice* today.

And if you've yet to read the previous adventures set on the continent of Providore, check out *The Singer Tales*! This completed series includes six connected but standalone fairy tale retellings featuring strong heroines navigating everything from miniature elves to brutish giants as they chase their own happily ever afters.

Join up to my mailing list at deborahgracewhite.com to be kept up to date on new releases, specials, and giveaways, such as bonus chapters. You'll receive some great freebies, too, including *An Expectation of Magic*, a novella which is a prequel to my completed YA fantasy series *The Vazula Chronicles*.

Plus, you'll receive *Dragon's Sight*, an 8,000 word prequel to my completed YA fantasy trilogy *The Kyona Chronicles*.

Again, thanks for entering the world of the Sovereign Realms! I hope to see you back again.

ALSO BY DEBORAH GRACE WHITE

The Kyona Chronicles: YA Fantasy

The Kyona Legacy: YA Fantasy

The Vazula Chronicles: YA Fantasy

The Kingdom Tales: Fairy Tale Retellings

ACKNOWLEDGMENTS

A huge thanks to my wonderful team for seeing me through another series.

My husband Ray and our four beautiful whirlwinds, thanks for your patience with me as I nutted out the details of this story (this one stumped me for a bit there!).

Thank you to my beta readers for being so engaged with the story, and giving such great feedback: Constance, Adrian, Alora, Dad, Mel W, Steph, and Mum. Thanks once again to Shae for the thorough and professional proofread. Any remaining errors are mine.

Thanks to Moorbooks for the cover and to Becca for the beautiful map.

To you, the reader, thank you for giving me the privilege of being an author.

And most importantly, to God, who puts the song in our hearts.

About the Author

I've been a reader since I can remember, growing up on a wide range of books, from classic literature to light-hearted romps. The love of reading has traveled with me unchanged across multiple  continents, and carried me from my own childhood all the way to having children of my own.

But if reading is like looking through a window into a magical and beautiful world, beginning to write my own stories was like discovering that I could open that window and climb right out into fantasyland.

I cannot believe how privileged I am to actually be living that childhood dream and publishing my own novels. I do so from my hometown of Adelaide, Australia, where I live with my husband and our four little ones.

I've never outgrown my love of young adult stories, so the genre of young adult fantasy was always going to be my niche. Feel free to email me at deborah@deborahgracewhite.com and introduce yourself! Or subscribe to my mailing list at deborah gracewhite.com for free giveaways, sales, and updates.